A SMALL INDISCRETION

A SMALL INDISCRETION

Denise Rudberg

Translated by Laura A. Wideburg

Published by

amazoncrossing

Text copyright © 2011 Denise Rudberg
English translation copyright © 2014 Laura A. Wideburg

A *Small Indiscretion* was first published in 2011 by Norstedts Forlagsgrupp AB as *Ett litet snedsprång*. Translated from Swedish by Laura A. Wideburg. Published in English by AmazonCrossing in 2014.

Published by AmazonCrossing, Seattle
www.apub.com

ISBN-13: 9781477817698
ISBN-10: 1477817697

Cover design by: Anna Curtis

Library of Congress Control Number: 2013917274

To my maternal grandmother, Ruth,
the brave, strong woman who will
always be my role model.

CAST OF CHARACTERS

MARIANNE JIDHOFF: A recent widow and legal secretary who spent the past year taking care of her dying husband.

TORSTEN EHN: A hardened investigator for the Swedish National Bureau of Investigation. He lives for good food.

OLLE LUNDQVIST: A brusque prosecutor who keeps everyone in line.

AUGUSTIN MADRID: A novice police assistant. His tailored suits are as unusual in the police force as his first name.

PAULA STEEN: A wealthy but lonely housewife.

ALEXANDRA BARANSKI: A famous prosecutor who wins case after case. Her opponents hope she'll finally have a losing streak.

NINA LARSON: Marianne's eldest daughter, with whom Marianne has a complicated relationship.

SIGRID LARSON: Marianne's second daughter, who runs a fashionable dressmaking shop.

PEDER LARSON: The baby brother in the family. He is finishing his university studies in Australia.

NOAH EHN: Torsten Ehn's teenage son, recently admitted to the Stockholm Ballet School.

PROLOGUE

I'm afraid that Hans is about to pass away, so you must prepare yourself."

Marianne blinked, trying to understand what the friendly nurse from Ersta Hospice was saying. Her entire body fought against this incomprehensible news about her husband. The whole family had been there just last night. They'd had a nice dinner together, and Hans had seemed more energetic than he had in weeks.

Today, Marianne and her son Peder had stopped by to see if Hans wanted to spend a few minutes in the sunshine. What had happened during the night? How could he have taken such a turn for the worse? Why hadn't the people from the Hospice called her earlier?

As if she'd been reading Marianne's thoughts, the nurse replied, "He woke up a few minutes ago and was in great pain. The doctor was just here and examined him—he has taken a bad turn. I'm sorry. This can happen quickly, much more so than we realize. I know this must be a shock to you."

"How is Hans right now?"

"He seems to know what is happening. I think he feels ready."

Peder looked straight ahead. Marianne squeezed his hand gently. Finally, she was able to absorb what the nurse was telling her.

"I'm just going to call my daughters," she said.

"Let me call them," the nurse said. "I think it's best for you to go to him now."

Marianne took a deep breath and stepped into Hans's room. The sun was shining, and, to her surprise, the window was open.

"Hans asked me to open it for him," the nurse said.

Marianne walked over to the bed to look at her husband. He was extremely thin. She could see that he was upset because he was unable to keep his mouth closed.

Peder sat down on the other side of the bed and took his father's hand.

Marianne watched her son. His jaw was clenched, and it had lost its color. She picked up Hans's left hand and rubbed it gently. She felt his wedding ring beneath her fingers, and that made her smile. He gave her a weak smile in return, and her eyes filled with tears. Marianne knew Hans hated it when she cried, but she couldn't help herself.

"The nurse is calling Nina and Sigrid."

Hans shut his eyes, and she felt a slight pressure from his hand. She understood what he meant: their daughters weren't going to make it in time.

Marianne cleared her throat and wiped her cheek to stop her tears from falling on the sheet. She tried to speak as strongly and clearly as she could.

"I love you. I'm here for you."

Hans's eyes were still closed, and he seemed to nod slightly.

Peder tried to strangle a sob.

Then, Hans opened his eyes to look at Marianne. He seemed to be trying to form sounds, so she leaned closer to him. Finally, he managed to say, "Irene . . ."

Marianne leaned even closer, looking at her husband quizzically. He made an extraordinary effort to say, "Irene. Where is Irene?"

Then, she saw the heartbreak in his eyes. Heartbreak over not being able to say what he wanted. She detected a feeling of loss, too. The kind of loss a boy has after he's decided to run away from his mother.

Hans looked around the room as if searching for someone, and just as Marianne started to ask about this Irene, his eyes turned empty. A weak sigh came from his mouth, and his hand quivered in Marianne's. His eyes rolled to the ceiling, and it was all over.

Marianne released his hand. Her own arms fell limply to her sides. She felt a pressure in her chest as if her lungs were going to burst. When she finally dragged in a deep breath, she saw that Peder was looking over at her with worry.

"Mamma, how are you?"

He helped her to her feet. They stood there for a long time—Marianne didn't know how long—with their arms around each other. She forced herself to look at Hans, but then she had to turn away. All she wanted was to leave this horrible room.

PART ONE

PART ONE

CHAPTER 1

Paula Steen let her arm slide down Jens's stomach, feeling his chest hair tickle her underarm. He jerked in his sleep, then turned over and muttered, "I have to get more sleep. I didn't get home until two thirty last night."

Paula spooned herself against his body and spoke softly: "We've missed you here at home. Especially me . . ."

She slowly ran her fingers underneath the band of his shorts, but he harshly pushed her away.

"Cut it out. I told you I need to sleep."

He pulled up the blanket protectively so she could no longer get at him. Soon she heard his deep breathing, and it appeared he was back asleep. Paula lay beside him, and tears ran down her cheeks. Her arousal had turned into shame.

Perhaps she was making too big a deal of the whole thing. Was she like these men who feel rejected when their wives are no longer interested? Just like them, she had no right to demand sex. She wondered if they felt as humiliated by being turned away as she did now.

Paula knew exactly how long it had been since the last time they'd had sex: four months and two days. It was the evening after they'd celebrated their eldest daughter's tenth birthday. Even then, Paula had taken the initiative, but at least he responded and they had a great time. Paula thought they'd gotten better at it as the years went by, so she didn't understand how it had come to this. Was there something he didn't like? Did he think she'd become repulsive, even though she worked hard to keep her body in shape? Her figure had hardly changed since the day they'd met fifteen years ago. Fifteen years and two pregnancies! He'd even mentioned once that he was pleased to have such an attractive wife who hadn't let herself go.

Jens had always fixated on appearance. Paula's friends were shocked when, on her fortieth birthday, he gave her plastic surgery for her breasts. But she understood. Jens took good care of his own body, so why shouldn't he expect the same from her? It was only fair. He'd used Botox for his forehead wrinkles and Restylane for his cheeks, but no one was supposed to know about it. Since Jens liked a natural look, Paula's breast operation involved only a slight increase. One hundred cc's in one breast and one hundred fifty in the other. The needed lift had created a small T-shaped scar, but that had started to fade right away and could hardly be seen now.

Paula still wondered why he'd insisted on the operation, since he'd never been all that interested in her breasts. He never touched them, not even when he was aroused. It almost seemed like he avoided that area. But really, the same thing applied to her vagina. Was her vagina too loose after having children? Was that the reason their sex life was dwindling? If that was the case, she was ready to undergo vaginal surgery to tighten things up. Her plastic surgeon performed those kinds of operations as well. But Jens had told her that her vagina wasn't the reason, and then he indicated the subject was closed.

Paula shut her eyes and wondered if she could fall back to sleep, but she realized at once it wouldn't work. Instead, she set her feet on the well-oiled wooden floor, put on her robe, and looked for her slippers. She was confused. They weren't where they were supposed to be. Had she left them downstairs by the television last night?

She spent a moment in the bathroom and went downstairs, letting her hand drag along the glossy white wooden railing. The girls weren't at home. School was closed on Thursday and Friday for a teacher's retreat, so they'd gone with friends to a neighbor's country house. The neighbors had often asked to host the girls at their place on Vaddö, and this long weekend had been the perfect opportunity.

Paula had tried to be relaxed about the girls being gone until late Sunday night. It was unusual to have them away for so long. But she had done her best to look on the bright side. She'd be alone with Jens, and she'd planned yesterday in great detail. Dinner was ready by six.

When Jens called to say that his plane would be late, Paula started to cry. Jens snapped at her, saying she should be grateful he'd called to save her a trip to the airport.

She apologized and said they'd still have time together that weekend. When they hung up, she drank a glass of wine, and after two glasses, she went upstairs and took out her dildo. She'd bought it in secret a few months back because her fingers were no longer doing the trick. As usual, she finished quickly. She cleaned the dildo with soap and water, and felt ill. She hurried back downstairs to drink up the rest of the bottle.

Now, she believed that the wine must still be affecting her head. She was dizzy when she reached the bottom stair, and she made a mental note to check to make sure she wasn't suffering from anemia again. The doctor had told her to eat more meat, but she didn't like the taste. In addition, Jens kept saying that meat was something modern people no longer needed.

Suddenly, Paula jumped in surprise. Her slippers were in the middle of the kitchen, in front of the refrigerator. She looked around, pulling her robe tighter around her body. She didn't remember going to the refrigerator before bed. Did she not remember because of that whole bottle of wine? She didn't usually snack in the evening, not even when drinking. Perhaps Jens had put her slippers there last night by mistake. He knew she liked to slip her feet into them the moment she got up—maybe he'd meant to take them upstairs but had forgotten them halfway.

Paula put on her slippers and opened the refrigerator. She took out soy milk to warm in the microwave and some Kusmi tea. She mixed the warm milk with granola and sliced in a third of a banana. When she found herself eating too quickly, she forced herself to chew thirty times before swallowing. It wasn't easy. The food wanted to go down much faster than she could control. Her reflexes were strong. Carbs were her biggest enemy: she had to keep strict control over how much she ate, and giving in to carbs could ruin her character.

Once Paula finished her breakfast, she stared at the empty bowl for a long time. She knew she shouldn't eat anything more, but she decided to make another half portion. While waiting for the soy milk to heat up, she looked outside her window. A teenage boy was riding past her house on a bicycle, looking up at her and running a hand through his hair. Paula guessed he was seventeen or eighteen. He was fairly good-looking—like Jens when he was younger.

The microwave beeped, and she opened the door at the same time her cell phone started to ring.

A message:

You look sexy when you're asleep.

She laughed as she read the text again. Then her brow furrowed. She didn't recognize the sender's number.

She smiled while walking upstairs to the bedroom. Typical Jens—he'd probably sent it from one of his work numbers. It was the kind of thing he used to do when they'd just fallen in love. She'd enjoyed his romantic surprises in those days.

Still smiling, she opened the bedroom door—but she was startled to see Jens in bed and in the same position she'd left him in. Confused, she whispered, "Jens, are you sleeping?"

He gave no answer. No reaction. Jens was completely asleep.

Slowly, she walked back downstairs, her cell phone in her hand. She read the text a few more times and then deleted it. Someone must have texted the wrong number.

CHAPTER 2

Marianne had just received a phone call from Olle Lundqvist a quarter of an hour earlier. He was in the neighborhood and wondered whether he could come up and see her. He had an important question to ask. Marianne reluctantly agreed but asked for half an hour to get ready. She was worried about the state of her apartment. In the three months since her husband had passed away, she'd barely left home. She had always been proud of keeping her home virtually spotless. But this summer, she just hadn't had much energy.

She looked around and decided that twenty minutes would be enough time. She vacuumed the hallway, and then just the living room and around the sofa where she usually had her evening sandwiches. The strong sunshine showed a thick layer of dust on the leather ottoman she used as a coffee table, so she wiped it down with her sleeve. The polished wooden floors were protected by a worn Persian rug, and she noticed that it was time to take the rug in to the cleaner's. No time now. She fluffed up the sofa—she'd slept there the night before—and realized it was time to change the slipcover from the white summer canvas to the blue-and-gray-striped one for the winter season. The French balcony doors needed cleaning, too, but her visitor probably wouldn't notice.

As she walked back into the large hallway, she rearranged the plaid blanket over the armchair by the fireplace and repositioned the candlestick on the mantel. In the hall she removed the pile of mail that had accumulated on an antique desk. The hallway was now presentable, although she still ran her finger over the rim of the golden mirror frame and frowned at the dust.

She closed the door to her bedroom. Olle wouldn't need to go there. Down the hallway were the three bedrooms she herself seldom entered unless she had to get something stored in there. The rooms belonged to her three grown children, and she hadn't yet started to redecorate them. That would have to be a future project.

With some irritation, she closed the door to the library. That had been her favorite room in the house, but she hadn't entered it since that day in May when Hans had passed away. Something was keeping her back. She just wasn't ready yet.

She went into the guest bathroom. The Josef Frank wallpaper looked worn, but it gave this room some character, as opposed to the somber look of the rest of her house. Little by little over the past decades, Marianne had come to discover her own personality in the house. The more Hans worked at his career, the more time she put into their home. This was also a hidden strategy on her part: the more elegant her home became, the more Hans felt lost in it. He'd brought only one thing into the house when they married thirty years ago—a wall clock he'd inherited from his mother's side of the family. The clock had never worked and wasn't all that attractive, either.

She found herself in her own bedroom. She gathered up all the dirty clothes she'd flung on a chair and put everything in the hamper. She smoothed the sheets and arranged the pillows against the brown headboard from Muscat. She'd changed the sheets a few days earlier and wasn't about to do it again. They were summer sheets, with light-blue stripes. It was highly unlikely that Olle would need to come in here, but still.

Marianne's daughters often teased her for decorating her home according to the seasons. They told her there was no reason to change sheets, slipcovers, and curtains just because the thermometer showed a different temperature. Marianne disagreed. It was important to keep track of the seasons. It made daily life better and made her appreciate her home even more. Probably it was a generational thing.

Time was getting short now, so she shed her rumpled sweater and pulled out a white linen blouse, which she'd hung over a gray linen pair of slacks. Her hair had grown fairly long recently. She'd never dyed it, so she felt even more bohemian-looking than usual. But what did it matter? She found a clasp and pulled her hair back. She had just put on a scarf and tied it in a soft knot when the doorbell rang. No time to worry about any deodorant or perfume. It was more important that Olle just tell her what he had to say and leave. She wanted the meeting over and done with.

—◻—

Olle Lundqvist took a sip of mineral water and set the glass down on a coaster with a map motif. He pressed two fingers to his mouth—a gesture he often made when he was about to plead a case. He cleared his throat, and Marianne realized he was embarrassed to ask for a favor directly.

"I know it's difficult making decisions now, but by the end of the week I need to know what you've decided. Your replacement has asked for the job permanently, and it will be hard to ask her to leave if you end up deciding to return. I know you think you've made up your mind—and I have your letter of resignation. But for my sake, Marianne, would you reconsider? Would you come back?"

Marianne's heart leapt, but she didn't know if it was from worry or relief. Most likely the latter. Her dry lips felt rough as she pressed them together. She smiled at the man she'd known as a good friend for the past twenty years.

"I understand your thinking, Olle, but you might as well give her the permanent position."

"Are you absolutely sure? I think that's unwise on your part. And sad. Well, I won't do anything until Friday, at least. I want you to come into the office and give your final answer in person. Damn it all, Marianne, I need you! I need your skill! Not a single one of the legal secretaries has a law degree. They don't have your experience—not by a long shot. You should feel responsible! Do you really think your replacement should come from a pool of temps? Do you understand the difference between your abilities and theirs?"

"This is starting to sound like bribery."

"Call it whatever you like. You've also had over twenty years of experience assisting Hans. I know you felt it was your duty since you were married, but you've learned a lot because of it."

Marianne could see that Olle looked tired—like something was weighing on him.

"Is anyone I know still around? Aren't there a lot of new people?"

"Yes, people come and go. You know that."

He steered the conversation in a different direction.

"How have you been dealing with the practical side of things? Do you need help with anything? How about your summer house on Dalarö? Are you keeping it?"

With a hard edge to her voice, Marianne answered, "I have no plans to sell my summer house. Hans never had much to do with it. He even hated going there. It wasn't just that he'd rather be working—to him, Dalarö symbolized everything he didn't like. He used to call it Snob Island. He wasn't much for status—it was a miracle I managed to convince him to move to Östermalm in the first place."

Olle nodded. "He never felt at home in your world."

Marianne shook her head and sighed. "Otherwise, everything is fairly well taken care of. Some paperwork left, but I need some forms from the tax office. Nina is taking care of it, actually, and my father is the executor."

"How is Harry, by the way?"

"I think he's getting more energetic by the year. It's almost annoying. He'll outlive us all! Last spring was his seventy-eighth birthday. I doubt there's a single charitable organization without him on the board. Recently, he even joined the board of some organization providing exercise classes for Östermalm's retirees."

Olle whistled. "It sure is hard to believe he's reached that age. He looked imposing at the funeral in his air force uniform. Is he still in contact with his military buddies?"

"Of course. They have lunch once a week."

The conversation paused. Marianne hoped that Olle had finally changed the subject now that the funeral had come up. She decided to let the mood hang in the room instead of putting him at ease.

She felt the need for a smoke. She kept a pack of cigarettes near the stove, on the top shelf of the kitchen pantry. She hadn't really smoked in over thirty years but liked having them on hand to offer guests. A few times she'd taken a puff or two. Now, she was surprised that the need to smoke had come on so suddenly and strongly. Drinking often brought with it the desire to smoke, but she hadn't even had any alcohol.

As she drummed her fingers on the armrest, Olle finally broke the silence.

"How are the girls taking it?"

"Nina hasn't changed. She still needs to organize everything and tell everyone else what to do. Sigrid lets her big sister be in charge. She takes things more calmly, and she's been able to lose herself in her sewing. She is opening a design studio on the first floor of this building. Nina was hit harder by Hans's death: she was her father's daughter. As the eldest, she's used to taking on responsibility. And right now she's having trouble understanding me. She thinks I'm not grieving for Hans properly."

"What about Peder?"

"He's heading back to Australia soon. He promised Hans he'd finish his studies. But to tell you the truth, I'm not sure how he's feeling. He doesn't show anything on the surface. I'm not even sure he cried during the funeral."

Olle nodded. "People grieve in different ways. Perhaps he'll start to deal with it once he's left Stockholm. And you? How are you doing?"

"Well, honestly, I really don't know."

As Marianne tried to ignore a memory playing in her mind like a snippet from a film, Olle looked at her with compassion.

"You don't have to tell me. I understand."

She surprised herself by blurting out, "I'm just so angry at him!"

Olle replied softly, "People often feel like that in the beginning. It's part of the grieving process. Being angry is perfectly normal."

Marianne's eyes narrowed, and she almost hissed back at him. She pictured Hans again on his deathbed, his words a final humiliation.

"I'm sure you're right," she said with a strained voice.

After a long pause, Marianne stood up.

"I'm sorry to be a bad hostess, but I need to shower and get ready for a doctor's appointment. I've also promised to make dinner this evening, and I need to do my shopping. Peder has been eating sandwiches for weeks, and I don't want him going back to Australia without having some of his favorite dishes. Pappa and Sigrid will be here, too."

"What about Nina?"

"She's going with her husband, Robert, to a friend's place. She needs to take a break from all of us. She's had too much responsibility for all this."

"We all choose our roles. I need to get going, too."

Marianne followed him to the entry hall and handed him his scarf. She could see in his eyes that he was debating whether to say something. Finally, he spoke.

"Marianne, I'd like you to come back. I really mean that."

Marianne examined his face, surprised by the deep feeling in his voice.

"Has something serious come up?"

Olle swallowed. He buttoned his coat but then stopped. He turned and strode back into the living room, sinking down in a chair and covering his face. For a moment, Marianne thought he might start crying, but he sat up straight and looked her in the eye.

"Marianne, I'll tell you straight. Please forgive me, but I don't want to mince words."

Marianne felt her heart flip-flop and got a sour taste in her mouth.

Olle continued, "We *have* had some issues lately. There's been a leak of confidential information. That's not a new problem, as you know, but it's never been as bad as we're experiencing now. It's out of hand. There have been leaks to different departments and the media, between local and national, and even to Säpo—though God only knows how they're getting their hands on it."

"And you have no idea who might be doing this?"

"We suspect a number of people. We're in the middle of setting up a new internal security system. But that takes time. I've devised a new strategy, and you're its linchpin."

Marianne was taken aback, but Olle went on.

"I want to keep this group very small. If people report only to me, we can keep things watertight."

"You can certainly find someone to take my place. A true assistant to the prosecutor. What about that new guy, Tommy, you mentioned before?"

"Listen to me, Marianne! It's *you* that I want! You know this organization inside and out. You know it from your own work and Hans's. I know this is a sensitive area, but . . . we both know that Hans was a fine person in his own way, one of the best we had in the Swedish legal system. Still, he had a weakness: women. I believe that's where the leaks started."

Marianne coughed and ran a hand down her thigh. She looked straight at Olle.

"What are you saying? Are you implying that he leaked sensitive information through some lover?"

"Honestly, I'm not sure exactly how it happened, but everything I've learned makes me think he was involved. I knew Hans well. I don't think he'd have willingly passed on information. But someone close to him could have been using him. I even suspect he was being blackmailed. So far, we have no concrete proof. It's an old story, especially in cases involving state secrets and espionage. This is just on a much smaller scale. What I'm trying to say is, I think someone got to Hans through his weak spot."

"How did you arrive at this conclusion?"

"I can't say right now, but—believe me—I wouldn't be telling you this if I weren't sure."

"So why do you think I'm the one who can help you? If he was able to hide his affairs from me during our marriage, I could hardly stumble on them now that he's dead."

"He didn't do much to hide them. I don't think he ever bothered. You just chose to keep your eyes shut."

The truth hurt. Marianne's instinct was to get up and leave. But she stayed.

"This is all very distasteful," she said.

"I think the leaks are still getting out, so it would be very helpful if you agreed to work with me in this special group. We're not going to bother with Hans's former lovers. We want to get to the heart of the matter and find out who else is leaking this vital information. I suspect it is someone high up in the ranks, or a group of people who might not even be working together. This is way beyond Hans now. I need your help because I know I can trust you one hundred percent. You are an intelligent woman—you know it, and you know how this affects us. These leaks hurt our work."

Marianne stood up. Olle looked at her questioningly.

She crooked her finger, saying, "Come with me to the kitchen. I need a cigarette."

—□—

Once Marianne closed the door behind Olle, she stood perfectly still, her feet planted on the coconut rug. She had agreed to go back to work the following Monday. How she was going to pull herself together by then was another question entirely. Today she'd hardly been able to get out of bed, let alone take a shower. Work, which would involve all her energy, seemed impossible at best. She sighed heavily and felt a strong tug of nausea. A second later, she was running into the guest bathroom to avoid vomiting on the hallway floor.

Before showering, Marianne contemplated her worn-out body. Without the proper support, her breasts looked sad against her white stomach. The right one had a pressed line from her robe and seemed somewhat knobby. Her stomach looked bloated, and her sides were flabby. Even though she'd increased the size of her underwear, her sides never managed to stay in place.

The bush between her legs was starting to look sparse. It was now a dull gray, unlike the steel gray of the hair on her head.

Her white legs were soft, and their youthful elasticity was long gone. To her, it looked as if her thighs were melting into her calves. She sighed as she looked down at her feet. There was only a tiny fleck of red polish on one of her big toes. It had been a long time since she'd had them done.

With a heavy heart, she pulled shut the shower curtain. The brown tinge around its bottom edge meant it was time to buy a new one. But today's task was a routine visit to the gynecologist. She'd already canceled her appointment twice. She didn't even want to think about how long it had been since her last Pap smear.

She turned the water on cold for a last blast, but that didn't energize her at all. Her exhaustion was debilitating. The morning had demanded more from her than she was ready to give, and she wished she could creep back into bed. Still, she couldn't cancel a third time. She hurried to find some clean clothes before she could change her mind. Just to be on the safe side, she misted a bit of perfume into her panties, even though she knew the doctor wouldn't care.

CHAPTER 3

"Are you absolutely sure? The local police are going to be furious," Torsten Ehn pointed out.

"I realize that," Olle said. "I wouldn't ask you to come unless it was the highest priority. A dead finance executive in Östermalm is going to whip the media into a frenzy. We have to keep absolute control over this one. I'm going to the crime scene now, but I told Brundin that you'd be on your way."

"I'll head over there now."

"Thanks! And give me a call as soon as you arrive. I want the news right from the horse's mouth. One more thing. I want you to get in touch with Marianne Jidhoff and keep her in the loop."

"Who?"

"Marianne's a close friend of mine. She'll be working on this case with us."

"What are you cooking up now?"

"Look, I'll send you her home number. Just make sure she gets all the information you find."

"Can't you at least tell me her role in this? Just to be sure I'm not doing anything illegal."

"Cut it out. Marianne has been the head secretary for the Prosecutor's Office. She's just been on leave for a while, but I managed to convince her to come back. She is one of the sharpest analysts we have. She figured out how to crack that shady lawyer's ring, although we got it through her husband, Hans Larson."

"That son of a bitch."

"You know Hans was a friend of mine."

"Friend? I knew he was your mentor, but I never thought you'd call him a friend. Maybe you had to stay on his good side, but he was a real son of a bitch. You know why I never liked him. He was a hypocrite, a power-hungry member of the Socialist Party. So, it turns out his wife was the real brains behind his legal genius."

"She had been studying to become a prosecutor herself, but then she had three kids, and you know how that goes. She's great. I want you to call her. And what I just told you stays between us."

Torsten Ehn hung up the phone. He turned off his computer and glanced at the heap of paperwork on his desk. Yesterday he'd told himself he'd sort through it all. He got up and took his jacket from its hook, wondering whether he should take his umbrella as well, but then decided against it. On his way down the staircase, he saw some colleagues on their way to play field hockey. Another match he'd have to miss. Perhaps it was just as well. The last time he played, he bruised his shins.

Torsten opened the door to his Toyota Corolla, glad that he'd cleaned it over the weekend. He'd spent quite a bit of Sunday in his brother's garage vacuuming the car's interior and getting rid of all the garbage. Since moving recently, he'd been storing things in his car that should have gone straight to the dump.

The car now smelled fresh and clean. He turned on the radio, which was playing music he recognized for once. This happened less and less. He exited onto Kungsholmsgatan and drove past the Court House. He'd put the note with Marianne Jidhoff's number on the passenger seat so he'd remember to call her after assessing the crime scene. He couldn't help being curious about what his boss Olle was cooking up—and how Hans Larson's wife fit in. As far as Torsten was concerned, Hans Larson had been a total idiot; God had given more sense to ants. Larson was also notorious for his bad fashion sense. Torsten shuddered at the thought of what Larson's wife must look like.

The victim was in the middle of a pedestrian crosswalk on Narvavägen, in front of King Oscar's Church, not far from Torsten's own apartment.

An older officer walked up to Torsten. "What are you doing here?" he said.

Torsten noticed that the officer had put on weight. He also looked more tired and worn than usual.

"Olle Lundqvist sent me."

"Damn nice of him. We need all the help we can get. By the way, you just missed him. I don't think he wanted to deal with that crowd."

The officer motioned toward a group of journalists crowding together with cameras and microphones.

Torsten hadn't expected that, but he kept his surprise in check. He and Olle shared the same instincts when it came to talking to the media. They knew what to tell and what to hold back. They were not about to jeopardize a case.

Torsten pulled up his jacket's zipper and said, "I might as well get to work. What do you have to show me?"

"He's lying over there. Jan is doing his best to keep the crowd back."

Jan Brundin was the head forensic expert for the National Police. Torsten wondered if Olle had called him in, too, or if he'd been requested by the local police. In his field, he was the best in the country. The fact that he was here at all showed this was no ordinary hit-and-run.

"Hi there, Jan. What's up? Do we know who this is?"

"His name is Christopher Turin. He lives right in that apartment building. Luckily, his family is away, so they didn't have to witness this. We've reached his wife in Mallorca, who's there with their three children. He's some kind of big-shot finance executive."

"How old is he?"

"He was born in 1964."

"So, just about fifty."

"Yeah. He works in the stock market, I believe."

"Any skid marks?"

"No, but the tire tracks show a fast start. I believe someone was in a car waiting for him to come home—just to run him over."

"Any witnesses?"

"Not that I know of yet, but at four in the morning there weren't too many folks out and about. Maybe we can find a newspaper-delivery person. There's hardly a soul in Östermalm after nine in the evening."

"So what was *he* doing out at four in the morning? Especially after a Sunday night? He'd hardly been to a bar or a party."

"No idea—I'm not up on the lifestyle of these people. I'll test his alcohol level. Or whether he was under the influence of drugs."

"Anything else? I have to talk to the vultures."

"My sympathies. How'd you get roped into that? I thought the local police would be taking on the media."

"So did I, but Olle asked me to do it."

"Must be a sensitive case. Whenever shit goes down in this neighborhood, it's a big deal. If this had been a hit-and-run in the poor suburbs south of Söder, we sure wouldn't be there."

"You're right about that."

Jan got to his feet and stretched his arms over his head. He turned his head so his neck cracked. He shook his shoulders and looked thoughtful.

"The first thing I thought was that he was leaving his home, but it looks like he was just coming back. I also think he was run over more than once. They backed up over him just to be sure."

Torsten looked at Jan in surprise. "So, first they hit him straight on, then backed over him again?"

"Sure looks like it."

–◻–

Torsten wrinkled his forehead. "I'd better deal with the media. Can you call me when you get lab results? Are you going to take a long lunch?"

"No, I'll have something quick at the office. I'll call you as soon as I have something."

Torsten gazed down at the sheet covering the victim, grateful that the victim's children were spared this sight. He ran his hands through his hair and massaged his temples. He would need to weigh each word he said with care—the journalists would be more bloodthirsty than usual. The victim was a wealthy, upper-crust man, which usually aroused speculations. Certainly, if this had happened in Rinkeby or Södertälje, the press wouldn't have bothered to show up.

—□—

"Do you have any witnesses? What kind of car are you looking for?"

"Our investigation is at an early stage. Our forensic experts need to run some tests. We'll make sure to give you the information once we have it."

"What can you tell us about the victim?"

"Not much at the moment, out of respect for the family. We can tell you that the victim was in his upper forties and lived in this neighborhood."

The vultures scribbled in their notebooks, and Torsten saw his chance to leave.

"You're welcome to come to the station as soon as we've finished our reports. Right now our investigation points toward fatal hit-and-run. I have to leave now, so thanks for your time."

He bowed slightly and turned away as quickly as he could. Reporters yelled questions at his back, but he was used to keeping his ears shut. If he let them, they'd keep him talking nonsense for hours. Sometimes he thought they stayed in the field as long as they could—it was a good excuse for avoiding their editors and dull colleagues back at their boring offices. He smiled at his own analysis while waving to Jan Brundin. Jan was packing up his portable laboratory case, and Torsten knew that when Jan called with lab results, he'd invite him to go out on his boat before autumn really set in. Since Jan had no family, he was just as flexible as Torsten. They could be spontaneous, letting the weather decide their course.

CHAPTER 4

Paula Steen tied the laces of her jogging shoes into double knots and checked her cell phone. She'd planned to run her short route but then decided she felt energetic enough to take the long one. That way, she'd be able to have bread with lunch. She really hungered for bread. Usually, she could resist carbs, but having so much wine the night before had made her crave them. Her friend Lotta would probably suggest they each have a cinnamon bun. Paula usually crumbled hers into bits. She never understood how Lotta could be so cavalier about food. Lotta was thinner than she was and had four kids. She ought to have gained weight. Instead, she usually ate big portions and didn't seem to gain anything at all. Paula suspected that Lotta's doctor prescribed weight-loss pills. Probably someone with a generous prescription pad in Spain, where Lotta and her husband had a summer house.

She tapped in the code to their alarm and listened to the familiar melody, hurrying outside and securing the two locks on the front door. Jens had thought an alarm system was unnecessary, but he changed his mind when a neighbor's two cars and riding mower were stolen. Paula had been afraid at night for as long as she could remember—and now she couldn't even imagine sleeping in a house without the protection of an alarm system. She had no explanation for her fear of the dark. And she was somewhat ashamed of it, especially when Jens would say she was passing her irrational fear to their girls. She worked hard at keeping her feelings under control, and the alarm system helped her stay calm.

Paula ran down the gravel path, adjusting the watch on her arm. The water of Svalnäs Bay was tinged gray with small whitecaps, even though the wind wasn't blowing that strong.

Before Jens had left for work that morning, she'd asked if they could have dinner in the city for a change. He'd shaken his head and said he had Japanese customers in the afternoon, and he was expected to have dinner with them afterward. She asked desperately if she could come, too. Jens had smiled and patted her on the cheek, telling her it was better if she stayed home, just in case the girls got homesick at the neighbors' country place. Paula agreed. The girls had actually done that before, and they'd had to rush to pick them up from a friend's house in the middle of the night. At any rate, she and Jens would have the rest of the weekend together.

Paula sped up to pass two teenage girls walking and laughing together. Seeing them made her miss her childhood friends in Gothenburg. Only one had moved to Stockholm, and she wasn't exactly one of her closest friends. She lived in Saltsjöbaden on the other side of town. Her other friends lived in Gothenburg suburbs—Särö or Örgryte—and had summer houses in Marstrand.

Paula once tried to convince Jens to look into renting a summer house on Marstrand, but he refused to even consider it. He had no intention of spending his free time in what he considered the backwaters of Sweden. He even had trouble with people from the city of Gothenburg. She'd smiled then and asked why he married one if he found them so disagreeable. Jens snorted and said he'd cured her of her small-town ways.

As Paula started toward home, sweat slid into her eyes. She pressed herself up the steep hill, and her legs shook from the effort.

The old embankment here was eroding, and she wondered when the district would come and fix it. They'd promised they would. The trees beside it were huge, and the undergrowth was so thick that it was impossible to see through. Paula was uncomfortable having such dense shrubbery so close to their house, especially for the girls. Who knows what might be hiding in there? She heard rustling as she passed by, but she didn't stop. She opened her front gate and rushed to her front door. When she turned around to look back, the rustling stopped. She had to collect herself. Being too neurotic wasn't an attractive trait. She took a deep breath and scolded herself, trying to keep her nerves in check.

Just then, she saw a shadow move behind her bedroom curtain. Someone was on the second floor.

CHAPTER 5

The medical complex on Odenplan was fourteen stories high. The last time Marianne had seen her gynecologist, her office was in a narrow, one-way street in Gärdet and decorated like an apartment. These days, her gynecologist worked only a few days a week, so she'd sold her practice and rented an office here.

Marianne squirmed when her name was called. She put down her magazine and was escorted to the examination room. No one else in the waiting room bothered to look up.

"You can sit here. Dr. Lundström will be right with you."

Marianne sat down and set her purse on the floor. She felt around her gums with her tongue and wondered if her breath smelled as bad as it tasted. Still, she wasn't visiting the dentist.

"Hello, Marianne! It's been a while!"

Marianne jumped to her feet to shake hands. Her doctor was a thin woman her own age with blonde hair—the same shade as when she'd taken Marianne as a patient six weeks after Peder was born.

"Yes, I'm sorry. Things have been crazy at home."

"I understand. Still, getting tests done is important, and it's been a few years."

Marianne sighed. "I know. But this spring my husband passed away with prostate cancer."

"I'm so sorry to hear that. You must have been through a difficult time. Well, it's been six years since you were here last. You weighed 140 pounds and you had a chlamydia test and a Pap smear. I also did a manual breast exam. Always a good thing to do, even if you get a mammogram. I suggest we do the same today. Please get undressed, and we'll get started. You can put your clothes on the stool behind the screen."

Marianne opened her mouth to say something, but nothing came out. Dr. Lundström looked at her over her glasses.

"Is there something you'd like to ask? Something else we should talk about?"

"Well . . . I haven't had sex since the last time I was here, so maybe the chlamydia test is unnecessary."

The doctor looked at her in surprise and placed her hands, palms down, on her desk. "Since chlamydia can be latent, I think we should go ahead with the test anyway, as long as you're here. I say the same thing to all the women I see. Why don't you go ahead and get on the scale."

Marianne went behind the screen and took off her clothes, but she left her panties on. She shivered as she stood on the glass plate of the scale. The merciless digital numbers on the screen showed 180 pounds.

Dr. Lundström typed the result into her computer. Then she asked Marianne to sit down on the examination table without her panties.

"If you wiggle a little closer, it'll be easier for me to reach. First, I'll do the chlamydia test. You'll feel a little pressure as I poke around. There we go. Now, the Pap smear. It'll pinch a little, as you know. Relax and take a deep breath, please . . . good. That's done. Now I'm going to take a look around. Well, what have we here? Are you aware that you still have your IUD?"

Marianne was surprised. "What? That's still there?"

She repressed a giggle. It reminded her of the first time she'd visited a gynecologist as an innocent seventeen-year-old, about to take her first lover.

"Yes, it's nice and snug, but I think we can remove it. There we go. Now I'm going to take a look with the ultrasound. We just want to make sure there are no unfortunate surprises on the ovaries."

The doctor pressed on Marianne's pelvis, and with a practiced hand she slid the ultrasound wand into Marianne's vagina. Marianne rested her gaze on the ceiling and tried to relax while Dr. Lundström looked at her and smiled.

"Well, Marianne, everything seems to be in good shape. Nothing unusual. You can get down now, and you'll find some tissues behind the screen if you need to dry off."

Dr. Lundström snapped off her latex gloves and walked back to her desk. Marianne spied the IUD discarded in a steel bowl. She hurried to dress and then sat back down on the visitor's chair.

"Well, Marianne, everything looks just fine. I'll let you know the test results as soon as they come in. How are things with your menstruation? Are you still having your periods?"

"No, they stopped over a year ago."

"Have you had any issues with menopause?"

"Not really. I had some hot flashes a few years back, but not enough to be bothersome."

"That's great. Many women have more difficulty going through the change. There's one thing I have to tell you, though, quite honestly. You've put on a great deal of weight. This is not good at your age."

Marianne felt her cheeks get hot and her heart speed up. She stared at the thin woman on the other side of the desk who'd just scolded her. She wanted to defend herself, but she didn't know how. Dr. Lundström didn't even look up from her screen.

"I suggest you work hard to lose the weight now. I know it sounds harsh, but I mean it in the most helpful way. You shouldn't weigh this much. It's especially hard on the body after menopause. This kind of weight can even cause problems such as incontinence. I suggest you contact your general practitioner for a prescription to help you."

"Diet pills?"

"There are many medications to choose from these days."

Marianne shook her head. "No, thank you. I'll try to lose the weight myself. I'm going back to work again, so I'll be moving around more. That should make things easier."

"Well, then, good luck. If you change your mind and want some help, just contact me or your general doctor. And make sure you add an exercise routine. We women suffer from osteoporosis. You can't skip exercise if you want to stay healthy."

They exchanged good-byes, and Marianne walked back into the waiting room. She took her coat from the hanger and felt odd, thinking it strange that most of the examination focused on her weight. Was it really all that bad that she'd put on some extra pounds? As she walked home along

Odengatan, she got upset. She did her best to not look at the pastry displays in the coffee shops and fight the urge to devour an entire Princess cake in pure protest. She didn't know how to shake the rage she felt. Preparing a family dinner now was the last thing she wanted to do.

She caught sight of her reflection in a display window. Her stomach protruded from her coat, and she could see a few bulges over her belt. She knew that her flat shoes gave her legs a stubby look, but still . . . she sighed. She already had enough to handle. How would she find the energy to deal with losing weight, too?

CHAPTER 6

Café Gateau was filled to bursting despite it being a Thursday. The patrons weren't harried workers checking their watches to get back to the office on time. Rather, this was a different clientele altogether: flawless women in their thirties and forties in colorful sweaters over tight jeans, wearing well-worn sneakers or Crocs in all the colors of the rainbow. Their fingers boasted glittering wedding rings, and their wrinkle-free faces were used to the most expensive creams. Very few wore makeup, and their hair was well taken care of—combed back and set up in ponytails.

Each had ordered her own special: a no-foam latte with soy, or a cheese sandwich with extra green pepper, no butter. *Could you be so kind and cut the cinnamon bun into thirds? Are you sure you don't have any liver pâté this morning? Could you have someone go procure some from the deli? Do you have lactose-free skim milk? Please give me a decaf latte with whole milk—and make it just hot enough so I can still hold the cup. Let me tell you how they make lattes in Italy . . .*

The special of the day was *croque monsieur*. Paula thought long and hard about whether to order it but decided no, at the last possible moment. Instead, she ordered a sandwich made of half a rye bun with ham and no butter. She ordered her latte with whole milk—she couldn't stand the aftertaste of soy—and she decided to satisfy her hunger with a bit of mustard on her ham. Lotta had ordered the *croque monsieur*, and she smiled down at her plate.

"This looks wonderful! Why don't we each have a cinnamon bun, too? They look so good today."

Paula nodded and felt the anxiety rise from the middle of her stomach. She couldn't resist eating that cinnamon bun this morning. But she could take a second lap this afternoon.

Lotta studied Paula with intense curiosity as she sat down.

"Come on! Tell me all about it! You sounded hysterical when you called."

Paula laughed. "Yes, well, now it sounds so stupid. I'd done my morning run and was coming through the yard when I saw someone standing in our bedroom. I panicked, as I was absolutely sure I'd set the alarm earlier."

"How scary! I'd have been frightened, too."

"I called Jens first, but he didn't pick up the phone, so I called you. Then our cleaning lady came out with the garbage. I'd forgotten that she was supposed to be there."

"She has the code to your alarm?"

"Yes, Jens gave it to her. I didn't want her to have it, but he said we have to trust some people. He thinks it's racist of me to be suspicious since I have no problem giving the baby-sitters our code. I just forgot we'd decided to switch days this week—so please forgive me for calling and sounding so frenzied."

"Don't think about it. I was worried. You were out of your mind with fright."

Paula shook her head. "I really have to get a grip on my anxiety. It's not good for a grown woman to have such fear at night. Jens is absolutely correct. It will affect the girls. I'm so glad they weren't with me today. What if they'd seen me lose it like that?"

"Maybe you'd have reacted differently if they were there. You were alone, so you gave yourself permission to be afraid. Tell me, do you want to go out with me tonight? Go to Velvet?"

"Oh, is that tonight?"

"Yes, and I bet you've never been there—right?"

Paula shook her head. Velvet was a once-a-month night-club that met at the exclusive Villa Pauli. She'd heard that the atmosphere was giddy. People who were no longer young enough for the "in" clubs at Stureplan now had somewhere to go.

"As long as Jens is out with customers, you should join us. There'll be five of us girls having dinner at my place be-forehand."

"It does sound fun. Let me just check with Jens first, in case he managed to change his evening plans."

Paula really wanted Jens to choose her over his custom-ers. It was also important to her to get his approval. It was a good idea, she thought, for spouses to check with each other before doing anything out of the ordinary.

"Aren't you going to eat your bun? I really do worry that you're not eating enough. It looks like you've lost weight. Are you doing all right?"

Lotta's words made Paula feel good. She smiled grate-fully.

"Thanks for your concern. You're so sweet, but don't worry about me. I just look a bit tired. You know how it is when Jens is working overtime so much. My responsibility for the girls is greater. I get exhausted not having anyone to share that with. But as far as eating is concerned—you're talking to someone who eats candy every day!"

She laughed to indicate how improbable it was that Lotta should think, even for a moment, that she was too thin. It was the best compliment that she'd received in a long time. She smiled at Lotta, continuing: "I'm just going to touch base with Jens and then I'll give you a call. It'll be great to get out of the house for an evening. But I've heard rumors things get pretty crazy there. What's it really like?"

Lotta laughed. "It's almost like the days when we were young and wild. The same guys stand around the bar popping champagne—except now they're almost fifty. Then they try to pick us up. Our neighbor, the one who got divorced last year, was caught having sex in the bathroom. How embarrassing! People so desperate for sex that they risk being thrown out of a bar! But there's a great deal of that. Velvet has the nickname "Wild Divorcées" in town. My sister says that the young guys she works with go there to pick up women because they know they won't get turned down for sex."

"Really? There's that much sex?"

"Come on, don't be such a prude. That's the whole point."

"I'm certainly out of the loop. Is it really going to be that bad for our daughters when they get older? How are they going to understand the real world?"

"Now, really, we're not all that old. We're not like our mothers when they were our age."

"Aren't we?"

Lotta laughed and then shook her head as she took a huge bite from her bun.

"No, we certainly are not. There weren't all that many plastic surgeons when they were our age!"

They both laughed and cheered each other with their coffee cups. Paula tugged at her sweater and hoped that Lotta's plastic-surgery comment hadn't been a subtle jab about noticing her breast operation. The she wondered whether going out with Lotta and her friends was a good idea. She didn't know if she was up for a night on the town.

CHAPTER 7

The Ica Banér grocery store was deserted, although there was seldom a rush at this midmorning hour. The faithful older ladies wouldn't come in to pinch the freshly baked loaves until early afternoon. The aisles echoed. A young woman at the register was reading a magazine. She nodded at Marianne with no sign of recognition.

Marianne paused to choose between a full-size shopping cart and a basket on wheels. Forty-five minutes later, she was lugging five fully packed grocery bags down the block to her front door.

She was relieved to see that Peder had come home. He greeted her in the hallway with a smile that made her think briefly of him at five years old. But Marianne couldn't ignore the major beard he'd grown while in Australia.

Peder peered into the bags as he helped her carry them into the kitchen.

"What are you making for dinner tonight? By the way, you're energetic today."

"Thanks. I realized that I hadn't made a single one of your favorite meals since you've been home. So this evening, I'm making Kassler Florentine, and I hope to make all the other ones before you leave for Australia. By the way, have you booked your flight?"

Peder looked a little apprehensive. "Yes, I'm flying out this Saturday. Is that all right?"

Marianne felt a pang in her heart, but she smiled anyway. "Of course. You need to get back to your life. That's the way it is. But tonight we are going to eat a wonderful dinner together, and then I hope you'll come home again soon so I can make your other favorites for you."

"What's your plan for dessert?"

"You can choose between baked pears and blueberry surprise."

Peder looked so happy that Marianne broke out into laughter. She patted him on the cheek.

"My sweet son—it has always been so easy to please you with food!"

She started to unpack the groceries. Peder's cell phone rang, and he chatted with a friend he was supposed to meet. Marianne wondered if it was Clara. Perhaps they'd already gotten together this visit. Clara and Peder had been close friends since childhood. Marianne secretly hoped he'd end up with her. She loved Clara almost as much as her own children. She had no explanation for this, except that there was something very special about her. She'd felt it the first time she'd seen the little girl at the parents' cooperative on Banérgatan.

"Hey, Mamma, I'd like to meet some of the guys downtown. Is it all right if I go out later, after our dinner?"

"Sure. You know I go to bed early. You don't have to stay home just to keep me company."

"Great! I'm looking forward to dinner, too, especially since I haven't seen Grandpa almost all summer. What does he do all day?"

Marianne sighed.

"I have no idea. It's impossible to keep up with him. He's always involved in some social event or another. I really don't understand how he has the energy, but people are always sending him invitations. The last one was to go hunting, but for once he had to decline. He hasn't been hunting for over thirty years! Otherwise the chairman of this or the petitioner of that is asking him to each and every charity event."

"That's not so bad. At least he's not sitting around alone all day."

"He's probably having the time of his life," Marianne said. "Not like me. I've hardly left home all summer long."

"Things will be different now. You should do whatever you want. You don't have to wait for someone else to give approval, right?"

Marianne looked into her son's dark eyes. They were framed by the kind of thick, black lashes most women would pay a fortune to have.

"Maybe so."

She knew that he was hinting at something else entirely. It wasn't just that she'd stayed cooped up ever since her husband had died. Peder was the only one who knew the truth. He'd been in the room with her when Hans said those last, hurtful words.

Peder wrapped his arm around his mother and kissed her on the forehead. She closed her eyes and leaned against his shoulder. *My little boy.*

CHAPTER 8

Torsten decided to take a drive to Djurgården, where he'd often gone to clear his thoughts and analyze his impressions from the crime scene. He found an open hot dog stand by Djurgård Fountain and had a plain dog while studying ducks floating along the Djurgård Canal. Then he drove onto the spit at Blockhus to sit in his car and stare at the water. But he didn't come to any new insights or a tidy solution.

Now he was on his way to Karlaplan, where he drove around the fountain and turned right at Karlavägen. He saw the classic sign *Frukt och grönt*—"Fruit and Veggies"— on his left. Since he planned to turn right at Skeppargatan, he grabbed an empty parking spot on the sunny side of Karlavägen. He walked across the wide boulevard, ignoring the "Keep Off the Grass" sign, and entered the small store called Karla Frukt.

He remembered the first time he'd ever been inside this store. He was with his mother, who worked for a family in Wittstocksgatan, and he'd gazed in awe at the beautiful glass jars filled with colorful candy and so many different chocolates.

Today the door was propped open—an invitation to step inside. Behind the counter the cashier—a woman his own age—was chatting with an elderly woman buying her week's rations of cigarettes and raspberries. Torsten was struck by the fact that the place hadn't changed much since his first visit as a seven-year-old boy.

The cashier behind the counter smiled warmly. She had straight blonde hair with bangs.

"Is there something I can help you with today?"

"Do you sell coffee?"

"Yes, is caffe latte OK?"

"Sure," Torsten said. "Just a small one, though. And I think I'll get something to go with it. May I help myself?"

"Absolutely. You'll find bags on the shelf next to the bins, and there's a basket with tongs and spoons."

Torsten grabbed a small, thin paper bag with the classic pastel bubble motif—and a pair of tongs to start digging into the bins. Two blue fish, one yellow caramel, three marshmallow bananas, a chocolate-dipped dolphin, a licorice pipe, and, finally, a *tomteklubba*, which he just couldn't resist.

"Let me count them for you," said the cashier, pouring the contents of the bag onto a silver tray. She counted out loud. Torsten thought that this must surely be the only place left in the city where candy in bins was sold by the piece.

"Adding the coffee, altogether it's twenty-eight crowns. By the way, did you hear about the horrible accident this morning on Narvavägen?"

Torsten looked up after fishing out two twenty-crown notes.

"Yes, I did."

"A real tragedy. He used to come here with his children when they were little. They'd come every weekend to buy the Saturday candy. Usually it's the dads who buy the candy for the kids on Saturdays, you know."

"So he came here often?"

"Yes, pretty much every week. He was so good to them. Dear Lord, what a tragedy. Who could do something like that? Hit someone with your car and then just drive off? It must have been a drug addict, don't you think? A normal sober person couldn't do that."

"No, you're right about that."

Torsten took his twelve crowns in change and stopped before stuffing them into his pocket, handing two back to the woman.

"I think I'll take one of those nougat pieces, too. They're two crowns, right?"

The woman smiled and said yes.

Torsten took a ball wrapped in red foil from the candy dish beside the cash register. He pulled off the foil and stuffed the nougat into his mouth. The taste blended perfectly with his sip of coffee. He stood for a moment, enjoying the scents of candy around him. He listened as the cashier helped another elderly lady, who was asking for pears and mint kisses.

Torsten drank the rest of his coffee and set the paper cup on the counter.

"Thanks very much."

"Thank you, and come again soon. Do you need any chocolate or fruit for the wife before you go?"

Torsten shook his head, smiling. "No, thanks, her new husband takes care of that now."

The woman laughed and waved good-bye as he left the shop. The stop at Karla Frukt had made him feel better, and he was looking forward to a quick visit to Escader, the store around the corner that specialized in Märklin model trains. From its old location on Gumshornsgatan, a small street behind Karlaplan, the owner had moved the shop and all its contents to a new spot on Östermalmsgatan. He'd even brought along some of the original interior decor from the thirties. Torsten found the place comfortable. For model trains, time was supposed to stand still.

Just as he turned onto Östermalmsgatan, his cell phone rang. Olle Lundqvist was on the other end.

"Have you spoken to Brundin yet?"

"Yes, I just left the scene."

"But since Brundin returned to the lab?"

"No, what's he have to say?"

"This guy wasn't just a hit-and-run victim. Somebody backed the car over him again. Twice. Brundin is already writing the report, and he is definitely labeling it a homicide."

"Hell. So now the Stockholm police take over?"

"No, they can't. They've called us in. They're up to their ears in last week's Nacka case."

Last week two motorcycle gangs had clashed and at least seven people had been severely beaten. There'd been massive coverage on TV and in the papers.

"But why us? This'll be a media circus—they've already gotten a whiff that we're involved."

The Stockholm Regional Police were judged just as competent to investigate homicide as the National Police. Torsten couldn't think of a single instance where the

Stockholm Police had willingly handed over a murder case. Each had its honor to consider. Neither was ever comfortable interfering with the other. If homicides occurred elsewhere in the country, the National Police were usually brought in, since local police units weren't equipped to handle such cases. They didn't have the experience. But it was odd, very odd, that Stockholm was ceding this case to them.

"What can I tell you? They asked us."

"I have nothing against that. I just don't want them second-guessing us and breathing down our necks afterward."

"I'm taking full responsibility. Hurry up and go to Brundin's lab. I'll meet you there. What have you said to the press already?"

Torsten told him, making sure to cover every detail. Olle was content.

"Perfect. We'll put together a press release while we're at Brundin's and send it out immediately."

Torsten frowned. Something else highly unusual: releasing information at this early stage. Then again, Torsten realized that Olle would not sit on his hands. This case would be a feather in his cap, and that just might irk someone.

Torsten cast a quick glance at the sign over Escader. He sighed and headed back to the car. As he turned on his police radio, he heard the rustle of paper in his pocket and felt happy that at least he had something to eat while driving across town. He pulled out the licorice pipe. It was as close as he ever got to smoking, and that was fine with him. When he was twelve, he'd sneaked a cigarette, just like lots of other boys in his school, but his father had found the butt in his pocket. He'd never gotten such a beating as he had that day. He still had scars on his arms.

He started the engine and called Marianne Jidhoff. He left a message for her to call him, reciting his cell number slowly and clearly. He hung up, thinking her voice sounded different from what he'd imagined.

CHAPTER 9

Paula smoothed her hair behind her head, luxuriating in the warmth provided by her terry cloth robe. Her second round of jogging had gone much better than her morning run, and she had renewed energy. She also felt better about having eaten the cinnamon bun. On the whole, she was in a much better mood. She threw herself onto the freshly made bed with its set of blue-striped Lexington sheets. They had been recently pressed through the mangle, which was a great addition to their laundry room—after the cleaning lady finally learned how to use it. Paula couldn't help touching herself at the same time she phoned Jens. She'd shaved away every hair and her skin felt soft to her touch. It would be good to get Jens's mind off his work. This was worth a try at any rate. She giggled as she asked Jens's secretary to put her through.

"Hello, darling, it's me. Guess what I'm doing right now."

"Glad you called. Saved me the trouble. My plans have changed. The Japanese want to go to the archipelago, so they've booked an overnight visit in Sandhamn. We'll be flying out by helicopter and then take the boat home tomorrow after lunch. So I won't be home tonight."

Paula pushed her hand into her robe pocket after sniffing to make sure her fingers didn't smell. She had to control her emotions so her voice wouldn't break.

"Why do you have to stay away all night? Can't you manage to just get home late?"

"It's not possible. No boats go at that hour, and a taxi boat would cost thousands of crowns. It doesn't matter, does it? We'll have tomorrow night. You can have time for yourself, and it might be pleasant not to have me around for a change."

"No. It's not pleasant for me. I don't like to be left alone so often."

"I know, it's happened a lot lately. But you know that's how my job works."

"You've been busy with all kinds of things . . ."

"If you're hinting that I should give up my yoga and meditation classes, that's completely unfair. You have all day to keep yourself in shape. I'm the one who's making sure you have a good life."

Paula sighed. She didn't want to start this same old discussion. It always ended the same way.

"You know I make sacrifices, too. I would like to find a job."

"Yes, yes, but we both know that that doesn't fit into the life we lead. Would you be so unkind to our girls? Do we really have to go through this again? I have to attend this event. There's nothing I can do about it. The Japanese are coming back from break. I have to go. I'll be home sometime after lunch. I love you."

He'd thrown out that *I love you* quickly, but the words made her happy. He hadn't said it for quite a while.

Frustrated, she threw her head against her pillow. She was just about to call Lotta when a text came through:

I can't stop looking at you. You're fantastically sexy. Too bad he doesn't realize it.

It was from the same number—the one she didn't recognize. Paula sat up straight. She looked around wildly but couldn't hear anything from inside the house. She looked out the window. The yard was empty, and she couldn't see a soul down on the road. She jumped back into bed, covering herself with her blanket, forcing herself to breathe normally. She called directory assistance to see if she could find out the name the number was registered on, but she didn't succeed. She was frozen in fear, but then she decided to take the bull by the horns. She found the text and called the number. Someone picked up but didn't say a word. She heard a slight buzz and then the sound of a train signal. Paula's entire body was tense as she whispered, "Hello?"

No reply. At the same time, she realized it was the same train signal that she heard every quarter hour in her own house. Then the caller hung up.

CHAPTER 10

The victim sure was run over thoroughly," Jan Brundin said with his usual dry wit. Torsten shook his head at his colleague's sense of humor. Jan continued, "The car first knocked him down."

"Can you tell what speed it was going?"

"I'd guess twenty, twenty-five miles an hour. My theory is that someone was waiting for him in the car. The minute he crossed the road, the driver hit the gas."

Torsten wrinkled his forehead. There should have been enough time for the victim to react.

"Was the victim taking drugs? Alcohol?"

Jan shook his head. "No drugs. I would venture to say that he'd never touched the stuff in his life. He seems to have been someone who took good care of his body. There was a small amount of alcohol—I'd guess red wine—but we'll know for certain when the test results are in. One glass or two at the most. Probably from dinner the night before."

"Can you pinpoint the time of the accident?"

"About four a.m."

"Why didn't he react when the car barreled down on him? He must have tried to throw himself out of the way, right?"

"Not that I can tell."

"Have you found his cell phone?"

"Inside his jacket pocket."

"So he wasn't on the phone, ignoring traffic."

Jan shook his head.

"Do you think he was waiting for a taxi?"

"Why would he be on his way home at four in the morning and then stop for a taxi in front of his entrance? It's not logical."

"Perhaps he'd forgotten something important back where he'd been." Then Torsten shrugged. "That's not probable. What if he recognized the car? What if it was someone he knew behind the wheel, and he didn't think he was in danger?"

"It's possible. Our driver certainly made sure that there would be no chance of survival."

"Revenge? Someone who has killed before?"

"Probably. Beginners don't act like this. If so, we're dealing with a dangerous individual, who could probably kill again. Could it be a hired killer?"

Olle Lundqvist rushed breathlessly through the door, asking for forgiveness with a wave.

"Sorry I'm late, but I was in a meeting that ran much too long. How does it look? Any chance that this was an accident?"

Jan Brundin shook his head. "No, I have no doubt that this was premeditated. Who's going to head up the investigation? I imagine you're too busy, Torsten."

Torsten looked down at the metal container—it held the victim's wedding band and a bracelet apparently made by a child, with colorful beads on an elastic band tied clumsily.

Torsten cleared his throat and looked away, "No, Jan, I'm on this case. Olle has to go and face the media vultures now. I'll talk to them later as the case progresses, but I've had my fill of them today."

"I can do that," Olle said

Jan Brundin excused himself to go back to his desk. The younger policemen watched his every move, so he always needed to follow protocol.

Torsten and Olle left the forensics lab and headed upstairs.

"So, who are you going to assign to me? Pia? Pelle? Or aren't you able to make that call? Do I have to ask Klaus?"

Olle peered at Torsten, running his thumb and forefinger down his nose. He was almost an inch taller, and thinner, than Torsten. A prominent nose and full lips dominated Olle's face. Torsten had heard that women found him extremely attractive, although not traditionally handsome Additionally, Olle moved with a natural elegance that Torsten envied. He always felt clumsy in Olle's company. Torsten liked Olle. He was the only person on the force who had never let him down.

Olle took a deep breath and shook his head.

"No, none of those. By the way, have you called Jidhoff yet?"

"I called on the way over here, but she didn't pick up. She'll probably call back when she can."

Olle cleared his throat to announce that he was raising a delicate subject.

"I was wondering if you would like to try working with a new guy."

"A new guy? Fresh from the Academy?"

"Yep."

Torsten sighed and threw up his hands, exclaiming, "What the hell is going on here? First you have me report to a confused widow, and now a new guy? Why should I take *him* on? What's going on here?"

Olle shook his head.

"Nothing at the moment," Olle said, "but I believe this new man is someone you can work with. He's a little different, and he needs someone like you. He has potential."

"Potential? I don't need potential. I need competence— not someone who'll be a good cop in five years."

"I know, but look at it like this. You prefer working alone, and this is the next best thing. He'll obey your every order, and you'll be completely in charge of the entire investigation. In return, I'll keep Klaus out of your hair."

Klaus Heikki was an officer Torsten had worked with for more than fifteen years. But now Heikki had decided to try to rise up the career ladder instead of working on the streets. He was already angling for one of the chief positions, and already a fairly good boss. Still, having a superior meant more bureaucracy for Torsten, which he'd rather do without. Things usually went faster and more smoothly when someone wasn't looking over his shoulder.

Torsten took a deep breath and shrugged. "OK. I get that I don't have much of a choice. What's his name?"

"Augustin Madrid."

"Excuse me?"

"Augustin Madrid. He finished his patrol duty at the Academy last summer, and he's been bugging me about a job every single day for the past two years. His dream is to work in our department."

"Why?"

"This is what he wants to do. His supervisor says that he was the best in his class by far. One of the best the past few years."

"That doesn't mean much. Does he want to move up the ladder, too?"

Olle shook his head. "No, I don't think so. I think he's the kind who wants to do the best at whatever he takes on."

"God help me, he'll be tough to work with. Why the hell are you throwing him at me?"

"Because I think you're going to like him. And I trust him. You'll see what I mean. Also, Klaus will believe I'm doing him a favor, and that can be useful later on. So how about lunch?"

Torsten could still taste his licorice pipe, but his stomach told him it was time for something more substantial. He said, "Yes, if you're paying."

Olle placed a hand on his shoulder. "Sure, and since you're such a good boy, I'll let you have dessert, too. I bet we can find ice cream with chocolate sauce."

"Thanks, Dad."

Heading out the doors and onto Kronobergsgatan, they laughed. The officer on guard duty gave them a nod from where he was sitting, his cell phone plastered against his ear.

CHAPTER 11

Marianne listened to the answering machine, wrinkling her forehead as she wrote down the number. As she tapped it into her cell phone, she had her doubts.

"Ehn!" the voice on the other end said.

"Hello. My name is Marianne Jidhoff. You were looking for me?"

"Yes, right, hi! My name is Torsten Ehn. I'm a detective for the National Police. Olle Lundqvist asked me to contact you. It seems we'll be working together on something."

"Yes?"

"Well, really, I don't know much more than that, but Olle told me to report to you, and that's what I'm doing. How much do you know already?"

"Nothing at all. I haven't even returned to work yet. I'm supposed to start Monday."

"I see. Well, then, I won't disturb the little lady any longer. I guess we'll wait to catch the killer once you're back. I'll call him and let him know."

Using a stern tone, Marianne replied, "You have no reason to be so disrespectful. I've been on leave for a while, and this is the first I'm hearing that I'm expected back at work already. You must excuse me for not knowing what you are talking about. What, exactly, are you supposed to report to me?"

"The stuff that I usually tell Olle. But he wants you to be some kind of communication central."

"That's more than I know. Yes, I'd better call Olle right away."

"I would think so."

Marianne sighed. She wondered what kind of idiot Olle had sent her way. Probably someone he couldn't stand, and she was supposed to act as a filter. Still, Marianne couldn't help being curious. She sighed again. Feeling idiotic she said, "If Olle told you to report to me, I think we should get started. Are you able to swing by Östermalm? I'm afraid I can't make it in to the station today."

"Sure. I'm heading that way anyway. I have to finish up something here first, but I can get to your place in about two hours. What's your address?"

"Banérgatan 8, Third Floor."

Marianne gave him the entry code and hung up. *What a strange person.* She didn't think she'd work well with this guy. On the other hand, she expected *some* static when she came back.

Marianne decided to call Chrisse Stierna, her oldest friend since childhood. They had started preschool together. For the past ten years, they'd kept in touch only by telephone since Chrisse had moved to Zurich with her husband. She'd opened a dentist's office there and rented her office of twenty years in Östermalm to another dentist.

Marianne wished that her friend would move back to Sweden. She really missed their Friday lunches, but talking to her a few times a week helped.

"Do you have time to chat?" she asked.

"I have a patient in half an hour, so I do have a few minutes. Just let me pour myself a cup of coffee."

Marianne heard the sound of coffee being poured into a cup. In her mind's eye, she could picture Chrisse and her well-coiffed blonde page. Chrisse had a year-round tan and legs to die for. Marianne thought that Chrisse should donate her legs to a museum. They were surely the best-sculpted legs on Earth—and they hadn't changed over the years. Despite being envious, she loved her friend with all her heart. Chrisse could keep her cool in the most dramatic situations and had an intelligent head on her shoulders. Her choice to go into dentistry had astonished everyone, including Marianne. People had thought Chrisse would remain a housewife, but once her third child was born, she decided to go to dental school and had gotten the highest grades in her class.

Marianne inhaled deeply on her cigarette.

"Don't tell me you've started smoking again!" Chrisse's voice rang down the line.

"I'm just having one. The pack's below the stove fan."

Marianne smiled at the sound of Chrisse lighting a cigarette and inhaling just as deeply.

"You can't be smoking in your office!"

"Where else would I? People don't care here in Switzerland. So tell me, what has Olle said to you? He wants you to come back to work, doesn't he?"

"That's right."

"How long did he give you to decide?"

"I've already agreed."

"That's wonderful! What made you change your mind?"

"There's a great deal going on there, and Olle's not exaggerating when he says he needs my help."

"Of course he does. He knows how smart you are. And what else would you do all day? How else would you fill those long hours?"

Marianne sighed. "I don't know if I'm doing the right thing, though. A detective is already on the way over here."

Chrisse laughed. "That sounds just like Olle. He's making sure you're already on a case so you can't back out. Smart guy!"

Olle had been in their same elementary-school classroom, so Chrisse knew him fairly well. As a young boy, Olle had been shier than most and didn't get into much trouble, but he'd certainly changed as the years went by. When Olle was first accepted in the Prosecutor's Office, Marianne's husband Hans had been his mentor. At that point, they included each other in their social circles. Marianne thought Olle's wife was a pleasant but introverted woman, and they'd never gotten to know each other very well. Olle was the one who kept in contact after Hans had died, and he was the one who'd called to express his sympathy. His wife accompanied him to the funeral, but she hadn't spoken to Marianne.

Chrisse was talking. "And, like I said, what else are you going to do? You certainly don't play golf. You have no grandchildren. Your husband is gone."

"I know, but I don't have much energy, either."

"Maybe it will come back when you start working again."

"Maybe. Olle told me many things to make me reconsider my decision. Still, I *had* decided I wanted to quit for good. Now everything is turned upside down."

"It's a sign. It's obvious! I was beginning to think you'd probably start driving your children crazy."

"What? Have they said anything to you?"

Chrisse was the godmother to Marianne's children. She kept in close contact with Nina and Sigrid, since her own daughters were similar ages and all were close friends.

"No, they haven't. Still, I know how quickly you'd start interfering out of boredom. I'd do the same thing myself. Otherwise, I'd take to drinking all day or give myself cancer from lying in the sun. I think I'd even get tired of playing golf. We aren't that old yet. In ten years, maybe things will be different. But now? We're only fifty-five, for God's sake. The same age as Madonna! Have you ever heard her talk about retiring?"

"No, but how am I supposed to keep up with Madonna?"

"That's not the point. It's that we're not old. Not yet."

Marianne took a last drag at her cigarette before holding the butt under the sink and throwing it in the trash. A few flecks of tobacco got stuck on the faucet, and she scraped them away with her fingernail.

"So you agree I should go back to work. What if I find it dull and boring?"

"Then tell them you're old and tired. Just quit if it doesn't work out."

"I think there's lots of gossip at the station about Hans. I don't know if I'm ready to face it."

"I'm sure they've been gossiping about him for decades. They'll lose interest now that he's passed away."

Marianne said, "Yes, and there's another thing. I went to my gynecologist today."

"Oh, no, tell me that you're all right!"

"There's no reason to worry. But she told me what I was doing wrong."

"Good Lord! Did you get an STD?"

"How could that have even happened? No, she was concerned that I'd missed several appointments and that I'd put on weight."

"What did she tell you?"

"That I have to get my weight under control. She even offered me diet pills. I had no idea those things were still around."

"I'm sure it's a big industry. But maybe you should pay more attention to her. Try that Danish Hospital Diet I usually go on before bikini season. And walk to work every day. The pounds will fall off."

"It sounds horrible."

"Yes, but it'll work, you'll see. Sorry, I have to run. I'd better air out this room before my patient arrives."

"I'll look into that Danish Hospital Diet. Talk to you tomorrow then? All right. I love you."

After they hung up, Marianne opened the pantry door. Next to her cigarette carton was a little box containing white-chocolate truffle nougats from Eje's Chocolate. She took out another cigarette and two of the nougats.

Her computer was on the dining room table, and she took it into the kitchen. As she let Google search for the Danish Hospital Diet, she stood by the stove fan and smoked, enjoying her delightful truffle nougats.

When she saw the recommended food intake on the website, she frowned. This was certainly classifiable as torture in another country. Well, obviously, the diet was supposed to speed up metabolism so the fat would dissolve.

Marianne took a deep drag. She decided the diet might be feasible since it lasted only ten days. Surely she could follow *any* diet for just ten days

She felt tired as she pulled out a pencil and a sheet of paper to write down the allowed staples. She'd have to go to the Ica Banér grocery store again. If she hurried, she'd be done before that Ehn guy showed up.

Chapter 12

Torsten read in his reports that the firm where Christopher Turin worked was on Biblioteksgatan. He parked in the elegant department store NK's garage, and since afternoon traffic was starting to pick up and more cars were leaving the garage than entering, Torsten snagged a spot on the first level. He took the elevator down to the street and exited at Regeringsgatan.

As he walked toward Mäster Samuelsgatan, the sun beat down on his head and he glanced up at the sky. Display windows offered the latest fall fashions of knitted scarves and thick sweaters. Torsten was in no hurry to get into the dark season of winter.

He turned down Jakobsbergsgatan and looked into one of the new Italian coffee bars that was supposed to be pretty good. Inside, men were jostling at the counter to request one of the tables in the sun. A number of them had taken off their ties, which now stuck out of their jacket pockets. Torsten wondered where all the women were. Didn't women drink coffee in this part of town?

He and a few other men his age reached the building's entrance at the same time. A bronze sign proclaimed that Carlfors & Malmström was located on the fifth floor. Torsten held open the whining elevator door for the others but didn't receive any nods of thanks. One of the men was overweight, although he tried to disguise it by wearing a welltailored, extremely expensive suit. The impression was ruined, however, by the tailor's tag still hanging on the sleeve. Even Torsten, who hardly ever wore suits—ones much less expensive—wouldn't have made such a faux pas. Torsten didn't mind suits, per se, but since he needed them so rarely—and his personal finances didn't allow for much extravagance—the two suits he owned usually hung in his closet, shabby and worn.

The two men next to him lowered their voices, and Torsten tried to appear as if he wasn't paying any attention. What were they thinking? Anyone could eavesdrop in an elevator nine feet square.

"You're absolutely sure? What does his wife say?"

"I heard she was still in Mallorca. The children are on school vacation, and she's there with them. Still, it sounds strange. Why would anyone have wanted to kill him? This is an unpleasant business."

Both men fell silent and seemed to imagine themselves right outside their homes, being run over on purpose in the middle of the night.

Torsten understood why these men needed to talk. The subject would be a hot topic at every dinner and cocktail party around here for quite some time.

The men got out on the fourth floor and Torsten continued up to the fifth. His Internet search on Carlfors & Malmström had told him it was a highly respected management-consulting firm. Many news agencies brought in people from this firm for their expertise and long commentaries. Torsten didn't know exactly what management consulting was, but he understood it had something to do with analyzing companies and giving advice about ways to make their business more effective. Christopher Turin had been a vice president of this firm for five years, and before then, he'd been a project manager. It appeared his position was very solid in the company—he'd spent most of his career here.

Torsten's appointment had been made with the highest level of administration, but he hoped that a few of the other employees would be around in case he needed to ask more questions. He needn't have worried. This office appeared fully staffed. Torsten couldn't see an empty desk. Everywhere, phones were ringing and printers were sliding out papers. There was feverish activity as far as the eye could see. It took a few minutes before a near-sighted receptionist noticed him and asked whether he needed assistance.

"Please excuse us today. It's pretty chaotic. One of our coworkers has died, and the phones are ringing off the hook."

"That's why I'm here. My name is Torsten Ehn, and I'm from the National Police. I have an appointment with Jonas Carlfors. Do you know where I can find him?"

"Please wait a moment. I'll tell him you're here."

The receptionist couldn't have been older than twenty-two or -three. She disappeared behind a glass partition and came back a few seconds later.

"He's on the line with Christopher's wife, but he's getting off. Can I offer you a cup of coffee or some mineral water?"

"A glass of tap water would be fine."

"Please take a seat over here, and I'll be right back. We have some magazines on the table if you'd like to read while you wait."

Torsten smiled as he sat in one of the armchairs close to the reception desk. The chairs were black leather with chrome edges. Torsten had read about the designer, but he couldn't remember the name. He was bad with names, but he never forgot a face. According to Olle, that wasn't unusual. People either remembered names or faces. This fit with Torsten's theory that no person was perfect, and even the most beautiful coin in the world had another side. Right now his job was to find out the other side of Christopher Turin's coin. And he knew he'd find it, given enough time and patience.

−□−

The ever-smiling receptionist served Torsten a glass of ice water. He drank it while flipping through a copy of *Dagens Industri*. In his mind he tried to form a picture of the personnel structure in this environment. Young men in dark suits and well-pressed shirts dominated the place. By now a few of them had removed their ties, but most had barely loosened theirs. There were a few women, all wearing dresses in somber colors. They sat at their desks with serious expressions on their faces, holding phones to their ears. Torsten noticed how different this workplace was from his, where everyone had his own office and the dress code was anything but strict. Still, the energy was similar. Perhaps that's how it was at most offices. Everyone was doing the same job, and it was only different on the surface. Every person was assigned a problem and had to find the best solution.

A man of about forty was heading toward him and was already holding out his hand in greeting. "Hello, I'm Jonas Carlfors," he said in a low voice.

Carlfors was average height and had short blond hair with bangs that fell in front of his light-blue eyes. He had a deep tan, and the wrinkles around his eyes were white in contrast. His muscular body was fitted with a tailor-made suit. Torsten imagined he was good at skiing, tennis, and golf—the three sports that demanded professional competence and social contacts. Torsten thought it would be depressing to have to live like that. But at any rate, he could never fit into such a regimen.

He took Carlfors's hand and clasped it firmly—but not *too* firmly—giving the man a warm smile at the same time.

"I'm Torsten Ehn."

"Do you need any coffee? Or more water?"

"I'm fine, thanks. Is there a place where we can speak undisturbed?"

"Absolutely."

Jonas Carlfors showed him to a corner room. Torsten noticed it was at least four hundred fifty square feet. The large, deep windows faced Biblioteksgatan, but not a bit of traffic could be heard. A gigantic desk sat throne-like between the windows, with overwhelming heaps of paper and folders.

"Excuse the mess. I've just had all the papers from Christopher's desk brought in, so things are a bit chaotic. I have to go through it all, and it's a huge amount of paperwork. I was the only one who knew what he was doing, so I guess I have only myself to blame. Please take a seat."

He pointed to a sofa and two armchairs, both made of light-beige suede. A cerise silk pillow was the lone occupant of the sofa. Torsten sat down in one of the armchairs and hoped that his clothes were clean enough not to leave a stain. He took out his notepad and pen from the inner pocket of his jacket.

"I should start by making sure you know this is by no means a formal interrogation. We aren't even sure what happened yet. All I need now is a description of the kind of person Christopher was."

"I understand. Of course, I'll do my best to be helpful."

Torsten knew that Jonas Carlfors had been through a difficult day. In spite of that, he seemed willing to help, and even grateful that Torsten had come. Torsten flipped to an empty page in his notepad and clicked his pen.

"So, Christopher Turin was a vice president here at Carlfors & Malmström?"

Jonas Carlfors replied, "That's correct. I founded the company along with my brother-in-law almost fifteen years ago. Christopher was with us from the very start. We studied together at Handels School of Business, and his wife is a good friend of my sister."

"So he's almost family, one could say."

"As good as family."

"Was he a part owner?"

"No. Just my brother-in-law and I own the company."

"Why is that?"

"We decided to keep control of the firm between the two of us. Christopher was well aware of this when we started. It's never been a problem. We made sure to pay him very well instead, and I believe he was happy with that. Last year we gave him a bonus of five million crowns—before taxes, that is. We've always understood that a guy like Christopher receives offers from other companies. Just a month ago, a competitor in London tried to lure him away."

"He told you that?"

"We always kept our cards face-up."

"So some places still give bonuses in these hard times? I thought the recession had taken away all that. Didn't our finance minister, Anders Borg, make new regulations?"

"That's not entirely true. It's a myth. No one in this field has ever taken those suggestions seriously. You'd hardly find any friends of Anders Borg here, ha, ha! It's almost comical how many of us are going to vote for the Socialists in the next election. Of course, we still have our bonus system, but we call it something else now—a commission. If you've done well, you're given your piece of the pie. Bad eggs try to get more than their share, of course, but all sorts of companies have those, even during economic growth. You have to realize that we're different from a bank. They're the ones who were speculating with other people's money. Anders Borg didn't intend to punish *our* field—we have nothing to do with the banks."

Torsten wanted to debate this but thought better of it. He wasn't about to argue. He simply thought extravagant bonuses were wrong, no matter what business the company was in.

"Did you see Christopher as a friend or a coworker?"

"He was an extremely close coworker. We hung out when we were still at college, but once we began working together, we actually saw each other less often. Perhaps because we both started families and had different social circles.

Christopher and his wife stayed in the city, while we moved to the suburbs. We bought a summer house in Torekov, and they decided to keep theirs in the archipelago. We lived different lives, you might say."

"You live where?"

"In Djursholm."

"Wife and kids?"

"Yes, two kids. Three and five."

"I see. You must be pretty busy these days."

They laughed for a moment. Torsten let his notepad rest on his knee.

"How would you describe Christopher's relationship with his wife? Were they thinking of separating?"

"No, not at all."

The answer was just a bit too quick, and Torsten blinked.

"So. No problems between them?"

"Not more than other people."

"How is his wife doing? I understand that you just spoke to her on the phone."

It was Jonas Carlfors's turn to blink. He looked away nervously, and Torsten knew that he was about to lie. Lying almost never worked. Torsten could read the body language of most people. He knew when they were lying, even when it was just a small white lie. Torsten pricked his ears in interest.

"She . . . seemed calm enough. Sad, of course, but also calm. The children had a restless night. Eventually they fell asleep. Isa is a woman with a strong family behind her. She's going through a rough time now, but she'll come out all right in the end."

"What does she do?"

"She does interior design."

"And you said she was a close friend of your sister?"

"Yes," Jonas said, "they call each other every day. There's only one year between me and my sister, so I've known her since we were small."

"Were you the one who brought the couple together?"

"You mean Isa and Christopher? No, actually not. They met in France one summer. It was all by chance. We were completely taken by surprise when we found out."

Torsten saw a darkness in Jonas's eyes, before Jonas blinked it away into a polite smile.

"Yes, Christopher was quite a stud at Handels. He had his choice of girls, if you know what I mean."

"So, he wasn't exactly the kind of man you'd have chosen for your sister's best friend?"

Jonas turned away for a moment, then cleared his throat.

"No, perhaps not. Still, he came around once they got together. Perhaps he was just sowing his wild oats. Isa got him in line, so it worked out all right in the end. They had three wonderful daughters who get the best grades and are good at sports. The middle one played the piano so beautifully at the end of the last school year that people were openly weeping. Christopher was proud of his girls."

Torsten took a deep breath and blew the air out slowly.

"How was he as a boss?"

"Great. Instinctive. Good at finding new talent and letting them shine. A real *A* boss."

"What is that?"

"An A boss employs A-caliber employees. B bosses employ C employees, because they're afraid of being outdone. Christopher wasn't one of those."

"And he didn't have anything going on here at the company? An affair, perhaps?"

"An affair?"

"Well?"

"No, no, hell no. He wasn't like that. He kept his nose clean here at work."

Here at work. Torsten took note of the slip and wondered how clean Christopher kept his nose *outside* of work.

"I think I have enough to go on for now. Can I call you if I need to ask any follow-up questions?"

"Of course," Carlfors replied. "Here's my card. My cell phone number is at the bottom. Call whenever you need to."

Torsten thanked him for his time, they shook hands, and then Jonas touched his forehead.

"Jesus Christ, what a mess. This whole day has been one big circus. And in the middle of all this, I'm grieving the loss of a friend. Damn it all, we've known each other for over twenty years."

For the first time since Torsten had met him, Jonas revealed his sorrow. Torsten said, "I understand. Call me if you think of anything else. You never know what might be important."

"I will. And call me if you find out anything more about the guy who did this. I can't imagine anyone doing such a thing."

"Well, that will be our job—solving that puzzle. But you'll know it when we do. Do you mind if I take a look around his office?"

"Of course, but it's kind of a mess, since we were in and out all day looking for paperwork. We've also tried to close down Christopher's Facebook page, but we couldn't.

We can't find his password, and it seems impossible to shut down the page without it. The person is dead—isn't that absurd?"

"Did you try to contact Facebook?"

"We did but had no luck."

"Strange. Unpleasant, too."

Jonas Carlfors opened the office door two doors down the hall from his own.

"This is Christopher's office. Please pardon the mess."

"Don't worry. I just want to look around a minute. I'll let you know if I find something I need to take. Our people may want to look at his computer, but the prosecutor will send a warrant if we need to do that."

"You can just take it now. I don't have a problem with that."

Torsten looked at Jonas Carlfors, searching for a sign of deception in his face. He didn't see one. He seemed to honestly be trying to help.

Jonas Carlfors left him as Torsten stepped inside. The room was disorganized, with heaps of paper and file folders all over the place. Books were randomly stuffed into the bookcase.

Two framed photographs were on the desk. One showed three smiling girls—they had to be the daughters. The other showed a woman with a huge head of blonde hair surrounding her pretty face. The woman was quite young and resembled a doll. The shot appeared to have been taken abroad. Torsten thought it must be Isa Turin, and he realized why Jonas Carlfors was dismayed when his college friend managed to whisk away his sister's sweet-looking friend. He put the photos back in their spots and left Christopher Turin's office.

Torsten headed for the exit, waving good-bye to the still-smiling young receptionist. He'd gotten some insight into Jonas Carlfors and wondered why he had made that slip about his friend. Something had obviously been bothering that man.

CHAPTER 13

Marianne began preparing her meal by peeling the King Edward potatoes she planned to mash. By the time they were bright and clean and ready to be dumped into the pot, her hands were red and wrinkled. Next, she shredded the cheese and fried the beefsteak tomatoes. After a while, the casserole was in the oven and the potatoes were boiling in the pot.

Today's newspaper was among a pile of magazines, and she pulled out the cultural section. The wine she'd opened the evening before was gone, so she decided to open a new bottle. She took a glass from the cupboard, noticing the dust on it. She rewashed the glass, thinking it made no sense to drink out of something that was dirty. *Might as well start drinking straight from the bottle in that case,* she thought. She hadn't sunk that low—at least not yet.

She flipped to the crossword and puzzle page, smoothing it down with her right hand. Soon, she got up and found her cigarette pack. She argued with herself before taking out her third cigarette of the day, but at least she would skip having a chocolate truffle. She'd already gotten the items for her new diet, which she would start tomorrow. She had no choice. Things couldn't get much worse. And even though she planned to eat heartily this evening, there was no reason to be gluttonous this afternoon. She'd have to stay away from the truffles for a while now, so she'd make sure to offer them generously after dinner and hope there wouldn't be any left to tempt her.

The day's difficult Sudoku was hardly a challenge. It annoyed her that the levels of difficulty varied so much. A feeling of emptiness swept over her as she entered the final number. It was no fun when the puzzle was too easy. Cigarette smoke hung over the kitchen table, so she opened the window as wide as possible. She drank some wine and stared outside, thinking she should put on some makeup— although that wasn't what she really wanted to do. She headed for the bathroom, almost against her will, and touched up her face with a dash of rouge and a bit of mascara. She skipped the lipstick and went back to the kitchen to sip her wine.

A creeping feeling of unease made her want to understand what frightened her about returning to work. The only strong emotion she felt was rage. She had been living with that night and day for the past few months. She was furious that her husband had willingly treated her so badly, hurting her even during his last minutes on Earth. His final words had hurt so much. She was still angry even if he didn't know what he was saying, and now she had no way to tell him off. It was beginning to make her crazy. She didn't know whether going back to work would give her a sense of redress, but she at least felt that her compass was pointing in that direction.

—□—

Just as the potatoes were finished and she'd guiltily poured herself another glass of wine, the doorbell rang. She had completely forgotten that the man from the National Police was stopping by. Here she was sitting alone and drinking! She quickly rinsed her mouth with water and headed toward the entry hall. In a jacket pocket, she found a wrinkled pack of Läkerol Special throat lozenges. She tossed a few into her mouth and hoped for the best.

The man on the other side of the door was her own age, perhaps a few years younger. His hair matched his grayish-beige jacket. It had been combed back, although there were curls at the back of his neck. He had steel-gray eyes, which gazed intensely at her. He was a touch shorter than average, and she could not tell if he was pudgy or in shape. At any rate, he was compact. He held out his firm, dry hand. Then, to Marianne's great surprise, he gave her a wide smile.

"Hello. I'm Torsten Ehn. You must be Marianne."

"Yes, that's right. Come in."

Torsten looked around curiously as he hung up his coat and wiped his shoes on the mat. Marianne was relieved that he didn't take them off, although that was the usual custom. She wasn't all that eager to see his socks—the odor of sweaty feet was always off-putting, no matter how charming the person in question might be.

"Can I get you something to drink? Coffee? Tea? A beer?"

Torsten looked up from his shoes. "A beer, please, and if you have some folk beer, all the better. I'm really thirsty."

"Of course. I also have some alcohol-free beer."

"That sounds great."

He followed her close behind into the kitchen and glanced at the kitchen table, where her wineglass sat beside the open newspaper.

"You like those puzzles? I've never figured out those Sudoku things. They're pretty hard, aren't they?"

"Not really. There's a code you have to break. Do you do the normal crossword?"

Torsten Ehn shook his head. "I don't do those, either. I'm the kind of guy who likes to do things with my hands. But my son likes crossword puzzles."

"How old is he?"

"Almost seventeen. How about you? What about your kids?"

Marianne answered as she poured the cold, alcohol-free pilsner into a tall cylindrical glass.

"Three. They're thirty, twenty-eight, and twenty-five."

"So they're all grown up. Does that mean you live here by yourself?"

"Yes, it does."

They both fell silent for a minute before Marianne added, "Let's go into the living room. It's more comfortable."

"No, this is fine." Torsten sat down on a chair across from where she'd been sitting. Stiffly, Marianne sat back down and tried not to look at her wine. She had to control the urge to move it aside and risk bringing more attention to it. What would he think of her—drinking wine before dinner?

Torsten sniffed the air. "What are you making?"

"Kassler Florentine. It's my son's favorite. He's going back to Australia soon, and I wanted to make sure he had the chance to eat it. He's studying there for the time being. We're having a family dinner in a few hours."

"It smells wonderful."

Marianne found her shoulders relaxing, and she smiled. "Maybe you're hungry, too? I can offer you a sandwich."

Torsten seemed reluctant to accept. Marianne hurried to say, "It really is no trouble."

"All right, then I'll have one, but only if you're fine with it."

Marianne got up and found the loaf of bread she'd bought for Peder's breakfast the next morning.

"What would you like? Cheese, liver pâté, salami?"

"Cheese and salami would be great."

Marianne took the ingredients out of the refrigerator and made two open-faced sandwiches with great care. She noticed him following her every movement and seeming touched as she placed a napkin at his place. The Danish rye bread was freshly baked, and the whiskey-infused ched-dar was well aged. She'd bought a quarter pound of sliced salami, and it had the pleasant aroma of smoke and a touch of salt. It would certainly suit his cold beer.

"Wow! These are great sandwiches!"

Torsten Ehn had torn off half of one sandwich in one bite. Marianne had to keep herself from laughing. Moments later, he'd already finished his first sandwich and washed it down with beer.

"So, the deal is, we have a man who was run over by a car on Narvavägen, just around the corner from here. He lived at number 8, next to King Oscar's Church. The man's name is Christopher Turin. The case is considered a homicide, since the driver not only hit him once, but backed over him again."

Marianne tucked a lock of hair behind her ear. She peered at Torsten and wished she could go get her glasses to help her concentrate. She couldn't remember for the life of her where she'd put them. Probably out in the hallway. She must have been wearing them when she was doing the Sudoku puzzle. She rubbed her eyes with her knuckles. As Torsten was going to continue talking, she decided to act.

"Excuse me for a moment. I need to get my glasses—I can't think without wearing them."

She was happy to find them in the hallway, and she grabbed the pen next to them, too. Returning to the kitchen, she opened the cupboard to get the block of paper she used for shopping lists. Torsten had finished his second sandwich and the beer. She didn't ask if he wanted more. She wanted to get to the facts of the case right away.

"So, let's start again from the beginning. I've learned through the years that the only way I can get to the bottom of these tricky situations is by writing things down."

"I'm the same way," Torsten said.

Marianne wrote as he spoke.

"I've just visited Christopher Turin's office. I've spoken to his boss, who knew him for years. They do management consulting, and I'm not sure what the hell that is. They're all connected through a complicated in-law relationship as well."

"That's not uncommon. People recruit other people they know. We do the same thing in law enforcement."

"True enough. I'll pay a visit to the other partner in the firm. He is married to the sister of the man I interviewed today. According to my files, he lives in Saltsjöbaden."

"Was the victim married?"

"He had a wife and three daughters, all of whom are on the island of Mallorca. They won't be home until tomorrow."

Marianne kept writing and asked, without looking up, "Do you think someone made sure the family was out of town first? Someone who didn't want them around?"

"That's a good thought. Brundin, our forensic man, thought the killer must have really hated the guy. The fact that he backed over the victim after he was on the ground indicates that he knew him or had some kind of relationship with him."

Marianne put down her pen for a moment. "It could also be someone who knew the victim without his being aware of it. A stalker of some kind. The world is full of crazies like that these days."

"That's also a good point. I've printed out the reports we have so far. I'll send the rest later by messenger. Are you aware of the latest security rules?"

"No, what are they?"

"We can no longer e-mail information concerning ongoing investigations, so it'll be easier to discuss this when you're back on Monday. By the way, why *did* you decide to return after your leave of absence?"

"Olle asked me to."

Marianne said nothing more, though it seemed Torsten was expecting her to elaborate.

"Well," he finally said. "Olle is good at getting people to do what he wants. For now, I should leave you to go over these reports in peace and quiet. We can keep in contact by phone. I'll make sure to call if something comes up. Phone me if you think of anything in the meantime."

After a moment's pause, he flung open his arms. "Fantastic place you have! It's huge. Those beautiful tile ovens. And those windows! How high is the ceiling?"

"About twenty feet. I've lived here my whole life. This apartment belonged to my mother."

"I see. I see."

"It is a bit much for one person, but I can't imagine living anywhere else."

"You should stay here—as long as you can afford to, of course."

CHAPTER 14

Marianne's father, Harry, and her daughter Sigrid wound up arriving at her door at the same time. It was routine for them, as they both lived in the building. Sigrid's two-room apartment had once been part of Harry's three-room. The apartments were divided when the pipes had been replaced.

When the doorbell rang, Marianne was in the bathroom trying to remove an eyelash from her eye.

"Peder, can you please get that? I'll be right out!" she called.

She managed to get the lash out and hurried to the entry hall.

"It's for you, Mamma!" her son said.

Sigrid held out a bouquet of gladiolus, which Marianne knew right away she'd bought at Norrmalm Square's open market. Hardly a single person who lived in Östermalm bought flowers at the market in Östermalm Square, even though it was geographically closer. The prices and the quality of the flowers were better at Norrmalm Square.

Harry held out a bottle of Italian wine. He never bought flowers unless there was a funeral. In honor of the evening, he was wearing his dark-blue blazer and gray flannel pants.

He'd added a colorful scarf around his neck and resembled a parody of Loa Falkman playing the typical upper-class man in a mediocre movie. His white hair was combed back perfectly. And he'd had a manicure. Marianne was often surprised by her father's vanity, but also proud of him. Many elderly fathers no longer knew how to take care of themselves. Marianne was certainly going to be too busy from now on to look after her father.

Harry looked around. "Where's Nina? She's usually the first one here."

Marianne shook her head. "She and Robert are out this evening with some of his friends from Handels. I think it's great she's getting out and socializing. For the past few months, they've just stayed at home."

Marianne heard Peder whisper to Sigrid, "Nice to be without her for a change."

Marianne cleared her throat in disapproval, raising an eyebrow at her son.

He shrugged at her warning.

"Come on, Mamma, we all know she can be a pain in the ass. Do you want me to bring out the champagne?"

—▢—

Five minutes later, they were all sitting in the living room and sipping champagne. Marianne wondered how much she should drink without it affecting her sleeping pills. Her friend Lola had assured her that if she stuck with one bottle and didn't drink before bedtime, there'd be no harm. Still, Marianne wasn't reassured. Lola had been a friend almost as long as Chrisse, and she could really count on her—she took on the task of always telling her the truth. If there was something Marianne was refusing to notice, Lola could be counted on to speak to her about it directly. Marianne loved her friend as if she were a sister.

Harry was flipping through a coffee-table book. He raised his eyes and looked Marianne over. "How nice you look this evening. You're wearing normal clothes for a change."

Marianne glared at her father and pouted. "Yes, I had to do some laundry."

Marianne had mostly worn pajamas all day long for the past few months. She knew it made her family worry about her—it was such a contrast to her normal, classic style.

Sigrid pulled at a loose thread in the rug, and Peder took advantage of the lull to refill their glasses. Marianne held her hand over her glass. She got up and headed to the kitchen, muttering, "I've got to check the oven temperature. The gas line really needs to be checked. It's probably time for a new oven."

Once she got into the kitchen, she turned on the faucet full force and let the hot water form steam over the sink. She knew they were whispering about her out there in the living room, but they were entitled to, as long as they left her in peace.

The top layer of cheddar had formed a light-brown crust on the casserole. Marianne took out two pot holders with perfect pink-and-yellow patterns. Nina had knitted them twenty years ago in fourth-grade home crafts.

As she hung them back in their usual spot, she spied her cigarette pack. She glanced quickly at the living room and turned the stove fan to the highest level before opening the pack and lighting a cigarette. After her sixth drag, she rinsed the butt under the faucet and threw it away.

Sigrid came into the kitchen and frowned.

"Do you have to have the fan on high? Oh my! Look at your hair!"

Marianne felt her hair and realized that it had formed a tuft right on the top of her head. Sigrid took a deep sniff of the casserole.

"It smells great."

Then she smiled at her mother. "You've been smoking, haven't you?"

"No, not at all."

"Oh, come on, does it matter? Are the Smoking Police going to burst down the door? Let me help you set the table. Where are we going to sit? The dining room?"

Marianne thought for a minute. "Why don't we sit in the kitchen for a change? It's just the four of us."

Sigrid took some fine china from the cupboard in the servants' hall, and Marianne noticed she was wearing a new dress. Sigrid tended not to sew dresses for herself, pleading too much work. But this ice-blue wool dress complemented her curves as well as her blonde hair, which hung down her back in a braid. Sigrid had rosy cheeks that reddened every time she made any effort, and Marianne had to resist her desire to pinch them lovingly. Ever since she was a little girl, Sigrid would cry, dismayed that so many people were always pinching her cheeks. Marianne would comfort her and try to explain why people were always tempted, while also understanding Sigrid's need to protect her personal space.

This evening, Sigrid had matched her new dress with a pair of elegant brown patent-leather shoes. Marianne knew that Sigrid had gotten tired of hearing that her beautiful clothes were made for well-shaped women. Sigrid didn't like her own body. She was in constant warfare with it as she tried one radical diet after another, and Marianne felt bad. She knew she'd passed on her own negative body image to her daughter. Here was her beautiful daughter, and she couldn't recognize her own beauty.

Not long afterward, they were all seated at the table. Peder piled a large portion of the casserole onto his plate, and Marianne smiled, seeing her hard work hadn't gone to waste. Sigrid was talking about her new atelier. As Peder started into his food, he began sharing his plans for the upcoming year. He would finish his last year of graduate school in Sydney and return to Sweden, as he didn't see much of a future in Australia. Marianne gave a sigh of relief. She had worried that he would settle down and maybe even start a family on the other side of the world. Of course, Peder had always been fond of his native country and loved Stockholm above all other cities, but Marianne secretly feared he might suddenly need to distance himself from his family. She was happy that her child's absence was coming to an end.

Harry had been silent through most of the dinner, but now he raised his glass.

"It is time to toast our hostess! I think that my daughter is looking absolutely wonderful this evening! And if I may say so, without your thinking less of me, it's about time. It has been painful to see my daughter hanging around the house like a ghost. And today, we can see the light at the end of the tunnel. So, let me be the first to say *skål!*"

Marianne made a face at her father, but she lifted her glass with everyone else. Putting her glass back on the table, she cleared her throat to get their attention. She patted her mouth with a napkin.

"I have something to tell you, too. I've decided to go back to work. Olle came by today and asked me personally. We agreed that I'll start on Monday."

There was silence around the table. Sigrid and Peder glanced at each other.

Peder asked, "So, you'll be working with Olle again?"

"That's the plan. I'll belong to a small unit reporting directly to him."

They were all quiet again. Marianne knew what they were thinking: How could she return to the place where both she and her husband had worked? Harry broke the silence.

"But that's absolutely wonderful! You will be a fantastic addition to the team. It is my hope that my daughter will have the career of her dreams and rise as high as she wants! So, another *skål* for that!"

Everyone laughed, and Marianne shook her head at her father.

"I hardly think you could call it the career of my dreams. But at least I'll be back to work. That's something."

"I think it will be great for you," Sigrid said. "You need to get out. What else would you do all day?"

"That's just what Chrisse told me. Then I talked to Lola and promised to come to her art exhibit next week. She has a big show."

Peder whistled. "Good for you, Mamma! You're really getting out there! You've gone from being a marmot in hibernation to a career woman and party animal!"

They all laughed again. Marianne loved this happy atmosphere around her kitchen table. She'd taken her first step back into the world and couldn't look back now. Truth be told, she didn't *want* to look back. Not when things were finally getting exciting again.

CHAPTER 15

As she turned toward the house, Paula Steen took a deep breath. Jens had just laughed when she'd told him about the text message. He told her she should look at the funny side of it. He thought there were two possibilities: The first was that someone meant the messages for someone else and got the wrong number. That someone was flirting with his new Internet date, not a sex-starved housewife from Djursholm. She'd brought up the sex-starved housewife bit herself, but Jens seemed to agree with it. The second alternative was that some neighbor was keeping an eye on her to see if she was interested in a little fling on the side. Perhaps one of the other fathers at school?

Jens thought she should see this second possibility as a compliment, but Paula didn't agree. She felt uncomfortable and thought this was strange and intrusive. She had tried the number a few times that afternoon. Why didn't the caller answer?

Lotta had invited her to stay in her guest room after going out that night. Paula didn't accept that offer right away but knew she would later. After a few glasses of wine, it wouldn't be so embarrassing. She didn't want to appear dependent, nor was she about to inform Jens. He'd just make fun of her.

Paula's stiletto heels crunched on the gravel driveway, and she did her best to make sure the gravel wouldn't rub the shine off of them. She'd chosen to wear her tallest heels—which she'd never worn out of the house. Only in the bedroom. She bought them to excite Jens, but he was just annoyed that she wanted to wear shoes to bed. He believed it was unhygienic—disgusting, even—although her elegant shoes with the bright-red soles were brand-new. The six-inch heels would have been impossible to walk in if the shoes weren't raised beneath the balls of her feet to provide some shock absorption.

Paula found it harder to walk downhill. She was happy when the driveway started to slope upward as she approached the house. She couldn't have made it much farther. She'd packed a pair of ballerina shoes in her overnight bag but didn't need them yet.

"Hello, darling," Lotta greeted her at the door. "Everyone, say hello to Paula!"

Paula waved at the company of women her own age. They all stared at her with interest. She'd met one or two of them briefly before, but most were new to her. Paula took off her coat, and Lotta smiled approvingly at her outfit. She was wearing a plum dress with a plunging neckline that revealed a good deal of her breasts. She'd also made the radical decision to leave her bra at home.

"Oh, my, what a babe you are tonight! Now hurry up and get a drink to catch up with the rest of us. We started with mojitos at five."

Lotta took Paula's hand and gave it a squeeze. Paula felt awkward as she followed her tipsy friend into the kitchen, where a young man with bronze skin and black hair handed her a glass with mint leaves and a straw. The drink's sweetness balanced perfectly with the alcohol. Paula took a cautious sip from the straw while casting a discreet glance at the clock. It was just past eight, and Lotta had said that Velvet didn't open until nine thirty. If she drank slowly, perhaps she'd get away with having just two drinks. She really didn't want to drink more calories than absolutely necessary.

The young man leaned toward her and laid a hand on her arm.

"Would you like more ice?"

Paula jumped and looked into his dark-brown eyes. He was so attractive, almost beautiful. She smiled and shook her head.

"No. Thanks. You made a perfect drink."

The young man held her gaze and gave her a big smile until she was forced to look away. What did he see in her that made him think he could so openly flirt with her? And here she was acting like a Mademoiselle at a seventeenth-century royal court. She raised her eyes and returned a big smile before going back to the women sitting on the sofas.

Lotta beckoned to her.

"Come sit down, Paula! This is Purran. She's just moved to Djurgården. Her husband is Michael and they have three kids, two dogs. They're in the middle of renovating their house."

Lotta pulled Paula down beside her and laid a hand on Paula's thigh. It seemed as if Lotta was making a point that Paula was her friend—like she was marking her territory.

Paula found it somewhat sweet—she'd never seen Lotta so open. Then again, this was the first time they were going out together without their husbands. With the men around, the women never let down their hair, never let themselves get smashed.

"Purran's like us. She doesn't have a job. She got tired of all the traffic into the city and the never-ending stress of finding time for the kids. We all know we can't depend on our sweet husbands, now, can we?"

Purran was short and had a wide face. Paula disliked her and mistrusted her fiery temperament immediately. And it appeared the feeling was mutual. Purran flashed a fake smile before saying, "So you're the one who's afraid of the dark. Lotta was just telling us about that."

Paula blinked and looked over at Lotta, who seemed not to have heard what Purran had just said.

"Yes," she replied, "although it's not as bad as all that. But I'm alone most of the day, and I tend to wind myself up a bit."

Purran seemed surprised by her honest response. She sipped her drink, taking in Paula's shoes and outfit.

"I decided long ago that I would never allow myself to be afraid of being alone at night. Why fear everything in life? You can saddle yourself with all kinds of phobias if you start down that road. Our alarm system goes off all the time. What if I panicked each and every time that happened? It would drive me nuts. So, what does your husband do for a living?"

"He's a marketing head. What does yours do?"

"He's a hedge fund manager, a self-made man. Yes, I believe I met your husband at school. He's the one who drives that old silver Porsche, right? My husband keeps saying he wants to get one of those antique cars, maybe next summer. He used to have an old MG after he finished high school, so now he's having flashbacks of those good old times."

Paula suddenly remembered who Purran was. Lotta had told her about a family that had recently moved here. The husband didn't do a thing at home and, according to Lotta, he tried to get into the pants of every babysitter north of the Stocksund Bridge. Purran was more concerned about keeping her social and economic status than anything else, so she turned a blind eye on his behavior. Paula didn't understand how Purran could live with herself. She wasn't sure she wanted to get into a deeper conversation with this woman who seemed eager to stir up trouble. Purran wore stretch jeans from Filippa K, and the sleeveless top she had on made her upper arms look strange. Paula forced herself to smile and asked, "So, where does your husband work?"

"He's just started a new hedge fund with an old friend. They mostly manage money from their own friends."

"That sounds awfully risky. Especially if the friendships end."

"Why would any friendships end? They're professional enough not to let that happen. Your marketing head—what does he do?"

"He's the international representative for a family-owned cosmetics business. He helps oversee their marketing campaigns and their media strategy. And what do you do, besides look after the children?"

Purran's expression hardened further, and Paula had to keep from moving away from her. Paula pressed her lips together, forcing them to turn up.

"I used to be the lead attorney at Apoteket," Purran growled. "But, as I mentioned, that was some time ago. I can barely remember those days. It was endless stress. What about you?"

"I worked as a designer at the same company as my husband. I designed products geared for a younger customer base. I'd love to get back to work. In fact, I received a fantastic offer just a month ago, which I had to decline."

Purran looked at her in surprise. "Why'd you turn it down?"

"We wouldn't be able to manage if both of us worked full time. Who would be home with the children? Especially if we both had to travel at the same time. Not to mention all the activities. I already hire a babysitter so I can manage to just get the two to all their activities! Those take place at times a working person could never manage. Who can get off work to take a child to ballet at two in the afternoon?"

For a half a second it looked like Purran might agree with her, but then her expression changed again, making her look ready for a fight.

"I think you're just making excuses. You might as well say it like it is. You want to stay home with your children. Any woman with any sense at all would rather be with her children than work. The ones who talk differently are secretly jealous."

"I don't agree. I do want to work. But Jens can't cut back his workload, so one of us has to compromise. Don't you ever miss working?"

"Sure, but not so much that I'd choose it over my children."

Paula's smile became strained as she shook her head.

"Then I must be a horrible person. I think it's sometimes stressful to be home with the children all the time. You never think so?"

"Of course not. Yes, there's stress raising children. But it helps to make it absolutely clear who is in charge. A mother must make sure that the children know she makes the decisions."

Paula glanced to see if Lotta had heard what Purran said, but she and everyone else were involved in their own discussions. Purran continued:

"Anyone who's read Anna Wahlgren's theories of child rearing knows how it works. If you follow her rules line by line, you'll never have any difficulty raising kids. The children will never be a problem at all."

Paula wanted to argue, but this wasn't the right time and place. She wasn't interested in any authoritarian view of child rearing. So instead of starting a fight, she took a large swig of her drink and wondered how she'd wound up here. This woman was the last person she'd ever want to hang out with. She suddenly longed to meet up with her old friends from Gothenburg. Paula turned forty-five degrees and gave her attention to Lotta, who was in the middle of a funny story about her three-year-old's latest escapades.

Before realizing it, Paula had finished her drink. Lotta quickly grabbed the enormous glass from her and made sure she got a refill.

"Come on, girls, drink up! Time to get in the mood for the evening!"

She turned up the stereo and gestured to everyone to get up and dance. The young man in the kitchen smiled dutifully as all the middle-aged women stood up and danced to "Mamma Mia." Lotta clapped along with the rhythm, and, although she didn't feel like dancing at all, Paula soon found her body moving in time with the others, even if she was dancing a bit more stiffly. Purran's compact body was totally in sync with the music, but Paula thought Purran looked grotesque with her thick thighs in her tight jeans. She should have chosen something that fit better. The other women also followed Lotta's lead, but—even with the alcohol—they had difficulty cutting loose.

"Oh, boy! We are going to have fun tonight! Just us girls!"

All the other women hooted in response, lifting their arms into the air.

This was the one day of the year when Lotta was on her own. Her husband had taken their three children to visit his mother in Halmstad, and they wouldn't be back until Sunday. Lotta could party all night and sleep in as late as she wanted. Paula had always envied Lotta's annual break from her duties. And now, here she was—also free.

Two taxis drove into the driveway exactly at nine thirty. Lotta was already fairly drunk. She kissed the young man serving drinks on the mouth before she left the house, and whispered to Paula: "He promised to stay until we got back. We can share him if you'd like."

Paula looked at Lotta in shock and waited for an *I'm only joking* that didn't come. Instead, Lotta leaned over and gave Paula a soft kiss on the mouth. Paula jerked back and sucked in a deep breath. Lotta looked at her tipsily, laying her head on Paula's shoulder, "Don't look so shocked. I know you want to," she said. She laughed and asked the taxi driver to turn up the music.

Paula realized that she, too, was pretty drunk. She'd had four mojitos! She looked out the window and felt Lotta's hair tickle her cheek. An image of Jens flitted through her mind, and she wondered what it would feel like to kiss that young bartender. Or even Lotta.

Another thought flew through her head. What if Lotta was behind those text messages all along? Perhaps she'd wanted to frighten Paula into wanting to stay overnight at her house. Could Lotta have actually plotted this? It seemed like a pretty big coincidence that all this was happening the same weekend Lotta had the house to herself. Perhaps she'd borrowed one of her children's cell phones? She'd ask Lotta later—after they'd had more to drink.

CHAPTER 16

Torsten threw himself onto the sofa and unbuttoned his pants, pulling off his socks and kicking them under the coffee table. The microwave buzzer let him know his veal rolls were ready. He'd taken them out of the freezer that morning before going to work. He was getting better at preparing food and freezing it. He and his son, Noah, liked cooking together and finding new recipes to try out, including this one.

Torsten put two rolls on a plate and poured some warmed-up sauce over them. The mashed potatoes were still a little cold, but he was so hungry he didn't care. He added a tablespoon of lingonberry jam to the plate and was pleased by the dash of color. He took his plate and a glass of alcohol-free beer into the living room. He was looking forward to Noah's return from visiting his mother. It was depressing eating dinner alone every evening. The food never tasted as good. But he did have to eat.

While putting his plate in the dishwasher, he wondered if a scoop of ice cream would put him in a better mood. No, he thought, it would be a shame to undercut the training session he'd had with Bertil earlier. They'd swum three thousand meters, ending with four lengths of butterfly stroke. He couldn't compete with Bertil, who'd come in half a length ahead. Bertil, though he was ten years older, was still in incredible shape. It bothered Torsten just a bit. Wasn't it time for Bertil to start aging like everyone else? Even if he *was* a super athlete? Torsten thought that his shoulder had suffered from the exertion, but it would probably heal itself overnight.

Visiting the Turin family home on Narvavägen hadn't given him much to go on, much like Christopher Turin's office. Their apartment building, next to King Oscar's Church, was an Art Nouveau fin-de-siècle building, and just stepping into it was an experience in itself. Ghostly hallways led him to the Turin apartment on the fourth floor. The apartment was modestly decorated and had few details. He could tell that the Turins had tried for minimalism, but they hadn't really succeeded. Instead of creating a roomy space, the impression was of someone having just moved out. Several areas were worn and untidy. Torsten decided that this was a messy family. He saw burns on the counter from pots set down without trivets. The refrigerator was covered with sticky notes about school, even though school had been out for weeks. And the well-designed furniture had seen better days: the white sofa at one end of the living room, for instance, was covered in stains showing these people ate dinner in front of the television.

After Torsten left and hopped back into his Corolla, he decided he'd visited a home with no soul. People ate and slept there, but not much more. It felt as if the owners had already moved out.

On the way home, Torsten stopped to buy two new potted plants for his balcony. Large, rounded chrysanthemum blooms looked good in early fall. He wanted Noah to come back to a house that looked presentable—and perhaps they'd still have a chance to eat dinner on the balcony before it got too chilly.

The news on channel four discussed a new gang that attacked retired people. Torsten wondered where they'd found that information. It was old news the stations must have dug up from the archives. Some old trash used to help a dry spell in the news. He felt sorry for all the old folks watching the program who were now frightened. This information helped no one.

After flipping through a few channels, he pulled the sofa out into his bed and crept into it. He had to get up early the next day, and there was no reason to stay up and stare at crap on TV.

Before falling asleep, he reflected on this last training session with Bertil. Bertil had been his mentor and father figure for almost forty years, ever since Torsten first signed up for the swim team. Bertil was the only one who understood how dysfunctional the Ehn family had been. Torsten's violent father saw it as his duty to beat his wife and children. One evening, Bertil had come to ring the doorbell to have a stern conversation with Torsten's father. Torsten never found out what was said between them, but his father moved out the next day. Torsten never saw him again. Later on, he heard his father had moved to Gothenburg. Several years after that, Torsten didn't even bother to attend his father's funeral.

When Torsten started hanging around an unsuitable group of friends, Bertil took him aside to explain how his life would turn out if he went down that road. Later, when

Torsten's swimming career ended, Bertil steered him toward the Police Academy. In all these years, they'd only had one serious falling out: that was when Torsten learned that, in his youth, Bertil had taken part in an armed robbery and spent six years at Kumla Prison. When he found out about it, Torsten felt betrayed. He couldn't understand why Bertil hadn't told him sooner. They argued about it for a while but eventually sorted things out. When Torsten was young, Bertil hadn't wanted to talk about his earlier mistake for fear that the boy would emulate him. And later, so many years had passed. Bertil had made a good life and put that part of his past behind him—so it almost never occurred to him to tell Torsten that story. These days, though, all that had long been smoothed over—and Torsten had a great deal of respect and understanding for his old friend. He also knew that swimming had straightened him out, and he was glad that life had brought Bertil to him. Now, lying on his sofa bed, he just felt gratitude for their friendship. As he debated whether to get out of bed for one last trip to the bathroom, he fell asleep.

Chapter 17

Paula loosened up in her dancing, and she saw Lotta sashay over to the bar, her hands over her head, swaying in time to the music. *Get into the groove, boy, you've got to prove your love to me.* The modern mix of this Madonna song had a throbbing, high-tempo beat, and the crowd sang along to lyrics they all knew by heart.

Villa Pauli was a club "open to members only," but exceptions were made for private parties and for the once-a-month nightclub Velvet. One had to be invited by another member, of course, but no one checked that closely.

The place was fine and traditional with a beautiful view over Askrika Bay and the north side of Lidingö. During the summer, its lawn reminded Paula of a well-kept garden in a park where cocktail parties never ended beneath the massive white party tents that held hundreds of guests.

On this September evening, the scene was different. Tipsy people between the ages of thirty and fifty bounced around. The men all wore colorful slacks or casual jeans. Their shirts were striped and starched, and they all wore loafers with tassels or pennies. The women had let loose in outfits they'd never wear in their conservative suburbs: short leather skirts ending just past their rumps; their stilettos, like Paula's, were six inches high or more and difficult to dance in. Most women had low-cut tops, and Paula wasn't the only woman who'd left her bra at home.

Plastic surgeons, a number of whom were at this party, could point to many of the evening's partygoers as examples of their best work. One of the most prominent women was tall with hair dyed a remarkable shade of blonde. Her thin dress clung to her curves. Her breasts had definitely undergone surgery. They hardly moved when she danced uninhibitedly, jumping up and down, losing herself in her wild gyrations. This woman wore a wedding ring, but several admiring males surrounded her. Paula thought she'd met the woman at a Midsummer party in the archipelago given by old friends of Jens. The woman had come to that party with her husband and children, gotten smashed, and started dancing on one of the tables—even though it wasn't *that* kind of gathering. The gossip afterward had been severe. Later that evening, she was found naked in the sauna with the host. Paula forced herself to look away, remembering what had been said about that woman: that she'd developed a serious drinking problem. On the other hand, the woman lived in Saltsjöbaden, where most residents had a reputation for being much too fond of drink.

The inside of Villa Pauli was traditional, but the heavy furniture had been pushed to the side to make room for dancing. Paula headed for the bar, following in Lotta's wake. She'd been dancing with the women from Lotta's party for the past hour, and her feet were tired. She didn't remember how many acquaintances she'd greeted, but it seemed like the whole suburb of Djursholm was cutting loose here tonight. Everyone was in a party mood and looking for attention. Perhaps they were tired of being seen as boring parents huddled around the soccer field; or perhaps they were just looking for someone to flirt with. Paula was reminded of Jens's theory that several fathers at school might be looking at her when their wives weren't around. It did seem that just half of any married couple was here tonight.

At one point, she found one of the fathers from school waiting for her when she came out of the bathroom. He was actually good-looking. He asked how she was doing and showed interest in her running. He, too, had been in a number of marathons. He had two boys. Paula had seen him around when dropping off her girls. She'd noticed him because he was so handsome and had a smile to die for. They'd never actually been introduced, so they went through the formalities that evening. His name was Carl-Fredrik.

He put a hand on her arm, said he'd gladly go running with her, then kissed her on the cheek. Obviously, he was interested in her. He said he looked forward to seeing her at school, but right now he had to head home. *This* must be the Don Juan who had sent her the text messages. Everything fit! Paula felt an involuntary warming in her privates as she watched him go. The text messages no longer seemed so threatening. He looked back at her and laughed. Paula wondered who his wife was and what she was doing this evening. She definitely wasn't here at Velvet. Paula was jerked out of her reverie as Lotta bumped her with her hip and cried, "Darling! Shots for everyone! Take one and pass them on!"

Paula helped hand out the colorful shots from the tray.
"*Skål! Skål,* everyone!"

Their group tossed back the shots, and the two men next to Lotta applauded, ogling the women. "Wonderful, girls! The next round is on us!" These men were in their fifties. When they introduced themselves over the music, Paula thought their names sounded like Knoll and Tott. Knoll and Tott bought three more rounds, and Paula was surprised that she didn't feel the alcohol anymore. Knoll— or was it Tott—put an arm round her waist and led her back to the dance floor. He was in fine shape. Most of the other men in their fifties had beer bellies or plump faces from all the conference food they ate on the job.

The man danced so close to her that Paula could feel his member against her groin. Lotta came dancing along with the other man, and Paula let her partner run his hands along her sides and then grab her ass. She threw back her head and laughed in Lotta's direction. Lotta was really getting wild. From the corner of her eye, Paula noticed Purran watching them with a sour smile. Paula couldn't help winking at her. Purran, in turn, said something to the other women from their group, and they all headed for the exit.

–o–

Paula had no idea what time it was as they stormed into Lotta's house with Knoll and Tott. She was so drunk she couldn't feel her own feet. Never mind that she'd walked the entire way back from Villa Pauli in her stockings. Looking through her bag, she hadn't found her ballerina slippers. Lotta stumbled toward the stereo system and turned it up to the highest volume. She started dancing by herself but soon was joined by Knoll and Tott, who sidled up to her and began fondling her breasts and ass.

Paula sat down on the sofa as the room started spinning. Then she went to the kitchen for a glass of water. Paula had difficulty forcing it down, and keeping it down. She peered at Lotta, who was kissing one of the men while the other one rubbed his face on her breasts.

Paula headed for the bathroom. She couldn't find the light switch, so she felt her way to the toilet.

As she finally flushed, someone gently knocked at the door.

CHAPTER 18

The morning was clear and the air fresh. Torsten left his apartment building and happily enjoyed the activity around him. Folkskolegatan was crowded with people on the way to work or to drop off children at school. People were pushing strollers and carrying parcels. Someone was pumping up a bicycle's flat tire. During his years living with Katrin in the suburb of Älvsjö, that hustle and bustle is what Torsten had missed the most. He'd longed to return to the lively energy of the city. In the suburbs, everyone just got into their cars and drove off. Hardly anyone walked on the sidewalks. Months could go by before you met a neighbor.

So when his divorce from Katrin was final, Torsten chose to look for an apartment in the city rather than elsewhere in the suburbs. Of course, he'd asked his son Noah for his opinion. As a newly divorced man, Torsten was dying of boredom in the suburbs. In the city, he could at least have the illusion of being part of a larger group. He felt younger than his fifty years in the city. But in Älvsjö, he always felt like he had one foot in the grave.

He jumped into his car and prayed that the Väster Bridge traffic would be moving smoothly. But if it wasn't, he had only himself to blame for driving at rush hour.

He'd woken at four in the morning and couldn't go back to sleep. By the time his alarm clock rang at quarter to seven, the tossing and turning had left him worn out. He couldn't figure out what was bothering him. During those early hours of the morning, he'd thought about his divorce and turned it over and over in his mind. Then he'd thought about his parents, which happened whenever he tried to think about the reasons for his divorce. Finally, thoughts about work tumbled around in his brain. All of it kept him from sleep.

Torsten's last major case had wrapped up two years ago. He'd had only minor ones to work on since. He also knew that his department was at risk of being shut down. He understood the reasons behind that, but it was still unsettling.

The worst thing that had ever happened to him, however, had been the divorce. When Katrin told him that there was no possibility that they would ever get back together, Torsten's entire world fell apart. Katrin and Noah had been his safe harbor, and he'd done everything he could for them. Now, in hindsight, he realized that he'd kept his real feelings under wraps during his marriage to Katrin—which was probably why she'd left him in the first place. Who wanted to be married to a doormat that never got into any argument and always agreed to everything? Katrin had explained that passion was important to her—and that she never sensed any passion from Torsten. What they'd had their first few years together was gone and was not coming back. She couldn't live without it, so she decided it would be better to leave. Torsten knew, then, that she'd found someone else. Yet oddly, that hurt the least. What hurt the most was losing the stable family life he'd dreamed of for Noah. He couldn't understand why she would choose her own needs over their son's. But he also realized he was projecting his own feelings onto Noah, which was wrong. Later, when Noah made clear that he thought his parents had made a good decision to separate, Torsten started to relax about it. Certainly, he could still see Noah suffering a bit from his parents' divorce, but Noah seemed capable of dealing with it. He was a calm, secure young man who was able to have a harmonious relationship with both parents.

Noah also liked living in the city and getting away from "the middle of nowhere," as he put it. This bothered Katrin to no end. Torsten wasn't big enough not to be secretly glad about that. At first, Katrin opposed Torsten's move to the city, but she finally gave up when Noah was accepted at Riddarfjärden Ballet School. And since moving to Norway, Katrin did not seem unhappy that Noah lived with Torsten most of the time.

Over the past spring and summer, Torsten and Noah carefully scouted for a great downtown apartment. But they had trouble finding the right fit, and Torsten was almost ready to give up and buy an apartment at Gullmar Square. His finances were limited, and he needed space for his teenage son. Torsten had calculated that he could only afford to borrow two million crowns at the most. Interest rates were low right now, but Torsten knew the National Bank would raise the rates. His income wasn't going to increase much in the next ten years, and he wanted to be absolutely certain he could stay in his home—even if rates went up as high as ten percent. He had two million crowns of his own to put into the purchase, as well as an additional three hundred and fifty thousand in an account he'd set up for Noah. Since Noah was born, Torsten had put two thousand crowns a month into a secret account he'd opened in his son's name—without Katrin knowing it. Some months, it had been hard on his wallet, but he wanted his son to get a start in life with some income.

When he told Noah about the money, Noah said they should use it for the apartment. But Torsten had insisted that course was only for an absolute emergency, and that money was for Noah when it was time for him to leave home.

After a sailing trip together in the archipelago, they learned that two apartments matching their requirements had come on the market. Both were in the Söder District, and both were approximately six hundred and thirty square feet. Stepping inside the doors, they turned away from the first apartment immediately—too many potential buyers had crowded in to take a look. The second apartment was the smaller of the two. It had only two rooms and a kitchen, and was a bad fit for Torsten and Noah. But the maintenance fee was just three thousand crowns. The apartment was on the third floor and faced the street. The kitchen was large enough to seat four at a table, and the original cupboards were stained in a warm, sunny color they both liked.

Four other parties were interested in the apartment. Torsten and Noah admired the large, well-lit space—and they loved the balcony running along the entire length of the apartment, opening, much to their surprise, on all three rooms. To be able to step outdoors from the kitchen, bedroom, or living room was a real luxury. The large bathroom had recently been renovated, although Torsten wasn't thrilled by the salmon-pink interior with fake gold-plate faucets. The toilet was definitely not new, but it wasn't in such bad shape that it had to be replaced. A tiled bathtub was the only decent fixture in the room. There was a stand for washing and room to make a laundry area if desired. The bedroom, located along another hallway, had built-in closets, and it was roomy and cool.

They left the apartment, each with a brochure, and Torsten suggested they eat an early Sunday dinner at a nearby pizzeria—Piccolo Angelo. Colleagues from Torsten's department often went there, and he'd been with other friends as well. The pizzas were famously generous.

"What do you think? Could we squeeze in there?"

Noah shrugged. He seemed doubtful. "Maybe."

"If we can, I'll start looking for a sofa bed right away. I can sleep there and you can have the bedroom."

Noah smiled broadly. Torsten realized that Noah hadn't wanted to make that suggestion himself.

"Are you sure?"

"Absolutely. There'll be a problem if you want to watch TV, though, especially if I need to sleep."

"That's no big deal. I usually use my computer to watch TV anyway. But won't it be rough for you to sleep on a sofa bed every night?"

"Why would it? I just have to make sure I fold it up every morning right when I get up. I have to say, I really liked that balcony."

Noah nodded eagerly. "That was fantastic. We could put out some garden furniture and plants there."

Torsten said, "We'll have to see what the real-estate agent says. He was going to call all the interested parties tomorrow."

By Monday, the apartment price had gone up by five hundred thousand, and Torsten sadly dropped out of the bidding. He felt bad that entire afternoon, waiting to break the bad news to Noah, but as he reached the parking garage after work, the agent called to say that the two parties bidding against him had dropped out. Was he still interested? Torsten was suspicious and asked why the others had dropped out. He received only a vague reply. He asked to call back. Two hours later, he phoned the agent and said he was interested in the place, but only at a hundred thousand over the asking price, no more. Two days later, the contract was signed and, as the apartment had been part of an estate, they'd gotten the keys that same day.

The next few months Torsten and Noah spent all their spare time renovating their shabby nest. They sandpapered and painted every single nook and cranny. Torsten rented a floor sander and, following Katrin's advice, stained the floor instead of painting it, using a shade darker than the wood. Katrin was right. The stain made the room seem warmer and the floor much more beautiful.

At first they thought they'd just trash everything in the bathroom and remodel from scratch. Then Torsten decided to wait awhile, keeping Noah's money in the bank and saving for a renovation. It tuned out to be a wise decision. Just before Christmas, water started dripping through the ceiling. The upstairs neighbor's washing machine had broken and leaked, and the water damage to the ceiling was pretty bad. All through January, Torsten and Noah had to put up with the stains from the damage, but they were able to celebrate when the neighbor's insurance paid for a bathroom renovation. Torsten's colleagues at the National Police joked with him, wondering what kind of screwdriver he'd used to sabotage his neighbor's washing machine.

A good sofa bed was more difficult to find. Torsten bought one from IKEA that looked attractive and comfortable, but after a few nights, he realized the bed was meant just for overnight visitors. When his back started complaining, he realized it had been a bad purchase.

These days, his conversations with Katrin were no longer hostile, so he called to ask her for help. Katrin was pleased, and when she saw the apartment, she said it had turned out well and would be a good place for Noah. She'd just gotten the job offer in Norway and would soon be moving.

Katrin headed out to all the bed manufacturers with Torsten and Noah in tow. Torsten had to curb his imagination—it was too easy to see them as the happy family they'd once been. Katrin's purposeful search ended well. They found a store north of Uppsala with sofa beds meant for full-time sleeping. They had to wait a few weeks for the sofa to be upholstered in the color Torsten preferred, but when the beige-striped furniture was finally carried to the third floor of the building on Folkskolegatan, Torsten found he could sleep the night through without the slightest twinge in his back. He'd even learned to appreciate making the bed immediately after getting up. He actually loved the transformation from bed to attractive sofa.

Torsten bought Katrin a bottle of champagne as a thank-you gift, and she seemed truly touched. She moved to Oslo the following week. Torsten still missed her, although they'd been separated for over a year. Still, Torsten didn't want someone who did not want him. He had his pride.

Nowadays his contact with Katrin was even more sporadic. Mostly, they just discussed Noah over the phone.

Today, Torsten looked forward to his son's return from Norway. He'd written a list of things he needed to restock the refrigerator. Noah had been with his mother for just over a week. Katrin had one week more vacation than her husband, and Noah's school was closed for planning sessions. It was the first time Noah had been out of the country for this long. Although he'd wanted to, Torsten didn't call all week. He didn't want to disturb them.

Torsten also felt nervous. What if Noah came home and said he'd rather go live with his mother? He'd just have to put up with it, although it would crush him. For his son's sake, he knew he would nod and smile and be understanding. But the thought of it made him break out in a cold sweat. He took a few deep breaths and reminded himself that this was a normal part of any child's growing up. He would allow Noah to make his choice without forcing his own selfish wishes on him.

CHAPTER 19

Marianne jumped when the doorbell rang. At first her body froze, but when the nerve-racking sound came a second time, she got to her feet. Her first thought was to call Peder and ask him to get the door, but then she remembered he was at the embassy renewing his visa.

The sun streamed into the bedroom where she'd fallen asleep again after breakfast, and her meal tray was still on the bed. She glanced at the clock and saw that it was ten thirty in the morning. She had only herself to blame that the dinner party had gone on so late. She really should have skipped that last glass of wine after everyone had gone home, but a nightcap in bed had been a pleasant end to the evening.

The doorbell rang again, but this time it was longer and more insistent. She called out, "Yes, I'm coming!"

She assumed it was her father, Harry. He was an impatient sort. If he'd been given the keys to her apartment, he would have already let himself in.

As she flung open the door, she found a young man wearing yellow overalls with a package in one hand and a signing tablet in the other.

"Marianne Jidhoff? I have a package for you."

"From whom, may I ask?"

The young man glanced at the signing tablet and said, "The Prosecutor's Office. Torsten Ehn and Olle Lundqvist."

She quickly signed her name and took the package. It was lighter than she'd thought, and she could tell by the feel that it was a stack of paper. With a heavy sigh, she closed the door behind her and rolled her eyes. Olle didn't miss a trick. If he was worried she'd jump ship, he knew exactly how to draw her in—her curiosity was her undoing. She couldn't help smiling.

To tell the truth, after the family left, she'd already spent some time sitting up in bed with the light on and jotting down notes from the information Torsten Ehn had given her. Probably that was why she'd allowed herself that last glass of wine. Just like when she used to assist Hans in his investigations, once an idea was planted in her head, she couldn't shake it even if she'd wanted to. Maybe this was part of her need to prove herself. Or maybe she was just stubborn. She just couldn't leave something unsolved—not even a Sudoku puzzle.

Marianne weighed the package in her hand and glanced at the closed door of her library. Without thinking, she placed the package on the hall dresser and firmly retied the belt on her robe. She resolutely opened the door, stepped inside, and turned on the lights. She drew open the heavy curtains hiding the French doors and tied them off at the sides with golden ropes. The daylight streamed in, and she opened the French doors as wide as she could.

Her beloved wingback chair that faced the street was ready for her, as was the footstool beside it. They'd been waiting for her like a faithful dog waits for its master. The floor lamp had been bumped, and the lampshade was askew. Her favorite blanket lay on the ottoman. That's where she often set down her papers after reading them. She picked up the blanket and lovingly shook it, watching the dust particles dance around the room.

The bookshelves along the walls were also fairly dusty, but there was only so much she could do about this. After all, it was her first visit to her library in many months.

She looked at the dining-room table on the other side of the room, which, when completely unfolded, could seat ten people. Marianne couldn't remember the last time the table had been used for dining—certainly it was before last Christmas. She'd located the surrounding chairs at various antique stores and flea markets and upholstered their seats in black to blend with the gray color of the table, a seventeenth-century antique. Hans had once irritably asked her why she'd bought a mismatched table that looked like it should be thrown out. But Marianne had fallen in love with it at first sight. It gave her a warm feeling.

The two silver candlesticks she'd set on it were tarnished. Some might argue that they needed a good polish, but Marianne preferred a little tarnish, as it showed the candlesticks were used. A worn Persian rug spread from the table to her armchair. The bookshelves were fastened to the wall and filled with volumes from the late nineteenth century to the present day. They gave the room its distinct character.

The room was magical, and she had loved it ever since she was a little girl. She would come here whenever she felt afraid of the dark, or when she wondered if her mother heard her when she talked to her. Marianne thought the library was the perfect place to have long conversations with her deceased mother, now an angel. Perhaps that's why she'd avoided the room since Hans's death. A voice inside had prevented her from entering, but now she told that voice to go to hell. She had decided to take charge of her library again.

She hurried to get her cleaning supplies and wiped away the worst of the dust with a cloth. Then she vacuumed the rug and the parquet floor around it. She leaned out through the French doors to shake the blanket more thoroughly; then she folded it neatly onto one of the arms of her chair.

From the servant's hall, she took two long candles and pushed them into the empty candlesticks. She didn't plan to light them, but they made the room more beautiful.

In the kitchen while pouring some coffee, she found her glasses—and a pen—sticking into her hair. Ignoring her diet, she took two of the white-chocolate truffle nougats from the box. They wouldn't make that much difference in her diet anyway. She set her coffee and chocolates on a silver tray that had handles in the shape of roses. The tray had been one of her mother's favorites. And Harry said that her mother had been served breakfast on that tray ever since she was a little girl.

Marianne balanced the tray in one hand and picked up the package with papers in the other. She walked into her library, set the tray on the ottoman, and reverently sat down in her armchair. It embraced her, molding to the shape of her body. The clear autumn air came in through the French doors. She shivered for a moment before drawing the blanket across her knees and taking a large sip of hot coffee. She knew the fresh air would help her think.

With her feet up on the footstool, she opened the envelope and pulled out documents identified by the case number and the date. She nursed her coffee and, with pen in hand, began to read.

CHAPTER 20

Torsten Ehn read through the reports one last time, then leaned back in his chair. He folded his hands over his stomach and stared into space. The image of the man run over in the pedestrian zone refused to leave his brain. He knew this was partially due to the personal details he'd gathered: The man was an interested father; he'd been married for nineteen years; he was liked by his coworkers; and he came from a family where respect and humility mattered.

Torsten couldn't get the picture to fit the situation. He knew he'd find the crack in this façade—it always came eventually. He just wondered where to start poking around. The best place might be the guy's office. Perhaps a client was unhappy, or a coworker felt overlooked. Competition and jealousy were often motivating factors. They could make people do the strangest things . . . although killing someone was rare.

Torsten thought another alternative might be undocumented labor. Perhaps the family had gotten a renovation and fallen out with the contractor. Lately, there had been incidents where low-paid manual laborers were tired of not receiving their pay, or impossible demands had been made on them. This happened often in the well-to-do parts of town.

Workers felt forced to take matters into their own hands, and violent incidents were covered up by powerful people in the business. Torsten felt this theory might fit. Perhaps the guy had ordered work on a summer house out in the archipelago, and the work had been shoddy, leading to a nasty conflict. He'd actually read that the victim and his wife owned a place on Värmdö, to the east of Stockholm, and, according to the tax records, it wasn't a tiny fishing cabin, either.

As Torsten lifted the telephone receiver to call the land management office, someone knocked on the door. "Come in!" Torsten called out, not putting down the phone.

A young man walked in. Torsten guessed he was between twenty-five and thirty years old. He was wearing dark jeans, a light-blue starched shirt, and a dark-blue blazer with suede patches on the elbows. The blazer looked expensive. The young man's hair was combed back and slightly longer at the neck. His face was perfect, with high, well-formed cheek-bones. For a moment, Torsten wondered if he was wearing makeup. The scarf around his neck was of a rough material in dark-blue stripes, and the color matched his eyes. He must have been over six feet tall and had a lean, patrician body. Torsten had to struggle to cover his surprise. He had no idea what this person, so different from the others in the police station, was doing in his office.

The man held out his hand and smiled, showing perfect white teeth.

"Hello, I'm Augustin Madrid. Olle Lundqvist sent me."

"Torsten Ehn. Just a moment, I've been put through. Go ahead and sit down."

Augustin Madrid sat across from Torsten's desk. He loosened his scarf, which Torsten imagined must be a bit too warm for today's weather.

The person on the other end of the line gave Torsten some of the information he needed. He would call back again within the hour.

Torsten hung up and said, "So Olle sent you here. How can I help you?"

The young man appeared confused. Torsten thought he saw a light touch of red on his smooth cheeks.

"He said he'd told you that I was supposed to assist you."

Torsten saw he couldn't keep the guy on edge for too long—he already seemed too nervous as it was. He wouldn't try joking with him, either.

"Oh, yes, Olle did mention that. I just didn't realize you'd be here so quickly. It often takes months for paperwork to clear here at the station, you know. What do you say, should we go get a cup of coffee? Then I'll show you around. Have they given you an office, or what?"

Augustin Madrid shook his head. "No—from what I understood, I was supposed to share this office with you."

Torsten stood up. "You know, I think we really need that coffee. There's a nice place not too far from here. So it's Augustin? What kind of a name is that?"

"My mother gave it to me."

Torsten was taken aback by his serious tone. Obviously he was tired of hearing that question, but it shouldn't have been unexpected. With such an odd name, people were going to ask you about it. He felt happy that he, himself, had been given such a common name as Torsten. Nobody ever asked him about that.

"So, why do you want to work for us, exactly?"

Torsten placed the two café lattes on the table and sat down in an armchair. It was much more comfortable than it looked.

"Because I know I can make a difference. I can be useful. I can see things other people miss."

Torsten looked into Augustin's dark-blue eyes. Was he trying to prove himself? It didn't seem like it.

Augustin continued: "I know I have to find the right answer right away, or I start to get bored. And I don't fit in just anywhere."

"But somehow you know you'll fit in with the National Police."

The young man shrugged. "You never know one hundred per cent, do you? I've helped Olle with many cases, and we've worked well together. He knows he can trust me."

Torsten managed to hide his surprise.

"Yes, Olle told me about you. What case that you worked on interested you the most?"

Augustin looked at him directly, then shook his head. "It's confidential, top secret. There were cases you had nothing to do with."

"Really!"

"For the Security Police."

No matter how much Torsten wanted to hide his surprise, he couldn't any longer. "So, you worked for Säpo under Olle? How'd that work out?"

"You can ask Olle, though I believe he's not cleared to tell you. He did say many times that he hoped I'd work for you one day. He said you have a great deal to teach me."

"What else did he say?"

"You prefer to work alone because you need your space to work a case. But I can run errands and take care of paperwork for you. I'm good at keeping people away."

Torsten laughed.

"So Olle thinks I'm not good at dealing with people?"

"No, that's not true. Just that you like to work at your own speed, and someone needs to keep the wolves at bay."

"And you can do that?"

Augustin said flatly, "Yes, I can."

"Okay, why not? Or perhaps I should say, what choice do I have? I do need assistance, but I'm going to hand over all the crappy duties to you. I have to warn you, I hate delegating and then having to go over everything again just to get it right. If I see that it's not working out, I'll tell you and Olle right up front. Then you'll have to find another job."

"I understand absolutely. I like it when things are clear."

"And the last thing I need is someone reporting to Olle behind my back. You have to tell me whatever you find out right away. If you don't reach me, wait until you do."

"Obviously."

"Good. Now I want you to write up a report—on yourself."

"What do you need to know?"

"Who you are: your background, who your friends are, the kinds of food you like—pretty much everything. I need to know."

"May I ask why? Do you think I have a criminal back-ground?"

"Not at all. If I'm going to let you work closely with me, I need to know all about your weaknesses and your strengths. I want to know if you have a complex about your mother. I want to know if you're afraid of spiders. I want to know anything, everything, that might tell me how you will handle your job, because these little things may be the difference between life and death."

"But I won't be receiving a similar report about you."

Torsten smiled at his cheeky reply.

"You won't need one. You'll find out all about me and my weaknesses. In our line of work, I'm responsible for you. *You* are not responsible for *me*. So give me every little shitty piece of information you can think of. I want your report by the end of the week."

"Sure," Augustin said.

"Also, you can go to the basement and find a desk. If we're going to share an office, you'll need somewhere to put your stuff. I'm used to spreading out. It's a big enough office, but I don't want us breathing down each other's necks."

"May I ask a question?"

"Not today. But think what you want to ask me and we'll take it up tomorrow over breakfast. I'll be here right after seven thirty, and I expect you to be here before me. Now . . . I have business in the fashionable part of town. So I'll see you tomorrow."

Augustin Madrid stood up and bowed, holding out his hand. Torsten waved back and left the café. He was looking forward to reading Augustin's personal report, not because he was worried about Augustin's competence, but because he was extremely curious. Who was this kid, mature beyond his years and looking like he was born to be Sweden's crown prince? What the hell was he doing inside a police station? Torsten smiled to himself. He was pleased with his report idea. The inspiration for it had just come to him. He imagined Olle would have a good laugh when he got wind of it.

Chapter 21

Marianne set her tray beside the sink. It was time for her half a grapefruit. For breakfast, she'd had just a soft-boiled egg and black coffee. To quell her desire for a cheese sandwich, she took four puffs on her cigarette, then left it on the side of the sink. She told herself she should be allowed to smoke during the next ten days. It wouldn't do any more damage to her health than it already had. She just wanted to get through this diet.

She pretended the two white-chocolate nougats hadn't happened. The grapefruit tasted sweeter than she'd expected, but her hunger didn't diminish. She felt more frustrated than ever. She relit the rest of the cigarette and thought that if things went on like this, she'd have to buy an entire carton of Davidoffs. That would make this particular diet the most expensive one she'd tried. She comforted herself with the thought of the grilled half chicken she was allowed for lunch.

She made her way back to the library, thinking about what she'd just read. She knew that the most important information was the stuff she hadn't seen yet—that's the way it usually worked. Perhaps she'd have more clarity when she finished all the reports.

She changed direction and went to the bathroom, hanging up her robe there. She brushed her teeth and pulled out the scale. It revealed the same depressing weight as the day before. She shoved the scale back under the sink with a bang. Maybe it was time to buy a new one. She climbed into the bathtub and grimaced at the old shower curtain. She wondered how long it would take before she got around to buying a new one. She hoped she'd remember to write that down on her to-do list.

Once refreshed and clean, she felt hungrier than ever. She sat back down in her library armchair, angry, and poured herself another cup of black coffee. She pulled the stack of papers onto her lap, bending her legs beneath her as she reached for her pen.

An hour later, she'd been through all the material. She eyed her notes in the margins. The fact that the crime had taken place just around the corner from her home made her feel alarmed, yet fascinated. She couldn't remember the last time something like this had taken place in her quiet neighborhood. Although she couldn't see his face, she had no trouble placing Christopher Turin. His type was so common. The only unusual thing about him was the fact that he'd been the victim of a brutal crime. Possibly, he could be part of a financial scheme gone wrong. But it was uncommon for people in his social class to be murdered over something like that.

Marianne eyed the autopsy report. She paused at the list of personal possessions found on his body. Nothing caught her eye immediately, but she felt like something was missing. She thought for some time before she wrote on the edge of the paper:

Eyeglasses? Did he wear glasses or contact lenses? Who kills someone in this manner? Experienced killer or inexperienced? Who were his influences? Internet search: combinations of similar materials. Permission to search crime register re: this?

She placed the reports to one side and stretched her legs. The air streaming into the room was warmer now. Traffic noise came from the street below. Trucks from the harbor going straight through the city on Strandvägen were getting caught in traffic. You'd think they'd learn to take another route.

She glanced at the papers with her notes and was filled with the sense that she'd actually accomplished something. She smiled weakly to herself. She was also glad that she'd spent an entire hour not thinking about her extreme hunger. Only three more hours until she could take out that grilled chicken and wolf it down.

CHAPTER 22

Paula turned the shower faucet so the water was as hot as she could stand. Her entire body ached from last night's activities. Her feet were blistered from her stilettos, and her genitals were sore.

She could deal with the physical pain, but as the alcohol wore off, it became more difficult to handle her ever-increasing anxiety. Flashbacks came of dancing with Knoll and Tott at Velvet; Purran's judgmental glares; those last shots at the bar she and Lotta took directly from mens' mouths; the walk back to Lotta's house, which seemed at first to be a wonderful idea . . . for the fresh air . . .

Her memories from Lotta's house were much dimmer. Knoll and Tott had practically thrown themselves at Lotta, who wasn't at all shy about being led into bed. And the young man who'd worked in the kitchen had visited Paula. What she'd done in the tiny guest room on the attic floor was more than Paula could comprehend. She couldn't count the times they'd had sex. They'd both been insatiable. She'd done things she didn't even have a name for. And of course, they hadn't used protection. All the while, they heard sounds from downstairs—of Lotta and the other men.

Paula leaned her forehead against the tiles and picked up the soap for the fifth time. She had no idea how she'd let all this happen. That she felt ashamed was an understatement. She was determined to visit her doctor as soon as she had a chance. Perhaps even today—to get all tests possible and demand the results ASAP. She'd read that you could get HIV-test results in just a day.

Then, she'd have to corral the gossip. Other women from the party witnessed some of her actions, and she and Lotta would have to devise an ironclad story. She dimly realized that Lotta and her husband may have come to an agreement about such things. Lotta had been perfectly comfortable about last night's goings-on. She felt that Paula was overstressing. What was there to worry about? Who would ever know what they did behind closed doors?

The young man—Passi—had woken Paula up that morning. He stroked her hair and laughed when her eyes widened in shock, but they had sex again. Paula was less ashamed then, since the damage had already been done. Passi kept telling her how beautiful she was, that he loved her body.

He gave her his number as he left the guest room. She took it but felt she would never call. Just to be on the safe side, she discreetly asked Lotta if she was supposed to pay him for the night, but Lotta just laughed and patted her on the cheek. She said she had no idea that Paula had such low self-esteem. Knoll and Tott had already left, and Paula had to sit politely and listen to Lotta's tales of her night's adventures. Ill from both the alcohol and what she'd heard, Paula walked back up the hill to her own empty house. For once, she didn't care about the hollow echo, or that the shoes in the hallway were in the same place she'd left them. She just went inside and turned off the alarm.

For over an hour she leaned over the toilet and vomited until there was nothing left but bile. Finally, she was able to rest for a bit on the side of the bed.

She knew she should call Jens to find out when he was coming home. She needed a plan to get through the day. She thought the sleeping pills she'd recently gotten for her insomnia might be a solution. She thought about taking another shower, but she settled on just doing a face peel. As she walked back to the bathroom, she saw the shadow of someone sitting on the toilet seat—and that shadow got up and ran out. Paula tried to scream, but the sound stuck in her throat. Then, everything went black.

CHAPTER 23

Torsten returned to his office at just after three in the afternoon. He had a strong urge for coffee, which was close to the Swedish norm. The meeting he'd attended had gone on for an eternity, and he'd had trouble keeping his eyes open. It was about the new structure they were expected to work under, and for the first half of the meeting, Torsten struggled not to explode at the idiotic suggestions. As the minutes ticked by, he turned listless. He started writing down his thoughts on the Christopher Turin case instead. He hadn't found anything of significance, but it was good to line up his thoughts. Writing the day's report on the case would be easier later that evening.

As he headed into his office, he was startled to see a second desk. His own desk had been cleaned, the paper piles neatly arranged. Even his pens and pencils had been gathered into a cup and set beside his computer. A lone lily adorned the windowsill, and its scent added a pleasant touch to the room.

Augustin Madrid greeted him from the new desk.

"I didn't get the coffee yet because I didn't know when your meeting would end. I'll run and get it now."

Torsten waved his hand and said, "No, thanks—I appreciate the offer, but I can get my own coffee. There's something I've forgotten in my car that I have to get, too, a report I need to take another look at."

Torsten began searching through the well-sorted stacks of reports and tried to mask his irritation at this invasion of his desk.

"If you're looking for Jan Brundin's final forensic report, it's on top of the pile closest to the computer. If you're leaving for the day, then the report about me is right beneath it. I completely understand if you want to go over it when I'm not around."

Torsten stared at the young officer, who was so articulate and extraordinarily polite. He wondered if the young man was playing with him.

"All right, well, thanks. I'm not leaving for the day. I'll be back in a while."

Torsten headed for the door with the two reports under his arm. He focused his gaze straight ahead to avoid the sight of Klaus Heikki waving from his office. Torsten needed a lot more coffee before he would be ready to talk to anyone. He was also curious to see what was in the reports, especially the one concerning his new subordinate. He grabbed the elevator before Klaus could catch up to him. Pressing the green button for the ground floor, he decided to head for the café around the corner, where he'd be able to work undisturbed.

As he stepped off the elevator, Torsten recognized two reporters from the crowd at the Narvavägen crime scene. He increased his pace so they wouldn't see him. They seemed to be fully occupied in talking to each other. Turning his head, he caught sight of Klaus, greeting the reporters with a big smile. He hoped Klaus would be able to keep his trap shut about the Turin case. But it looked like the journalists were there to talk about last week's motorcycle gang case. Klaus had been working in a different unit that concentrated on such crimes, and he was seen as an expert. Now Klaus was trying for a well-paid administrative post, perhaps because of all the threats he'd received the past few years. Torsten could understand that, but he still felt annoyed by him. But then, who was he to judge? Klaus wasn't exactly a bad superior—it was just that Torsten preferred to work on his own without other people messing things up. Only Olle was capable of not interfering. Olle was never an encumbrance—he always helped figure things out. Olle was one in a million, one of the few who made Torsten's job easier.

The café on Bergsgatan, at the corner of Pilgatan, was empty except for an older man that Torsten suspected had fallen asleep behind his newspaper. The man was making sounds suspiciously like snoring. The café's decor was the exact opposite of the jail and the police station. Its clean, white furniture and romantic country details gave the impression of an old manor-house parlor. This was one reason Torsten made it his haunt. None of his colleagues were inclined to enter such a place, which made the café secure to think through his ideas in peace. Not to mention the baked goods, a good step above the usual plastic-wrapped stuff in other nearby cafés. Here everything was made from scratch. Even if the interior was a bit on the frilly side, Torsten felt at home.

He snagged a table by the window with his steaming-hot coffee and took a big bite of his cinnamon bun. The taste of cinnamon and melted salt butter spread through his mouth, and the pearl sugar crackled beneath his teeth. His taste buds gave him jolts of happiness. He couldn't help taking a second bite immediately. His craving satisfied, he began to read his reports.

CHAPTER 24

When Peder had packed his bags the night before, Marianne helped him fold his clothes. The lump in her throat returned whenever she saw his suitcases. She wanted nothing more than to have all her children together. Especially now.

Before putting on her robe, she couldn't resist quietly stepping onto that hateful scale. Peder was still in the shower. She held in her stomach, although she knew that was useless. The pointer swayed back and forth before landing at the same spot, especially if she leaned to the left. She'd have to give Chrisse a call and see if she'd really tried this diet herself. It appeared not to be working for her. Marianne donned her robe and wrote on a memo pad: *SCALE!* A few moments later, she added: *NEW SHOWER CURTAIN!* She ripped off the top sheet and placed it by the bowl with her keys. She ought to remember it there.

–◻–

Hardly more than an hour later, she was waving good-bye to Peder. She tried to blink away her tears, but he'd already noticed them.

"Don't be sad, Mamma. I'll be back for Christmas break."

"I know, I'm just silly. But I'll miss you."

"My sisters are still here, you know."

"That doesn't mean I won't miss *you*. Are you sure you have enough money? I put enough for your rent for the next half year into your account. Promise to let me know if you need more."

"I promise. And I'll call when I get there. You know, I'm so happy that you're going back to work. It's not good for you to hang around at home."

"You're probably right, though it doesn't feel good right now."

She received his long hug, and the memory of that moment in May returned to her. Stroking his cheek with the back of her hand, she said, "Don't forget to call if things get rough. I know I wasn't much use while Pappa was ill, but you know that I'll always be here for you."

Peder nodded as he picked up his suitcases. A moment later, the door closed and he was gone. She listened to his footsteps descend the stairs. Marianne felt her nose start to run, so she went for tissues in the guest bathroom. It took her a long time to calm down. Her heart was heavy. Peder would be away for most of the next year. He would be dealing with his grief and the loss of his father all by himself, and Marianne didn't like the thought of that at all.

She was just about to head into the kitchen and foreswear her diet when the phone rang. She ran to her bedroom to pick up.

"Marianne, is that you?"

"It is."

"Ehn here. Torsten. May I swing by later? I'm going to see Turin's colleague in Saltsjöbaden now—the other part owner of the firm. I'd like to hand you the report right after that. Olle will compensate you for your time since you haven't officially started back to work. But with this case, we have to get going to stay one step ahead of the media."

Marianne frowned while Torsten took a deep breath. Why in the world did he need to come moseying over to her place? Couldn't he just give her a quick call when he was done? As if reading her thoughts, Torsten continued: "I know I'm being a bit presumptuous here, but I feel we need to run through all the material together before the weekend. By the time Monday rolls around, we'll need to jump right in. You'll be able to hit the floor running, so to speak, on your first day back."

Marianne paused before replying. "Okay, but when will you be dropping by?"

After they hung up, Marianne sat down heavily on her bed. She had no desire to get dressed or have anyone in her apartment. She just wanted peace and quiet, to be alone until evening fell. She had planned to sit in her kitchen and drink wine and feel her sorrow over the fact that her son had just left for Australia. Peder had been home for three weeks before Hans died, and then he'd stayed on through the rest of the summer. The nights he'd gone out with friends, her daughter Nina had stayed in the house and slept in the big double bed beside her—although Marianne said that was unnecessary. Perhaps they were overly concerned, but it still had made her feel better. It had even become a little frustrating that she never had a moment to herself. Now, all she wanted was to gorge on her own unhappiness this Friday afternoon—alone. But this Torsten Ehn guy was going to come over and stuff information into her head. She wouldn't be able to get it back out, either—she'd ruminate on it all weekend. Still, what he'd said about being able to jump in feet first was taking root. She had enough of a need to be in control that being a step ahead was appealing.

Tired, she headed for the bathroom. Perhaps she'd offer Torsten Ehn some of the leftovers from last night's dinner. He'd been so eager yesterday, sniffing the casserole in the oven. She didn't wait for the water to entirely heat up and just contented herself with a lukewarm shower.

CHAPTER 25

Paula was sitting with a bath towel wrapped tightly around her when she heard Jens open the front door. She didn't bother to get up. She no longer had any feeling in her lower body, and she was so cold, her teeth were chattering. Jens's sharp steps in the hallway showed his irritation. She closed her eyes. She didn't think she could endure being yelled at. How could she ever get Jens to understand what she was going through? The problem was that he didn't want to understand. She didn't move when he banged on the bathroom door, yelling at her to open up. She didn't answer even when his anger turned to concern and he called her name. When he was finally able to spring the lock from the other side of the door, he was both worried and angry.

"What the hell is going on with you, Paula? You can't behave like this! What if the children had been here?"

Paula let him circle his arms around her body and try to rock her. Perhaps she'd let herself fall into this fear because the children were gone. Maybe *she* needed to feel small and childlike.

Jens pulled her to her feet and led her to the bedroom. He carefully laid her down on the bed. The cover he tucked around her body smelled comforting and familiar. She wished he would lie down beside her. Instead, he sat on the edge of the bed and patted her cheek tenderly.

"Darling, what is happening to you? Why are you feeling like this? How could you ever imagine there was someone in the house? Why would anyone want to come in? There are hundreds of other houses around here, and most of them are empty during the day. You've got to get control of yourself, or else you'll have to see a doctor. We can't have you like this. Do you understand?"

Paula felt a wave of nausea and pressed her jaw shut. She wanted him to just be quiet and sit there. She had no strength to listen to him. She knew what she'd seen. She'd gotten a good look at him, and he had seen her.

CHAPTER 26

Torsten deliberately let his finger linger on the doorbell just a second too long. He couldn't resist antagonizing Marianne just a little. Something about her peevishness made him want to stir her up—not to be nasty or start a fight, but to see that spark in her eyes that showed she wanted to say something she fought to control. He wanted to push Marianne Jidhoff off-balance, to find out what was behind the shield she'd built around herself—a shield that showed up in her strict posture and stubborn integrity. He knew why she was like this—anyone who'd been married to Hans Larson would have been the same way. Hans Larson had that effect on people: making them stand at attention and do exactly what he demanded. His wife had certainly been no exception.

The door opened, and he noticed that she looked even more tired than the day before. He recalled her saying she'd be sending her son off to Australia—perhaps it had hit her hard.

"Sorry, I haven't had a chance to deal with these magazines and newspapers," she said.

Torsten looked at the newspapers piled by the front door and decided there were two weeks' worth of them. He smiled as he bent to untie his shoes.

"As I mentioned, I have a teenage boy myself. So . . . how was your family dinner?"

Marianne wanted to skip the personal chit-chat. "It was pleasant," she said. "In the end, it was pretty nice. That's life."

"You mean, because of Hans?"

"No, because Peder had to leave. Actually, Hans seldom attended our family dinners. I can count on one hand the times he was able to come."

"That's right, you did tell me your son was leaving. It must be difficult for you."

"I certainly don't want to cry over the children and keep them from leaving home."

"You don't seem to be the kind of mother who ties her children to her apron strings. But it would be strange if you didn't feel sad about not seeing your son for an entire year. I'd wail like a stuck pig."

"Pigs wail?" Marianne laughed. "I thought they squealed. Speaking of dinner last night, I'm warming some leftovers in the oven. It would be unfair not to offer you some of the casserole you were longing to try yesterday. Or do you have to go home for dinner?"

Now it was Torsten's turn to look surprised. "Leftovers? Here I've called and gotten myself an invitation to dinner, although I didn't mean that you'd take it like that—giving me dinner, that is."

"I understand completely, but I thought you might be hungry."

"Me? Hungry? I'm always hungry. It's one of my worst faults."

"Yes, I know that already."

They went into the kitchen and Torsten was filled again with a feeling of peace. Although she decorated in a conservative style, Marianne Jidhoff knew how to make people feel at home. Her home was very welcoming.

Marianne pulled the casserole out of the oven and set a plate before Torsten. Marianne knew from experience that the Kassler potatoes always tasted better on the second day. Torsten was amazed by the large portion she ladled onto his plate. He opened his napkin and laid it on his lap.

"I can't believe I'm being served something so elegant!"

Marianne laughed.

"This is the first time I've ever heard anyone call Kassler Florentine elegant!"

"Good home cooking is always a luxury in my book. Can I dig right in?"

"Go ahead. I'll be eating some grilled chicken later tonight."

"That seems a shame to me, with such delicious food so close at hand. But nobody is happier than I am right now."

Marianne noticed that Torsten handled his knife and fork well, in spite of his rough hands. She'd thought he might have had trouble using the delicate silverware. She gave him time to finish a good part of his portion before she moved to the topic at hand.

"So tell me how things went at Saltsjöbaden. Any new leads?"

"Pretty much the same as from Jonas Carlfors. Carlfors's sister Hanna is married to Tom Malmström, the other partner. Talk about a family business! Still, Jonas Carlfors was sympathetic and polite. This business partner of his was exactly the opposite."

"That's often the way."

"Right. Tom Malmström was a boor. He never let his wife or me get a word in edgewise. He kept saying how things should be—whether it was the coffee they were serving, or Christopher Turin's marriage. He had an opinion about everything—kind of refreshing in a way, but fairly exhausting. His wife was more discreet and had no desire to broadcast her opinions the way he did."

"So what opinions did this Tom Malmström have? It sounds to me as if he already knows who the suspect is."

"Yes, he does, and he is absolutely sure of it, too. He insisted that Christopher Turin's new lifestyle was getting him on the wrong track. He was probably tricked into something or other."

"What did he suggest?"

"Christopher Turin enrolled in a lot of courses the past few years. Tom Malmström insisted that these 'courses' were actually some kind of cult. Malmström ripped into alternative therapies of all kinds, saying that the people who called themselves 'coaches' were just opportunists without any kind of real education."

"I must say, I agree with him there. I can't tell you how many sleazy salespeople are out there."

"Well, I guess it all depends on how you look at it, and how the people involved feel about it. He was not at all sympathetic toward Christopher Turin. All his sympathy lay with Isa Turin, the widow."

"Why did they let Turin continue as a vice president if Malmström had so little confidence in him?"

"That's an interesting thing—and it didn't come up in the conversation with Jonas Carlfors yesterday. Our friend Tom said that if Christopher hadn't up and died on them, they probably would have fired him in the next few weeks. They'd already made the decision—they were just looking for a good excuse to fire him and trying to decide the amount of the severance package."

"Do you think Jonas Carlfors was trying to keep all that from you?"

Torsten thought a moment and said, "No, I think he was uneasy bringing it up on the same day that Christopher died. Perhaps he didn't want to, with everything else going on. The mind does funny things after a shocking bit of information—and I think that's what was going on with Jonas Carlfors. Tom Malmström, on the other hand, didn't seem to mourn his former college friend's death all that much."

"Still, that doesn't sound like a reason to murder him, does it?"

"I don't think so. They had enough capital to replace him—even if buying him out cost them a bit of cash. The amount of money actually wouldn't have been all that much, and Tom didn't seem like the sneaky type."

"He's probably much too concerned about his social status to even risk any criminal act."

"Probably. So we still don't have much new. By the way, let me compliment you on this dish. I can understand why it was one of your son's favorites. It's absolutely wonderful."

"It's not all that special, but it does the trick."

"Does the trick? You're kidding! It's a delicacy! Actually, may I be so bold as to ask for a second helping?"

Marianne was pleased by his compliment, even if she hid it well. They chatted some minutes, before Torsten forced himself up from the table. He would have gladly stayed the rest of the evening if he could, opening the bottle of wine he saw on the kitchen counter. But he knew not to overstay his welcome. They said good-bye in the hallway, and Torsten thanked her again for letting him stop by—and for feeding him such great food. When he closed the door behind him, he had to sigh contentedly. Just like her casserole, Marianne Jidhoff gave him the desire for another helping.

CHAPTER 27

"You don't dive?"

Augustin shook his head and stiffly stepped down the ladder into the water. Torsten stared at this slender young man. He had such an athletic body that a Greek god would have wept from pure envy. Augustin started to swim toward the other side of the pool with small, paddling strokes.

"What? You can't do the crawl, either?"

Augustin shook his head. He was struggling to stay above the surface.

Torsten stepped to the side of the pool and dove in. He caught up to his new colleague with one stroke. Augustin fought as hard as he could, while Torsten floated leisurely at his side.

"When did you learn to swim?"

"A year ago."

"Excuse me? How the hell did you manage to get through the Police Academy without learning how to swim? Didn't you have physical tests?"

"No. Well, I mean, yes, but I always made sure I was absent when it was time to go into the water. Nobody checked."

Torsten snorted, then burst into laughter. He heaved himself up on the far edge, looking out over the empty pool.

He shook his head. "So, you're telling me you actually have a weakness? I wondered when I'd find it. You must know I was a part of the Junior National Team?"

Augustin said yes and did the best he could to turn at the wall without grabbing the edge. Then, he went beneath the surface.

"Come on, get out of there. Let's go to the sauna instead. I really didn't mean to torture you."

Augustin used the ladder to climb out. His entire body was shivering from the cold. He gave Torsten a grateful glance. "Sorry I disappointed you."

Torsten gestured his apology away, and they headed toward the sauna. On the way, they crossed paths with some colleagues who jumped into the pool, screaming "Cannonball!"

The air inside the sauna was dry, but a tad too cool. Torsten liked it hot enough that the dry planks almost hissed against his thighs when he sat down.

"So how come you never learned?"

Augustin undid his thin gold wristwatch and laid it on a towel beside him.

"I've been afraid of the water ever since I was small. I'd faint just entering a place with a swimming pool. My parents did everything they could, but I had a panic attack every time."

"Did you fall in once and almost drown?"

"Not that I can remember. I even refused baths. Until I was ten, I only took showers."

"Jesus! What a phobia!"

Augustin shrugged. "Maybe, but I think it was harder on my parents than it was on me. I didn't really care."

Torsten started to laugh again. "Sorry, but I can't get it out of my head that you played hooky from water training in the Academy. It must be the first time someone ever got away with it. The Academy is filled with all those coarse super-athlete types!"

"Yes, it was strange. Nobody seemed to care, though. I didn't try to make many friends there, anyway."

"And why not? Those guys were going to be your future colleagues."

"I've never fit into big groups. It's just not me."

"But from what I read in your report, you have no trouble with authority. How does that make sense?"

"Is it supposed to?"

"I always thought so, but obviously not, judging from you. Do you think you were making enemies instead?"

"No, not that either. I'm just not the type that people make friends with. I'm kind of an oddball, so it's no surprise I wouldn't fit in."

"And despite this, you think you'd make a great police officer."

"Maybe because of it. I'm convinced that the police corps must have all kinds of people. There are some instances where police can't just walk in and join the party. There have to be inconspicuous people who can slide right into a group—I'm one of those."

"What kinds of groups do you just slide right into, if I may ask?"

"Immigrants, especially, because of my looks. I speak Spanish and Portuguese. And the upper classes—also because of my background."

"I read that your father was a professor of languages. What was your mother—?"

"My mother is deceased. She taught psychology at the University of Barcelona."

"Why didn't you mention her in your report?"

"Because I knew you would ask, and I would rather talk than write about her."

"Then go ahead and talk."

"She died when I was ten. After she passed away, we moved from Spain to Sweden. Pappa got a position at the University of Stockholm—he had many friends here. A large gang of them came to Sweden in the seventies."

"Your father is originally from Chile?"

"Yes, and Mamma was from Brazil."

"And that is the reason you learned capo—capowera?"

Augustin laughed. "Capoeira. It's a martial art from the streets. People arranged cage matches back in the day."

Torsten shuddered. "Why are you involved in such an aggressive sport?"

"It's not really aggressive—more like intense, and fairly demanding. Seven of us started a club in Stockholm a few years ago. We had already learned all kinds of martial arts, and then we found a spot in one of the guys' basements. It's still a small club, just forty members. The guys who began it are still involved in training others. It's fun. We already have a few thirteen- and fourteen-year-old kids who are re-ally getting good. They keep off the streets, and they're training hard."

"I certainly can support a club like that. Maybe I should drop by and see what you do. What about your father? Do you have a good relationship?"

"Yes, we go out for dinner sometimes. He lives just a few blocks away from me."

Torsten drew his hand through his hair. He noticed the sweat pouring down Augustin's face. "Too hot for you?"

Augustin smiled, shaking his head. "No, I'm fine."

"And about the swimming thing. We're going to have to fix that. I have a friend you ought to meet. When things go down, I need you to be able to leap in the water, not climb down some damned set of stairs."

Augustin nodded. His face was serious. "I'd like to meet your friend. I know I have to solve this problem."

"Come on, let's get going. I want something to drink. Do you drink beer, or does it have to be some wine of the proper vintage?"

Augustin laughed. "I do like a nice wine from a good year, but not after a sauna. I'll have a beer with you."

—◻—

Torsten thought hard as he dressed. Augustin seemed like a pleasant person with a range of knowledge far greater than his own, but he wondered why Olle wanted to bring the two of them together. Olle was working on some kind of plan, but he hadn't told them about it yet. Of that Torsten was absolutely sure.

CHAPTER 28

Paula Steen brought her knees up to her chin and adjusted the blankets so no cold air could come in. She was watching an episode of a reality show where the host saved people from their financial idiocies. She wondered if people ever really got back on their feet after being on the show.

Jens slumbered beside her. She stroked his hair lightly. They'd had a good evening together. As the alcohol and the anxiety it caused left her body, she'd begun to relax, realizing that she must have been seeing things. There hadn't been anyone in her house. It had been a phantom from her own confused brain—due to her exhaustion, or the alcohol.

As far as her "night's adventure" was concerned, nothing dramatic happened after Jens came home. Slowly, as when one's bowl is filled with sour milk, Paula had come to realize that she really wasn't worried about it, either. If she'd had a one-night stand with a much younger man in Lotta's house, then there it was. She also was beginning to feel that Jens wouldn't even care. Perhaps he'd even be relieved. He might even regale her with all his own escapades. She wasn't a complete idiot: she was convinced that was part of their problem. Of course Jens was getting some outside action.

Why else wasn't he interested in sex with his wife anymore? Paula was starting not to care about whom he'd been with or how often. She just knew that she loved Jens and liked when they were together. As long as their marriage continued, even if they had sex with others, she would be content. At any rate, that was what she told herself this Friday afternoon.

Lotta had called and said that Passi had asked about her. He said he hoped she'd get in touch. Paula smiled and told Lotta she had come to feel much younger than her forty years. Although she'd firmly decided she'd never contact him again, she was beginning to change her mind. Calling him and arranging another meeting seemed an exciting idea. Maybe she would invite him here when Jens was traveling. Perhaps during the day, when the kids were at school. Spending an hour or two with Passi in bed would be a comfort she might enjoy every now and then—if he wanted her, of course.

Paula quietly disentangled herself from the blanket on the sofa. She poured a glass of water, drinking it all in one go.

Her cell phone on the kitchen counter showed she had a message, and it was from the same anonymous person as before.

You weren't imagining things. I watched you when you were taking a shower. Don't let him think I don't exist. I see you everywhere. Wherever you go, I will be following you. You never need to be alone. I am beside you. I know you need me. Soon it will be our time.

Paula grabbed the countertop so hard she broke a finger-nail. Staring at the message, she heard Jens snore.

Outside in her yard, the night was dark. There was a rustling sound beneath a birch tree by the patio. She didn't dare look outside, and she erased the message.

Although she should have shown it to Jens to get him to understand that someone was stalking her, she decided not to wake him. The fact that she could prove it to him made no difference.

Instead, she sneaked into the bathroom and locked the door carefully. She sat down on the edge of the bathtub. Her fingers shook as she tapped the number she'd saved earlier that morning.

"Hello, Passi here."

"Hi. It's me, Paula. From last night."

PART TWO

CHAPTER 29

He had no new car yet, so he thought it would be safest to ride his bike. He had no desire to use public transportation all the way to Djursholm. Not so much because it was always crowded, but simply because he didn't want anyone to notice him. Not yet, anyway.

His front tire needed some air, so he used the pump strapped to the frame. After checking the back tire as well, he threw on his backpack and led the bicycle through the courtyard and out the gate. He biked up Narvavägen, and when he passed the accident site, he couldn't see any trace of the "tragic hit-and-run," as the newspapers called it. He smiled to himself. It did feel good.

He had two sandwiches and a sports drink in his backpack. He thought he'd be waiting for quite some time. As he crossed Valhallavägen and turned up Erik Dahlbergsgatan, his cell phone rang.

"Hi, it's me. What are you up to?"

He cringed and realized he had to come up with a sensible lie on the spot. He took a deep breath and said, "I'm going to a lecture. What about you?"

"I got off to a late start. Too bad, I thought we'd see each other—I miss you."

"Hmm, maybe later this evening? I'll be alone."

"You will? Can I come over and study? I have a test to-morrow."

"Sure, but I don't know when I'll be back. Maybe about nine or so?"

He ended the call and slid the phone back into his jacket pocket. The call had disturbed his focus. Next time, he'd skip answering and just reply later with a text. That girl was going to be a problem. It could ruin everything.

Lill-Jan Forest was quiet, and just a car or two passed him. The air was clean and clear, and he breathed deeply, filling his lungs. He had always enjoyed the fall. Everything felt pure—school was starting and things were returning to normal. This year, his studies would be tough and demand a great deal of his energy. He had no desire to be a loser—he was going to continue to get the highest possible grades. All the rest was irrelevant.

He passed the tall light-blue buildings of the University of Stockholm on his right. He had to push harder going uphill past the National Museum of Natural History.

He wondered when the funeral would take place. He wondered whether he should attend. He didn't think a funeral would be held quietly with just the family. It was hardly their style. They'd invite all kinds of folks to honor his memory. *Honor!* He wondered if that man had felt so honored that morning—or if he'd even understood what was about to happen.

He thought their eyes had met, but that could just have been his imagination. Wishful thinking. But the more he thought about it, the more he realized that is how truth is written. Their eyes *had* met for a second, before his fear and panic over what was about to happen took over.

That's how he wanted to remember it.

CHAPTER 30

Marianne had already been awake for over half an hour when the alarm beeped. She sat up on the edge of the bed and stretched her arms over her head, her breasts sluggishly following her movements. Through her nightgown, her nipples clearly showed that they didn't appreciate the cold air outside the blanket.

She wrapped her robe around her body and slipped her feet into slippers, whose sheepskin lining had been worn down with use. It was high time to buy a new pair. No sunlight appeared in the kitchen yet, so she turned on the lamp above the stove. She switched on the coffee machine and headed into the hallway. The newspaper had gotten stuck in her mail slot, and the first page of *Dagens Nyheter* was torn.

Over the weekend, Marianne had prepared, mentally and physically, to start work. She had bought a new scale with not only digital numbers but also a memory system, whatever that could be good for. At a new store called Gertrude, she bought a new shower curtain. She loved the abundance of beautiful bed and bathroom sets and had difficulty choosing from the wide selection. The friendly saleswoman had guided her through the store and helped her decide between a striped and a rose-patterned curtain. She'd chosen the one with the roses. Hans had always hated anything with flowers on it, and he would certainly have hated how much she'd spent. He'd hated excess in all its forms. Marianne felt a bit childish making such a strong statement with that purchase, but she realized she'd soon be over that phase.

Her daughter Sigrid had helped her go through her wardrobe, also checking her own clothes, to find suitable work outfits. They chose outfits that weren't too striking— the Prosecutor's Office wasn't a place for outlandish fashion.

Part of her weekend had also been devoted to staving off the feeling of starvation. It hadn't been easy. Although she was still skeptical about this diet, she followed it rigorously, and she had lost about one and a half pounds. The result seemed to mock her efforts. In desperation, she had gone with her father, Harry, for a long afternoon walk on Sunday. She had already begun regretting it by the time they reached the Djurgård Bridge. Harry stopped to chat with every person he knew, and Marianne finally begged him to stop. They were out to exercise, not to have a walking cocktail party. Harry scolded that she could hardly force him to act like an idiot. In seething silence, they walked across the bridge and then back. As they approached Djurgård Bridge the second time, it started to rain. Marianne hadn't felt tired at all after the five-kilometer walk, but now, this morning, her legs were slightly sore.

She decided she'd avoid the scale for a few days, not wanting to give herself an excuse to stop the diet. Perhaps the pounds would fly off before the tenth day.

The aroma of freshly brewed coffee hit her when she returned to the kitchen. She reverently poured some steaming, black liquid into her favorite cup. Then she boiled her egg, placing it on a napkin next to her newspaper. The radio was playing a concert by the London Philharmonic, which she thought might be a reprise from last week. Nothing in the paper made her raise an eyebrow. On the other hand, the fall season of the City Theater looked promising. Marianne liked to alternate between the City Theater and the National Theater. A number of her friends would never set foot in the National Theater, but Marianne liked to provoke her friends' snobbery. This was also true of her choice of the daily paper. Harry still thought that only Communists read *Dagens Nyheter*, and he couldn't understand why she had a subscription. Marianne thought *DN* was fresh and exciting, although she couldn't see much difference between the two morning papers any longer.

Marianne had remembered to buy panty hose, which she pulled on over suitable underwear. The fashionable trousers of the day demanded the right kind of underwear. Marianne hated the thought of panty lines or a muffin top. At work, one's behind should not call attention to itself—she felt that was true for both men and women.

Her trousers fit well, but she worried they'd be itchy if the weather turned warm. She'd just have to make sure she didn't run around too much. At any rate, she couldn't picture herself jogging through the hallways.

She'd been told that the department had been reorganized, affecting how the offices were laid out. Perhaps a change would be useful, although Marianne had her doubts about the open floor plan. It could hardly induce peace and quiet.

Marianne checked her purse one last time, then locked her door behind her. She took the stairs down and, stepping outside, she breathed in the fresh September air. She followed Storgatan up through Östermalm Square and past Sibyllegatan. She stopped to wait for Bus 62 in front of the ancient shop selling ladies' undergarments and the now almost-extinct "day dress." That's when she realized her new routine was now a fact. Many months had gone by since she'd last taken this bus to work, but it now seemed like only yesterday. The bus came six minutes later. Marianne smiled at the driver as he stamped her multiple-ride pass. He had a gray beard and kind eyes. She had thought she'd walk to work every morning, but she changed her mind. She would walk home instead—at least on this first day. She needed to keep everything under control.

CHAPTER 31

Harsh sunlight beat down upon the Stocksund Bridge. The wind tugged at his bicycle, and he had to hold on tightly to the handlebars to keep from hitting the railing. Once across, he took the exit toward Stocksund, which was more pleasant for biking, and he preferred the smaller roads. His body signaled that it wanted coffee. For a while he'd been drinking several cups a day, and he'd gotten addicted. He thought it almost sweet that his body had a will of its own. It was not at all interested in the sports drink he had in his backpack. Where could he buy some coffee but go unnoticed?

He steered his bicycle onto Djursholm Square, where groups of schoolchildren laughed and talked. Two boys were chasing a girl, and when they caught her, they lifted her into the air. He thought they were ridiculous. It was so obvious what they were playing. Childish. With a snort, he parked his bicycle on the other side of the street and made his way through the kids to a café.

The line was long and straggling. He stood patiently at the back, forcing himself to think about the coffee he'd soon be drinking. That kept him occupied during the long wait. When he finally reached the counter, the girl behind it smiled. Her hair was blonde and in tight corkscrew curls, wildly framing her somewhat round face.

"So, your number?"

"What?"

"We have a number system. Take a number from over there."

The blood left his face, and his rage bubbled up. The girl must have noticed the shift in his expression, and she hurried to say, "Don't worry this time. I'll take your order now. What would you like?"

Stammering slightly, he asked for two caffe lattes to go.

"Which size?"

"Large, please."

The girl hurried to make the coffee and soon came back with two paper cups with lids.

"Seventy-two crowns, please. That is, unless you'd like a sandwich or a cinnamon bun?"

He shook his head and pulled a hundred-crown note from his back pocket. As she handed him his change, she looked him in the eyes flirtatiously and said, "Come back soon."

He lowered his eyes and hurried out. He decided to walk his bicycle with the paper cups of coffee in the basket. Two Asian women were ahead of him. He suspected they were from the Philippines and probably on their way to cleaning jobs in the large, fin-de-siècle houses in this neighborhood, which seemed to be Svalnäs. He remembered reading in the tabloids about a female bank executive who'd bought a house here. It had been nicknamed Fort Knox because of all the alarm systems she'd put in. He imagined it would still be easy enough to break into her place. Swedish alarm systems were worthless compared to the ones in Italy or the United States. In those countries, people took potential threats seriously—probably due to experience. The latest brochures for alarm systems boasted direct connections to the police, not to some useless office building with inexperienced security guards whose uniforms did nothing to scare off serious thieves.

So what if an entire SWAT team was on his own trail? What could they do? He'd have to show firepower for them to use force—otherwise they wouldn't dare shoot. He knew they were incompetent cowards. In his latest issue of *Lethal Weapons* magazine, he'd read that in trial runs, police officers were outgunned by serious criminal gangs. The latter never hesitated to shoot. *Shoot first—ask questions later.* The police had tried to justify their terrible performance, but as far as he was concerned, they gave the weakest excuses.

CHAPTER 32

Marianne took a deep breath as she entered the Main Police Station. There was no possibility of turning back now. Somehow, the thought calmed her.

"Hello, I'm Marianne Jidhoff, a secretary for the Prosecutor's Office. I'm coming back from leave."

"And you're in the system?"

"I don't know. Olle Lundqvist would take care of such matters if he remembered, but that I doubt."

"Chief Prosecutor Lundqvist?"

"Yes," Marianne said, and the receptionist typed on her keyboard.

"Jidhoff. One *F* or two?"

"Two—just as it sounds."

Marianne bit her tongue. She didn't think her last name was all that unusual.

"Yes, here you are. Do you know your way to the office?"

"I think so. They've moved things around since I was here last."

"Take the first elevator to the fourth floor and then take a right. I'll give you a pass card, so you can open the door yourself."

"Has anyone else come in yet?"

"Yes, Olle Lundqvist came in earlier this morning. Alexandra Baranski is also here."

Marianne's brow furrowed. She couldn't put a face to the name. Baranski . . . Hans had probably mentioned her, but Marianne didn't know how she fit in.

"If you would stand against the wall, please, I'll take your picture."

Marianne stood against the yellow stone wall and tried to look calm. She knew that the picture would look terrible no matter how she stood, so she kept her mouth shut and hoped that the worst flaws—like the dark circles under her eyes—wouldn't stand out too much. She hadn't tried to cover them with makeup. Her sad hair color seemed to make them worse. Sigrid had pointed out that women do dye their hair these days, but Marianne had pretended not to hear. Luckily, the pass photo was in black-and-white. It was hard to make out her wrinkles, and her name was spelled correctly.

She took the elevator, which smelled like sweat and stale air, up to the fourth floor. Anxiously, she sniffed near her armpits to make sure the odor wasn't coming from her. She smelled her own deodorant and a trace of moth repellant from her jacket, but nothing offensive.

She wondered when she'd see Torsten Ehn, who'd said they'd have a chance to talk on Monday.

The investigators of the National Police seemed like the children of the house. They were in tight with the Prosecutor's Office even fifteen years ago, when Hans was Lead Prosecutor—before he climbed the career ladder and became Attorney General. Marianne was skeptical about his political career, but that's where Hans felt most at home.

His close buddies operated in the upper levels of the Social Democratic Party and the Workers' Movement, where Marianne—with her upper-class background—could never have entered. Even if she'd been more saintly than Mother Teresa, she couldn't have opened those doors. Hans, on the other hand, had grown up in Knivsta with a drinker of a father and a hardworking mother who did her best to keep the family together. He had no difficulty fitting into that scene, and he used his working-class background to his advantage. He worked his way into the Prosecutor's Office. He'd not been born with a silver spoon in his mouth. Even though both Hans and Marianne knew their backgrounds weren't so simple, Hans made this version public for political reasons. Marianne felt it wasn't her place to protest, although it seemed to her that Hans's social climbing had long ago taken him out of the working class. Marianne could never really comprehend the distance he'd traveled or why he had decided to marry a woman from the social class he publicly denounced. He certainly had never refused any of the advantages he received from her background whenever it suited his needs. Their relationship had always gone according to his wishes, and Marianne had learned to accept it.

Marianne adjusted her jacket and turned to the right, as the receptionist had told her. She looked around and realized that she needn't have worried so much about the open office space. The length of the hallway was lined with doors that could be shut to discourage random visiting. That fit her style perfectly. She didn't expect work to be like a cocktail party.

She heard voices from farther down the hallway and then saw Torsten Ehn and Olle Lundqvist leave an office together. They were speaking in low tones. Olle's body language told Marianne that he liked Torsten and had confidence in him. Olle caught sight of Marianne, excused himself from Torsten, and hurried up to her.

"Marianne! Welcome back!"

He gave her a hug, holding her just a shade too long for comfort. She disengaged herself and then held her hand out to Torsten. He took it, smiling.

"Here you are! I was just telling Olle that we'd met over the weekend."

Olle gave Torsten a thump on the back. "Nobody can escape Torsten. He's like a pit bull. Perhaps you two can get going on the case while I make some phone calls. Marianne, you'll be fine without me, won't you? I'm trying to shake free an office for you. You'll probably be able to get into it after lunch."

Torsten looked after Olle and shrugged. "Well, I really don't have anything new to tell you. Why don't you take a look around, and I'll find you if something turns up. Do you need any help?"

Marianne looked around for a place to hang her jacket but shook her head.

"No, thanks. I'll be fine."

Torsten smiled and winked at her. If she had been anywhere besides the Prosecutor's Office, she would have thought he was flirting. She managed a stiff smile as he hurried off. She truly hoped that Torsten Ehn hadn't gotten the wrong idea—she hadn't been sending out signals as far as she knew. That would be painfully embarrassing. She certainly didn't want the reputation of a merry widow.

CHAPTER 33

Friggavägen was deathly quiet as he led his bicycle up the hill. One of his paper cups was now empty, so he tossed it into a ditch.

On his left was a level area, once a railway bed. It housed a grouping of large trees that allowed him to be invisible.

A garden sloped away from the house, and the lush, green lawn rivaled the grass you'd find at the poshest golf course. He'd already noted that a gardener came twice a week. Flower beds looked as if the flowers grew naturally, but their perfect color combinations revealed the hard work behind them. At the very edge of the enormous yard was a smaller house. It had probably once been the servants' quarters, but now it was used just for storage.

He laid down his bicycle in the ditch, where he knew it couldn't be seen. Then he headed to the edge of the railway bed. A large oak towered over a grove of birch trees. Still wearing his backpack, he climbed to the most comfortable branch, which gave him the perfect view of the house on Friggavägen. He'd learned a great deal about the people who lived there: what they ate for breakfast, the children's schedules—all their routines. He leaned against the trunk and watched for a while. Then he saw her.

She walked into the garden dressed in her jogging clothes, and she was talking to a friend. In a loud voice, she related an incident at the children's school. Her every word floated up into his tree. The other mother responded unpleasantly, saying that her children must not be well brought up. He smiled and closed his eyes. His body tingled with anticipation. From his perch, he felt in control. He could watch everything they did. And sometimes—like now—he could hear everything, too.

She stopped talking as she walked through the gate onto the gravel road. She had left the porch door open: perhaps there was still someone home—a cleaning woman or a babysitter? The woman started jogging on Friggavägen toward Svalnäs Bay. He resisted his impulse to follow her and learn her route. He really didn't need to know it, as long as she came back. And in the meantime, once he figured out all that went on in the house, he'd be able to get inside and accomplish his plan.

CHAPTER 34

Marianne found an empty desk and hung her jacket on a hook just as Olle returned.

"That Ehn is a fantastic policeman," Olle said, "one of the best we have. Not everyone can see it, but he's sharp as a tack. I often wonder if the guy is psychic. I'm happy the two of you had the chance to get acquainted—you complement each other. But now, my dear Marianne, let me show you around. Few people have arrived so far, but you'll meet everyone in time. As you know, I'm in the office on the left, all the way down the hall. Baranski's office is next to mine. You should have the one next to ours. I'll move the two secretaries in that room closer to the prosecutors they work with."

"Won't that be stepping on a few toes?" Marianne asked.

"I think everyone will just be grateful that you're lessening their workloads. I've made it clear that we need to rearrange this department, so this won't come as a shock to anyone. You already know many people, but some young women will be new to you."

"Any assistants?"

"Yes, two new ones. I've already told them we're offering them proper training. I'd like them to stay a few years and really learn something. Lately, as soon as the assistants learn a little, offices in other parts of the country pluck them away, even though they're so green they can barely carry their own law books. The two we have now are really good, though: Tommy Lööv and Eleonor Rydman. They attended school and took the bar together. But enough of that. Let's go see Alexandra. She's probably done with her phone calls now."

Olle gently knocked on the frosted glass pane beneath the sign "Prosecutor Alexandra Baranski."

"Alexandra, I want you to meet Marianne."

Alexandra stood up. Marianne was surprised to see that this woman, in her early forties, was much taller than Olle. She had dark, wavy hair with red highlights. Her dark-brown eyes were serious. Marianne saw how they might scare the life out of a tough criminal. She was the kind of attractive woman who couldn't walk across a square without everyone noticing—her figure was like that of a fifties-era Hollywood star.

"Hello, welcome back to the department. God knows you're needed. Olle has talked about how talented you are. I'm looking forward to working with you. I was so impressed with your solution on the lawyer case—I'd heard about you even then."

To her annoyance, Marianne felt that she was blushing. She stammered a reply: "Thank you. We'll have to see how it goes. I don't want to disappoint you. Since I've been out of the loop for a while, maybe don't expect too much from me at first. I wasn't alone in cracking the lawyer case. Others contributed."

"But you found the common thread in those reports, which meant your husband could break them in the interrogation."

"It was just an accident—simply a fresh pair of eyes looking at material that had gotten stale from being read over and over. I was simply carefully examining the text."

"In that case, I hope you'll use your 'fresh eyes' to examine all my reports."

Alexandra laughed and shook her head and continued. "I never understood why someone like you would just up and quit for good. But, my condolences on the death of your husband. I understand you've gone through a difficult time. How are your children dealing with their loss?"

"They are grown, all three of them. Since Hans's illness was drawn out for some time, we could prepare ourselves for it."

"I know things can be hard. As for me, I'm divorced with three young children."

"Sounds tough."

"Yes, especially as my ex has a new wife and family and isn't really interested in his first three anymore. My boys have found that difficult. Still, my mother lives with us. That's the only way we could make it work. It's not a good situation to be forty-seven, single, and living with your old mom!" She laughed, but Marianne could feel the seriousness behind it. She appreciated Alexandra's openness, not hiding her ambitions or trying to make things seem easy. Working with Alexandra Baranski wouldn't be a problem at all.

"Do you have time for a cup of coffee with us?" Olle asked Alexandra, but she shook her head decisively. "No,

I have to prepare an argument. I'll be in court after lunch. But, as I said, it's really nice to have you here, Marianne."

Alexandra excused herself, stepped back into her office, and closed the door behind her. Olle steered his way to the kitchen. The coffeepot was half full.

"She's a tough one. Her divorce was particularly nasty. Her husband just up and left her and the three boys. I don't know how she does it all, but she's worked out a pretty good life for herself and the kids."

"She seems talented."

Olle said, "This is just the first step for her. She'll go a long way. But she already has a few enemies. She's not exactly what we'd call diplomatic."

"Who would dare oppose her?"

"You'd be surprised. Still, she lets it run like water off a duck's back. You'll be working for both Alexandra and me, as well as with Torsten Ehn. We'll take things slowly."

Then, from the tone of his voice, Marianne realized he needed to discuss things further outside the department.

"Alexandra's going to start working with Lillemor Rootander. Alexandra and Annelie have had some differences of opinion, so it's become absolutely necessary to reshuffle things. I know that Annelie, for instance, thinks this is a tender point. You should know all these nuances. I'm still convinced that in the end everybody will do their best to make you feel welcome. And, of course, Lillemor Rootander coming back to work is changing things around."

"You mean 'The Root' is working here?"

Olle looked pained and turned to the coffeemaker.

"Yes, she started here some months ago."

Marianne tried to keep a straight face. "Well, it's probably good for her to be back in Stockholm."

"You can look at it that way. Do you want milk in your coffee?"

Olle took Marianne around the entire department and explained the reorganization of the Main Police Station. Marianne tried to listen, but she soon found herself answering with a nod or a "yes" or an "I understand." So Lillemor "The Root" Rootander was back . . . She understood why Olle hadn't mentioned this earlier. It had been a long time, but the wounds still hurt. Lillemor had been one of Hans's first paramours, and their affair had lasted a long time. Olle knew that. Lillemor had been deeply in love with Hans and demanded that he leave Marianne and the children. Hans had considered it, too, and Marianne had never known why he decided not to. Perhaps it was political. A divorce wouldn't have helped his career.

Lillemor had called Marianne to tell her everything. She wanted Marianne to know the man she was married to. Marianne was holding Sigrid on her lap, listening to Lillemor's slightly hysterical rationalizations. Finally, she hung up and pulled out the telephone jack. When Hans came home that evening, Marianne simply said that if that woman ever called again, they would have to change their phone number. Hans was shocked. He promised he'd never be unfaithful again, and they had a few good months after that. They laughed together and made love every day, and Hans became more actively involved with the children. But when the summer ended and vacation was over, Hans disappeared into his work, leaving Marianne and the children behind. A few years later, Marianne heard that Lillemor

Rootander had taken a position as Head Prosecutor in Gothenburg.

"Well, I think we're done with the tour. Do you want to move into your office right away or wait until the others have cleared their things?"

"It would be better to wait. And a computer . . . how do I get one?"

"I'll call our tech guy. He'll make sure you get all the codes and accessories you need to work with our new systems. You'll learn it all quickly."

The tech guy found Marianne and said, "Why don't you follow me to storage so I can sign you out on everything you need."

Before obediently following the young man, Marianne debated whether she should take her purse or leave it behind. She took it with her.

The young man, who Marianne guessed to be about twenty-five, introduced himself as Ulrik Carstens. He had short, unkempt hair, a small, perky nose, and extreme acne. His gangly limbs seemed difficult to control, almost as if he were a teenager instead of a grown man. But he dressed well, in a well-pressed summer jacket with light-blue jeans. This added an aura of respectability to his appearance and signaled interest in his career. He turned toward her as he pressed the "B1" button for the basement storage level.

"Is this your first time here?"

Marianne shook her head. "Yes and no. I've been on leave for a while, but I was here for twenty years before that."

"Twenty years? I was only five years old twenty years ago!"

Marianne smiled and realized she was not far off estimating his age.

"Are you a prosecutor, then?" he asked.

"No, I'm the secretary to the prosecutor. I work for Olle Lundqvist."

Ulrik said, "You seem to have a lot of work up there these days. Do you know anything about computers?"

"I know how to start one and how to turn it off. And send e-mail. That kind of thing."

Ulrik nodded, as if he'd just plugged her into the category of middle-aged women unaware of common technological advancements.

The elevator reached the basement.

"How big of a screen do you want? And do you want a laptop?"

"I think a laptop would be good. People will probably want me to connect from home. But I'm not too picky when it comes to the screen."

The tech guy looked at her thoughtfully. "In that case, I'll get you a laptop that can easily connect to the stationary computers in the building. What kind of computer do you have at home?"

"A Mac."

"Why's that?"

"I like to avoid the viruses on PCs."

The tech guy seemed to undergo some inner turmoil changing his assessment of her.

"Sorry, but we only have PCs here at the station. You'll have to learn how to use them. Will that be a problem?"

Marianne winked and said, "Not in the least."

CHAPTER 35

"You sure about this?"

Augustin shook his head. "No, not at all. It's a rumor going around town."

"So Jonas Carlfors was having an affair with Christopher Turin's wife. It's a truly bad cliché."

"That's the rumor going around anyway."

Torsten wondered where Augustin had heard the rumor, but he knew he wouldn't get an answer to that. It wasn't all that important, anyway.

"Think we should bring him in for questioning?"

Augustin squinted straight ahead as he ran his hand through his elegant hair. Then he shook his head. "No, but we could have a little chat, just to see where it leads. Maybe there's something in the rumor that he could explain. But I can understand why he didn't want to bring it up when you were talking to him."

"Why is that?"

"He was probably still in shock. I don't think Jonas Carlfors ran the victim down."

"How can you be sure? You haven't even met him."

Torsten watched Augustin, interested to see how he'd formulate his thoughts. Actually, Torsten was just as convinced that Jonas Carlfors wasn't their suspect.

"He has nothing to gain. He hasn't been pushed into a corner, and nothing seems to be driving him over the edge. There's nothing in the interviews I read or in your reports indicating that he's psychotic."

"Psychotic?"

"That he was going off the deep end. You know what *psychotic* is."

"Yes, I do. I just wanted to check if you had the same view of it. I never know what you young people call things these days. So, why don't we pay a little follow-up visit to Carlfors & Malmström?"

"Do you want me to come with you?"

"That would be preferable. Are you ready?"

"Absolutely!"

"According to our sources, Christopher Turin's widow returns from Mallorca today. I've asked her to come by the station later this afternoon."

"Do you want to meet her on your own or would you like me there as well?"

"You certainly can attend."

Augustin stood up and reached for his jacket. "Your car or mine?"

Torsten remembered his parking problems last time he visited Carlfors & Malmström.

"Yours."

Augustin whirled the ring of car keys around his finger as he opened their office door. He smiled and bowed. "After you."

CHAPTER 36

Marianne's new computer was installed with the software she needed. She'd carefully written down all the passwords and codes for future use.

Olle trotted past the bare desk where she'd settled in and asked if she needed help with anything, but he hurried away as soon as he saw she had everything she needed. "I've called a meeting at ten for everyone," he said. "In the kitchen."

Marianne checked her watch and saw that she still had a half an hour. She got up and quietly knocked on Alexandra's door. "Is there anything you need me to do right now? I have a computer, and I can help with anything urgent."

"Yes, please," she said. "I need several printouts of this argument—and then we have an entire investigation to go through. It arrived this morning. I have no idea where it will lead, but we have to enter the whole thing into our journal. Annelie has done some of it already, but I would like your input. To be safe, please go through the whole thing."

"What kind of an investigation is it?"

"It's been Torsten Ehn's case for about two years. There are many well-known names involved, as well as drugs and prostitution, spiced with bribery and fraud. It's politically explosive, you might say, and certainly not anything we want to find leaked out before the next election. Unfortunately, Torsten isn't finished, and he's lacking quite a bit of information. We might have to shut this investigation down for now. Torsten will be disappointed, although he surely suspects which way the wind is blowing."

"He was here earlier this morning."

Alexandra said, "He's a great investigator. Handpicked from the Police Academy for the Huddinge group during the seventies. He's absolutely fantastic at interrogation. But I think stopping this investigation will take the wind out of his sails."

Alexandra handed over a thick folder. Marianne would need both arms to carry it.

"Another thing. If people give you any trouble, come right to me. Olle sometimes closes his eyes to interpersonal matters, but promise me you'll speak up if there's any difficulty."

Marianne agreed and left the room, taking a deep breath as she walked to the desk. She sensed there were hidden currents around here, but she certainly couldn't just sit and worry about it. She might as well get going on her work. She'd just handle each problem as it arose.

Half an hour later, Olle returned.

"Let's go, shall we?"

They walked to the kitchen, and Marianne noticed Olle mentally preparing himself for the meeting ahead. His body language indicated he was expecting trouble. His shoulders were tense and he was rubbing his hands nervously. All the calm certainty he used in the courtroom was gone. People were coming out of the offices and looking at Olle curiously. He cleared his throat once everyone was in the kitchen:

"Does everyone have their coffee? I'm going to make this short and sweet. We have a returning employee, Marianne Jidhoff, whom some of you know already. For the rest of you, let me tell you that Marianne had been part of this group for a long time, and fortunately I was able to persuade her to return instead of retiring. Marianne will work directly with Alexandra and me. She will have the office where Annelie and Sussi are now. *They* will move to the office next to the kitchen, nearer Stefan and Lillemor, as they will be assisting them. I've asked some staff to come by after lunch to help you transfer your belongings. I do hope, and also expect, that you will make Marianne feel welcome."

A voice spoke up, "What about Linda? Is she going to lose her position as a substitute?"

"Well, unfortunately, we have no funds to pay for her promotion, but I believe she'll be fine. We need Marianne's competence and experience on our team."

The woman questioning Olle was about thirty-five years old. "And if we need a new temp, will Linda get that job?"

Olle was definitely uncomfortable. "We'll have to see. Right now, Marianne has returned and I just hope we all stay healthy so no temps will be needed. Would you like to say anything, Marianne?"

"No. Thank you. I'm fine."

Olle headed away to his office, and Marianne looked around. The woman who'd spoken had blonde, spiky hair; she looked like a remnant from the eighties. She was tall and had an hourglass figure, which was neither fat nor thin, but her hips were a bit too wide and gave her a clumsy look.

Her voice was deep for a woman. Her hand was cool when she introduced herself.

"Annelie Hedin. So you're going to take Linda's place."

"Linda was a substitute for *me* during my leave."

"Let me introduce Karin. She works mostly for Lillemor. I guess I will now, too. And we have Sussi, who is assigned mostly to Stefan. You know Stefan and Lillemor?"

Marianne tried to tell from Annelie Hedin's eyes whether she knew anything about Hans and his lovers—and she decided that she knew everything.

"I haven't met Stefan, but I know Lillemor."

Annelie's steady gaze revealed that she did, indeed, know all about that old, sordid story. As she kept speaking, her tone of voice didn't change. "Ingrid Björk works here, too. She is the Head Administrator. She rose up in the National Prosecutor's Office, but she's off today. I believe her grandchildren are being christened."

"Well, it seems you are really in the loop about the people here. I hope I can call on you when I need to know about someone."

Annelie Hedin didn't answer but smiled in a way that wasn't difficult to interpret—she wouldn't help Marianne at all, come hell or high water.

"Let's see, you've been gone for how long now?"

Marianne looked at the three women—Annelie, Karin, and Sussi—and took a deep breath. "I was home caring for my husband. He died just before the summer. Thank you for this nice chat, but I've got to get back to work. Olle told me that you are a hardworking group, and I don't want to disappoint."

Annelie, Sussi, and Karin looked at her with great skepticism. As she left, she knew they'd be gossiping about her. She understood. To them she was an interloper. She'd gotten their office and a higher position. All the names and faces she'd been introduced to swirled around in her head. It wouldn't do to forget anyone. She had to keep her eyes open. There was no room for mistakes.

She wondered how much they all knew about Hans's relationship with Olle—how they'd been best friends—or at the very least, extremely close colleagues. Did they know Marianne lived in a large apartment all by herself? In Östermalm, to boot, and in a building she owned outright? That she was wealthy and didn't need this job to pay her bills could certainly be the reason behind Annelie Hedin's chilly reception. Poor little Linda, who certainly needed a secure position, was being jettisoned, just so Marianne wouldn't have to stay at home all day in her robe. Marianne completely understood their doubts. She had difficulty accepting the situation herself.

Chapter 37

Augustin lifted his glass of mineral water, smiling at Jonas Carlfors. Torsten had situated himself in an armchair somewhat out of the line of fire between the two men in well-tailored suits. He tugged at his gray sweater and hoped his mismatched socks weren't too obvious. Jonas Carlfors tilted his head to one side, peering at Augustin curiously. "Have we met before?" he asked.

Augustin took a sip of water before saying, "Yes, I believe we have met a few times."

Torsten studied Jonas Carlfors, whose head seemed ready to burst with the effort of trying to place Augustin, but Augustin offered no help. Instead, he went straight to the matter at hand.

"Why didn't you mention your relationship with Isa Turin when my colleague was here before?"

Jonas Carlfors twisted in his seat. He looked away while saying, "What do you mean?"

"I mean your intimate relationship."

Jonas Carlfors swallowed hard and pressed his lips together. His face turned deep red as he pulled at his starched shirt collar.

"I didn't know how to bring it up. I didn't think it had anything to do with Christopher's death."

"You never know what's important."

"To be honest, I was afraid. My wife knows nothing about it. I'd be extraordinarily grateful if you kept her out of this."

Augustin leaned forward and pulled at the cuff links on his light-blue shirt. "To be honest—just between us—I think the rumor will reach her soon enough."

"People are talking about it?"

"Yes, that's how *we* found out. You know how people talk."

Augustin leaned back in the sofa and wrapped his hands around a knee. Torsten was amused at this young officer who could change his manner so quickly and never give the impression he was green or unsure of himself. Augustin was in his element.

Jonas Carlfors's eyes flashed as he hissed, "So you're here to interrogate me over a rumor you heard in the city!"

"Well, no, we're not interrogating you, per se, but rumors are often helpful in our work. That appears to be the case here, am I right?"

Jonas Carlfors looked as if he wanted to go after Augustin that minute. Torsten did his best not to smile.

"We weren't having the usual fling," Jonas growled. "Our relationship grew over time. We've supported each other when times were rough. It's not some dirty little affair, if that's what you're thinking."

Torsten looked up from his notebook. "Are you going to leave your wife for her?"

Jonas Carlfors took ten seconds before he replied, "No. That is not possible."

Augustin rested an elbow on his knee. "Why not?"

Jonas Carlfors looked at Augustin with disgust.

Augustin made a calming gesture. "Take it easy. We're not here to ask you about all the details. Neither of us thinks you're behind Christopher's death. I said as much to Torsten as we were driving here. But what we need to know is what motivated a person to kill him. We're convinced it is someone he knew. We need to know all about Christopher's contacts, both at home and at work."

"What does this have to do with my relationship to his wife?"

Augustin changed his tone, as if he were talking to a stubborn five-year-old. "It indicates that their marriage wasn't that good and that he, in turn, might have someone on the side. We have to know those kinds of things. Did he have another woman?"

"A while back, but they broke up right before Christmas. I don't know of anyone since then."

"Would he have told you?"

"He would have earlier, but this past year he kept mostly to himself."

"Was that because he found out you were poking his wife?"

Jonas Carlfors realized Augustin was trying to provoke him. His eyes darkened, but he remained calm. "No, our physical relationship began almost two years ago, before he started to draw away from me."

"For two years? Tell me again why you haven't left your wife?"

"Because she's sick."

Torsten flinched and felt something sour rise up in his throat. Before he could ask a stern question, Jonas Carlfors continued.

"I know it sounds terrible. But my wife suffers from mental illness. She is a manic-depressive, or *bipolar* as they call it these days. The illness began when she was pregnant with our first child. Looking back, she might have had it earlier, but not as severely. She's asked me to leave her, but I can't. I want to be around our children. They haven't had an easy life. My wife suffers both from her illness and her medication. We had no intention of having a second child, but we slipped up, so to speak. If I had known her second pregnancy would make her condition even worse, I would have asked her to terminate it. She's tried to take her own life several times."

Augustin and Torsten sat silently, watching a man who—from the outside—seemed to have the perfect life. But he was actually in a miserable situation. Neither of them envied him at all.

Jonas Carlfors continued, "You can imagine how painful it is for our children. They say they understand that their mother is ill. Since Christopher's wife is their godmother, she's often been an extra mother for them. She helped us a great deal, and her own children have also been wonderful. I don't know how I would have made it through the past years without them. Isa and her children even lived with us at times. You must understand that I never would have done anything to hurt Christopher. I didn't have time or energy for such a thing. I love his children like my own, and I'd never think of doing anything to hurt them. *I* know just how hard it is for a child to lose a parent."

Torsten noticed a shine in Augustin's eyes when their eyes met. They were in agreement. Jonas Carlfors had nothing to do with the murder of Christopher Turin. They would have to look elsewhere for his killer.

Chapter 38

They decided he would come to her place. It was a gamble, but Paula knew that the probability of Jens canceling his business trip to London was small.

The girls had come home happy after their long weekend in the countryside, talking all evening about their trip. Jens drove them to school early that morning, and Paula explained she would pick them up from gymnastics at five o'clock, as usual. This meant she had the entire day to herself. She invited Passi over for lunch, and he accepted since he had some work in the neighborhood. He also told her he was studying economics, which was why he took so many extra jobs in Djursholm, so close to the university.

Paula knew it was ridiculous to pour so much emotion into her meeting with Passi, but she couldn't keep her excitement at bay. Everything he said to her made her feel a resonance in her own body. The more they talked, the more she felt they had a special connection. She didn't ask him how old he was, and he didn't ask her, either. At this point, it was completely irrelevant. This was a game, and not knowing was part of the thrill.

Paula dressed in the torn jeans that gave her figure the right look and a white T-shirt without a bra. Her nipples showed through the thin fabric. Jens had thrown himself at her in a similar outfit early on in their relationship. She hoped she'd have a similar effect on Passi today.

She made a Caesar salad for lunch and put a bottle of white wine into the refrigerator. A good Chablis—it would calm the nerves. Even if Passi wasn't nervous, Paula was. She examined herself in the bathroom mirror and hoped he wouldn't be turned off seeing her in daylight. Her panties were a thong—just some string and a triangle—that she thought made her look sexy.

Her cell phone beeped at eleven thirty. It was Passi, wondering if he could come a little early.

Paula forced herself to breathe deeply before answering the gentle knock at the door. He was taller than she remembered, with wider shoulders. She swallowed heavily, smiling as she let him in. He threw his jacket and backpack on the chair by the door and stepped out of his shoes.

"You're looking good. You have more style than the usual women at Lotta's place."

Paula laughed and rolled her eyes. She tried to ignore her heart, which was bursting like a rocket inside her chest.

"Thanks! Do you want anything to drink? A glass of wine? I've made a salad."

Passi looked around briefly and said, "Sure."

Paula opened the refrigerator and took two glasses down from the cupboard. She noticed him following her every move and tried not to let it throw her off-balance. Still, her fingers shook as she pressed the corkscrew's tip into the soft cork. He smiled at her.

"Let me."

He took the wine bottle from her, opened it, poured the white wine into the glasses, and held one to her.

"*Skål.*"

"*Skål.*"

She had just put her wineglass on the counter when he was on her. One of his hands held the back of her neck as his lips pressed onto hers. She could feel that he was already excited, and she couldn't help a sigh escaping her lips.

A moment later, they were on the sofa. He'd taken off her jeans and unbuttoned his own. His tongue licked her down to her panties, which he pulled off with one hand. Then he took her thighs into his hands and plunged his tongue deep into her. It felt like he wanted to eat her up. She was so surprised that she couldn't help coming immediately. She closed her eyes and hoped he hadn't noticed, while her insides clenched tightly. He kept licking, and his excitement increased as he noticed how wet she was.

Very soon, she realized she was ready to come again, but she wanted more control. She pulled Passi up to her and took his member into her hands. It tasted salty, and it was so silky. She had to keep herself from biting it! It filled her mouth, and she tried to relax her jaw muscles to fit more of it in. As he panted harder, she stopped. He sighed deeply and threw himself back on the sofa. Paula straddled him and he pulled her down, making her sink all the way in. Her orgasm was more intense than her first one. He needed more, so she rode him until he exploded. Afterward he took her hand, saying, "You're unbelievable. It's like you were born to fuck."

He smiled and again moved inside her, but slowly. She quietly enjoyed that for a while until she realized he was hard and ready for another round. Paula, who wasn't counting on a third time, began to heat up as he touched her clitoris in just the right way. Before their tempo increased, he asked her to turn. She sat with her back to him, riding him as hard as he asked while his fingers continued stroking her clitoris. When she finally came the third time, her orgasm was long and slow, almost painful, and he came right along with her.

CHAPTER 39

With a sigh, Marianne sat down at her empty desk and set her coffee cup next to the keyboard. The hallway was empty. No one felt comfortable approaching her. She had expected she would need courage getting used to her routines again, and now this, how she was received this morning. It was nothing new under the sun, however—Marianne knew she was the kind of person that was never welcomed with open arms.

She took a sip of coffee and began to go over Alexandra Baranski's investigative reports. She skimmed through the first part, which made a case for opening the investigation, and she understood what Alexandra had told her. If this was real, Sweden was in for an enormous political scandal. People in various police departments would be affected. She knew at once that Olle couldn't be eager to continue this investigation, especially in an election year.

She lost herself in the reports until lunch, pretending to ignore the moving guys clearing out the room so she could claim it as her office. The room was light and had two large windows. It would be nice to put some flowers on the wide windowsills. Perhaps she'd walk over to Rosendahl during the weekend and pick out a few potted plants.

She could hear Annelie Hedin bitterly complaining on the phone that being moved out of her office had ruined her entire day. Marianne could tell that she was speaking to someone in her family. Annelie's ring finger was bare, but Marianne remembered seeing a photo of two children on her desk. Perhaps she was in a long-term relationship. Marianne had removed her own wedding ring and dropped it into her drawer with her underthings. It was a simple gold ring. Nothing her daughters would want to pass on to their children if they ever got married. Lola thought that Marianne ought to melt the ring down for some cute earrings—it would be a waste of the gold to have it just sitting there. Marianne had rejected the idea, but now she was beginning to think the idea wasn't half bad. She'd been so angry with Hans after his death that she'd contemplated throwing the ring into his coffin just before his cremation. But in the end she changed her mind, and she was glad now. After all, she had paid for that wedding ring herself.

At noon, Alexandra Baranski stopped by Marianne's desk and thanked her for the printouts and edit of that afternoon's final argument. Marianne told her she'd been happy to help and began to think about lunch. She assumed she'd be having it on her own, something she'd often done before she'd gone on leave. Many people ate bag lunches in front of the computer so they could leave work early. Marianne thought she could probably do the same, but not this first day. She hadn't brought anything with her, so she might as well go out.

Nobody noticed her leaving. The elevator was full of people eager to get some last rays of sunshine before the weather closed in. When she stepped out on the street, she felt lost. She wandered without a plan, crossing the street to the other side of Bergsgatan and heading toward Pilgatan. To her joy, she saw a pleasant-looking café. She decided to keep to her diet at breakfast and dinner, and this lunch would be a normal meal. It was cool outdoors in the shade, but Marianne reserved a chair outside with her shawl. At the antique cash register, she found platters of baked goods in all shapes and colors. She felt her mouth starting to water. A blackboard described the lunch special: one of two soups with a sandwich on the side. Marianne chose the vegetable soup and a large cheese sandwich. Another blackboard proclaimed that all the food was made in-house and was completely organic. The cinnamon buns gave off a delicious aroma, but Marianne decided to limit her calorie intake to the cheese sandwich, and she hurried to pay to avoid the temptation. Just as she was carrying her tray away from the cashier, someone cleared his throat behind her. It was Torsten Ehn.

"How's the first day going?"

Marianne almost dropped her lunch. A small grimace flickered across her face.

"Well, so-so."

"That bad?"

They laughed, and Marianne set the tray on her table, shaking her head. Torsten gestured to the empty chair.

"You want to be by yourself, or may I join you?"

Marianne looked at him in surprise, then she hurriedly smiled and said, "Of course. Please sit down."

"Let me just go inside and order something first."

Torsten came out with a similar lunch.

"I rarely meet people from work here."

"Well, perhaps it's too charming for the average police officer."

Torsten laughed. "That's exactly what I think, which is why I choose to come here and avoid them all!"

"And here I come and destroy your safe haven."

"Not at all, especially since you're not a police officer. Although, you'd probably be the best of them if you joined the force. You're kind of a legend over there."

"What? What do they say about me?"

"That you have amazing analytical skills."

Marianne took a bite of the delicious sandwich. She shook her head, but she was smiling.

"I'm an administrator. No more than that."

"Weren't you going to become a prosecutor yourself once?"

Marianne hesitated before replying. "Yes, well, that was a long time ago. I was young and naive, wanting to change the world. I've let most of that go now."

"That's too bad. I believe you would've gone far."

Marianne took a spoonful of soup. "How did you hear all this?"

Torsten laughed. "I have my sources. It's my job to poke around in everybody's business. They what they pay me for!"

"But most of the stuff you hear is just rumors."

"You can call it rumor, or you can call it information. It's what I work with. You'd be amazed how far a rumor can take you in any investigation."

"I'm sure you're right," Marianne said. "Speaking of investigations, your recent one landed in my lap, too. I've gone through it this morning and will read it again more thoroughly this afternoon."

"You are quick on the draw."

Marianne looked at him. "It's a heavy file. You've been on this for a long time."

"Yes, more or less around the clock for the past two years," Torsten said. "But you think they're going to shut it down, don't you?"

"Well, I can't answer that."

"Or put it on ice."

Marianne said, "Whatever they decide, you've done an outstanding job."

"That doesn't mean shit, unfortunately. This was great soup . . . they have good food here. What do you say—should we have a cup of coffee? Do you want it with or without cream?"

"A touch of cream would be nice."

Torsten got up and returned soon with two cups. "We interviewed Jonas Carlfors again this morning. It turns out he's had a long affair with the victim's wife."

"Yes, there seemed something not quite right about Turin's marriage."

"What do you base that on?"

"Well, his wife was alone on Mallorca for two weeks with the children."

"Why is that so strange? Don't all you upper-class people travel whenever you feel like it?"

"No, actually, not during the school year. That's quite unusual. I'd guess she went away with the children because a divorce was in the works."

"His colleague didn't seem to think so."

"Check if he was involved in any kind of therapy. Counselors, that kind of thing."

"We're going to meet her this afternoon," Torsten said. "I'll remember to look into it." The way he gazed at her made Marianne wonder if he thought she'd brought up a red herring or if she'd just contributed something important.

Suddenly, he sighed, and looked out over Kronoberg Park.

"Do you sail?"

"Excuse me?"

"Do you sail? You know, on a sailboat."

"No, I'm a landlubber. At best I can row a few yards in a rowboat."

"All I can think about in this beautiful weather is how much I want to head out on my boat."

"Then why don't you?"

"Because I have a job to do."

"Well, just hang your jacket on your office chair. People will think you're nearby if they look in."

Torsten had to laugh. "Great tip. But I don't think I'm the kind who can get away with that."

"How long have you been a police officer?"

"Almost thirty years. It's crazy when you think about it."

"Well, if we're going to form a mutual-admiration society, I've heard you're one of the best investigators on the force."

"It doesn't matter how good I am. Most of the time, it's wasted effort. And you? Do you miss your husband much?"

Marianne was so taken aback she couldn't keep her mouth from dropping. "Well . . . I guess I do."

Torsten studied her intently.

"We had a complicated relationship. What about you, are you married?"

Torsten shook his head. "No, I'm divorced, and I have a son. I think I mentioned that before. He's sixteen. Almost seventeen. Most of the time he lives with me. His mother moved to Norway."

Torsten glanced at his watch. "Oh, hell. I promised to pick up my colleague on the other side of town. I've got to run. I'll check in with you this afternoon after we've chatted with the widow."

He surprised her with a pat on the arm, and she couldn't help recoiling at his touch. She watched him cross the street and almost get hit by a honking truck.

Marianne took another sip of her coffee, which had cooled by now. She'd enjoyed company for lunch. Obviously, Torsten Ehn was passionate about police work, and she respected that. She also liked talking to him. It was easy and effortless. She watched him turn the corner onto Polhemsgatan. His jacket blew in the wind as he tried to button it. He had an admirable body, even if he wasn't what you'd call elegant.

CHAPTER 40

Augustin waved both arms over his head to catch Torsten's attention. Torsten couldn't help smiling. There was something disarming about this young man. Despite his stiff and formal ways, Torsten saw the eagerness and engagement in his work. He reminded Torsten of a Labrador puppy. Pleasant, happy, and a touch naive, even while exhibiting great intelligence.

Torsten crossed Narvavägen and walked over to him.

"You had no trouble getting here?"

"No," Augustin said, "I met my father here for lunch anyway."

"How nice."

"We try to meet up once a week."

Torsten pressed the buzzer at the entrance, and the door opened.

"All right, let's go."

Looking serious, Torsten and Augustin walked through the long hallway leading to the elevator, and Torsten pressed the button to the fourth floor. The grill on the elevator door had been cut into skillful patterns; they saw beautiful landings pass by with tasteful Art Deco wall paintings. Despite all the beauty, Torsten shuddered. Something about this

elegant building felt dark and threatening, and not just because one of its inhabitants had just been murdered. The
atmosphere seemed to have embedded itself into the walls
decades before. The bronze signage indicating the servants'
entrances to the kitchens bothered him—probably because
he knew they were still part of everyday life here.

Augustin whispered to Torsten, "I imagine she's a hell of
a beauty."

Torsten lifted an eyebrow, nodding. They stepped out of
the elevator and Torsten rang the bell at the Turin's apartment door. A woman of about forty opened the door. Her
hair was honey-blonde, slightly on the brown side, and it
was elegantly blown dry to hang straight to her shoulders.
Torsten liked the curly hair she'd had in the wedding photo
better. She was thin to the point of skeletal; her collarbone
jutted from the collar of a gray sweatshirt matching a pair of
tight gray jeans that hugged her legs. Her clothes appeared
common enough, but they were probably from a pricey designer. Torsten didn't get these semi-starved women who
only ate crumbs to keep their thin figures.

Isa Turin was tanned, probably from her recent visit
to Mallorca. There wasn't a trace of makeup on her face,
and she wore thick socks on her feet. Torsten surmised that
because she had so little body fat, she must be constantly
freezing. Her left ring finger still wore two rings with bright,
shining stones. Torsten wondered if such large rocks inter-
fered with her housework. Did she take them off? Did she
have a cleaning lady? Isa Turin held out her right hand.

"Welcome. I'm Isa Turin."

"Thanks for seeing us. My name is Torsten Ehn, and I work for the National Police. This is my assistant, Augustin Madrid."

"Madrid . . . the name sounds familiar. Have we met before?"

Augustin held out his hand. As he'd said to Jonas Carlfors, he replied, "I believe we have."

He didn't elaborate, so Isa Turin didn't pursue it. She just put on a strained smile.

"May I offer you anything? Coffee or tea?"

"No, thank you. We're fine." Torsten said.

"Then let's go inside and sit down. You have to excuse the house. It looks like a storm hit it . . . we're in the middle of moving. I don't know what the future will hold, but we had been planning to move."

Torsten felt that his earlier suspicions, when he'd visited the apartment on his own, were confirmed.

"Where are you moving?"

"A few blocks away. Torstenssonsgatan on the other side of Narvavägen. There's so much traffic here. When we heard that apartment was coming on the market, we jumped on it."

Torsten coughed into his sleeve.

"So you were planning to move together?"

Isa Turin stared at him, hesitating, then her eyes filled with tears. She blinked several times before continuing. "We hadn't yet decided how to arrange it, but I decided to move nonetheless. We were going to take it from there. Are you sure you don't need anything? I need a cup of coffee."

Torsten smiled. "If you're already going to the trouble, then sure."

Augustin said, "Yes, please. By the way, this is a terrific painting. Who is the artist?"

"Cita Theander. She's a Swedish artist who also lives in New York. The Americans pay tons of money for her work. Cita is one of our friends."

Augustin walked over to the enormous painting and studied it carefully. Torsten thought the painting looked interesting, but no way would he pay a fortune for something just to hang in his living room. Yet, he was hardly someone who understood art.

They followed Isa to the kitchen, where she stuffed small capsules into an espresso machine.

"Latte or pure espresso? Caffe macchiato?"

Torsten shook his head. "What does that last one mean?"

"Espresso with just a touch of cream on the top."

"Well, then I'll have one of those."

"Mr. Madrid?"

"A simple espresso, please."

Isa took out three small cups and placed them on matching saucers; then she turned to Augustin. "I remember where I met you. You used to go out with Nilla Martin, right?"

Torsten was surprised, but Augustin didn't move a single muscle in his face. His voice was as neutral as ever: "You could say we were going out."

Isa gave him a flirtatious look, and she turned the handle on the espresso machine. She wasn't ready to drop the topic. "That's right, you were at the Midsummer party Nilla's sister gave. Everyone was talking about how Nilla had just gotten a divorce and then met you. I hope I'm not being too rude if I say you're quite a bit younger?"

If Augustin was embarrassed, he didn't show it. Torsten saw no trace of a blush on his cheeks. Still, a slight rising of his voice indicated he wasn't entirely comfortable.

"It is possible, but I usually don't worry about a woman's age. I concentrate on more important things."

Now Isa Turin seemed embarrassed. She giggled in a way that made her seem more human to Torsten. Still, her flirtatiousness seemed odd for a recent widow. Did she forget every now and then? He couldn't help but be impressed by Augustin's reply.

Isa poured the coffee into the cups and gestured to the living room.

"Let's sit down."

Augustin sat on an orange chair made of hard plastic and shaped like a bean. Torsten sat on the long sofa, avoiding a stain that looked like tomato sauce. Isa sat next to him. He took a sip of coffee and tried not to grimace. The coffee was terrible. Quickly, he gave a friendly smile and said, "Great coffee."

Isa Turin smiled back. "That machine is worth its weight in gold. Christopher thought it was ridiculous that I bought it, but he didn't even like coffee. Tea was his drink."

Torsten looked straight at Isa. "How would you describe your marriage?"

"Besides the fact that I drink coffee, and he drank tea? Our entire marriage was like that. He was more spiritual, and somewhere we lost our connection."

"What do you mean?"

She shrugged, swallowing. A tear trickled down her cheek and she wiped it away.

"We started to have problems after our third girl was born. We'd been hoping for a son. That's when everything started. Don't think we're not grateful for our daughter, but a rift opened between us. Christopher had always worked a great deal, and I didn't mind. But then he started to work *all the time.* I found myself alone with three small children, and he had no interest in helping me at all."

"Would he have been more involved if you'd had a son?"

Isa hesitated before answering, "Yes, I believe so. But as things were, he started worrying about other things besides the family."

"Such as?"

"Such as where we should go on vacation. What kind of furniture we should buy. Gray or white tiles in the bathroom—or all black. Lots of small things that would blow up into big arguments. We used them to take sides, like on a battleground. Typical problems for the privileged."

"Did you fight more often?"

"Yes, certainly then. We fought a great deal. Christopher thought we should do something about it, so I agreed to go to that camp with him that was supposed to help our relationship."

"A camp?"

"Yes, or a course, or whatever they call it. The place is called Right Now. It's all about mindfulness and how to be present in the now, within a relationship."

Augustin interrupted to inform Torsten: "Right Now is a conference center in the archipelago, pretty far out in the Baltic. A couple—a man and a woman—decided to change their lives by purchasing an entire island where they began

Right Now. They both survived the *Estonia* ferry disaster and decided to do something meaningful with their lives."

Isa Turin added, "Yes, and it's very trendy to go there. TV personalities, pop singers, famous actors in ads . . . In the beginning I thought it would be good for us."

"But—"

"But then Christopher started going there on his own. I think he took every course. They had everything from Find Your Newborn Self to . . . Reclaim Your Sexuality."

"How long are these courses? How much do they cost?"

"They're pretty expensive. From ten thousand crowns up to a few hundred thousand."

"A hundred thousand?"

She nodded. "Yes, but *those* courses go for a full year. I really can't tell you what they do, because I signed a confidentiality agreement when I enrolled."

"If it makes it any easier to speak to us, we understand the need for confidentiality. Especially if it's something relating to our investigation."

"Well, the first course is called Open Your Window. It's about learning to understand yourself. You sit in a ring in silence. Then you have to tell your deepest secret to the others in the circle. When you're finished, everyone thanks you for sharing. Then the next person talks."

Torsten thought it sounded suspiciously like Alcoholics Anonymous. He'd attended with his brother before.

"Then we go around hugging each other. The lights are turned off, so it's completely dark. The idea is to let go of aggression. One girl in our group began to sob, and one guy couldn't be talked to for the rest of the evening. As far as I was concerned, it was too touchy-feely, but Christopher and

I actually did feel closer to each other. It broke down our defenses, and we were able to get through and communicate with each other again."

Torsten looked at her as if trying to understand what she meant. "And how about later?"

"Christopher wanted to take more courses. I didn't. I went to two more with him, but I wasn't interested in them at all. Christopher thought I was just stubborn and unwilling to open myself up. I thought it was too weird, especially going around in the darkness and not speaking for days on end. And then that one course . . ."

Isa looked troubled and twisted around a little. "That Find Your Newborn Self stuff was too much. They put us in diapers to get rid of our feelings of shame. They wanted to go through all of human development, from birth to the present."

Torsten made an unintentional smirking sound, and Isa jumped.

"I'm sorry, diapers?"

Isa threw up her hands. "The whole thing was disgusting. I'd call it fetishistic—not some form of self-development, as they put it."

"But Christopher thought it was good?"

"I know he found that diaper thing off-putting, but as far as the courses themselves, he thought they helped him find out a great deal about himself. I grew tired of hearing about it, though. Every time he returned from Right Now, he had a new insight and understood everything so well."

"What about the children? How did they react to all of this?"

"That was what was so wrong about the whole thing. He was always leaving home to spend more time 'in the now,' but he distanced himself more and more from his daughters. That was my main argument against it."

"So you're saying he wasn't present for his daughters."

Isa hesitated again. "Well, I hate to say it, but he wasn't. Christopher's own father had never been home, and Christopher was sent abroad to boarding school. I think he was incapable of getting close to anyone."

Augustin happened to put his coffee cup down hard, and it rattled.

"I'm sorry," he said. "We have met Jonas Carlfors. He told us all about your relationship."

Isa was taken aback. She drank the last drops of coffee in her cup. Torsten was about to do the same, but then remembered just how bad it was.

"Jonas and I have been close to each other all our lives. His sister is one of my best friends. We've helped each other quite a bit lately. His wife is extremely ill, and I had my own problems with Christopher. We found we had so much in common—especially when I began to suspect Christopher was also depressed. We spent lots of time together with the children, and we still do. We go to the country, make dinner, or go out fishing. Sometimes it feels awfully sad that we got close only after marrying other people. But you surely don't suspect Jonas would have anything to do with Christopher's death?"

Torsten looked right in her eyes. "Do you think we should?"

Isa Turin waved away the thought, then shook her head vigorously. "Absolutely not! Jonas would never do anything to hurt the children or me! Never!"

"Perhaps not. But he did say that you all might feel better without Christopher in your lives."

Isa said, "No. He is much more intelligent than that. He'd never even consider taking those ridiculous courses in the archipelago. Christopher used to complain that Jonas only saw the surface of things, but in truth Jonas is a thousand times deeper and more philosophical than anyone else. He lives inside his emotions and doesn't have to pretend. He can look me in the eyes and tell me how much he loves me. Christopher could never do that, even if he drank all night."

Torsten steadied his right hand on his leg, remembering yet again to steer clear of the coffee.

"About alcohol. How much did Christopher drink?"

"He drank socially. Less than average, actually. Once he started Right Now, he drank less and less. Instead, he drank various kinds of purifying teas. At Right Now, no alcohol is allowed. I suspect that many of their so-called leaders smoked—and I'm not talking cigarettes. But I think that was also part of their ridiculous theories."

The more Torsten heard about Right Now, the more he suspected that it was some sort of cult—and a silly one at that.

"Is it true that Christopher was having his own affairs?"

Isa took a deep breath and twisted her hands. "Yes, and definitely more than one. After Jonas and I started our relationship, I stopped caring. At Right Now, they often find so-called soul companions—twin souls, spiritual friends, or whatever you want to call it—and they have passionate sexual relationships. Then they go home and tell their partners that they've 'found themselves.'"

Tears started streaming down her cheeks, and soon her entire body shook with sobs. Finally, she said, "I don't understand why anyone hasn't investigated them as some kind of sex cult. No one ever talks about what really goes on there. Almost everyone who is drawn into it goes nuts and gets a divorce. They decide to overhaul their lives by starting yoga studios or organic gardens. And the founders just sit there, raking in the dough on these lost souls."

"What do you know about the founders?"

"Not much. I believe the man was in advertising, and I have no idea what the woman did before."

"Do they live on their island year round?"

"I don't know, but they're always there for all the courses. What they do the rest of the time is anybody's guess. They say they both have families, and I know the woman has a son. I've seen him."

"You believe Right Now changed Christopher in a negative way?"

Isa Turin nodded emphatically as she blew her nose.

"Absolutely. I'm not saying our marriage would have been great, but he was more communicative at first."

"When was the last time he went to Right Now?"

"I have no idea. Probably about a month or so ago. We stopped talking about it."

"It sounds to me as if the two of you were just coexisting. Why didn't you go ahead and get divorced?"

Isa blew her nose a second time, stuffing the tissue under one of her legs. "Logistics. We hadn't yet talked to the children, and we wanted to do it together. I'll never tell them about it now. It's bad enough they've lost their father so tragically."

Torsten agreed that she had made a wise decision. "Is there anyone you think might want to hurt Christopher? A married man jealous about an affair Christopher was having in Right Now? Or an undocumented worker? Some kind of renovation gone awry? Or a conflict with someone at work? Anything at all you can think of?"

Isa shook her head. "I've gone over and over it in my mind, but I just can't think of anyone who would want to hurt him. People liked him in spite of his faults. He was easygoing. He wasn't the kind who easily made enemies. His problem was trying to please everyone too much."

"No strange phone calls or letters?"

Isa shook her head. "None. Of course, we weren't checking each other's phones—that was one of our silent agreements. On the other hand, I do know one of our daughters got some strange text messages for a while. It seemed like someone thought her phone number belonged to a different girl. *That* girl's old boyfriend must have been trying to terrorize her."

"Thank you for all your time. We'll be back again if we have any more questions. Please call us if you think of anything else."

"I promise. But don't suspect Jonas in this. I know it's not him."

Torsten patted Isa's arm. "We'll clear it all up so nobody has to live under a cloud of suspicion. And thanks so much for the coffee."

Isa Turin followed them to the door. She smiled weakly at Augustin. "I'll give Nilla your regards."

Augustin bowed slightly. "Please do. She is a fine woman."

Torsten and Augustin took the stairs down, silently walking through the long entry hall and out the door. Once they reached Narvavägen, they both took deep breaths. Torsten shook his head.

"I can't believe the things people do. Diapers? Jesus."

Augustin agreed. "I think we should go check out this Right Now place. What do you think?"

Torsten replied, "Let's do a web search on it back at the station. Then we'll take a ride out to the island early tomorrow morning. Tell me—what's your impression of this recent widow?"

Augustin shook his head. "Honestly, I don't know. But I think she knows more than she is saying."

Torsten agreed. "She's holding something back, subconsciously or not. But I have to tell you, I didn't think she was all that good-looking. Much too thin for my taste."

"I know. I remember her with a bit more weight."

"That woman . . . Nilla . . . she mentioned."

Augustin raised an eyebrow. "Yes?"

"Will that relationship affect this investigation?"

Augustin smiled weakly, shaking his head. "No, no, don't worry. I lived next door to her apartment for a while, and she often invited me out to events as a cover."

"A what?"

"Yes, well, she was recently divorced and was tired of people feeling sorry for her. Her husband had left her for a younger woman."

Torsten laughed. "So she invited you along to play the boy toy? What a woman!"

Augustin smiled. "Yes, she has a great sense of humor."

"Well, I have trouble believing you were just her cover."

"That's all I'm going to say, Torsten. We don't get together anymore these days. I'm telling you, our investigation won't be affected in the least."

"Was *she* part of Right Now?"

"I have no idea," Augustin replied, "but I'd find that hard to believe. She wasn't the type."

"Maybe you can call her and ask a few questions?"

Augustin looked doubtful. Finally, he said, "I guess so, why not. But I'll tell her that I'm part of the investigative team. I don't want to be duplicitous."

"Sure. And perhaps she has inside information about the Turins."

They got into their respective cars. Torsten drove up Narvavägen and decided to swing by Karla Frukt again as long as he was in the neighborhood. Perhaps that cheerful blonde with the bangs would be working today. He liked chatting with her. He also craved one of those licorice pipes. Maybe he'd buy two—one for Marianne Jidhoff. He hoped he wasn't being too pushy. But she seemed like the kind of person who both appreciated gestures like that and liked licorice.

CHAPTER 41

In the end, Torsten decided not to go back to the office. He called Marianne to give her a short update; then he headed off to the airport. He tried to remember which terminal Noah was arriving at, and he finally found a one-hour parking spot. Reaching the terminal, he saw Noah coming out the electric doors, dragging his suitcase. His head was drooping, as if he hadn't slept in a while. Noah's eyes always turned red when he'd had too little sleep.

Torsten hurried over, grabbed his suitcase, and gave his son a hug. Just a month or two ago, Noah had grown taller than his father.

"Hello, my boy, how are you doing?"

"Not so good. I think I'm coming down with something."

Noah coughed, and Torsten realized his son was avoiding eye contact. Torsten put an arm around Noah's shoulders as they walked to the car. He heaved the suitcase into the trunk.

"You mind if I change the channel?" Noah asked as they started for home. "I don't get how you can listen to radio with ads."

"Well, the ads *are* nerve-racking."

They sat silently, and Torsten kept glancing worriedly at his son. Noah kept his eyes focused straight ahead.

"How's your mother?"

"Fine."

"Her guy, Peo? How's he?"

"Fine."

"Were his children there, too?"

"No."

Torsten drummed his fingers on the steering wheel and said, "I bought some groceries, but maybe you want to eat out tonight?"

"On a Monday?"

"Why not? Celebrate that you're home and all."

"No, thanks. I just want a sandwich. I'm not that hungry."

"That's fine. That'll work."

—□—

They were quiet for some time and Torsten wondered what to say. Finally, he spoke up. "I've been handed a new case."

"What about the old one?"

"I'm still on that one, too, but I think it's going to be shelved if I don't find out more. This new case is a murder in Östermalm. It's complicated, because the Stockholm police should have jurisdiction, but Olle wanted us to handle it."

"Cool."

"And I have a new colleague."

"Working with you?"

"That's the idea. He's a young guy, pretty much right out of the Academy. Olle says he's one of a kind, but I'm going to wait and see."

"Sounds familiar. What else can you do?"

Torsten laughed as Noah broke into a smile. Ever since Noah had decided to live with him, Torsten liked to keep his son up-to-date on his work. Torsten thought if he was open about his job and responsibilities, his son would be open in return. At least, that's what he'd hoped.

"You're right about that," Torsten said. "Are you sure you're not hungry? We could go to Ho's for some Chinese food."

Noah stopped smiling. He shrugged. "Sure, but I'm really tired."

"We'll just eat something quick, then we'll go home and relax. Do you need to prepare for class tomorrow?"

"No."

Torsten parked close to their apartment, and they walked down the long street to one of Stockholm's most popular Chinese restaurants. They ordered two hot dishes with glasses of milk and ate in silence. Torsten kept biting his tongue. He wanted to ask Noah what the hell was wrong with him but knew that was the wrong tack, so he concentrated on eating his rice with chopsticks, an extremely difficult task. Noah had told him before that eating Asian food with a fork and knife was in bad taste—he'd demanded Torsten learn to eat with chopsticks. Torsten found it almost impossible in the beginning, but he finally got the hang of it. Still, rice was difficult to pick up, especially when it was covered in any kind of sauce.

Noah ate his food but wanted no dessert. He usually loved Ho's fried banana with vanilla ice cream. Torsten wondered if he should order the fried banana for himself but realized that Noah really wanted to get home. He asked for the check, and they walked home to Folkskolegatan. Torsten got the suitcase from the trunk while Noah headed up to the apartment.

Torsten spent a few moments collecting the trash that had accumulated in his car, and when he got into the apartment, he heard sounds from the bathroom.

"What's wrong, son?"

"I'm feeling really bad!"

Noah bent over the toilet bowl and vomited with such force that his body shook with violent spasms.

Torsten handed him some toilet paper to wipe his mouth, and flushed the toilet for him. "Come, let's get you to bed," he said.

He led Noah to his room. He had already put clean sheets on the bed, and Noah lay down, exhausted. Torsten hurriedly opened the French doors to the balcony for some fresh air. Then he pulled the curtains. The sun had set and the glare from the streetlights came in at an unfortunate angle, right onto Noah's bed. Torsten sat down and put his palm on his son's forehead.

"Should I get you any medicine?"

Noah shook his head. "No, thanks. I just want to rest. I'm so tired."

"Do you think it was the food?"

Noah shook his head weakly.

"Tell me if you need anything. I'll be sitting up."

"OK."

Noah closed his eyes, and Torsten got up. He hoped his expression didn't show how worried he was. Noah was rarely sick. He hadn't been this ill since having the chicken pox at age ten. Nowadays, with swine flu and God knows what else, Torsten knew that a person could very quickly become seriously ill. He'd see how Noah felt during the night. He hadn't detected a fever, but he planned to call the doctor if Noah wasn't feeling better in the morning.

CHAPTER 42

Paula heard the girls giggling, so she stuck her head into the room she'd let them both sleep in. "Hey, girls, don't keep talking too long. Otherwise, you'll have to go back and sleep in your own bedrooms. After that long weekend, you need your sleep. I'll bet you were up late every single night."

"But, Mamma, please? Can't we just talk a little bit more?"

Paula smiled and shook her head. "Not tonight, sorry. Sleep tight, now. I'll pack a special snack in your lunches for tomorrow."

The girls were taking a field trip—outdoors in the woods—and they liked the change of routine from the usual school lunch. Paula remembered it well from her own childhood. She would make them pancakes and give them thermoses with hot chocolate. She hesitated at the door, but then decided to go in and give each girl a kiss and pat on the forehead. She inhaled their scent, so happy to have them home again. It made the disruptions of these past few days easier to handle.

Passi had left the house twenty minutes before she picked up the girls from gymnastics. She'd vacuumed and scrubbed all the places they'd been during those hours after lunch. Her vagina was raw, and she wondered if people could tell what she'd been up to just by looking at her. She thought there might be too much happiness in her eyes, so she did her best to look more neutral.

Jens called from London to wish the girls a good night. When Paula took the receiver to say hello, she thought she heard a woman in the background trying to keep from coughing. After they hung up, she considered calling back to ask him directly what was going on, but she decided she really didn't want to know, not yet.

She started down the stairs, stopping halfway to listen if the girls had quieted down. When she reached the bottom, she heard the rain lashing against the patio doors. It made her want to yell to the world that she was no longer afraid. She had someone on her side who had listened to her fear.

Passi had asked to come over tonight once the girls were asleep, especially if she was afraid during the night. She had looked at him tenderly and thanked him. She said she'd set the house alarm to loud before going to bed in case anyone tried to open a door or window or moved around on the ground floor. She could set it from her bedroom. Passi had hugged and rocked her, saying that no woman should be so frightened, especially in her own home. They'd slept for a while, dozing in each other's arms until Paula woke with a jerk, assured once again that his arms were still around her.

Now she looked out at the darkness in her yard, wondering what would unfold in her life. What would happen after this? She knew that things were about to change, but she wasn't ready to think it through. She wanted to practice living in the moment and enjoying it.

Paula sighed, then sat down in front of the TV to watch a documentary, unaware that someone was sliding open the patio doors behind her. That someone was wearing a black ski mask to better fit in with the darkness—and he considered darkness his best friend.

CHAPTER 43

Good Lord, it's not that complicated. You're making a big deal over nothing!"

"You're completely sure about all this?"

"I do it every month! It's really easy! You mean to tell me you've never dyed your hair before?"

Marianne sighed, looking at her reflection in the mirror. Lola stood behind her wearing plastic gloves and holding a bottle. Marianne gave her a bored look. "All right, let's do it."

Lola smiled and got to work. Energetically, she rubbed the dye into Marianne's hair. She'd mixed it according to the directions on the box, ignoring Marianne, who told her she was afraid her hair would turn out too black. Lola looked fantastic with her raven-black hair, but that color might not work with Marianne's paler coloring.

"Why don't you ever go to a stylist?" Marianne once asked.

Lola looked at her as if she'd lost her mind.

"Why pay some young thing a few thousand crowns every month if I can do it myself for just a hundred? I refuse! I get my hair cut twice a year, and that's good enough. I can manage the rest of it myself perfectly well."

Despite being mature, Lola could be stingy about certain things. Hairstylists were on her list of things the rest of humanity had no trouble paying for but that she wouldn't. So were cars. Lola still drove the car she'd bought upon returning to Sweden after many years in Germany. She'd no doubt drive it until it literally fell apart. One of her Skeppsholmen neighbors, an older gentleman, kept it running. She paid him one thousand crowns each time, no matter what he did to it.

Another thing Lola never spent money on: shoes. She thought it was vulgar how much young women paid for shoes these days, and she bought all her shoes secondhand. Sometimes, she even found a pair in her size. If she found one she liked in a different size, she'd have a shoemaker alter them. Marianne found all this a bit odd, but Lola always just snorted. Her logic was perfectly clear to her.

It was hard for Marianne to discuss these kinds of things with Lola, knowing that Lola spent a great deal of money on other luxuries. For instance, she bought makeup only from Chanel, insisting she was "allergic" to *all* the other less-expensive brands. She also spent a fortune at Östermalm Food Hall. Neither Lola nor Marianne's father could be reasoned with when it came to gourmet food. Both just got angry whenever she brought it up.

Suddenly, Marianne cried, "It's burning my scalp! Is it supposed to do that?"

Lola sighed as she dug her fingers further into Marianne's hair. She accidentally scraped her scalp with a fingernail.

"Ouch!"

"Your scalp isn't turning red at all—it's fine. I don't know why you're so worried about a little hair dye. You've certainly been through much worse."

"You're right about that."

Marianne's plain gray hair had become an issue for Lola, and for the rest of Marianne's family. Nobody understood why she'd stopped putting in highlights. But it was simple: she just didn't want to fuss with it anymore, especially since Hans thought she looked better with gray hair. He said it gave her character. She'd liked that he approved of something about her, even if it made her look unnecessarily older, especially since she'd developed laugh lines around her eyes. She luckily didn't have many other wrinkles yet. It probably helped that she was a bit plumper than average. *Lola* was always complaining about her own wrinkles. Yet Marianne suspected that Lola had had Botox treatments once or twice. Of course Lola would never admit to that—not even to herself. Denial was one of her dominant traits, but Lola knew what she was doing and if it made her feel happy, who was Marianne to talk?

"Do you have any wine?" Lola asked.

"Of course I do. What do you want, white or red?"

"Red, naturally. Have you ever seen me drink white wine?"

Marianne found a bottle of Ripassa in the servants' hall and poured Lola a large glass.

"Aren't you going to have any?"

"I'll wait until we rinse out my hair. It smells so bad."

"Just ten more minutes. I can't wait to see how it turns out."

Marianne thought it felt uncomfortable. "Come out into the kitchen while I have a smoke," she said.

"Why do we have to go into the kitchen?"

"I only smoke under the stove fan."

"But why? You live all alone in this apartment."

"So?"

"Don't you realize how strange that is? Why can't we just smoke in the living room?"

"What if the girls come home? They'd notice."

"Why would they care?"

"It just doesn't feel right."

"But this is your home! Nobody else lives here. Nobody can tell you what to do. You can smoke wherever you want. Your children won't kill themselves because their mother has taken up smoking in her old age."

"But I *want* to smoke under the stove fan. I don't want my entire apartment to reek of smoke. Come on—otherwise I won't be able to finish my cigarette before we have to rinse. I don't want this awful stuff sitting on my head any longer than I have to."

Marianne found her cigarette pack and offered one to Lola. Lola shook her head.

"You know you have to stop doing things like this?"

"Like smoking?"

"No, like living according to the rules Hans made for you."

"Oh, I've broken one or two already!"

Marianne turned on the fan. Lola shook her head, sitting down at the kitchen table.

"And I'm inhaling, too," Marianne added.

They laughed. The smoke went down wrong, and Marianne coughed. "I know, I know, I shouldn't smoke. But I *have* started to diet."

Lola stared at her. "What?"

"My gynecologist told me to lose weight and Chrisse suggested this diet. It's called the Danish Hospital Diet."

"So what are you supposed to eat?"

"Lots of grilled chicken and boiled eggs. Grapefruit and green beans. Black coffee. And smoking is allowed."

Lola raised an eyebrow. "Hmm, healthy enough I guess. Have you lost any weight yet?"

"No, but I promised I'd stay on it for ten days. Of course I already broke my promise at lunch today. I had a sandwich with my vegetable soup. This diet is perfectly horrible. I'm hungry all the time. That's why smoking helps. It distracts me."

"I hardly think a sandwich with vegetable soup is all that bad, and I don't think smoking instead is really better. Still, I guess it's a phase you have to go through since you've become one of them."

"One of whom?"

"The kind that diets. But maybe it's a good thing. You have put on some extra pounds lately."

"Thanks, I already noticed that. I've hardly moved all summer long. The only things I've eaten were sandwiches, and there's not much good nutrition there. Becoming a widow isn't exactly a health cure, let me tell you."

Marianne sniffed the air and wrinkled her nose at the strong ammonia smell from the hair dye.

"That's it! Get this stuff off my head."

They went to the bathroom, and Marianne bent over the edge of the bathtub. She rinsed out the stinking goop.

"Hand me a towel, please. I think I've gotten most of it out." Lola obliged and Marianne dried her hair. She said, "OK, let's see how this turned out."

Suddenly, Lola looked tense and moved into a corner of the bathroom. She murmured, "Remember—it has to dry before you can see the real color."

"I know. I did used to have my hair dyed."

Marianne pressed at the turban she'd made with the towel and then unwrapped it. Simultaneously, both women screamed. Marianne's hair had turned bright orange.

"Lola! What have you done?"

Lola looked frightened. Then, a few seconds later, they started laughing. Marianne sank to the floor of the bathroom and shook her head. "What am I supposed to do now? I have to go to work tomorrow morning!"

Lola hiccupped from laughing, turning back to Marianne and laughing again.

Marianne gasped, "It's like when we were twelve and tried to pierce our ears with a pin and a cork! How could I have been so dumb as to let you at my hair?"

"Don't blame me!"

"Who else am I supposed to blame?"

"We'll have to go back to the store and complain."

"I am not leaving the house looking like this! Besides, people at the store will just tell us that every person's hair reacts differently. Mine obviously likes to turn orange. I'm going to call Sigrid. She'll think of something."

"Well, if you're all right, I'd better hurry home. I promised Philippe I'd be home by ten."

"You're leaving me like this?"

"You'll figure out what to do. Maybe you can wear a scarf over your head at work tomorrow. People did that all the time in the seventies."

"Yes, and back then people willingly dyed their hair this color, too."

"Call me tomorrow and let me know how you solve it. And, don't forget to come on time tomorrow evening. Six o'clock sharp! You're welcome to come a few minutes early."

"I'll see what I can do. I hope you understand if I decide not to show up looking like this."

"Come on, now you're exaggerating. You'll fit right in with the cultured crowd."

About three hundred people were expected for an opening at Lola's gallery. Her openings were always well-attended. Many people would gladly pay a great deal just to get an invitation.

CHAPTER 44

Torsten walked into the kitchen for a tall glass of water. He flipped through the local paper and sat down on the sofa, listening for any sounds from Noah's room. All he heard was his son's deep breathing.

He turned on the television to catch an episode of a series he'd been following on TV 4 and had a sudden feeling of déjà vu. He remembered when Noah was a newborn. Katrin had been accepted for a course of study, and they'd both thought she should go for it. Torsten stayed home three nights a week during the hours she was gone. It gave him the chance to be alone with Noah. He missed those evenings even though he always had one ear tuned for any sound of something wrong. Baby Noah usually slept soundly, though, and Torsten became relaxed with his son as time went by.

When the commercial break started, Torsten grabbed some crackers. Then he rummaged through the refrigerator for suitable cheese. When he returned to the sofa, he was surprised to find Noah was there, wrapped in a blanket.

"You're awake? How are you feeling?"

"So-so. A bit better."

"Was the food bad?"

"No, I don't think so. I felt nauseated even on the plane."

"Would you like some crackers?"

Noah eyed his father's plate. "I don't know, maybe just one for now."

Torsten knew how that would end—no crackers for him. Still, he was happy Noah wanted something to eat. They watched the show together. During the third commercial break, Noah said, "It was really strange being in Norway."

"What was so strange about it?" Torsten was tense but tried not to show it.

"Well, it's hard to say. Mamma was bitchy, and it was, like, she didn't want me there. Oh, it was OK sometimes, but as soon as Peo came around, she acted all weird, like I was in her way or something."

Torsten's stomach churned. He didn't like hearing such things.

"Perhaps she was nervous? She wanted everything to be perfect but it didn't work out that way?"

Noah shook his head and grabbed the last cracker. "No, it wasn't like that. I thought that maybe he was jealous or something. Peo's kind of a snob. I don't get what Mamma sees in him. But it's, like, how *she* acted around *him*. It was embarrassing. She'd laugh too loud . . . stuff like that."

"People do that when they're nervous."

"I don't know. She'd snap at me to stop talking nonsense whenever I spoke to Peo—like I'm her embarrassing little brother instead of her son."

"So what did you end up doing?"

"Mostly I stayed in my room and played computer games. That seemed to make her happy. When it was time to leave, she said it was time I learned to take the train to the airport

241

by myself. I mean, she didn't even want to drive me. And she said she couldn't just drop what she was doing every time I needed a ride."

Torsten had to bite back the impulse to call Katrin and give her a piece of his mind. He also wondered if this was just Noah's delayed reaction to the divorce. Katrin couldn't have possibly treated him that badly—could she? Noah kept talking.

"I actually know why she didn't want to drive me. She and Peo were invited to a party. I can't figure out why she even wanted me to visit if she thinks I just get in the way."

"Maybe it was such a new experience for her, too, having you there. Maybe she'll adjust."

Noah shrugged and shook his head. "I have no intention of ever going back there. That Peo was angry all the time. And he *definitely* thought I was in the way."

"I do think you should give your mother another chance."

"No way. I won't go back there. If she wants to see me, she can come to Stockholm. Remember what she was like before? Remember when we were invited to the neighbors'? The ones with the pool she always went on about? And how she insisted you wear a *jacket?*"

Torsten remembered that incident well. A new family had moved into the fin-de-siècle house on the hill in Älvsjö. They'd completely remodeled and put an entire spa in the basement and a pool in the backyard. The neighbor woman liked to go on and on about how wonderful it was being a full-time housewife, especially since her husband was often away on business four days a week. Katrin had gone into a tizzy when they'd received the invitation to their *glögg* party that winter.

Noah's description of his time in Oslo disturbed Torsten. Just like that incident with the wealthy family, Katrin's social ambitions sometimes took over. But it was unforgiveable for her to make Noah suffer. Torsten took a deep breath.

"I think you should tell your Mamma what you just told me. Be honest and give her another chance."

"She'll just lay into me and tell me *I'm* wrong."

"Then it will be her problem. Start by telling her what's bothering you. Take it from there."

Torsten knew that Katrin would call after hearing from Noah to accuse him of turning their son against her. He tried to examine his own conscience. Was he wrong not to demand that Noah return to Oslo? Noah was old enough to make his own decisions. He couldn't be forced to visit his mother in Norway. She'd made her decision to move out of the country even though her son was a minor, and it wasn't because of her work: Katrin had had a fine job at the thorax clinic at Karolinska Hospital, a position she'd wanted for years. It was *only after* she met Peo and moved to Norway that she'd been offered a much better job as chief surgeon there with a higher salary. Torsten tried not to judge her decision to move. But she could have stayed in Stockholm, and she and Peo could have flown back and forth. It wasn't a great distance. Instead, they'd decided to force their children to travel to them, including Peo's two daughters from his first marriage who lived with their mother in Saltsjöbaden.

"I'll call her tomorrow," Noah said.

"Why not wait a few days and see how you're feeling? Sometimes it's better to let things take their time."

"No, or it will just be the same thing. I—"

Without warning, Noah burst out crying. His face, with its recently sprouted peach fuzz, became streaked with tears. Torsten pulled Noah into a hug. He felt his sixteen-year-old son shaking and sobbing and had to blink away his own tears. He stroked Noah's hair and said:

"It'll work out. You'll see. It's good you've decided to talk to her. She's probably just as sad as you are that the visit didn't go so well. Maybe she was nervous about your first visit to her new home. Did she do a good job on it, by the way? How did she decorate it?"

"It felt, like, exaggerated," Noah said. "Like being in a museum. You know, that Peo got all upset about the littlest things, too. Once Mamma put her cup on the coffee table, and he went into a real rage about her being more careful. He said the table cost a lot of money and the rings would ruin it. Stuff like that."

Torsten was worried. Katrin had been the fussy one during their marriage. She always wanted things in perfect order—from pillow arrangement on the sofa to the jars of jam in the pantry. He couldn't imagine anyone accusing her of being careless. He decided to stop thinking about it. Katrin wasn't his wife anymore, and she was responsible for her own life. Still, he didn't like how this affected Noah. That was going too far. He decided to tell her when she called, and he didn't care how angry she'd get. She could scream at him as much as she liked—he'd just tell her that she wasn't the one who had to comfort his son after the long weekend visit with *her*.

A movie came on after the TV show, but Torsten and Noah were both yawning. They said good night, and Torsten listened to Noah brush his teeth. When he came out of the bathroom, Torsten went to him and gave him a big hug.

"How about we do something really fun this weekend. Or do you have plans?"

Noah shook his head. "I was going to ask if we could go out on the boat. What's the weather going to be like?"

"The weatherman said it would be great. You really want to go out on the boat? Do you want to take a day trip or go for the whole weekend?"

"The whole weekend. Isn't it almost time to bring the boat in for the winter?"

Torsten smiled and said, "OK, let's do it. I'll take Friday off so we can leave Thursday evening. I have lots of comp time."

Torsten brushed his teeth, looking at his reflection in the mirror. He felt sorry for Katrin. It couldn't be easy for her, either. She was the one who'd wanted the divorce, but he couldn't blame her. No one was to blame after the love was gone. Her situation, now, could be due to a great number of things that he knew nothing about. It was none of his business. Still, the fact remained: she risked losing close contact with her son. Torsten was almost crazy with happiness that his son wanted to spend the weekend with him on his little old sailboat, and he realized part of this was because Noah had lost closeness with his mother. He didn't mind reaping some of the benefits, but he still hoped that mother and son could find a new way to get along. It wouldn't help anyone if their relationship went sour.

Torsten made up the sofa bed and crept between the cool sheets, looking forward to his weekend sailing trip with Noah. Closing his eyes, he tried to put Katrin from his mind. Instead, he thought about running into Marianne Jidhoff at lunch. He hoped to see her again soon.

CHAPTER 45

She was in the kitchen wearing nothing but a thin T-shirt and panties. Her pink slippers were in such contrast to the clean style of the rest of the house. He watched her in fascination as she emptied the dishwasher, storing plates and glasses in the upper cupboards. Her hair was swept up in a messy bun, while a few strands tickled her neck. She closed the dishwasher and poured a glass of water. With great care, she chose several pills from a collection of bottles she had on the counter. He watched her swallow them methodically, impressed.

The woman jumped and turned as if looking for something. She reached for the windowsill and picked up her cell phone. At first she smiled and it looked like she was saying, "Hello, darling!" But then her face darkened, and her mouth hardened. He watched as she seemed to ask, "Why?"

A moment later, she put down her phone and leaned on the counter, hanging her head between her arms. He wanted to stroke her hair and had to restrain himself from touching the glass of the windowpane that separated them. It was almost time for him to go inside—he wanted to be there when she needed him.

CHAPTER 46

As promised, Sigrid rang Marianne's doorbell at six a.m.—and she stared in shock at her mother.

"Mamma! What the hell?"

"Now, now, stop it. I already told you it was a catastrophe," Marianne said.

"That is an understatement. What was the name of the color?"

"Ginger. But they told Lola it would be dark red, not orange."

"Well, they were obviously wrong. We'll have to hurry. The taxi is already waiting downstairs."

"You're absolutely sure this hairdresser is good?"

"How can you even ask that question when you were crazy enough to let Lola touch your hair! What were you thinking?"

Marianne snorted at her daughter's concern but then jumped at her own reflection in the mirror. "I have to agree with you." She packed a few personal belongings to help perk up her office and locked the door.

Marianne paid for the taxi ride to Nybrogatan. They could have walked those few blocks, but she didn't want to force Sigrid to do more than she had to so early in the morning. As they walked up Riddargatan, Nybrogatan was quiet and empty. There was one light on; the other store-fronts were dark. Sigrid steered Marianne toward the lit shop.

"Here it is, and remember, this is a favor. My hairdresser is usually booked a month or two in advance. He's only do-ing this for me so he can ask for a favor in return."

"Not *that* favor, I hope."

"Don't be ridiculous. I promised to sew him a tuxedo coat."

Marianne hurried inside behind Sigrid. A forty-year-old man with black, curly hair greeted them.

"Go ahead and hang up your coats," he said.

He studied Marianne's hair without a word, and Marianne thought that showed professionalism. She was given a protective cape to cover her shoulders and told to sit on his stylist's chair. Sigrid sat on a regular chair beside her. The hairdresser brushed Marianne's hair and took a good look at the top of her head.

"I suggest we start with removing the dye, then I'll mix in two or three highlights."

"Which colors?" Marianne asked, nervously contemplat-ing her reflection.

"I promise you will be satisfied. You'll even be able to turn back the clock a bit. How long has it been since you stopped coloring your hair?"

"Five, six years maybe."

He didn't even change his expression. "It's great that you've kept your hair long, but now it's time for a good cut. And you have to be at work at eight? Let's get started. Would you like coffee or tea? We also have wine, but I'm assuming it's too early in the morning for that."

The hairdresser smiled for the first time. Marianne was quick to smile in return. He led her to a black shampoo station, and she leaned back in the chair.

After a while he said, "The de-colorization is complete. It was actually easy to get rid of that color. Now I'll mix up your new ones."

More time went by before she was ready to sit in the stylist's chair again. She stared uneasily at Sigrid, whispering, "Are you sure this is a good idea?"

"Just relax. Read a magazine."

"But will I make it to work on time?"

"Don't *worry!*"

Sigrid stared her down, obviously not interested in her mother's whining. She ignored her by reading a magazine. Marianne sighed and looked in the mirror at her hair now covered in foil tabs. She wondered what in heaven's name she'd gotten herself into.

Forty-five minutes later, she was ordered back to the shampoo station. With the push of a button on the chair, she even got a back massage. Then, as the scissors worked their way through her hair, she started feeling better. He was quick and effective, and in no time, he was blow-drying and finishing the top locks with a brush. Marianne could not believe her eyes. The color was the same as she'd had as a young woman, long before it ever started going gray. It was so shiny, too, and had impressive volume due to the hairdresser's expert use of the round brush. Maybe it was a bit too stylish for work, but since she was going to the art exhibit later that evening, it would suffice.

Marianne turned to Sigrid and smiled. "How much should I pay?"

"I told you, I've already arranged it. Wow, you look fantastic. A little different from Lola's attempt, don't you think?"

Nybrogatan was no longer empty as they walked along. Sleepy people were hurrying to work. At a side street beside Östermalm Food Hall, a recycling truck stopped with a deafening noise to pick up a week's worth of glass. A smaller truck parked to unload huge wooden crates of seafood. Marianne and Sigrid walked into Café Baresso, where the line already snaked along, and they joined those already patiently waiting for their orders. Sigrid yawned, and Marianne petted her cheek.

"Poor you. Go home and take a nap. I'm sorry I got you into all this."

"Oh, stop, it was fun. And I'm not really tired. I have important customers today. A bride with four bridesmaids."

"Four? In my day, people didn't have bridesmaids."

"Yes, I know, you've told me that a thousand times. Still, I think bridesmaids are nice. They certainly help my business!"

"That's true," Marianne said. "Is it someone I know?"

"You don't know the bride, but one of the bridesmaids is Clara Edenstam."

"Peder's Clara?"

Sigrid nodded.

"What's she doing these days?"

"She did cultural studies at Uppsala, and now she is chief editor at some book publisher. I don't remember which one."

"She's not the kind you have to worry about. Is she as cute as ever?"

"Oh, yes. She's living with her boyfriend now. I ran into them on Djurgården awhile back on a Sunday afternoon. They were coming home from visiting Clara's parents."

"What kind of a guy is he? Is he nice?"

"He's cute, but a little too much of the silent type for my taste."

"I can't see why Clara would want that. He won't get a word in edgewise."

"Still, you've got to give her credit. He's kind of French looking, though he grew up in Bromma. He works in advertising."

They had all wanted Peder and Clara to get together. Although time had shown that was not to be, Marianne suspected Peder still had a soft spot for her, the first girl he'd ever had a crush on.

Marianne felt the pain of missing Peder as they reached the head of the line. She disliked him staying in Australia, but she wouldn't mention that to Sigrid. She didn't want to be the type of clingy mother who never cut the apron strings.

CHAPTER 47

Torsten knocked softly and peeked in at Noah, who was sitting up in bed.

"I'm going to make breakfast before I go. What do you want?"

Noah rubbed his eyes, still sleepy.

"Hot chocolate, or chocolate milk?"

"Hot chocolate, thanks."

Torsten went to the kitchen and pulled out some bread, cheese, and sausage. He put a glass of milk into the microwave and glanced at the clock. Augustin would pick him up in about a half an hour, so he wasn't in a great rush. He wondered if he should make a lunch for himself. There probably wouldn't be any restaurants open in the archipelago now that summer was over. He decided to make a number of different sandwiches. He also started the percolator and soon had enough coffee to fill his big thermos.

When Noah came out of the bathroom, breakfast with boiled eggs and two sausage sandwiches was already on the table. Torsten lit a candle, then mixed chocolate powder into the warm milk. Perhaps he should have packed hot chocolate to go instead of coffee? Sweet things taste good when you're outdoors. So while Noah peeled his egg,

Torsten heated four cups of milk and poured that into a second thermos. Noah looked up from his egg.

"You're really going to town on that lunch. Where do you have to go today?"

"Somewhere in the north end of the archipelago. A taxi boat is picking us up at nine from Blidö."

Noah said, "Having a new partner is doing you some good."

Torsten looked at his son in surprise. "You think?"

"Look at you, making lunch. And aren't you happy you're not just staring at the walls in your office today?"

Torsten sat down across the table from Noah and took a bite of his sausage sandwich. "I guess you're right," he finally said. "I haven't been at the top of my game at work lately. I owe Olle a lot of thanks that he didn't send some idiot my way."

"So you like this new guy?"

"Sure, I like him well enough. But I'm not sure he'll live up to the job. We'll have to see. I've been disappointed before."

They chatted as they ate breakfast and started to plan the boat trip for the coming weekend. Torsten hurried out when he heard Augustin honking from the street below.

Augustin seemed even more properly dressed than the day before, if that were possible. Torsten noticed his gloved hands. Cognac-colored suede. Augustin pointed to the back seat. "I have a couple pairs of rubber boots back there. I dressed up because I'm attending an art exhibit with my father this evening."

Torsten patted his backpack and set it on the floor between his feet. "I packed us a lunch."

"Great, thanks. I bought some cinnamon buns on the way over. We can have a party in this car."

Torsten chuckled, realizing they both felt slightly foolish. It was unusual for two police officers to bring food for each other as they headed out on duty.

"I've programmed the route to Blidö on my GPS. If there's not too much traffic, we should be there in about an hour."

"Perfect . . . nice car you have here. Very comfortable."

"Yes," Augustin said, "it has special ergo dynamic racing seats, but they can be uncomfortable if you have to go a long distance. What radio station do you like?"

"Go ahead and choose something. I'm not too picky. Isn't that the unwritten rule of driving? The driver picks?"

"OK."

Augustin turned on the radio and, not surprisingly, classical music began to play. Torsten usually didn't choose P2 but thought the music was pleasant.

Augustin headed toward Roslagstull, and fifteen minutes later they were on the highway toward Norrtälje.

CHAPTER 48

Paula pressed the red button of her remote control; then she entered the code to turn off the alarm. She'd slept all night without waking even once.

The girls heard that she was up and stormed into her bedroom. They had a late start today since they were going on their field trip. It would be less hectic than usual this morning.

"So, what do you say, girls? Shall we get up and make some pancakes?"

The girls yelled in agreement, and Paula laughed. She was proud that her difficulties with food didn't affect her girls. She was careful never to emphasize the subject of food: and she never commented on what they ate or on their appearance. They would surely clue in to all that when they were older, but so far, she'd been able to keep them free of any guilty feelings about food. The girls ran downstairs, and Paula hurried to catch up with them. At the bottom step, she noticed an unusual smell.

"Mamma, what's that? Something stinks!"

Paula felt her stomach tie into knots as she began mixing the pancake batter. She scanned the room for the source of the odor. It smelled like cigarette smoke.

While the girls ate, Paula went into the hallway and unlocked the door to get the newspaper. On the windowsill, between two potted plants, she spotted them: six cigarette butts, burned down to the filter.

CHAPTER 49

Marianne stepped off the elevator onto the fourth floor. She was pleased to notice that it wasn't yet past eight. She and Sigrid had enjoyed their coffee, and Sigrid had also had a sandwich before they each went their own way. Marianne intended to stick with just coffee until lunchtime, although she'd brought an apple with her to stave off any hunger pangs. In addition, she'd had a cigarette after she'd gotten off the bus. If she had to, she could sneak out for another one.

Her office was still empty. It was time to truly move in and get down to work. Marianne set down the large box she'd brought with her. She looked around and thought that the first thing this office needed was a thorough cleaning. Instead of waiting for the janitor, she went to the cleaning closet and took a bottle of cleanser and some rags. She pulled open the blinds and opened the window as wide as it could go. Then she started attacking the dust. The cleaner she used did wonders cutting the musty smell. Finally, she finished the floor. Once it dried, she looked for some furniture. She found a desk that was light enough to move herself, though getting it in, she had to tilt it on edge and ease it through. Once it was in place in the middle of the floor, it looked nice. She missed seeing a rug on the floor but decided that would be too much trouble for the cleaning ladies. One corner looked lonely. Marianne surveyed her office from all sides before calling the super.

"Hi—Marianne Jidhoff here. On the fourth floor. I hate to trouble you, but is there an unused armchair in storage somewhere? I thought there might be some in the basement."

Ten minutes later, Marianne received word that a number of armchairs could be found down there She took the elevator down immediately and met the super, and they ended up taking a rather square moss-green armchair back up.

"Maybe a lamp would be a good idea, too," the super said. "I'll see if I can find a floor lamp that would fit."

Marianne thanked him warmly. No one usually cared about interior decoration in such a bureaucratic institution.

She took a vase from her box as well as two glass cups, setting tea lights in the cups. That would make the coming dark winter mornings more cheerful. During her lunch break, she intended to go to a florist on Fleminggatan and fill the vase with beautiful flowers. She would also try to remember to bring a throw from home for the back of the armchair. It would be nice to have something to pull around her shoulders. She headed back into the hallway to collect her files and a bookcase. Some of her colleagues greeted her, asking what she was doing. Annelie Hedin, however, just stared at her sourly and walked past—and Marianne had to try not to openly cringe at the sight of her. Instead, she dragged the bookcase into her office and set it against the narrow wall next to the armchair. A cough behind her back made her jump. She turned to see the super holding a floor lamp.

"That's a great one! Where did you find it?" she asked.

"It was in the basement with all the other surplus stuff. If you give me some time, I think I'll be able to find a small table for you, too. There are lots of odds and ends that people haven't touched in years. As soon as people order new furniture, they send the old stuff downstairs. I found an extremely comfortable armchair for my office, too."

"Thank you. I'll have to stop by and try out your armchair."

They smiled at each other, and after he left, Marianne continued to sort the bookshelf, then finally, she set up her new computer on the desk. The IT guy had shown her how to connect all the cables, and soon she heard the jingle indicating that her machine was up and running.

Marianne surveyed her new office again and decided she'd made it quite attractive. The armchair and the curtains gave the room a softer look. The floor lamp really belonged in that corner and stood ready to illuminate her reading. The only thing left to do was remove the fluorescent light from the ceiling. She found a ladder, climbed up somewhat shakily, and managed to get the cover off. She eyed the light tube and realized that removing it would be too difficult. Annoyed, she screwed the protective plastic covering back on. She decided, for now anyway, to give up the idea of finding a more pleasant ceiling lamp. The rest of the room had been sufficiently transformed.

Her hard work had made her hungry. To avoid chewing the furniture, she decided to have her second cigarette of the day. It was the perfect excuse for taking a stroll in the middle of the morning. She found her purse, put on her coat, and hurried out of the building toward a café on the corner. Obediently, she waited her turn in line, then asked for two fruit Danishes and two cinnamon coffee cakes. She hesitated for just a moment before ordering an additional two pounds of mixed cookies. She knew she was buying too much, as usual, but perhaps they'd last more than a day. Once back on the street, she lit her cigarette, hoping to drive away her hunger for the baked goods. She was only torturing herself by buying and not eating them. She'd read somewhere that people on diets often bought too much for others. After a last, slow puff, she rushed back to work.

By now the department was buzzing with people. She hurried to the coffee machine in the kitchen and arranged the goodies on a tray. She found there was no milk, so she threw on her coat and dashed back to the café. The friendly cashier agreed to sell her two liters of milk even though they usually didn't sell that to customers. Marianne promised it wouldn't happen again. On the way back, she resisted the impulse to have another cigarette. She realized she was already smoking too much and took a deep lungful of fresh air instead. That would have to hold her until lunchtime, when she could dig into her piece of grilled chicken.

CHAPTER 50

He decided to call in sick for the rest of the week. Nobody would suspect him of cutting classes. After all, he was a good student, and his teachers knew he always made up work if he was ill or absent. During the two weeks he'd been traveling, he'd made sure all his work got in to his advisers before he returned to Sweden. Everyone thought he might as well have skipped it all since he was visiting his father, but he really wanted to get everything done. He'd gotten the highest possible grades on all his examinations but one. That low grade was because a teacher was playing games with him to throw him off-balance. He was convinced that incident with that teacher in the cafeteria last year was the reason. If that bastard hadn't been such an idiot, he wouldn't have had to punch him. Unprovoked, he never hurt anyone. Well, he certainly didn't need that idiot's approval.

He steered his bike over Djursholm Square and parked it close to the real-estate agent's office. He found his wallet and walked over to Café Gateau. The girl with the funny corkscrew curls was behind the counter, and he shuddered. It was stupid to come back here. A group of young people came in, and he slipped between them before he took a number. Perhaps he would melt in with them, and not look like a loner. To his relief, a different girl served him. She had greasy red hair and tired eyes and didn't seem to pay much attention when he ordered two lattes, two ham-and-cheese sandwiches, and two butter ball cookies.

"Here or to go?"

"To go."

He wondered whether to pour the coffee into his thermos now but decided it would bring too much attention. He paid and was just about to leave when the girl with the corkscrew hair gave him a big smile.

"Hey, do you work around here, or what?"

Why the hell did she want to talk to him? She wasn't even the one serving him.

"Excuse me?"

"I'm just wondering. You always ask for two of the same thing, so I thought you worked around here and were, like, picking it up for your boss, too."

"No, I'm still in school."

"Where? I just graduated from Sammis last spring."

How could he have been so stupid? He looked at the red-haired sleepy girl, but she'd picked up a magazine now that the other customers were gone.

"I'm just finishing up some classes."

He shrugged and forced a nice smile. She licked her lips and smiled back.

"Too bad. If you worked around here, we could have lunch sometime."

She winked, and he was flattered by her invitation. He felt his guts fill with disgust but smiled again anyway.

"Maybe we could still meet for lunch. I'll be back."

He raised his coffee cup in farewell as she smiled in return.

Back at his bike, he took a deep breath. He'd messed up big time.

CHAPTER 51

The aroma of freshly brewed coffee met her as she stepped off the elevator. Most of the department was there circulating around the trays with the attractive goodies. People were wondering what the occasion was.

"Oh, nothing in particular," Marianne said. "I thought, since there are so many new people here, it would be nice to offer something. Bribe my way back into the group, so to speak."

She smiled and invited them to have whatever they wanted. She put one of the milk cartons on the table and the other in the fridge.

Annelie Hedin entered the kitchen and appeared not to notice the display of treats. She opened the cupboard and took out a mug on which "WORLD'S BEST MAMMA" was printed with Annelie's picture beneath. In it Annelie was laughing at the camera, and it seemed to be summertime since she was tanned and her blonde hair was bleached by the sun. Marianne smiled, relaxing as best she could.

"Help yourself," Marianne said. "I thought it would be good to tank up on a Tuesday morning."

Annelie Hedin filled her mug with water.

"No, thanks. I'll have tea."

Marianne's smile froze. She wanted to say something stupid, but she restrained herself. "How about a cookie with your tea?" she asked.

Annelie Hedin looked at her coldly. Marianne couldn't help noticing she used way too much gel on her spiky hairstyle.

"No, thank you. I had breakfast."

Annelie put her mug into the microwave, then walked straight back to her office next door. Karin followed her, although she cast a longing glance at the tray of cookies.

Marianne sighed and took a coffee mug for herself, filling it to the brim. She couldn't restrain herself any longer. She picked up a slice of the Danish and took a huge bite, regretting it the minute the wonderful taste spread through her mouth. She took another quick bite and threw the rest into the garbage under the sink.

"Wow! Did you bring all this? What's the occasion?" Alexandra Baranski said, walking into the kitchen.

"It was nothing. I thought it would be a good way to start the day."

Alexandra picked up a slice of the cinnamon coffee cake. She almost got the whole piece down in one bite. Then she stared at Marianne for a second, exclaiming, "My goodness, what have you done to yourself? You're looking great!"

"Oh, I just got a haircut."

"Come on, you colored your hair, right? What a difference. You look fantastic. I'll have to try a piece of the Danish, too. I was supposed to start a new diet today, but let's just forget that for the moment. I can start next Monday—my usual routine, I have to add."

"With your figure, you shouldn't waste time dieting. I just broke my own diet a minute ago."

Alexandra sighed and tried to pull in her stomach. "All this wasn't there before. I have to blame all the late nights I stay up working. It's impossible to stay awake without snacking. My Mamma lives with us, and it's her life's mission to feed me as much as possible. I think she's even managed to put a few pounds on the boys. The way they do sports, you'd think that would be impossible."

"Still, it must be nice that your mother is willing to help out. Or does it work better in theory than in practice?"

Alexandra gave an even deeper sigh. While picking up yet another slice of Danish, she said, "It's unbelievably difficult but a huge relief, too. I never could have made it without her. I was worried at first that she would spoil them, like she used to do when they were little. But it works—they respect her and do what she says. I think they listen more to her than to me."

"Do they listen to your ex?"

"He's too busy starting his new family. They'll have their second child soon, and it's no exaggeration to say that he's seen the boys just four times this year. They're beginning not to care about him one way or the other. In the beginning it was hell. They missed him so much it hurt, but he didn't give a damn. The strange thing is, he was a great father when we were married. Then, when he met that new girl, all that just stopped."

"Do you think it's just temporary? Maybe he'll pay more attention to them again."

Alexandra finished her coffee and quickly poured herself a refill. She shook her head.

"In the beginning, I hoped things would change, but I think that train has left the station. It's been four years since we separated. His time away from them is getting too long. They're turning into strangers."

"How about your contact with him?"

"What can I say? He's a big asshole. I understand he got tired of me, and I accepted that fairly quickly. But I could kill him for what he did to our boys. I shouldn't put it in these words, being a prosecutor and all, but I hope he gets what's coming to him. Maybe something like gonorrhea? Who knows."

They laughed, and Marianne rinsed her cup before putting it in the dishwasher.

"His punishment will come, sooner or later. I'm absolutely convinced of it."

Alexandra nodded slowly. She knew Marianne spoke from experience.

"Well, what will be will be. By the way, I looked through that report and made some changes, especially in the conclusion. I marked them in red."

"Great, thanks. Yes, I guess it's time to get back to work. And thanks again for all of this."

Alexandra reached over the tray and picked up a cookie.

Annelie Hedin passed them as they walked through the hall. She gave Alexandra a chilly smile and avoided looking at Marianne. Marianne wondered about this young woman as she turned into her office. It was unusual for someone to show such hostility, especially at work. Annelie Hedin didn't even seem to care about showing it in front of Alexandra, her boss. Marianne wondered. Either Annelie had some devious plan, or she was simply showing her true nature.

Perhaps she had low self-esteem, and she took revenge by trying to throw others off-balance. Marianne decided to get to the bottom of it. She had to be prepared in case Annelie's animosity went too far.

Chapter 52

Torsten woke up momentarily confused about why he was in a car. The classical music had probably put him to sleep. The GPS announced a mile and a half to go until they reached their destination, and Augustin was following the arrow as he turned off the highway. Torsten decided he should invest in a GPS for his own car.

He cleared his throat, but he couldn't rid his voice of its huskiness. He asked, "Did you ever get in touch with your old flame?"

Augustin smiled. He didn't take his eyes off the road. "Old flame? Tell me which century we live in again? Yes, I got in touch with her. She told me a lot that could be of interest."

"Did she attend Right Now herself?"

"No, but her sister went, and left before the course was finished. She thought it was unnatural, artificial. She also didn't feel comfortable taking off all her clothes, which some of the exercises encouraged."

"All their clothes?"

"The way I understand it, they were encouraged to take off as much clothing as they felt comfortable shedding.

They were supposed to release the inhibitions and shame modern culture imprints on us."

"What a bunch of shit! I take it they just wanted to see naked ladies. Or how would you interpret it?"

Augustin laughed. "I tend to agree with you. They seem to concentrate too much on sex. Addressing sexual inhibitions is the impetus behind most of their exercises. Perhaps there's a good reason, but the entire business sounds off. Don't *most* people feel inhibited in large groups?"

Torsten shook his head. "What else did she say?"

"Many of their friends went there," Augustin continued. "Many also refused to go along with what they were expected to do, although attending Right Now is the in thing."

"Maybe the novelty is wearing off. Did she mention Christopher or Isa Turin?"

"She said the same thing as everyone else. Their relationship wasn't going well—that they were both open about seeing other people but neither wanted to hurt the children."

"I've gotten the same impression. They both seemed to really care for their children."

"Afterward, I did a little research on Right Now. They have kept their accounts in excellent shape. They seem to be aware that their finances could be examined at any time, and I couldn't find a single flaw. I also found out about a group protesting Right Now. They say they want to help people leave—that it's a cult—and they can help relatives deprogram those lost souls. I thought that all seemed just as sketchy as Right Now itself."

"You are the son of a psychologist. What do you think about all of this? Why don't they have a doctor on the premises? Why are there no professional psychiatrists or psychologists on staff?"

The GPS announced they'd reached their destination. Augustin steered the car into a parking spot and took a deep breath.

"I think we will see more of this phenomenon in the future. People today need more support, and they're fumbling around in the dark for it. There's the Institute for Self-Actualization, or ISA, which is a similar institution. It's supposed to be the successor to the Forum, which was active in the United States. There's also the Journey: a sort of 'eternity project.' They bring in members with all kinds of mumbo jumbo about taking mental life journeys. Behind all these groups are founders who make loads of money. Lots of people take these three-month courses from what they call coaches—it's an enormous business. There's Humanova and other minor groups—some of them are much worse than others. How can a person, after just a few months of training, become qualified to help people undergoing deep life crises? And what is a coach, really? Many of them say they use their own experiences to help others in the same situation. Can anything be flimsier? But, some people do feel better, and then they truly believe they are able to help others in the same situation. It's tragic that they all feel they are helping others. We know that a lot of people are in it for the money."

"Profiting from the misfortune of others."

"Exactly," Augustin said. "That's my analysis, for what it's worth. Still, I don't know if the idea was so bad in the beginning. But I'm uncomfortable with their belief that they can open wounds that are very difficult to repair later. Some people are struck down with depression or even psychosis after taking these so-called courses. They ought to have seen a psychiatrist instead. Still, it's symptomatic of our times to look for a quick fix. Solving deep psychological problems can take a long time, even years. Thinking mental illness can be solved with a snap of the fingers is naive at best. Crazy, I know. And it's not a question of being cheaper. Not everyone can afford a psychiatrist, but what they're charging for those courses is beyond the pale. Ten thousand crowns for a one-day course? That's a huge amount of money."

Torsten sighed and slammed the car door behind him.

"It'll be interesting to actually see what they're up to on that island."

Torsten pulled out his backpack. Augustin was carrying a large bag from Valhalla Bakery. He looked out over the ominously gray water.

"When's the taxi boat getting here?"

"A half hour at the latest."

Torsten beamed. "Great! Then we can have some pastries and coffee. I'm desperate for a cup."

They sat down on a bench where the steamboats pulled in by the dock. The breeze was hitting them, but the temperature was still reasonable.

"I have hot chocolate and coffee with milk. Be honest, now. What do you want?"

Augustin looked at the two thermoses. "Hot chocolate. I can't remember the last time I had it."

Torsten smiled, pouring the steaming hot chocolate into a cup, and Augustin blew on it before taking a slow sip.

"This is great. I should drink this more often."

Torsten poured his coffee, then opened the sandwich container. "Cheese and sausage with herbs, or egg and caviar?"

"I don't know which to choose. Did you really make all these this morning?"

"It's not a big deal. It's just a few sandwiches."

Augustin shook his head. "Just a few sandwiches, he says. I haven't had a brown-bag lunch this good in ages. No one ever made me a brown-bag lunch. Ever."

"Well, they taste good, too. Here, I made enough so we can have one of each."

They began to eat the egg sandwiches, and Torsten glanced at his watch. He'd eaten breakfast just two hours ago, but it felt like an eternity had passed. He packed the cheese sandwiches for lunch and figured he'd stop at the bakery for some cardamom buns to round out the meal.

"Valhalla Bakery is around the corner from my apartment."

"Forgive my ignorance, but where exactly is your apartment?"

"Wittstocksgatan 17. It's near where it loops around Gustaf Adolf Park."

"Oh, my mother worked for a family on Wittstocksgatan when I was a boy. What a neighborhood. Does your balcony face the park?" Torsten asked.

Augustin nodded. "Yes, indeed. Does your place have a balcony?"

"My son and I were sold on our balcony when we bought our apartment. We're just like everyone else. I read in the newspaper most people in the center of the city want balconies. We're not unique, and I never said I wasn't an average guy. Do you have a big place?"

"Big enough for my purposes. I live by myself."

"Two-room apartment?"

Embarrassed, Augustin said, "A three-room."

"How many square feet?"

"About nine hundred."

"Jesus, that's enormous," Torsten exclaimed. "How did you find it?"

"I bought it with the money I inherited from my mother. She came from a wealthy Brazilian family," Augustin explained.

"I see. Well, I don't have those kinds of relatives. All I inherited from my mother was her Gustavsberg china, and my wife took that when she left me."

They laughed and Torsten drank the last of his coffee, pulling out a napkin and cleaning his cup before returning it to his backpack.

Augustin pointed to the boat heading toward them. "That should be it, right?"

The taxi boat docked and tied up, and they hopped on board. Augustin started to shiver and he buttoned his coat. Torsten realized Augustin's elegant light-wool suit was much too thin for being out on the water, especially as the wind picked up. His own fleece jacket kept him quite warm, and he was glad he'd worn a pair of outdoor pants.

The boat trip took thirty minutes. Torsten wondered if Right Now escorted their guests. Maybe they had their own boat? He leaned toward Augustin, who was shivering next to the heater.

"Do you think Isa Turin is capable of murder?"

Augustin looked at him, surprised, then wrinkled his brow thoughtfully. "It depends. I think she could if her children were in danger."

"Let's say Christopher wanted sole custody after his sporadic attempts at being a father. Would she do it to regain the children?"

"I don't know. Maybe."

"Have we checked? Did he apply for sole custody?"

Augustin shook his head. "I could call someone now."

Torsten peered into space for a moment, then he slowly shook his head. "No, let's wait. I know the person we should call, but it looks like we don't have a signal here."

Augustin shot him a serious expression. "It's too bad things have come to this."

"What are you talking about?"

"All the leaks. No one can trust anyone. The system will fall apart if this continues."

"Yes, it's bad right now," Torsten agreed. "I've always been careful, even if it seemed like overkill sometimes. I just hope we can stop the leaks, or soon we'll be in pretty bad shape."

They were quiet as they got ready to jump onto the dock. The taxi boat was supposed to pick them up three hours later, and Torsten hoped that would give them enough time to finish their inquiry. The island seemed empty on this early autumn morning. They'd told Right Now they were coming, and they'd expected someone to meet them, but there wasn't a single soul. Torsten took out his cell phone and placed a call to the station.

"I'd like to speak to Marianne Jidhoff, please."

Augustin looked at him with curiosity while adjusting his scarf.

Torsten broke out in a wide grin.

"Hi, there! Torsten Ehn here! Thanks for the company yesterday!"

He laughed, then continued, "Sorry for bothering you. Something I'd like you to check for me. Could you check on the custody arrangements in the . . . yes! That's it. Thanks so much, Marianne!"

He ended the call and smiled. Augustin gave him an inquisitive look.

"Marianne Jidhoff works for Olle. I report directly to her, by the way. I'm not exactly sure if Olle will rearrange our team in the long run, but we'll see."

"I don't believe I've met her," Augustin said.

"She used to work here, but she's been on leave for a while. She's extremely attractive—a bella donna for sure!"

Augustin sighed. "Bella donna? Someone must update you on today's slang. Especially for women. Still, now that you mention it, I do remember Olle mentioning her name. He wanted her to come back to work instead of retiring, I believe?"

"That's right. She is a recent widow. I can't even imagine going into retirement at just fifty plus. It'd be like giving oneself an early death."

CHAPTER 53

Lotta came to pick up the girls. They were alarmed, but Paula hoped they didn't yet grasp the gravity of the situation. Lotta had told her to wait inside the house while she drove the girls to school. She returned at the same time as the police.

The officers were a strong-looking young blonde woman and an older man with a mustache. Both appeared disinterested. The young officer took extensive notes. She'd taken a careful look at the alarm box and the remote control, picked up the cigarette stubs with a pair of tweezers, and put them in a plastic bag taken from a black case.

"I really ought to have an investigator come by, but no one is available. You understand that breaking and entering is not a high priority for us."

"Excuse me? Isn't this more than just breaking and entering? Someone came in here when we were sleeping!"

"Sorry. You weren't harmed, so it falls under breaking and entering. Probably it was a homeless person wanting a warm place to sleep for the night, or some kid trying to make a little trouble."

"Entering a house protected by an alarm in the middle of the night? And so cool about it he smoked six cigarettes while he was here?" Lotta burst out laughing, and the female officer nodded in agreement.

"It's strange, all right, but I've seen stranger things that later had a natural explanation. Your husband is away on business, you say? Where is he?"

"London."

"We'll take a look at these cigarette butts, and we'll get back to you. But I doubt we'll find much. At any rate, if I were you, I would stay somewhere else for the next few days."

"Why? Do you think something will happen to me? Can't you protect me?"

"You might feel more secure not being here alone. Maybe you can borrow somebody's dog?"

Paula started chewing on a fingernail. She stared into space and shook her head before saying absently, "My kids are allergic."

The female officer shrugged and gave Paula a sympathetic look. Her male colleague seemed eager to get going.

"That's all I can suggest right now. If it happens again, call us."

"You've truly helped me feel safe and secure," Paula replied sarcastically.

The police car drove off.

Lotta hugged her. "Don't worry. We'll get through this. As long as Jens is gone, you and the girls can stay with us. We'll make it fun, like a pajama party. The children will love it."

Paula smiled gratefully at her friend. "Thanks, you're a sweetheart. Right now, all I want to do is sell this house and move far away from here."

"I know what you mean. Let's go to Café Gateau. I'm starving. We deserve our cinnamon buns, don't you think?"

As she reached for her purse and cell phone, Paula said, "Yes—and today I think I'll even have two."

CHAPTER 54

Torsten felt reenergized. He walked so swiftly that Augustin, tall as he was, had to jog to keep up. Augustin was amused. They headed toward a large building in the classic archipelago style: it had a wraparound veranda and looked a great deal like a house made of gingerbread. The house was painted red with white trim, and it appeared to be well cared for. Torsten noted a large cupola on the roof, somewhat hidden by the chimney. Two smaller buildings on either side seemed fairly new, but they'd been built in the same style. The building had two porches lined with rubber boots of various colors and sizes. Torsten assumed they were for the guests' use. The entire picture was one of pleasure and welcome. It was probably time soon for a new course to begin. Nobody would have left all those boots in this weather to deteriorate. He saw a quick movement behind one of the curtains and whispered to Augustin: "Don't look now, but someone is watching us."

Augustin didn't shift his gaze. He replied so softly that Torsten could hardly hear him. "I saw that, too. Silly question, but do you have your gun?"

Torsten had to laugh. "Yeah, I'm not that stupid!"

Augustin smiled. "Just checking."

"I agree, it feels isolated out here. Hey, look, someone wants to talk to us after all."

A man of about sixty was walking toward them. He had dark-gray hair combed back into a ponytail. He wore black linen trousers and a thick, beige, knitted sweater. During his youth, he must have been extremely attractive. Even now he was still an elegant man. He greeted them, holding out his right hand.

Torsten thought he looked like a stereotypical cult leader, but he hoped to be proven wrong. Whenever his prejudices were confirmed, it never ended well.

"Hello, I'm Torsten Ehn, an investigator from the National Police. This is my colleague, Augustin Madrid."

"I'm Ushtanga Erik Bergström."

"Sorry, I didn't quite catch that."

The man sighed, smiling. "Ushtanga. It's my Sanskrit name."

"I get it. It's like my middle name, which I never tell anyone. It could be used against me."

Torsten laughed at his own joke, but Ushtanga Erik barely smiled. He gestured toward the main building.

"We can talk inside without being disturbed. We have a course of study beginning in about three hours, and some of the participants will arrive soon."

"How many people are taking your course?"

Ushtanga Erik replied without looking back. "It depends on the subject and level of the course. We don't offer one unless we have at least ten participants."

Torsten made a quick mental calculation and decided that Ushtanga Erik had no trouble financing his lifestyle. They were shown into an austere white entrance hall and invited to hang up their coats. Torsten set his backpack on the floor as he hung up his fleece jacket, but then he picked it up and brought it inside with him. He had no idea what kind of people he was dealing with here. He'd seen seemingly simple situations end with listening devices or bombs being set off.

They walked through a large auditorium and were seated in large armchairs next to a crackling fireplace.

Torsten hadn't noticed any other color in the building except white, and he asked:

"Did you paint every single area in this building white?"

The man looked like he was struggling with sarcasm, but then he stopped himself. "Yes, we think white makes a room more harmonic. What colors are in your home?"

"Mine? Sand beige, I think it's called. Almost white. But do you see this place as your home or your workplace?"

The man gave him an exasperated look, and Torsten returned it as innocently as possible.

"My home is wherever my soul is. Material circumstances are unimportant. We don't focus on the material surface here."

"So, the color white is just a material surface? It has no significance?"

Ushtanga Erik's eyes darkened.

Pleased to have made his point, Torsten calmly continued: "According to the tax authorities, you are divorced and have two children. Is that correct?"

Ushtanga Erik nodded.

"Is it also correct that you own this place with a woman named Christina Filipsson?"

"Christina now calls herself Tchinti."

Torsten couldn't stop a wide grin from forming, but he didn't dare say anything until he had himself under control. "I see. According to the tax authorities, she is still legally Christina Filipsson. The question remains. Are you two partners in this business?"

The man's gray ponytail wagged as he nodded yes and shifted in his armchair.

"Can we meet with her?"

"She's preparing for her course. She needs time to meditate and enter the right mental state."

"I understand, but we really don't need more than a few minutes of her time. We've traveled a good way to come see you both."

The man realized he wouldn't win this round, either, so he said, "I'll ask her to come down. But can we wait until she finishes her meditation?"

"That's fine."

"How did the two of you decide to start Right Now?" Augustin asked.

Ushtanga Erik relaxed noticeably. He smiled at them.

"Fifteen years ago, I was on the *Estonia* ferry, part of a kickoff celebration with my advertising firm. Most of my team had already gone to bed, but I had difficulty sleeping. I was living a demanding lifestyle filled with stress. I decided to have one last drink in the bar before going to bed. As I neared the bar, there was a tremendous bang."

He took a deep breath. Torsten suspected that this dramatic pause was well rehearsed. This could hardly be the first time Ushtanga Erik had told this story. Torsten was curious to hear how it played out.

"The furniture began to move around, and I had to avoid the chairs flying through the room. A man was pinned behind a refrigerator. The girl at the bar and I gave each other a quick glance and realized the situation was bad. When everything turned over, we ran for the stairs. People were coming out of their cabins, and we had to pull ourselves up the steps. Near the deck, a fat lady hung on to the stairs in front of us. She screamed that she couldn't hold on any longer. I threw myself to the side and held myself as close to the wall as I could, pressing the girl from the bar against the wall, too. The woman fell all the way down and took a number of people with her.

"Once we reached the deck, the ferry shifted again, and we could see the cabin windows sinking beneath our feet. The ferry sank even more quickly, and we did our best to keep climbing up. Finally, we saw that we were out of time and a second later, a wave swept over us. The only thing I was able to think was that I would lose the nice new watch I'd just bought. When I came to, I was hanging over a lifeboat and a man was struggling to pull me on board."

Ushtanga Erik paused and looked at them in a state of contemplation. Torsten was impressed. He heard Augustin's voice.

"What happened to the girl from the bar?"

Erik said, "Miraculously enough, she landed in the same lifeboat as I did. We both made it. We sat with our arms around each other to keep warm. It was freezing with the storm. We promised we would do something to make the world a better place if we survived."

"So, Christina was the young woman from the bar?"

Ushtanga Erik nodded, folded his hands in his lap, and blinked.

Torsten said, "Very impressive. How lucky you two were. I can understand how your life was changed and that you wanted to do something important."

"Of course. I was already in the middle of a divorce before the *Estonia* sank. I sold the advertising firm afterward and bought this island with the money. We still hadn't decided what to do, but after we took a long trip to India, our idea was born."

"And your idea was?"

"To help people live in the moment with *mindfulness*, as it's called. In our modern consumerist world, it is a way of life we have difficulty practicing. We want people to break free of their negative ways and dare to follow their inner voices."

The unctuousness in the man's voice made Torsten so angry that he felt an urge to punch Ushtanga Erik in the face. He knew hypocrisy when he heard it. Torsten's voice shook as he asked, "And you believe people are generally capable of changing?"

Ushtanga Erik closed his eyes for a long time. Then he replied, "No, unfortunately not. Many people are used to running in their little hamster wheels, unaware of their basic needs. Only when their bodies can no longer hold on, when they crash into a wall, do they realize they are burned out and need to change."

"And what exactly do you do here?"

"I can't go into that, out of respect for our companion souls."

"Companion souls?"

"That's what we call the people who learn from our courses. Now, perhaps, you can tell me why you are here?"

"You don't know? I thought I was clear when I called earlier."

Ushtanga Erik was obviously surprised. "No, nobody told me why you were coming."

"We're here because one of the participants in your course has died. In fact, he was murdered."

Ushtanga Erik's mouth dropped. Then he took a deep breath.

Torsten continued. "Christopher Turin. From what I understand, he's been taking your courses for years."

"Yes, absolutely, he was a devout participant."

Torsten noticed the switch from "companion soul" to "participant." Ushtanga Erik didn't seem to notice his slip.

"What happened? How did he die?"

"He was hit by a moving car."

"But murder? It wasn't an accident?"

"No, in this case, it was deliberate."

"That's awful," Usthanga Erik said. "How is his family doing? He has a number of children."

"We have been in touch with the widow."

Torsten wasn't going to say anything about Isa Turin to this man she certainly didn't care for. "How would you characterize Christopher's situation?" he asked instead.

"His 'situation'? What do you mean?"

"How he was feeling, what he was doing up here. What were his needs?"

"That's a difficult question. I don't think I am the right person to answer. You should ask Christina."

He didn't call his companion by her "new name." Torsten took this as additional proof that this was all mumbo jumbo. Erik Bergström stood up and looked at them gravely. "I'll go get her at once."

–□–

Torsten watched the man stride through the wood-paneled hallway—painted white, of course. He turned to Augustin and whispered, "What a bunch of shit!"

Augustin rubbed his hand over his face and said, "It's actually kind of sad. I can't decide whether he believes in his own blessed gifts or he's just an extremely savvy business-man."

"He has a great story, even if he's used it much too often. But odd things can happen. Let's check his background to find out what he's up to. Same thing with his partner. Even if they feel reborn, there's bound to be some stuff we can dig up. No one can avoid time, but that old guy is in great shape. He surely has enough neurotic upper-class women to keep his engine going. He talks about their souls and gets into their pants. The minute a spouse comes to their part-ner and says they're going to take a Right Now course, all you have to do is count the days until the divorce. Here they come."

Torsten took a deep breath, and they smiled at each oth-er. Augustin took a pack of gum from his pocket and offered a stick to Torsten, who shook his head. The woman who walked beside Ushtanga Erik was strikingly beautiful. Her skin was olive and her curly, golden-brown hair fell past her slender shoulders. Her green eyes were in stark contrast to her black lashes, and her eyebrows were beautifully formed.

She wore no makeup, but she made a strong impression. Her white tunic over her dark-gray linen pants looked good against her skin. She was barefoot, and her feet and hands were well manicured. If the women went crazy for Erik, the men must be even more affected by Christina Filipsson. Even Torsten had to fight off his immediate attraction.

She held out her hand, saying, "I'm Tchinti."

"Torsten Ehn, National Police. My colleague, Augustin Madrid. According to the tax authorities, you are Christina Filipsson—and you are divorced with a son?"

She nodded yes.

"We've just talked to your partner about one of the participants in your course—Christopher Turin, who is recently deceased."

"Ushtanga told me. It's terribly tragic. Christopher was a close soul who had come far. It's painful that he's left our plane of existence."

"Yes, he was murdered. Someone ran him over on purpose."

The woman studied them, then said, "So how can I help you?"

"How did you 'experience' Christopher? What were his needs?"

"I found him a lost soul when he first came here. He gained strength the longer he was with us. He needed to break free from his former way of life."

"How did you help him here?"

"We don't believe we *help* people. We can only show them how to increase mindfulness in the present."

Torsten was losing patience. "So you decided that he was feeling bad?"

Christina looked at him with steel in her eyes. "Yes, he felt bad. And he felt better after he started coming to us."

"I would hope so. He paid a fortune for your courses. Can you tell me exactly how much money he invested in your operation?"

Ushtanga Erik frowned, answering brusquely. "He wasn't an investor. He took our courses. He owns nothing here."

"I mean, how much money did he pay you?"

"I wouldn't know, but I believe that would be confidential information. If you want it, you'll probably have to get a court order."

"That won't be difficult. My boys will come here and turn this place upside down. It's up to you how you want it done. Besides, we can always contact the widow for the information."

Augustin quietly entered the conversation. "How does this operation work? Do the two of you have equal shares in the firm?"

The partners looked at each other. Erik replied, "I own the island and the buildings. The firm is registered in both of our names. We share the expenses and profits equally."

Torsten scratched his cheek, looking at Christina Filipsson. "Are you romantically involved? You are both divorced and according to the tax authorities, there are no spouses or partners registered at your addresses."

Christina Filipsson raised an eyebrow.

Neither of them replied.

Torsten sighed and wrote something in his notebook. "I'll take that as a yes. Don't you find it difficult to always be so opaque? Or have you been so affected by all this crazy stuff that it seems normal now?"

Ushtanga Erik Bergström replied drily, "We live according to the way we interpret the world—and that may not agree with your worldview."

Augustin entered the conversation quietly, asking, "Many participants in your courses have said there's lots of sex going on here. Is that true?"

Christina gave Augustin a gentle smile. "Sexuality can be interpreted in many different ways. We do whatever it takes to rid ourselves of stress. Sexuality is one of our tools. It doesn't mean that we're all down on the floor having orgies."

Torsten was amused to see Augustin blush in response to the woman's charming offensive. Augustin continued in spite of his red cheeks. "So you have a free interpretation of sex?"

"Everything depends on your interpretation."

"Doesn't it sound logical that a participant's partner might feel threatened by their spouse coming here and having sex with other people?"

"I told you, that's not how it works here. That is your own interpretation."

"Yes, and it's how some people in your courses interpret it, too. Don't you think that you as leaders shouldn't encourage sexual relationships between your disciples, or whatever you call them? Psychologists and doctors would lose their licenses doing that."

Ushtanga Erik hissed at Augustin, "This has gone far enough. We have never claimed to be psychologists or doctors. We practice an alternative to the usual forms of therapy. That doesn't mean we have sex with our participants. If you'd like to take us to the station for questioning, go right ahead. But otherwise, this conversation is over."

Torsten focused his gaze on the man with the ponytail. In a forceful tone—but with a smile—he said, "I'm the one with the authority to conclude this conversation. As I said, this place will soon be crawling with police officers doing a thorough search. We're asking these questions to find the motive for Christopher Turin's murder. We really don't give a damn what you all do up here. We don't care about your sex orgies and diapers and God knows what else. But we do need you to answer our questions. If you don't cooperate, I *will* need take you down to the station immediately. Then you can forget all about your courses for a good long time."

Christina Filipsson looked shocked, and she no longer appeared so beautiful. Her appearance seemed to wilt with each passing second.

"Are you saying that we are suspects?" she said.

"Not at this time. But I'm going to need a list of all the participants in these courses from the day you opened. And I need to know who was in each course. There's indication that the murder was somehow connected to this place. Meanwhile, my colleague and I will take a look around."

Ushtanga Erik Bergström's eye twitched, and he clenched his jaw so tightly that Torsten worried his teeth might break.

"Of course," he said. "Would you like one of us to escort you, or do you want to look around on your own?"

Torsten smiled. "We'd appreciate it if one of you could show us around."

Ushtanga Erik turned to Christina. "If you could meet the incoming participants, I'll have the office put together this information. Let me show these gentlemen around."

Relieved, Christina turned toward all three of them. "Then I'll take my leave. I'll be in one of the other buildings if you have any more questions. Erik can tell you where I am."

As she left, her bountiful hair swirled around her back. Ushtanga Erik walked her out, and Torsten noticed not a hair in his ponytail out of place. His linen clothes were immaculate and without a single wrinkle, despite the fact he'd been sitting in a chair.

Augustin plopped back into his armchair. "Good God in Heaven, I'm exhausted! I don't know how you do it."

"Do what?"

"Get them to open up, to say stuff. How do you keep them on the right track? I'm completely wiped out from the tension."

"Oh, you get used to it. You put in a few good questions yourself."

"Well, I wanted to take part. Do you think he's gone to hide things now that he's in his office?"

"Probably. What he likely doesn't get is that makes it easier for us. We'll find whatever he's hiding, and then we'll know right away that's what we're after. But maybe he gets that and he'll show us everything we need. That'll mean we have our work cut out for us. We'll have to bring in some experts, or other help, if we have to sort all that out."

Augustin looked at him in amazement but said nothing. Torsten grimaced and motioned toward the hallway. "He's already coming back. If he hid things, he's impressively fast."

They got to their feet, and Ushtanga Erik Bergström took them on a tour of the property.

CHAPTER 55

S o, what did Purran say?"
"Not much. She just asked how long we stayed out. I said
we left right after she did, and that we were really wasted."

"That wasn't an exaggeration."

"No, but it's far from the truth. So how was it? Have you
two gotten together since?"

Paula hesitated before replying. She hoped Lotta
wouldn't notice she was lying. "No, I haven't called. I
thought I would at first, but I didn't know where it would
lead. I have enough problems already."

"Oh, go on and call him."

Paula took a bite of her cinnamon bun and chewed
slowly. She looked at Lotta. "How do you and your husband
manage things? Have you come to some agreement about
sex with other people?"

Lotta pressed her lips together. "Not exactly. But I found
the bill from his last business trip. He spent a lot of money
at a certain kind of club, if you know what I mean."

"Strippers?"

Lotta shrugged. Her voice was hard. "Or prostitutes. I
don't know, and I don't care. I went through his stuff and
found bills from previous trips, too."

"Yuck. Have you asked him flat out?"

Lotta shook her head. "No, and I'm not sure I want to know. If he confesses he goes to whores, I'll have to divorce. What kind of person would I be if I didn't? As long as I don't know for sure, I can put up with a great deal."

"You can put up with it? Come on, isn't life more than that?"

"Well, what about you? Aren't you just putting up with things, too? Your husband comes home from a long business trip and goes right out to the archipelago for one of his strange courses . . . and his yoga . . . and God knows what else."

Paula cringed. Lotta had assessed her marriage so clearly. Hearing it from someone else made it sound so much worse. "I know. I'm putting up with things, too."

"Think about how life would change if we didn't! Not being able to see the children as often as we want? Maybe losing the house? Let me tell you, some strange woman would be moving into my house the minute I finished packing, and then I'd have to live in a terrible apartment in a terrible place like Mörby Centrum. How would I ever deal with that?"

Paula said, "So your strategy is to have a little something on the side to help you put up with all his shit?"

"That's about right. But I'd never tell the world."

"What if you meet someone special?"

"Then I'm out of here."

Paula felt ill. She didn't know if it was from the stress-eating of two cinnamon buns after a hefty lunch, or from seeing the picture Lotta painted for her.

Suddenly, there were loud voices. The sweet young girl who had just waited on them and always knew what Paula wanted was getting harassed by some woman patron.

"I'm very sorry, but we can't accept your credit card unless you show some ID."

"You've got to be kidding me. Are you stupid or something? I'm *always* in here. Do I look like a thief to you?"

Without thinking, Paula got up and walked to the cashier. "Excuse me, but this girl is not in the least bit stupid. Can't you hear how you sound to other people? She didn't make the rules. You should carry your ID when you leave home. How can she know if this is really your credit card? Do you truly believe that every human being on the planet knows who you are?"

The woman stared at Paula in disbelief. Paula herself actually couldn't believe what she'd done. The entire crowd at Café Gateau had fallen silent. Realizing all eyes were on her, the woman threw the bag of bread on the counter and stormed out.

The young clerk smiled gratefully at Paula. "Thanks— that was so kind of you to step in like that."

"Well, she was being particularly unpleasant."

"If you and your friend want free refills, just ask."

Paula went back to her chair. The girl's next customer was a young man. The girl motioned toward Paula, and the young man turned to look at her with a particularly intense stare. Paula thought there was something familiar about him.

Lotta interrupted her. "Can you believe that lady? What an idiot!"

"Oh, I shouldn't have been so hard on her. I don't know what got into me."

"It was the right thing to do. She had no right to chew that girl out. So, what do you say? Shall we get our refills?"

Paula nodded. As Lotta got up, Paula pulled out her phone. She knew it was wrong, but she couldn't help herself. The only thing she wanted after that morning's terrifying discovery was to lie in Passi's arms and inhale his scent. Before Lotta returned, she quickly texted:

I want to see you again./Paula

CHAPTER 56

Marianne called the family court offices and after being put on hold four times, she finally reached a person competent enough to send over the required information. A few minutes later, the material arrived via e-mail. She had already finished Alexandra Baranski's assignments and recorded the day's results from another investigation. She called the tax authorities and asked for Gunnar Blad.

"Hello, Gunnar. Marianne Jidhoff here. Sorry to bother you during your coffee break."

"Marianne! How nice to hear from you! Have you returned to work?"

"Just yesterday."

"Please accept my sympathies for your loss. I saw Hans's obituary in the paper."

"Things have been difficult. But I have to tell you, it feels wonderful to be back at work. I've been surprised by that."

"I can imagine. I think I wouldn't have any trouble playing golf for the rest of my life, but, really, having a routine makes life meaningful. The thought of retirement can actually be frightening."

"I've begun to realize that retirement isn't everything it's cracked up to be. How is your wife doing?"

"She's having an operation to take out her gall bladder. But I assume you didn't call me to ask about her. What can I help you with?"

"I'm working for Olle Lundqvist again. I need some information to complete a preliminary investigation."

"Name and tax number?"

"Just a minute . . . there are several names."

"Send them, and please send the authorization code in a separate e-mail."

"Another thing, Gunnar. Don't tell anyone about this. Everything in this specific file is confidential, even internally."

"Is this a part of Olle's new system?"

"Well, partially."

"You can trust me. I've also set up my server to eradicate everything five minutes after downloading."

"That's good. Thanks for all your help."

Marianne noted this on a Post-it as she hung up. She e-mailed the list and the authorization code while calling Eje's Chocolate Factory.

"Hello, Marianne Jidhoff here. I would like to send two boxes of truffle nougat—yes, that's right, the middle size— one is for a hairstylist on Nybrogatan and the other is for Gunnar Blad at the tax authority on Södermalm. You can choose the delivery service. Just make sure they're delivered today. Yes, please put it on my account. Write the same thing on both cards: 'Warmest greetings from Marianne Jidhoff.' No, sorry, I won't be ordering anything for myself today."

Marianne wasn't sure what to do next. She drummed her fingers on her desk. She had sworn she wouldn't do this, but her fingers started working on automatic pilot. She typed "Irene" into the search engine, but the results weren't useful. She knew she shouldn't dig any further into this subject. How could it lead to anything good? She had nothing to gain from knowing more about Hans's greatest love. Her destructive side wanted to know, but her sensible side said to put it all behind her. The painful truth would reveal itself soon enough.

While waiting for Gunnar Blad's reply, she decided to visit the ladies' room. She looked in the mirror and saw that her hair still fell in place. The hairstylist definitely deserved that box of chocolates. Suddenly, she heard voices outside the door.

"Have you seen what she did to her office? Where did she find all that furniture?"

"I assume it was specially ordered for her. I'd like to know how much money she's making."

"Me, too. It's horrible how Olle tiptoes around her, as if she's better than the rest of us. It's embarrassing. And did you hear Alexandra this morning? *I looooove your new hairstyle!* What's up with that?"

"You know Alexandra. She brownnoses those on the way up, and kicks the others downstairs. She's the most spineless person in the entire department."

"I can hardly believe she's ranked higher than Baranski. It's probably because of where she comes from. She's a long way from royalty, though. I think it's reprehensible. And poor Linda. What is she going to do now?"

"I talked to her yesterday. She still hadn't heard anything about another temporary position."

"Well, I sure hope she gets one."

The voices subsided and Marianne heard Alexandra's voice. "Have you two seen Marianne? I need her for something right away."

Marianne had to smile as she pressed down the door handle and walked out of the bathroom. Annelie Hedin and Sussi Kjell stared at her.

Alexandra exclaimed, "Oh, there you are! I need you to check something for me."

"Absolutely. Just let me get a cup of coffee first."

Marianne walked past her female coworkers without a glance. She would have loved to look back to see their faces, but she restrained herself. She hurried toward the kitchen and was sitting at her desk when Alexandra came in with an armful of paperwork.

"Something's wrong with the math in this report. Could you check it for me again?" she asked.

"I'll do it right away," Marianne said.

Alexandra smiled widely. "You're an angel."

Marianne studied the documents and frowned. Something was definitely off. She read through the reports again and went through the statistics, only to reach the same conclusion as Alexandra. Alexandra looked at Marianne in puzzlement when she returned to her office.

"How strange. I wonder how those figures got in there. Annelie Hedin must have missed it. She did help me with the initial report."

"Maybe it's not her fault. She may have received wrong information from the investigators."

Alexandra shook her head. "That's hard for me to believe. I double-checked everything. Well, we'll let it go this once. I am so grateful you're here."

Marianne smiled as Alexandra slid the papers into her dark-brown portfolio and struggled into her red coat. "Let's go out one evening for a glass of wine," Alexandra said. "There's got to be something fun about working here, right?"

"I'd enjoy that. Just say when. I have the feeling your schedule is more booked than mine."

"I'll check with my mom back home," Alexandra said. "We won't see each other tomorrow because I'm in court all day. Thanks again for all the treats this morning. It was nice of you."

She hurried off, and Marianne walked back to her office pondering the information in those reports. She wondered who had something to gain by manipulating the numbers. Would it influence a judgment or compromise Alexandra in some way? Marianne remembered Olle telling her that she already had some enemies. She clicked to make a copy of the document in question, saved it, and hid it in a folder behind another containing different information. It was best to be on the safe side here.

Her e-mail pinged to announce that Gunnar's message had arrived. Curious, she opened the documents to read about the six people involved. It was interesting reading. She called Torsten Ehn, who answered after two rings.

"Ehn, here!"

"Marianne Jidhoff. I have what you wanted."

"Wonderful. Can we meet at the same place we ate yesterday? Let's say at four p.m.?"

Marianne ran through her schedule in her mind. "That should work."

She had received a new pile of research concerning Olle's investigation, and it demanded her attention. An hour later, she put it aside in order to warm her piece of grilled chicken in the microwave and return to eat in front of her computer.

The information was well organized, making it easy for her to sift through, and she found items that were definitely pertinent to the investigation. She ate the chicken as slowly as she could, but it left her still feeling hungry. She needed a smoke. Grabbing her coat, she took the stairs down.

Out on the street, she saw that the sun had disappeared behind some clouds. The temperature had sunk remarkably quickly since yesterday. She turned left on Polhemsgatan and looked up at the hill, which was part of Kronoberg Park.

On a park bench near the top of the hill, Marianne spied the backs of two people, Lillemor Rootander and some man. They leaned closer and a moment later they were kissing. Marianne's entire body shuddered. She couldn't see how anyone would want to kiss that woman, although she knew she wasn't exactly impartial. She lit a cigarette and slowly walked onto Bergsgatan. A few moments later, she passed the café where she'd soon meet Torsten Ehn and his partner.

In front of the passport office, people were standing around, bored, some of them drinking coffee. The waiting time to get a passport was ever longer these days. Marianne realized that she probably needed a new one herself, although she hadn't been abroad in over ten years.

She turned into the tiny park and walked past the entrance to the Kronoberg Baths. She turned the corner again to Kungsholmsgatan and then crushed her cigarette stub, wrapping it in tissue to throw out later.

When she walked back into the station, Olle was on his way out, looking extremely stressed. Though a taxi waited for him, he stopped to say, "I heard you had a chance to talk to Torsten. That's great! I have to run, but can I ask you to stay behind and hold down the fort? I'm supposed to be on call for the rest of the day, but I have to meet some guys from the EU meeting."

Marianne agreed.

"Thank you, Marianne. I'll text reception my cell phone number. Let's hope nothing serious happens. If it does, I'll come right back."

Taking over Olle's on-call duties wouldn't be as dramatic as it sounded. Mostly Marianne would answer any press calls that came in regarding ongoing investigations. If nothing big was happening, the journalists never called after office hours.

She got another cup of coffee and sat down in front of her computer, happy that her hunger pangs had subsided. She was just about to turn on the computer when she realized that something wasn't right.

Someone had been in her office.

She looked around carefully. Nothing had shifted or been removed. As the computer warmed up, she could see that someone had accessed it—with her correct user name and password. That person had logged out just two minutes before her return. What the person didn't know was that Marianne arranged the monitor at a certain angle whenever she turned her computer on or off. She never wanted it to be in direct sunlight, a habit she'd picked up at home. She'd heard it wasn't good for the screen, and now the screen had been shifted so the sunlight hit it.

She thought about calling Olle but changed her mind. Maybe it was nothing. Perhaps the IT guy came in to see if her machine was working. Until it happened again, she would just keep it to herself. She didn't want to be thought of as a paranoid old woman.

She wondered: Did this person find what he or she was looking for? Marianne thought it couldn't have been easy, as she used a system for hiding documents within her file system. The question was, what was the person looking for in *her* system. What did he or she think was there?

CHAPTER 57

Shivering, they boarded the taxi boat and hurried toward the covered passenger cabin. They were both freezing after waiting half an hour for the boat. The tour of the Right Now property hadn't revealed anything new. The place was aesthetically pleasing, and Ushtanga Erik had told them— in as few words as possible—everything that took place in each room. Returning to the Right Now office, Ushtanga Erik handed them a thick folder containing a list of participants in various courses.

"Handle these with discretion," he said gravely. "I hope nothing appears in the press."

"We will. Thank you for your time."

Ushtanga Erik had smiled weakly, turning on his heel and not bothering to show them to the door. Back outside in the wind they noticed someone was studying them from behind the curtain, yet again.

The taxi boat rocked more than it had on the way out. Torsten noticed Augustin beginning to turn green, but finally, the boat docked and they hurried to Augustin's car. When Augustin started the car, he sighed deeply and steered out of the parking lot.

Torsten smiled. "I know. Forgive my French, but that place is fucking weird."

Augustin shook his head. "I can't put my finger on it. Everyone was very friendly on the surface. At least at first. But the moment I got there, I wanted to run away screaming. It felt like a mental hospital with a strict warden who makes sure nobody escapes."

"I agree. It would be hard to slip from his claws, especially if he wanted to hold on to you. Let's see what Marianne Jidhoff found out about his previous life. By the way, I still have vacation days to use up, and I want to take Friday off. Can you hold down the fort in case something important comes up?"

"Certainly," Augustin responded.

Once they passed Roslagen, Torsten noticed autumn's effect on the city. He hoped it wouldn't be too cold to stay overnight on the boat. Noah wasn't the type to complain, but they'd better make sure they took enough warm clothes.

CHAPTER 58

Marianne made one more foray through the office. It was hard to let go of thoughts about her secret visitor. Who was it? Some people could be eliminated right away. Annelie Hedin, of course, was one of the most likely suspects. But it was doubtful she'd be so foolhardy. Mouthing off to the boss and being unfriendly to a new colleague weren't in the same league as hacking into someone's computer.

Marianne walked through the hall, peeking into each office. Most people were in front of their computers or on the phone. Some looked up when she poked her head in, and others ignored her. Her stroll didn't give her any leads, but it was good to stretch her legs. She walked back to her office and reviewed the last files of the day. With the information she'd found, she made a special file and printed two copies on her printer. It was more than she realized. She put everything in a plastic folder and carefully slid it into her purse. A quick bathroom visit, and she put on her coat and got ready to leave. She made sure her computer screen was turned away from the window. Perhaps she was just being silly.

Annelie Hedin was by the coffee machine. "So, leaving already?"

"Yes. Have a pleasant evening."

She held her head as high as she could without getting a pain in her neck, pressing the button for the elevator, and when she turned back around, Annelie Hedin was standing next to Karin and Sussi, gesturing while she talked. Marianne took a deep breath and pressed the button again. She took out her cell phone and wondered whether to call Olle. She wanted to make sure that he'd redirected his calls, and she decided that he surely must have done so. There was no reason to bother him. It was in his own interest for her to cover him.

She walked the same route she had earlier and soon reached the little café at the corner of Bergsgatan and Pilgatan. Torsten Ehn was already sitting on one of the sofas, more sloppily dressed than yesterday. Next to him was a young man whose clothing was in elegant contrast. He wore a tailor-made suit and handmade shoes and looked like a picture cut straight from an Italian fashion magazine.

Torsten got up and smiled. "Great you could get away. I thought it would be better if we met here. This is my new colleague, Augustin Madrid. Olle pinned him on me."

Marianne smiled at the stylish young man and held out her hand. "Nice to meet you."

Augustin's soft hand gave a firm handshake.

She sat down and pulled out the plastic folder, which Torsten eyed curiously.

"This is what I was able to find. Go ahead and look through it."

"You have to get a cinnamon bun. They're freshly baked and wonderful. Augustin and I just polished off ours."

Marianne smiled and sat down between the two men as they intently studied the material in the folder. Augustin looked up.

"This is highly informative. Isn't it strange that Isa Turin didn't mention any of this to us? They've been waging a custody battle for over two years. It's gotten worse lately, and the fighting was getting dirty."

Torsten looked up and said, "She probably thought there was no reason to bring it up now that he's dead. But she should have realized we'd be looking into everything. Didn't she know there'd be official documents?"

Marianne had to agree. "I know. It's strange, especially because she has a law degree. Why didn't she bring it up? Could she have simply forgotten to in her grief?"

Torsten shrugged. "I don't know. Could you forget something like that?"

Torsten suddenly looked embarrassed.

"I'm sorry. I wasn't meaning to ask you that directly. It just came out. Forgive me for being clumsy."

Marianne smiled. "Don't worry. I didn't take it personally. I do think she might have had so many other emotions going on that she just didn't think it was worth mentioning."

Augustin wrinkled his brow. "She didn't seem that sad to me."

"She even sort of flirted with me," Torsten said. "I think we should press her on this and the rest of it. What did you find out about our cult leaders?"

"A number of interesting things. Look all the way toward the back.

Torsten was flipping through the papers when his cell phone rang.

"Ehn here!"

He was silent with his cell phone to his ear for a long time, until he finally said, "I understand. We'll be right there."

He turned to Marianne and Augustin. "That was Olle. They've found a young woman murdered near a jogging path in Djursholm. Olle wants us to head there right away."

Marianne's cell phone rang.

"Marianne Jidhoff speaking."

"Olle here. A woman has been found murdered in Djursholm. I want you to stay at the office. I'll need your assistance. I'm going to wrap up this meeting and get over there right away. I really need you to stay."

"Of course. We've already agreed on it."

"I know, but I didn't expect anything like this. I also want you to call Torsten Ehn and give him any assistance he needs."

Marianne had to cough before saying, "That shouldn't be a problem."

"And keep this under wraps. It's the same deal as with the man on Narvavägen. We don't want any leaks. Don't talk to anyone beside Torsten and me. I promise to get back to the office as soon as I can."

They all stood up, and Marianne put her cell phone back in her purse. Torsten's face was filled with emotion.

"I imagine that was Olle. Augustin and I will head right to the crime scene. We'll call you later. Damn it all, I hate it when a young woman is killed."

Marianne wanted to lay a hand on his arm to comfort him, but it wouldn't be proper.

The trio broke up. Marianne went back the way she'd come and called Lola as she walked. She would have to miss tonight's gallery event. There would be other openings. With a deep sigh, she lit a cigarette and inhaled. It was going to be a long night.

PART THREE

Part Three

CHAPTER 59

Torsten turned toward Augustin.

"Is it OK if we take your car? You might have to drive me home pretty late tonight."

"That's fine."

They didn't say anything more. It took fifteen minutes to drive over the Barnhus Bridge, continue on Dalagatan to Odenplan and then onto Sveavägen, crossing both Norrtull and Roslagstull before reaching Norrtäljevägen. At Stocksund Bridge, Torsten said quietly, "It's not going to be a pretty sight."

"I understand."

When Augustin's GPS showed there was just a mile to their destination, Torsten's stomach cramped. Many of his colleagues said they'd become hardened over the years. Torsten found just the opposite: it was more difficult with each passing year, especially where women and children were concerned, and this made him more determined to solve these cases.

Olle had told Torsten over the phone that the young woman was found under a boat. The owners had brought it ashore the previous weekend and turned it upside down for storage. That's when they made the macabre find.

Without taking his eyes off the road, Augustin asked Torsten if anyone had informed her family.

Torsten said, "A crisis team has been sent to their home. Thank God we won't have to do that. The team has special training in talking to the bereaved. When I was at the Academy, we hardly touched on it, but I believe your generation learned more than we did."

They fell silent and Augustin slowed the car, parking on the side of the road behind a police vehicle. Torsten locked his hands together and stretched his shoulders. He needed to step out of the car but couldn't yet bring himself to do it. To Augustin, he said, "Have you ever seen a dead body before?"

"Yes. I was with my mother when she died. And I was one of the few people in my year at the Academy who chose to attend an autopsy."

"So you know what to expect."

Before he could change his mind, Torsten quickly climbed out onto the damp asphalt, while Augustin locked the car and pulled up the collar of his thin coat. They walked toward the white lamps where Brundin was standing in his overalls.

Torsten gave Brundin a short nod and said, "All right to take a look?"

Brundin blinked. "Sure, I'm finished."

Torsten and Augustin walked over to the boat that covered the corpse. The female victim was lying on a black bier of rubber. Torsten guessed she hadn't yet reached her twentieth birthday—not yet an adult, really. Torsten turned his head away, and Augustin took a step forward, looking more closely at the deceased. He then called over to Brundin, "Do we know yet how she was killed?"

Brundin was about ten feet away, packing his bag. He shook his head. "I see no blunt trauma and nothing to indicate she was poisoned. My first guess would be suffocation. I won't be able to tell until I've finished the autopsy."

Torsten wrinkled his brow. "Suffocated? I don't see any blue marks on her face."

"They don't always show up. I'll take a look at the lungs. It's not always easy to tell from the outside. I'll call you as soon as I find anything."

Augustin looked at Jan Brundin. "Do you think she came here to commit suicide? Or was that boat put over her after she died?"

"The latter, most likely. Someone killed her and then used the boat to hide her body. I doubt very much she would crawl under there to kill herself."

"Maybe she was hiding, and then something went terribly wrong."

"Possibly, but I'll stand by my first impression for now: suffocation. Someone hid her body under the boat, and she died here."

Torsten laid a hand on Augustin's shoulder. "Come on, let's get going. We'll get all the information we need later. Let's try to solve this murder."

To Brundin, Torsten said, "Her father came? How did he react when he identified the body? Is he a suspect?"

"I doubt it, but I've been wrong before. I'm going to the lab to begin the autopsy."

Torsten and Augustin waved good-bye as Jan Brundin began instructing his team on how to prepare the crime scene and transport the young woman.

On the way back to the city, Augustin turned off the radio. They drove in dark silence. When they reached Scheelegatan, Augustin turned to Torsten. "I assume we're going to the station to start investigating this right away."

"Yep. Might as well. We'll have to get a report together before Olle faces the media vultures. They will have us for breakfast if we have nothing to show them. We won't trouble the family, however. I'm going to call the crisis team and ask them to tell the family we'll be over there by lunchtime tomorrow."

Their footsteps dragged as they headed into their office. Torsten rubbed his eyes with his thumbs and smoothed his hair back, massaging his head. The scent of the lily Augustin had put in the window was too strong. He had the urge to throw it out. Still, Augustin had placed it there out of the goodness of his heart. Torsten didn't want to insult him. He moved his chair a bit farther away and massaged his neck.

"Let's start by creating a timeline of the girl's life. Where did she go to school? Where did she live? Who were her friends? Did she have a jealous boyfriend or a stalker? Which one do you want to start looking into first?"

They divided the areas of inquiry and leaned forward to their computers. For the next few hours they stayed there preparing for interviews, occasionally reaching for the phone. By seven, Torsten tiredly lifted his head from his work to call Noah's cell phone.

"Hello, my boy, it's me, Pappa. I'm still at work. There's been a murder north of the city, a young girl. Have you found something to eat? Do you mind my staying here a few more hours? I don't think I'll be home before midnight."

Torsten glanced at Augustin.

"Noah was studying with a friend and didn't seem to miss me. I think they're having a good time."

"Sounds like a great kid. Just the fact he's studying without being nagged is proof of that."

"Yeah, though I have no idea where he gets it from. You practically had to force me to study at gunpoint, and as far as I know, his mother wasn't much better. But something good came out of our genes.

"So, why don't we put together what we've found into a timeline? But maybe we should get something to eat first. One of us should call Olle and give him a preliminary report. The journalists must be licking their chops already."

"You call Olle, and I'll run down and buy some food. What do you want?"

"Just a hamburger for me, thanks."

Augustin disappeared and Torsten punched in Olle's cell phone number.

"Hello. You've reached Olle Lundqvist's cell phone," said a female voice.

Torsten jumped. "Marianne? Is that you?"

Her voice was stiff and formal. "With whom am I speaking?"

"Torsten Ehn. Are you on call?"

Her voice softened and she laughed. "Yes, I am. Olle just called. He's still stuck in that meeting with the EU guys. I'll have to hold down the fort a little while longer."

"Are you here at the station?"

"Yes, and it's been busy. The phone hasn't stopped ringing. I finally released a press statement for Olle."

"What did it say?"

"That we can't release any information until the press conference early tomorrow morning."

"That's a good idea. It gives us a little more time. I was afraid he wanted to give one out this evening. Have you had any dinner? Augustin is out buying hamburgers. We could bring one to your office."

"That sounds good, but I'm on a diet right now."

"Nonsense," he said. "A diet? You've got to be kidding. We'll bring you something in fifteen minutes. And we'll need your help. We have a lot to sort through, especially if Olle wants something definite by nine tomorrow morning."

Torsten called Augustin right away to add to the order and tell him they'd meet at the entrance.

CHAPTER 60

Paula took a deep breath before turning the key in the ignition. Jens's return had made the girls very happy, and he hinted to her that they were obviously relieved because she'd failed to make them feel secure.

They endured dinner stiffly, artificially. Afterward, Paula felt forced to take two migraine pills. Since Jens had hardly seen the girls the past week, it was his turn to read to them and put them to bed. The girls knew how to read, but they insisted on the bedtime-story routine, so he would read them a chapter from whatever book they chose.

Paula loved that part of the day. Tears came to her eyes when she thought how a divorce would take away some of these moments. The idea of divorce had been whirling through her head all afternoon. She was somewhat shocked by her own thoughts. How did she jump to them so quickly? Had she been subconsciously debating the issue all the time?

Before bedtime, Paula told Jens that a Gothenburg friend had taken a quick trip to Stockholm and wanted to get together for a glass of wine. Paula saw Jens's relief at the thought of being alone. He told her she should get out more often. The girls gave her a slew of kisses before she left, saying she was the most beautiful Mamma in the world. They liked seeing her with her hair down.

Her car slowed through the traffic circle leading past Djursholm Square. All the shops were closed. Two police cars were parked near Café Gateau. Paula wished the police would do more than just park there, that they would actually patrol the place. But that would be asking too much, of course. At least they were making an appearance in the neighborhood.

She drove over Stocksund Bridge and looked out over the bay toward Lidingö. The sun had just set on this beautiful September evening. She reached for the radio, but then changed her mind and enjoyed the silence. Her body thrilled to the memory of her phone call. He'd called right after seeing her text message. Lotta had given her a strange look as she walked outside to talk. He asked if she could find an excuse to come over that evening. At first she'd laughed and explained it would be impossible, but he managed to convince her. She'd memorized his address and the entrance code for the main door: Värtavägen 148—the third floor, the first door to the left of the elevator. He explained he was subletting a studio with less square footage than her entryway. She told him about finding the cigarette butts inside her house and how frightened she was. He'd asked her bluntly why her husband wasn't taking her seriously and said that would be scary for anyone, even him.

She turned right by the Statoil gas station and drove into Lill-Jan Forest. She slowed to a stop at the crossing below the hill to let two horseback riders cross. A lone jogger took advantage of the moment to cross as well. Paula realized that this was the first day in a long time she'd missed her morning run. She'd followed the same routine for at least a year without a break, running even when she had a cold. Perhaps a day of rest was fine, after all.

She took Tegeluddsvägen past the ferries to Estonia. Some obviously tipsy women, about fifty years old, staggered along the sidewalk. One of them lost her shoe, and the rest laughed so hard they almost fell over. Paula couldn't help frowning at the scene. She parked in front of Värtavägen 18 and walked about ten feet from number 14. At the entrance, she took a deep breath to calm her racing heart. Then she pressed the door code and went in.

The stairwell could have matched any housing-project design from the seventies. The elevator door was heavy, and the elevator itself stank of cigarettes, despite the small metal sign forbidding smoking. The door opened on the third floor as she took out her cell phone. She thought about how she hadn't received those anonymous text messages for a while. Perhaps the terrorizing had come to an end. But the invasion of her house left a much worse impression. With her thumb, she put the cell phone on silent and locked it.

As the doorbell echoed and she heard steps coming close, she couldn't help smiling. A laugh bubbled up the moment the door opened. He smiled widely and pulled her close. She closed her eyes and melted into his embrace. At last she felt safe.

CHAPTER 61

Torsten and Augustin entered Marianne's office bearing food, papers, and their laptops. Marianne had Olle's cell phone to her ear, explaining to yet another journalist that she could say nothing more than that the victim was deceased and had just passed her twentieth birthday.

She hung up. "They'll call again. It was the fourth time Aftonbladet called. They don't get that they can't fool me just by putting a different journalist on the line each time. Wow, what a feast!"

Augustin had set the burgers and fries on a tray, and he handed them their sodas with straws. Marianne sighed at the thought of her new scale grumbling at the result. What was she supposed to do? She couldn't work the rest of the night on just a grilled chicken thigh for lunch and a boiled egg for breakfast. She was human after all. She decided to enjoy her hamburger. She couldn't remember the last time she'd had Coca-Cola. Then, she nodded at the stack of papers they'd brought in.

"What do you have for me?"

Torsten washed down a mouthful of food with some Coke.

"We haven't spoken yet with the girl's family, but we have updates from the crisis team over there now. We've also done quite a bit of research. There's nothing unusual. The girl's name is Ellen Nyhlén, born July 18th, 1990. Both parents raised her and her younger sister in Näsbypark. She graduated from Viktor Rydberg Gymnasium last spring, and she's been working at Café Gateau on Djursholm Square ever since. She'd just given notice and was planning to go to France for six months to study French and ski. She didn't have a boyfriend, or, at least, not one her friends knew. She was a responsible person; she partied at times but never let it get out of hand. The crisis team told us that her parents and her friends believe she had never tried drugs—which doesn't say much. What have you found out, Augustin?"

Augustin tapped some keys on his laptop and picked up a few sheets of paper. "According to her school, Ellen wasn't an outstanding student. She was seen as a good friend and had slightly above-average grades. The only thing unusual is that she started a demonstration a year ago. A guy in a neighboring school was going to be shipped back to Iraq with his family, and Ellen organized a successful protest to make sure he could stay. The boy and his family received permission to remain in the country. There's a newspaper article about it. Could this have upset someone? A neo-Nazi, perhaps? Other right-wing groups?"

Torsten's forehead wrinkled. "Possibly. We'll have to check on that. I'm sure someone's thought of it, though. I can see the headline now: Girl Slaughtered By Nazi. The only thing that makes that unlikely is that a Nazi would have killed her in a splashier way. Nazis are publicity hounds—perhaps they'd mark the body up. They'd be more likely to beat her up in a subway tunnel or something like that."

He sighed and stuffed a handful of fries into his mouth.

Marianne asked to read the papers they'd gathered. Augustin handed over his, which already had notes written on them. She put on her reading glasses and drank the last sip of Coke. While her stomach gurgled in protest, her eyes caught a sentence that she read aloud:

"'Ellen Nyhlén is a true revolutionary, and has always fought for the rights of the weak. This makes her a perfect candidate to be the Student Body President.' A revolutionary? Could she have been part of an organization or political party? Perhaps her parents didn't know about this? It sounds as if that protest group wasn't the only thing she was involved in. She could have annoyed quite a few people, especially conservatives. The only place with more Nazis than Skåne is Djursholm. My friend Chrisse used to live there, and she said when people meet for lunch, they talk openly about how much they hate immigrants. I would have thought educated people had more sense than to utter such embarrassing opinions in public."

Torsten agreed with her.

"Augustin, could you look into that? I'll find out more about her workplace. Just to be on the safe side, I'll find out more about her family, too. Even if they seem perfectly normal, some strange things have come out in other investigations. Oh, these are great burgers. I'm sorry, Marianne, that you're missing your gallery opening."

Marianne looked up surprised. "Gallery opening?"

"Weren't you going to the opening at Carlsdotter's on Skeppsholmen?" Augustin said. "I usually go there with my father. He knows the gallery owner."

"Lola is my best friend. I was going there this evening, but there will be other openings."

Marianne wondered who the young man's father could be. She didn't mention that she was meeting Lola for dinner the following evening. She didn't want it to seem like she was dropping names. The tradition Lola had was to go out for dinner the evening after an opening. Lola would invite the artist as well as a few close friends and colleagues. They would celebrate the opening and discuss the reviews, if there were any. Sometimes, if the reviews hadn't been good, the dinner guests were in the mood to argue. Once Lola had invited a famous newspaper critic. His review had been terrible, but the critic had the nerve to show up to the dinner anyway. The dinner turned into a fistfight before the hors d'oeuvres were even finished. Marianne valued the place she had in Lola's life and found events like this truly entertaining—probably because they were so unlike her usual daily routine.

Her eyes wandered over the reports, and she stopped at one of Augustin's notes.

"Augustin, you wrote here that perhaps she was trying to hide under the wooden boat, and then she was murdered. What do you mean by that?"

Augustin looked embarrassed. He waved toward the sheet of paper. "Oh, I was just jotting down an idea. Torsten thought it wasn't likely, but I wanted to be thorough."

Marianne shook her head. "It's not unlikely at all. That's something we ought to check. Perhaps she *was* trying to hide."

Torsten and Augustin glanced at her doubtfully, but she continued her train of thought. "Let's say she did have a boyfriend. Perhaps they decided to fool around, and the boat was a good hiding place."

Torsten smiled. "So you think that they could have both gone there willingly, and then the guy just happened to kill her?"

"Stranger things have happened. Sometimes young people have a difficult time with both parents at home keeping an eagle eye on them. They have to find secluded places to make out."

"You could be right," Augustin said. "We can try to find any young men she might have been dating."

Marianne took a French fry and pointed at the paper. "Definitely. Look for someone her age. Or a year or two older at the most."

Torsten stared into space, chewing on his pencil and thinking about what Marianne had said.

Olle's telephone rang again, and Marianne gave her stock answer. Then Olle called in to say he'd stop by at midnight to check on their results.

Torsten took out the trash and called Brundin, who answered at the first ring.

"Damn it, there's something not right about this," Brundin said. I can't put my finger on it, but it's different from any case I've ever dealt with."

"In what way?" Torsten asked.

Brundin sighed. "I thought I'd find more during the autopsy. There was nothing. She wasn't raped. She wasn't injured in any way. It is as if she suddenly just stopped breathing."

"But if you were to guess? Was the murderer male or female? Or could it be suicide?"

"Definitely not suicide. I would have found poison in her stomach—or elsewhere in her body. I'll take another look, but I really don't expect to find anything."

Torsten hung up, wrinkling his brow. He felt the same as Brundin. There was something odd about Ellen Nyhlén's death. He'd thought it had to do with her youth, which touched him deeply, but now . . .

When Torsten returned to Marianne's office, Augustin looked up. "What did Brundin have to say?"

Torsten shook his head. "Not much. I know this sounds far-fetched, but I'm getting the strange feeling that this death is connected to Turin's on Narvavägen."

Augustin stopped chewing. "Now I'm lost. Why should the two murders be connected?"

Marianne finished another phone call and said to Torsten, "Really? It's not common for two people to be murdered within a few days of each other. But it's not impossible. We should look at that long list of people who've been at Right Now and see if there's a connection. I'm sure many Djursholm residents have also gone there. There could very well be a link."

Torsten and Augustin looked at each other and nodded.

Marianne continued. "If you want, I could go through the lists myself. Then you can keep on with what you're doing."

Soon, all three were busy. Marianne still had to answer the phone every few minutes, and finally, at just past eleven p.m., Jan Brundin called. He'd finished his report. Torsten got up and put on his jacket.

"I'll head downstairs, but Augustin, you stay here. There's no reason for both of us to see such a sad sight."

Augustin nodded gratefully as Torsten walked to the elevator.

Marianne thought having their company was pleasant. She admitted to herself that she was slightly less afraid. It wasn't much fun to be alone in the middle of the night in an empty office, having to answer questions from journalists about a murder.

She smiled at Augustin.

"Why don't we have some coffee? And there's still some coffee cake in the cupboard. I was trying to soften up my colleagues this morning, but they didn't really appreciate it."

She shrugged. Augustin had to laugh. "Already that bad, is it?"

Marianne rolled her eyes. "That's just the half of it. But I have only myself to blame. I've popped up like a jack-in-the-box and stolen someone else's job."

"I understand. But you can soften me up with some coffee cake. And the coffee that goes with it."

"How nice. I think you and I are going to get along well."

She walked to the kitchen and started the coffeemaker. A sudden noise came from down the hall. It sounded like someone was trying to open a door by the bathrooms. She stepped quietly back to her office and whispered to Augustin: "I think there's someone in the bathroom. I heard a strange sound. Did you see anyone go in there?"

Augustin got up as quietly as he could and peered down the hallway.

"Were you alone up here when we got here?"

Marianne whispered, "Yes. The last person left right after six. I'll check with the security guard to see if he let someone in. Did you hear anything?"

Augustin shook his head but kept his eyes on the long dark hallway in front of him.

"I'll sneak up and check."

Suddenly there was a crash. The bathroom door flew open, and it sounded like a body fell out. Both Augustin and Marianne instinctively ran toward the noise. Then they heard someone retching. Augustin hit the light switch, and they saw Lillemor Rootander huddled on the hallway floor. She'd vomited quite a lot already. Her straggly hair covered her face, and her eyes were shut. The stench of vomit mixed with alcohol was overwhelming, and Marianne and Augustin flinched. Meanwhile, the elevator door opened and Torsten strode into the hallway.

"What the hell?" He looked shocked at the heap of human being before them. Marianne didn't know what to do. She felt sorry for this woman she'd hated for so many years. Anyone would be mortified to be found drunk and throwing up at work.

"I'm calling an ambulance," Marianne said. "She really must be seen by a doctor."

Torsten and Augustin agreed. Torsten bent over Lillemor and said gently, "Lillemor, can you hear me?"

There was no answer, just heavy, ragged breathing.

Torsten shook his head. "Jesus, I knew Lillemor liked the bars. But this . . . someone ought to call Olle as well."

Lillemor moved slightly, groaning, and turned her head toward them. "Not Olle . . . not Olle . . . please."

Her voice was weak, but she pleaded, "Please don't call Olle . . . please."

When Marianne returned from the telephone, she looked into Lillemor's devastated face and said softly, "I've called an ambulance. You have to see a doctor. I think you might have alcohol poisoning."

Lillemor Rootander closed her eyes and let her head fall back. The ambulance medics arrived quickly, as they'd been parked nearby, outside the jail. Lillemor was unconscious by the time they lifted her onto the stretcher. Marianne looked on worriedly as they began to take her away.

"Does one of us need to go along?"

"Any of you close relatives?" a medic asked.

"No, we're just work colleagues."

"It's better if you stay here. We'll contact her family."

Marianne opened her mouth to protest but quickly closed it again. It wasn't her responsibility to take care of this woman who'd been involved with her husband . . . yet she did feel that she had to do something.

"Take my number in case you don't reach anyone. I'm not sure she has a family," Marianne said.

The man nodded, and she hurried to find pen and paper.

"Where are you taking her?"

"To Karolinska Hospital. They're the only one with open beds tonight."

Torsten looked at Marianne as she returned to the office.

"How was she?"

"Passed out. I wonder how long she was in the bathroom."

Torsten shrugged. "I have no idea. I knew she liked her liquor, but I had no idea it was that bad. How well do you know The Root?"

Marianne looked away and shook her head. "We knew of each other, not more than that."

Torsten studied her, then decided to say nothing.

"I just feel extremely sorry for her," Marianne said.

Torsten said, "We still have to tell Olle about this. He *is* her boss. Keeping him in the dark wouldn't do her any favors. It's better if she's forced to confront her problem."

"That's probably true. But what drama! She must have been in there since this afternoon! I'll have to go take a look."

The bathroom was spattered with vomit and other fluids Marianne didn't want to think about. She found a pair of rubber gloves on a shelf and went to work. She felt like vomiting herself from the smell. From this mess all over the bathroom, she figured that Lillemor Rootander had drunk an incredible amount. It took Marianne forty minutes to clean the bathroom, and still there was a slight stench. She thought it should disappear by morning. She'd also found a bottle of Rosita behind the toilet. Marianne remembered seeing Lillemor Rootander on the bench in Kronoberg Park. Perhaps she was already tipsy by then.

Marianne's cell phone rang. She hurriedly stripped off the rubber gloves so she could answer.

"Marianne Jidhoff here."

"Darling! You're such a loyal worker! I must tell you that you've just missed *the* gallery opening of the decade! I missed you, and so did lots of other people . . . especially one person in particular! But since I am your very good friend, I will make sure you two have the chance to talk tomorrow!"

"I'm so sorry I missed it. It's been absolute chaos here. I'm happy the opening was a success."

"You *are* coming for dinner tomorrow, right? I will make that Olle Lundqvist regret it if he forces you to work tomorrow night, too!"

"I promise, I'll be there, but I've got to go right now."

"So you don't care who wanted to meet you?"

"Of course, but I'll let it be a surprise for tomorrow."

They hung up, and Marianne smiled slightly as she plopped down into her chair. Augustin was finishing a phone call in the hallway. Torsten put his hands together and rubbed the bridge of his nose with his thumbs.

"I just thought I'd quickly go through Brundin's report with you, and then we can summarize what we have."

Marianne said, "Sure. I'm just going to get some more coffee. Does anyone else want a cup?"

The other two smiled gratefully. Marianne was soon back with three cups along with a plate of cookies.

Torsten yawned and rolled his shoulders. "Thank God for coffee. Am I the only one here who's tired? I feel like I've been hit by a truck. I guess I shouldn't complain. Unfortunately, Brundin found nothing of interest. The girl died. That's all he has. Someone suffocated her by holding a hand over her nose and mouth. Perhaps using a cloth— maybe a piece of clothing—though no fibers were found except those from her sweater. No fingerprints. All Brundin found at the site were bicycle-tire marks, and unfortunately, it wasn't an unusual bike—just a standard model. Nine out of ten Swedes have it. There are no signs of resistance, which, to Brundin, indicates that the attack was a surprise. There were many footprints around the boat, but that's a well-used path along the waterfront. Brundin says there's nothing more he can find. So we have nothing."

Marianne said, "Except for the fact that she didn't resist. That is a big clue. I believe it shows she trusted this person, either because he seemed trustworthy or she knew him."

Torsten said, "Yes, that would point to her father, or a boyfriend no one knew about. What have you found, Augustin?"

"Not much. As far as her work on the Iraqi boy's asylum issues, I see nothing to indicate anyone was upset. I think nobody took her seriously, not even when the deportation was annulled. People seem to think the only reason she got media attention was because she was young and attractive."

Torsten raised an eyebrow. "And that isn't deemed worthy of respect?"

Augustin shrugged. "I really wouldn't know, but at any rate, she had no enemies to speak of. I dug and dug, but there's nothing. No threats to her of any kind."

To Marianne, Torsten said, "How about your lists? Anything useful?"

"Yes. I've gone through them all. I've cross-referenced them and seen who changed addresses and so on. Eight people living in Danderyd township, which is where Djursholm is located, have also attended Right Now courses. Four of them are married. I see no direct connection to Ellen Nyhlén, but that will be up to you to find out. Many of these people are wealthy and famous. I can understand why the Right Now people didn't want to give you participants' names. It's explosive stuff if it gets leaked to the media. I also have the information you wanted about the founders of Right Now, but I think we can wait on that. I assume Ellen Nyhlén's case is a higher priority."

Torsten sighed.

"Most likely. Still, I want to see that information as soon as possible. Perhaps after tomorrow morning's press conference. I need to head home, now. Noah is alone, and I am exhausted. Augustin, I suggest we meet at eight—before the press conference. We can go through all this material again before Olle has to speak, and perhaps something more will turn up during the night. The local police from Danderyd township are combing the neighborhood. They might find something, though I doubt it. Something tells me this devil knows how to keep under the radar. Marianne, I assume you'll stay here until Olle arrives? See you tomorrow, then. Aside from all this, I hope The Root realizes that you literally cleaned up after her, and she has enough manners to thank you. Will you be all right alone?"

"I'll be fine," Marianne said, smiling. "Olle will be here any minute. I also have the feeling that not much more is happening tonight. Go home. You need your rest. You're going to be working hard tomorrow."

Once they'd gone, Marianne looked at the clock. It was just before midnight. She picked up her phone and asked to be connected to the emergency room at Karolinska Hospital.

"I'm calling about Lillemor Rootander. She came by ambulance an hour or so ago."

"Are you a relative?" a voice answered.

Marianne hesitated a moment, then said, "I'm a close colleague from work. I was the one who found her."

"One moment. I'll connect you to the ICU. She's under observation."

A few moments later, someone at the ICU picked up. "Nurse Lena here."

"Hello, I'm Marianne Jidhoff. I'm calling about Lillemor Rootander."

"One minute. I'll take a look at her chart."

Nurse Lena came back after a minute or two. "Lillemor Rootander has informed us that she has no family, and she doesn't wish to have any contact with people from her workplace."

"I just wanted to know if she's going to be all right. I'm the one who found her this evening."

"Lillemor will contact you when she is released. I must care for a patient, now. Please excuse me."

Marianne frowned as she put down the phone. She knew she ought to discuss what had happened with Olle, but all she could remember was Lillemor's desperate look when begging them to leave Olle out of it.

She stared into space for a while, finally deciding to work on the material she'd promised Torsten. She went through all the information Gunnar had sent and made her own notes, hoping Torsten would be able to read her scrawls. On the computer, she added the addresses of the Right Now participants and put everything in a private folder, which she hid inside another folder. She carefully deleted the irrelevant data on her computer. Then, an idea struck her. She could plant some red herrings to see where they turned up. She might discover who'd been poking around in her office. She already had a good idea who it might be: it was probably no coincidence that Lillemor Rootander had been hiding in the bathroom.

She inserted random documents into a prominently visible computer file and gave it the title CONFIDENTIAL, with today's date. She almost giggled over her own cleverness. She hoped it wouldn't be too obvious that she'd set a trap.

She heard the hum of the elevator, and a few moments later, Olle came rushing in.

"Forgive me, Marianne. How have you been holding up? I heard that Torsten and Augustin kept you company. Can you brief me on where the case stands now?"

Marianne took out her notes, and she and Olle went through them for almost two hours. Marianne noticed that Olle smelled of sweat, just a bit. She hoped she, herself, didn't smell too bad. They each poured a cup of coffee and continued to prepare the release for the press conference. Olle had changed the time of the conference to seven a.m. since he didn't want to keep the journalists waiting for too long. Without facts, they'd start inventing things to write about. Better to release what they had now. Perhaps it would prompt a witness to come forward with more information.

The telephones started ringing almost as soon as Olle entered the building, and Marianne suspected that many journalists had camped out in the reception area just waiting for him to appear. Nearly an hour passed before they stopped calling. Olle finally took off his jacket and undid his tie.

"I am eternally grateful that you've come back to work. You can't imagine how much I missed working in a partnership like this."

"But why don't you have more assistants?"

"I do, but I can't call them in the middle of the night, and they don't have your knowledge. They have no idea how to talk to the press, and no clue how to keep information to themselves. That's a profession in and of itself."

"And your press secretary?"

"I use her only when we're further along in a case. In the beginning, everything must come from me. I know how much Hans valued having you at his side."

"That was the only good thing about us. We worked well together."

"You're underestimating yourself. I know he loved you very much," Olle replied.

Marianne looked at Olle seriously. "I imagine that he did, in his own way. But he cared much more for his work. Of course, he loved our children. But I believe that if he'd had to choose between me and his job, the job would have won out."

Olle blinked. "Hans always said he wanted to change. That was his mantra. He was very sad at times. I don't believe he would have risen as far as he did without making some sacrifices."

Marianne swallowed. She knew there was a hard gleam in her eye as she said, "Would you sacrifice your own children?"

Olle jerked. "Actually, sometimes I do just that. Tonight, for example. A murderer is on the loose and someone has to make sure he is caught before he kills again. I do this for the sake of my children, as well as society. Sacrifices have to be made. I'm probably no better than Hans. I'd never be able to do this work without my wife's help."

"And do you have other women on the side?"

Olle looked down at the desk, then back at Marianne. "I know Hans hurt you. I know he promised again and again that he'd change and that this affair would be the last. He was weak—and not just concerning women. But despite all of that, I know he loved you—and the children."

Marianne gave Olle a firm look. "How do you grieve for someone when you're angry at them, too? It is terrible."

"I understand."

They fell silent, and Olle's cell phone rang. As he headed into the hallway to answer, Marianne watched his bulky silhouette in the darkness. She realized he hadn't answered her question.

CHAPTER 62

Paula looked at Passi's profile on the balcony, and she sighed over the contoured muscles of his upper body. The glow from his cigarette shone on his face every time he took a drag. Paula pulled the synthetic blanket closer to her body and closed her eyes. The cool autumn air coming in through the open balcony door made her shiver. He smiled as he came back into the room, closing the door behind him. He threw himself on the bed.

"Can't you stay?" he urged. "You could say you're spending the night with your girlfriend."

Paula looked at him, then kissed the top of his strong nose.

"I don't want to go home, but my girls might start to wonder about me."

He stroked her hair and pulled her closer. Paula reached for her cell phone. She tapped in a text message:

Went later than I thought. Lots to talk about. Staying at Anna's hotel for the night. Get the girls to school tomorrow morning. Tell them I'll pick them up from gymnastics. Sleep well. /P

She drew a deep breath and felt her heart beat strongly. Quickly, so she wouldn't change her mind, she sent the message. She instantly regretted it. She threw her head back on the pillow and exhaled through her teeth. Her cell phone blinked. Jens had already sent a reply.

The girls went to sleep at 9:30. Asked when you'd be coming home. I'll take them to school. I'd appreciate it if you went grocery shopping. There's no food in the house. Please take my car in for service tomorrow morning, too. One of the headlights is loose. Make sure it's ready by Friday.

Paula exhaled again and showed the message to Passi. He read it and shook his head. "Is he always like that? Giving you orders?"

Paula shrugged. "I don't even notice anymore. Perhaps I'd be like him if I went out to work all the time and he was home with the children. I'm just one of many he delegates his work to."

"But you are his *wife*! That's sick. You know he doesn't appreciate you."

Paula curled up next to him, laying her head on his chest. "At least I can stay here tonight. If I may."

"Of course! I don't want to let you go! And say, are you hungry? I haven't had dinner yet."

"You poor thing. I had a bite to eat before I left home."

"I'll make some pasta."

"You know how to cook?" she asked.

Passi laughed. "Why not? Doesn't your husband cook?"

Paula shook her head. "Not often. When he does, it's only refined food."

Passi laughed again. "I like cooking. We always cooked in my family. But my family isn't Swedish. Maybe that's why."

Paula pretended to look insulted. "So you think we Swedes can't cook?"

"Well, your people can't make food as well as we can. And you don't cook as often, either. All we Chileans do is eat and talk about food. We're worse than the Italians."

Passi got out of bed, and Paula couldn't help admiring his body. She felt ashamed. She was just like all the middle-aged men looking for younger women. Here she was, a sex-starved housewife of forty, lusting after this young male body. What was the difference between her and those men?

Passi took a number of items from the refrigerator, and after fifteen minutes, a wonderful aroma wafted out from the kitchen. Passi lit two candles in their candlesticks. He then put down silverware.

"You have to excuse the fact I don't have a dinner table. I usually eat in front of the television. I hope you don't mind."

"Of course I don't mind!"

A few minutes later, Paula was curled up on the IKEA sofa, wrapped in a bright-red throw, and eating pasta with tomato sauce and mozzarella.

"This is delicious!"

It's my specialty," he said.

Paula smiled and raised an eyebrow. "So this is what you offer all your girlfriends?"

Passi gave her a serious look. "I've never had a woman in my apartment before."

Paula blinked. She stopped in the middle of lifting her fork to her mouth. She believed he was telling the truth. He felt just as strong an attraction to her as she did for him! Still, it all seemed impossible. Maybe because it *was* impossible.

Paula finished her dinner and tried to remember how long it had been since she'd eaten something with so many carbs. As Passi did the dishes, Paula went to the bathroom, fighting her way past a large mountain bike to get there.

CHAPTER 63

This press conference was more chaotic than the ones Marianne remembered from the past. Hans was always in his element speaking at one, but he'd end up like a wrung-out dishcloth when it was over. Olle didn't look much better when he came back to Marianne's office.

Marianne had a metallic taste in her mouth. She wished she could go have breakfast. For the past hour, she'd been dreaming of the freshly baked cinnamon buns at the corner café, but she hadn't had even a few minutes to go get some. Olle gave her a tired grin.

"Everything went fine, thanks to you. Good preparation is the key. Now I have to find Torsten and go through everything with him. Then I'll go home and sleep for a few hours. I'm scheduled for court all afternoon."

A voice came from the hallway.

"What about Marianne? How much has she slept?"

An energetic Alexandra Baranski poked her head through the door. She looked accusingly at Olle. "I've heard she's been up all night. If I were her boss, I'd order her to take the rest of the day off and not come back until tomorrow afternoon."

Olle's smile was tinged with exhaustion. "Yes, I was getting to that. Marianne, thank you. It's time for you to go home. As Alexandra said, I don't want to see hide nor hair of you until tomorrow after lunch. You need a good night's sleep. It's more than likely you'll have to be on call tomorrow night again."

"You're fine if I leave?"

Olle nodded. "I need you rested and full of energy tomorrow. Go home and sleep now."

Alexandra nodded. "I notice you also finished quite a bit of work on other assignments during the night. I didn't expect my stuff back until next week. Go sleep in good conscience!"

Marianne packed up her things and set up her computer as she'd planned during the night. It would be easier to simply change her password, but she thought it would be more interesting to see if the spy fell into her trap. She shivered a little as she struggled into her coat. Lying awake at night as she'd done so often during Hans's illness had been exhausting, but working all night had brought a different kind of tiredness. She felt dizzy. She drank a full glass of water, expecting her body to be screaming for fluids after all the coffee during the night. With her purse strap over her shoulder and her cell phone in her pocket, she headed past the bathroom. There was no indication of last night's events; she smelled nothing more than cleanser. Marianne pressed the elevator button, wondering if she'd done the right thing not telling Olle about Lillemor Rootander. She'd called Torsten Ehn, who was wide awake, and asked if he could keep quiet about it. He told her he respected her decision and that he'd call after talking to the young woman's family.

On the street, the usual rush hour traffic was under way. She breathed in the morning air and decided to walk home. Surprised at her decision, her feet seemed to move with a will all their own. She enjoyed the exercise after having been bent over paperwork almost the entire night. She passed the Klaraberg Viaduct and looked out over Sergel Square. The sun was starting to rise behind The House of Culture. The air was clear and cool, and she suspected that there might have been frost during the night. Her footsteps became lighter as she walked down Hamngatan. She smiled at NK's display windows showing Nordic fashion designs. She wondered if Sigrid had seen them yet.

Norrmalm Square was being renovated, and she hurried past the noise of bulldozers and jackhammers. She looked into Richie restaurant, where two men in white uniforms were busy cleaning. They'd soon set the tables for the lunch rush. The former Smålandsgatan, which had been rechristened Ingmar Bergmans Gata, smelled: it appeared to have been used as a toilet by people walking out of bars the evening before. Nybrogatan was much more pleasant. Marianne appreciated that it was now a pedestrian walkway. In her opinion, more of the old streets in the innermost part of the city should be turned into pedestrian streets.

Soon she found herself on Riddargatan, and she walked past the Army Museum just as the Hedvig Eleonora Church bells chimed nine. She headed up the hill toward Skeppargatan and peeked into the Riddar Bakery, thinking about whether to stop for a sandwich. The line was long, and she had to admit that her appetite was gone. She decided to just drink another glass of water once she got home and lie down. Drinking water was certainly a good way to lose weight.

She followed Riddargatan all the way to Banérgatan. She hesitated a moment and then went into the Ica Banér grocery store. She quickly found a carton of eggs, a grilled chicken, a package of green beans, and a huge piece of ox fillet.

Tired, but pleased that she'd walked home, she staggered into her apartment and kicked off her shoes. She called Sigrid and told her daughter's answering machine about the night's dramatic events. Then she headed into the kitchen and put away the groceries. She called Nina, who sounded tense.

"I'm just about to head out the door. We're going to the archipelago. Robert and I decided to take a few days off."

"How wonderful. You certainly deserve it."

"How was work?"

"Well, it's a bit of a shock working with all sorts of people instead of being alone all day."

"Do you think you made the right decision to return?"

"We'll have to see. I hope so," she replied.

"What do you think Pappa would have thought? Would he have wanted you to go back?"

Marianne noticed tension creep into her body. She went on the defensive.

"What do you mean by that?"

"Well? Did he give you any advice?"

"About how I was supposed to live my life after he died? No, he did not."

"I didn't mean it like that. I mean he always thought you were good at your job."

"I don't know. If he had to choose, he probably would have told me to retire. He always preferred that I stay out of his world."

"Maybe he just wanted to protect you?"

Marianne wondered if Nina really understood what she'd just said. She forced herself to bite her tongue. Nina knew nothing about Hans's last moments or about the lies that had darkened their marriage. Marianne had been extremely careful to hide all the dirty laundry. She had asked Peder to keep Hans's last words to himself, and as far as she knew, he hadn't mentioned it to Nina. Marianne had never asked her children how much they knew about her marriage, and she had no intention of doing so now. She felt ashamed of her own part in the charade: not that she'd been lied to and rejected by her husband, but because she saw herself as a bad role model. What kind of mother was she not to stand up for herself and leave a bad marriage? Letting herself be the martyr was just as bad as her husband's affairs. She didn't want to pass this on to the next generation.

Nina cleared her throat and said, "I have to go. Robert's honking the horn. I can call later if you'd like."

"No, sweetie, you don't have to do that. Enjoy your vacation and call me when you get back. Sigrid's here if I need anything. Take good care of yourself, and say hello to Robert."

"Thanks. Bye. Oh, Mamma . . ."

"Yes?"

"I love you."

"I love you, too. Sorry if I sounded upset. I haven't slept all night. Bye, now."

They hung up and, as usual, Marianne had to fight the unhappy feeling that things always seemed to go wrong between her and her firstborn daughter. She accepted the blame. She just felt that Nina always put her under a microscope. Not that Nina didn't have the right to criticize her—that was part of a mother-daughter relationship. Marianne should be able to handle it. But she seldom could, and she hated herself for it. Her eyes were too tired to fill with tears, and she stifled a sob in her chest. She hoped Nina knew that she loved her. She quickly visited the bathroom to brush her teeth. Then she fell into bed. Thank goodness her curtains blocked the sunlight.

Finallly, she fumbled for her cell phone, turning it off.

Chapter 64

He watched the man pack the children into the car. The man was yelling at the youngest girl, and she seemed downcast. As he got behind the steering wheel, he slapped it with both hands, then got out and ran back to the house. He threw open the door and strode inside. The man had probably forgotten his cell phone. When he slid back behind the wheel, he hit the gas so hard that the wheels of his silver Porsche smoked, reversing full speed onto the gravel road.

He watched the girls in the backseat, holding their backpacks. They looked sad.

His footsteps were silent as he walked to the front door, and then he stood still for a few minutes to make sure no one had seen him arrive. He had the key to the door in his pocket. He'd made a copy of it at the Mörby shopping mall. The cleaning lady had left it on the hallway dresser.

He put the key into the lock, pressed down the door handle, and opened the door. He listened for the familiar sound of the shower upstairs, but all he heard was silence. He sneaked into the kitchen to look around.

A teacup was on the counter. He touched its edge with his fingertip and then bent over to sniff the tea. A half-eaten ham sandwich was on a napkin next to the teacup. He looked at it with interest, then picked it up and took a bite. Silently, he drank a large sip of tea. It was sweetened with honey and reminded him of his grandmother. The cup clattered more than he'd intended as he set it down. He looked up toward the second floor, but there was no sound up there. He suspected that she wasn't home. But he didn't dare go upstairs to make sure: perhaps she was just sleeping in. He wouldn't want to disturb her. She'd need her sleep for what was to come.

He sneaked back to the entryway and closed the front door behind him. The husband, as usual, had forgotten to set the alarm. This gave him more freedom to come and go during the day. He pulled his bicycle from the thicket and looked around to make sure nobody saw him riding away.

CHAPTER 65

Marianne didn't remember falling asleep, but she woke up confused—and enormously hungry. Her clock showed she'd slept just over four hours, and she decided she'd have to be content with that. She sat up on the edge of the bed and rolled her shoulders. Fortunately, they no longer felt so sore. When she pulled up the shades, the sun shone directly on her face. She blinked as she opened the window. She liked a little bit of street noise. Her dinner with Lola would be at seven o'clock, so she had plenty of time to get ready. Her cell phone showed five missed calls, four of them from Torsten Ehn. The fifth showed a number she didn't recognize, so she called that one back first. A weak voice answered on the third ring.

"Lillemor here."

Marianne gasped and swallowed hard before saying, "It's Marianne."

She didn't receive a reply. "How are you doing?" she asked.

Lillemor made a strangled sound. "Sorry, not too good."

Both women fell silent, and Marianne held her tongue so she wouldn't start chattering out of sheer nervousness. That was not her role in this conversation.

"I'm very sorry for what happened yesterday. I . . . I don't know what got into me."

Marianne couldn't hold back. "Perhaps it was something you ate?"

"Yes, a bad shrimp, right?"

They both chuckled a little. Marianne said, "I want you to know I didn't mention it to Olle."

She wondered whether Lillemor realized that Torsten Ehn and Augustin Madrid had also witnessed the event. She figured Lillemor probably didn't remember that they'd been present.

"Thanks. Yes, in my medical report, you were the one who called for an ambulance."

"Are you still at the hospital?"

"No, they let me go home. I'll be on sick leave for a while."

"I see." Marianne realized her tone sounded snotty, so she hurried to say, "That's probably a good idea. I was actually worried about you."

"Yes, that must not have been a pretty sight. Well . . . that's all I wanted to say. Thank you for your help."

"Don't worry," Marianne said. "Call me if you need anything else."

"I will," Lillemor replied.

After they hung up. Marianne wondered how Lillemor would find help for her problem. Would she attend a program for alcoholics or go to rehab? Well, it wasn't any of her business. Her thoughts were still darting around in her head when she called Torsten Ehn. He picked up on the first ring.

"Ehn, here."

"Yes, Marianne Jidhoff."

"Oh, damn. I'm sorry I called so often. I didn't realize you'd gone home to get some sleep. I've called Olle a few times, too."

"Don't worry. I had my phone on silent."

"I can't believe you worked all night. I'm impressed! I couldn't hold out past midnight. Well, we've got more information, and I was hoping we could go through it all."

Marianne wrinkled her brow, smiling at the same time.

"I didn't intend to come in to the station today. I assumed you and Augustin could manage on your own."

"We probably could, but I want your input."

Marianne laughed. "Well, you'll have to come here. Buy some coffee cake on the way over. I don't have anything to serve you."

"We'll be there in an hour."

Marianne shook her head and then charged her cell phone. Out in the kitchen, she turned on the coffee machine. She started to boil water, and when the water was ready she put two eggs into the pot. After five minutes, she reverently ate the eggs with a teaspoon of caviar on top. She didn't realize how heavenly two eggs could taste. So simple and so good! Her coffee was just as delightful, and she relished the sensation of the warm liquid going down her throat. She realized she needed a shower, which would not only warm her shivering body, but was a high priority in case her body smelled.

She turned the water on as hot as possible and soaped herself up twice to make sure she was clean. She even rubbed body wash between her toes. As she toweled off, she remembered the new scale. She took it out even though she'd decided not to look at her weight until finishing her diet. She stepped on and off a few times to make sure she'd read the numbers right. The scale reported she'd lost four pounds. How could that have happened? She'd just had breakfast, not to mention the hamburger the night before. Happy as a puppy, she returned the scale to the cupboard and looked at her naked body in front of the mirror. Four pounds were gone. It was a miracle. She didn't look all that different, but her stomach appeared a little less bloated, and she did seem to have more energy. Her face wasn't as droopy as it had been, either. Perhaps that was due to her new hair color. Her blowout still looked good, despite having been slept on.

She chose a gray skirt and a dark-lilac cashmere sweater, both of which Sigrid had given to her, complaining they no longer fit her. Marianne didn't believe that for a minute; she knew that Sigrid just wanted her to have a few nice pieces of clothing. She had to admit that the sweater looked good on her.

As usual, her nylons got twisted when she tried to put them on, and she had to start over. Instead of putting on her slippers, she found a pair of natural leather loafers she hadn't worn since the previous summer. Perhaps it was high time she returned to dressing properly, even at home. No reason to look like a schlump. She unpacked her computer, and when she logged into her e-mail, she couldn't help smiling. Someone had logged into her mail program earlier and read her incoming messages. Since she had set it up to divert any sensitive mail before landing in her inbox, no valuable information was compromised. It would be interesting to find out who was behind this.

The doorbell rang and she hurried to answer it. Torsten Ehn and Augustin Madrid stood at attention, and she let out a chuckle.

"Well, you're right on time, you two. It looks like you brought something interesting with you."

Torsten smiled and waved a paper bag. "You can say so. Cinnamon buns."

They came in, and Augustin looked around with curiosity. "What a beautiful apartment! How long have you lived here?"

"Since I was born. This is my childhood home. My mother grew up in this building, and I inherited it when she died."

Torsten exclaimed, "You own this entire building?"

Marianne laughed. "Well, I did. Now I share it with my children. I do have some renters in some of the apartments as well."

"I can understand that. Well. I never would have guessed."

"Guessed what?"

"That you were independently wealthy. You don't seem the type."

They laughed. Torsten looked around while Augustin pulled out his laptop. He asked where they should sit, and Marianne pointed to the living room. "We have sofas in the living room. We could also go into my library, where I have a dining table and we could spread out our paperwork. Perhaps that would be better? Would you like something to drink? Coffee? Tea?"

Marianne walked quickly into the library and shivered. She opened the tile stove to throw in some logs from the basket beside it.

"It gets so cold in here. I have no idea why. It doesn't matter whether it's summer or winter. I'll start a fire, and soon it will be much more pleasant. Go ahead and sit at the table, and I'll go heat some water."

Augustin put his computer on the table and smiled at her. "I'll have coffee, thanks."

Torsten followed her into the kitchen. He placed the paper bag on the kitchen table, watching Marianne as she took cups from the upper cupboard and set out napkins for the cinnamon buns. She looked at him out of the corner of her eye. "What's wrong? You're looking at me so suspiciously."

Torsten shook his head as he opened the pantry door. He looked at all the items she stored inside. "Not suspicious at all. I just think it's fascinating."

"What is fascinating?"

"That you ever married Hans Larson. I can't put it together. You enjoy your food and seem to enjoy life. In my eyes, Hans Larson was a sour old man who only thought about himself. A full-time egoist, however you look at it. Did he even like to eat?"

Torsten made such a face that Marianne had to laugh. "You're bad!"

"But Marianne, I can't imagine him in this place. In your life. He couldn't have felt at home in this elegant apartment. That man couldn't even dress properly. All his suits were ill-fitting, and that's being kind. They were even worse than Olle's, if that's possible. And you. You are always put together. You seem to enjoy the good things in life."

"How did you come to that conclusion?"

"I just glanced through your pantry. The different olive oils, the balsamic vinegar, the spices from around the world. You use imported jams and jellies—and I see that you grow your own herbs on the windowsill. Hans Larson was just an everyday sausage-in-a-cafeteria kind of guy. Nothing wrong with that. But you're something else. You don't have to say anything. I see you know what I mean. How the hell did he manage to land you?"

Marianne smiled, pouring coffee into three cups.

Augustin looked up when they came in, happy to see the coffee.

Torsten had already finished one of his cinnamon buns and was looking at the plate, wondering if he should take another. Marianne sat down at the head of the table. She looked with great interest at the papers, and Augustin moved in her direction.

"So what happened in Djursholm? What did you find out?"

Having finished his internal debate, Torsten took a healthy bite from his second bun and was too busy chewing to reply. Augustin spoke instead.

"We met Ellen Nyhlén's family. Her parents were devastated. It was hard to communicate with them. Her little sister seemed to be in shock. We think they'd been given sedatives, and that must have influenced how they reacted to us. We have no indication that any of them were part of the murder. The parents seem to have devoted their lives to their daughters."

Marianne shuddered. "How horrible. What about a boyfriend, or an admirer?"

Torsten took a long sip of coffee, which went down the wrong way. He coughed for a few seconds. Then he picked up from where Augustin left off.

"We haven't found any. The little sister had a boyfriend, but Ellen did not. And, yes, we did check into the little sister's boyfriend. He studies in Gothenburg, and we found through our channels that he was there at the time of the murder. Ellen's work is a bit complicated. Her boss was bullheaded and sometimes didn't pay his employees for weeks. Ellen decided the staff all needed to join a union, and he didn't like that."

Marianne smiled, impressed at their work. "She sounds like a special girl. Have you met with the boss?"

"He's extremely upset about what happened. And although Ellen fought him about the union, she was one of his best workers. He found her the most responsible of all the girls working there. He depended on her. Today the place was closed, and we've talked to all of them but one. We're going to meet her later today. All the girls were extremely upset."

Marianne's brow furrowed. "There must have been lots of people going to that café every day."

Augustin said, "The girls told us that customers often ask them out. Young guys, because there are a number of schools nearby, as well as married men who want a little whoopee on the side."

Torsten snorted. "Whoopee? Where'd you pick that up? And you tell me *I* use old-fashioned slang!"

Augustin glared at him, then turned to Marianne. "There could be something there. A married man who wanted some side action and then thought he'd gotten in too deep."

Marianne looked at him doubtfully. "It seems odd. She was so young. I have difficulty believing she'd be a demanding lover. And what would she want with a married man? In her eyes, he'd be, well, *old*. I don't think she's the kind of girl who'd be seduced by roses or small presents. But perhaps I'm being naive?"

Torsten shook his head. "I think you're right, Marianne. Ellen Nyhlén wasn't that type. Still, we should definitely check into the customers. I also want to check what we've found out about Christopher Turin and Right Now. This afternoon, we're going out to talk to the last girl on our list from the café, and we'll also stop by some of those addresses of the Right Now participants in Djursholm. It may be a long shot, but it's worth a try. I also think we need to visit Erik Bergström and Christina Filipsson again. Their business adventures have been extremely interesting. Erik Bergström, as it turns out, sold his advertising business in a sneaky way, not aboveboard at all, while he was divorcing. He certainly didn't want to go into detail about it when we had our little chat. His ex-wife reported the shady dealings, which broke a few legal precepts. Christina Filipsson may be working legally now, but she hasn't always. There have been many legal twists and turns because of her various debts, although most of them are from twenty years ago. Still, it shows that she wasn't always careful with money. Also of interest, she has another small business on the side. I wonder if Ushtanga Erik is aware of it. Her website shows she has customers from the finance and advertising worlds. I wonder what she helps them with? She calls it 'lifestyle coaching,' but hell if I know what that is."

Marianne said, "Personally, I think that the *Estonia* story is just that. A story. It would be interesting to track that one down."

"You think they're not telling the truth?"

"I don't know, but it seems too much of a miracle to me. And wouldn't we have read about an incident like that in the papers? I've read about various heroes who helped save people, but I don't remember reading anything about those two. Wouldn't people remember them?"

Torsten said, "Yes, and even if the story is true, it's in bad taste to boast about how he survived. It's not proper. I think we'll also want to call in Isa Turin again to find out more about their custody battle. We might as well bring in Jonas Carlfors, too. We'll find two more officers to help us with the interrogations. I'll check around. And . . . am I completely out of line if I take a third bun?"

Augustin shook his head and sighed. "Yes, you are."

Torsten shrugged and grabbed it anyway. He sighed contentedly and took a big bite. Marianne looked through the papers and then her finger stopped.

"Do you have more information about the car used to drive over Turin?"

Torsten shook his head.

"Brundin couldn't tell us more than that it was a smaller vehicle, due to the damage on Turin's shins when he was first hit. So it's not a jeep or an SUV. Brundin looked for evidence at the scene, but he didn't find anything specific. Hit-and-runs are hard to solve, even if we know the driver intended to commit murder. It's a damned shame, but in both cases, we don't have any evidence to follow up on. That makes me think that the two cases are linked. The person who drove over Christopher Turin and suffocated Ellen Nyhlén knew exactly what he was doing. He must have studied up on the best way to kill someone without leaving any evidence. But on the other hand, it could be an unfortunate coincidence."

Augustin looked skeptical, "I have trouble seeing a connection. The methods were completely different. Running over someone and suffocating a person aren't similar actions at all."

"I agree that in theory, there should be no connection," Torsten said. "But we'd better leave now if we want to interview everyone. Marianne, is it all right to call you later this afternoon to keep you in the loop?"

"Of course. But get in touch with Olle for any real emergency. He's on call tonight. Make sure he doesn't feel left out."

Torsten nodded, patting her on the shoulder. "Don't worry. We won't bother you on your night off."

Marianne felt sure that she was blushing, and she hoped no one would notice it in the soft light of the library. For some reason she felt found out, even though she hadn't mentioned her dinner plans.

Marianne locked the door behind them and went back to the library. As she picked up the serving tray, she couldn't help smiling. She hated to admit it, but she liked feeling needed. She liked it very much indeed.

CHAPTER 66

Passi closed his eyes. His breathing was deeper, quicker, and Paula moved slowly so it wouldn't go too quickly. She touched herself at the same time. Jens had never liked it when she did that, but Passi didn't mind. He watched her fingers in fascination. She was tender from the activity of the past few hours, and her tenderness made her more excited. She felt everything in a beautiful, more intense way.

Passi pulled her closer and enclosed her breast in his mouth, grunting when her nipple hardened. Paula knew this would make her come before he did, but she let it happen. Passi continued to move, slowly and carefully. His penis was slippery from her wetness. He pulled up her knees and slid his fingers into her as well. Paula lay still and let him penetrate her so completely. She was amazed that he had such control over his lust. Much more than she did.

Afterward, they stood together in the tight shower stall. Holding him close, she whispered, "When you were away earlier, I had no idea how I'd get through the day."

He smiled and kissed the tip of her nose. "I just needed some groceries."

She closed her eyes and shivered. "It will be difficult to be alone tonight."

"I understand," Passi said. "Did the police say anything about patrolling the area?"

"They said they'd drive by regularly, but what good does that do?" Paula said. "Jens called the police and told them I was overreacting."

"If you want, I can call someone I know—maybe he can help."

Paula reacted with fear. "What? Not to kill anybody!"

Passi laughed. "No! What do you think? I know someone who works with these kinds of incidents. If you want me to, I can ask for his opinion."

"Perhaps. Let's wait and see. Maybe it will stop. Those awful text messages stopped."

Passi nodded. "Things will calm down. You'll see. Maybe it was just some crazy dude who wanted to see you naked. I can't really blame him . . ."

Paula pinched his middle and smiled. "Females are probably stalking you all the time!"

They kissed.

Paula knew she should have already left for home by now. She'd have to drive like a maniac to get to the girls on time. She hadn't taken Jens's car to the shop, as she'd promised. Nor had she picked up any groceries. She'd just have to order pizza for dinner.

CHAPTER 67

Torsten's cell phone rang just as Augustin parked outside the tiny house.

"Hi, my boy!" Torsten said. "Sure, when should I pick you up? . . . Okay, I'll be there."

Torsten stepped out of the car. "We have to wrap it up by eight. I promised Noah I'd pick him up from school at eight thirty. Per and Anki are scheduled to help with the interrogations tomorrow morning, so we can tear through them all before lunch. We need to speed it up a bit. Olle starts to get jumpy—everything is on his shoulders."

"I'm impressed that you still make time for family, even with a case like this."

"Make time for my son? Of course!" Torsten said. "That goes without saying."

Augustin shook his head. "Not everyone does, especially police officers."

"I think people's attitudes will change in the future," Torsten replied. "I've been on so many cases that I know avoiding burnout is crucial. We have to sleep, to have a private life. Otherwise we become useless, and we're no good for anyone."

"So you didn't get divorced because you spent too much time on the job?"

"No," Torsten said. "She left me for completely different reasons. By the way, tomorrow morning, when Anki and Per come in, we should split up with them."

Augustin smiled. "So we can keep an eye on everything?"

Torsten shrugged, smiling back. "That's the idea."

They were walking through the garden of a one-family house right on the border between Stocksund and Danderyd. The house was a far cry from the palatial mansions usually found in this neighborhood. The doorbell gave out a weak sound, so Torsten used the knocker. A young woman with red stripes in her hair opened the door. Her eyes were red from crying, and she was holding a paper tissue to her nose. As Torsten introduced himself, she looked at him in fright and shrunk back.

"You're Josefine, aren't you? Is it all right if we come in to ask you a few questions?"

The girl stepped aside to let them in.

"Are your mother and father home?"

"No, but Mamma will be home soon. She works at Mörby mall."

The house was clean. Most likely, it had been renovated around the beginning of the nineties. The walls were sponge-painted in pastel colors, and stripped wooden furniture dominated the interior. The atmosphere was cozy and snug, though Torsten knew quite well that for Djursholm it was outdated. He wondered whether Josefine cared about that. They sat down at a kitchen table with only a mint-green tablecloth. On the wall beside the table, a kitchen calendar with puppies on it hung from a hook. The weekdays were marked with *M* and *P* and a time. Torsten guessed that was when the parents returned from work.

"As you must know, we're here to talk about Ellen. I need you to describe her for us. How did you like working with her? What kind of a person was she?"

"She was reliable. She'd tell me off if I was careless with the espresso machine. But she'd been there longer and knew how to run it better than I did."

"Was she always on time?" Torsten asked.

The girl replied, "Yes, and she was the one who closed most often. Our boss depended on her. When I counted out the money at the end of the day, I always had trouble. I'm not that good with math."

"So, did you hang out together outside of work?"

"No, we didn't. Sometimes we walked together to the train, but she lived in Näsbypark, so we usually went off in opposite directions. And she rode her bike most of the time."

"So she'd bike the whole way home? Even in autumn?"

"Yes, well, it's not far."

"Did she take her bike yesterday?"

Josefine said that she had. Torsten glanced at Augustin.

"Do you know if she biked home, or if she maybe left her bike at work?"

"No idea. My shift ended at three, and she was closing."

Torsten looked at her seriously and said, "Were there any customers who acted odd? Anyone waiting for Ellen? Maybe someone unpleasant?"

"No, not that I know. Sometimes customers *are* difficult or angry . . . but . . . well, not so they'd want to murder anybody."

"Can you tell me more about any difficult or angry customers?"

"I just mean customers who just complain about their coffee. If it's too cold. Or someone ordered a cake in advance and it wasn't perfect. But, wait—there *was* one young guy who acted angry with Ellen. He came this week and he seemed mad at me, too. He was cute—but kind of strange."

"Can you remember what he looked like?"

"Not really. He was a bit taller than me. I'm five-seven. He had dark-blond hair, a little on the long side. Not long enough to put it in a ponytail or anything, but kind of behind his ears."

"What was he wearing?"

"A gray jacket with one of those racing-car decals. Dark jeans, kind of on the expensive side. He was a little snobby."

"Was he from Djursholm?"

"No idea. Yes, he was odd, but he didn't look the type to murder someone."

"But you noticed him."

"Yes."

"Do you often notice your customers?"

Josefine shrugged. "Sometimes."

"Why him? Did you see him earlier?"

The girl thought deeply, and her red, swollen eyes blinked a few times.

"I don't know. No—I hadn't seen him before."

Smiling, Torsten stood up and held out his hand.

"Thank you very much, Josefine. You've been a great help."

She looked at them in surprise. "Is that all? I thought we'd be talking for hours. And you'd have hot lights and stuff like that."

"You're thinking of interrogations. No, we just wanted to ask you a few questions. We don't need lights for that."

He smiled and hoped her mother would be there soon. He thought the girl could use a shoulder to cry on.

−□−

Once they were back on the street, the rain started up. Twilight had come.

Augustin started the car. "So, should we start with the missing bike?"

"Yep. I'll call our guys and tell them to start looking for it. And then we need to look into this odd customer."

"But then the connection to Turin is broken."

"I'm not so sure about that. The devil's in the details. Rest assured, we'll find the connection. I feel that this case is about to break."

"We have to find that guy."

"We'll knock on doors from the list Marianne gave us, just as we planned. Also, we should send the girl to one of our artists. I'll ask Anki to arrange it. We've had a lucky break. I believe Josefine noticed him because he was attractive. A teenager noticing someone can be a good witness—they are good at spotting details. So, what should we do now? Who is the first person on Jidhoff's list?"

"A woman on Ysätervägen. Let's hope she's home."

"Of course she's home. The women around here don't go to work. They congregate in pleated skirts at soccer games to cheer on their spoiled kids. That is, when they're not busy getting their nails done."

Augustin laughed. "I think you have a few stereotypes of your own. But you've got a point. I've read somewhere that Djursholm has more housewives than any other city in all of Sweden."

"Doesn't surprise me in the least."

Augustin's cell phone rang. "Madrid here. Hey, dude, what's up?"

Torsten smiled. Augustin's speaking style had abruptly changed. He could fit into any neighborhood in Stockholm. Torsten understood exactly what Augustin meant when he'd said his strength as a police officer was fitting in. Torsten took a moment to check his own messages and saw that Katrin had left one. She was trying to sound neutral and relaxed, but she didn't fool him. It must be about Noah. But he had no desire to call her back. He needed more mental fortitude for the task at hand.

CHAPTER 68

With Torsten and Augustin finally gone, Marianne sat down on the sofa. She spread a throw over her legs and picked up the printouts to read through. She thought deeply about the case but found she wasn't getting anywhere. She dozed off with the reports woven into her dreams. Hans appeared, as if still alive. He looked at her judgmentally and said she'd been sloppy with the facts. He yelled at her to look more carefully, and she woke up in a cold sweat.

She decided to take another shower and then thought a bath might be more pleasant. She took the reports with her. She had to laugh at realizing she obeyed Hans's commands even after his death. She pored over the papers again, frowning. She knew she was missing something. Something among the lines of text. It was like a Sudoku puzzle—sometimes it was better to put it away and come back to it after her subconscious mind had a chance to work on it.

She let the water drain out and took a quick cold shower to wake up. She had forty minutes to get ready. She thought she'd wear the black dress she'd bought for the funeral. It was the only dressy piece she had that wouldn't make her look frumpy, although people might think she was still in mourning for her late husband.

As she slid her fingers through her new nylon stockings, doing her best not to create a run, she realized that it would have been a good idea to shave her legs. Good Lord. The hair on her legs stuck out like that of a wild boar. No time now. She'd try to remember to do that before the next party.

She'd have to put razors on her shopping list, as she didn't even have any in the house. Hans had always used an electric razor, so she knew she wouldn't find any of her razors with his things. That's when she realized it was time to start sorting through his belongings. She couldn't put it off forever. She longed to know what home would look like shorn of Hans—yet she worried about it, too. Would she even notice a difference? She would ask Sigrid for help. Nina had offered, but she didn't think that was a good idea. Nina was welcome, though, to come by and choose any of her father's things she wanted. Sigrid had said she wanted just one item: Hans's father's old bear gun. She had no desire for anything else. If it were up to Marianne, everything would be thrown in the trash.

—□—

Her dress was hanging, pressed and ready, still in the plastic bag from the dry cleaner's. This time, she could pull up the back zipper without too many acrobatics. It bothered her that designers made clothes without considering how people were supposed to put them on by themselves. Not everyone had someone around to help zip up a zipper. She thought she should point this out to Sigrid at the next opportunity, although Sigrid would probably just laugh and tell her to worry about more important things.

She found some powder and rouge in the back of the medicine cabinet and fought to bring life to her pale face. When she finally put on a few dabs of mascara, she had to admit, she looked more than passable—and, in fact, she looked quite nice.

She wrapped her gray shawl around her shoulders and hoped she wouldn't get too warm in it. She'd set her attractive shoes by the door so she wouldn't forget and wear something more comfortable instead. It wouldn't do to appear at Lola's event in everyday flats.

At five minutes before seven, she was ready to go. It was her first party since becoming a widow. She wondered how it would feel. Would people treat her differently? In earlier days, the recently widowed used to stay isolated so others wouldn't be confronted by their grief. Marianne made sure her purse had everything she needed. She was just about to call for a taxi when she realized she didn't have a gift for Lola. In her eagerness to make herself presentable, she'd completely forgotten. People didn't come to Lola's empty-handed. It would be like going into Saint Peter's Cathedral without an offering.

"Hi, it's me. Are you home?"

"No, I'm in the studio looking for a measuring rod," Sigrid replied. "Aren't you supposed to be at Lola's dinner party?"

"Soon. And it looks like I've forgotten to find a present. Do you have anything I could take? It can't be a bottle of alcohol, or Lola will complain I've been lazy. She hates getting a bottle of wine for a dinner party."

"I have some scarves that might work. Emilia started sewing them when she didn't have anything else to do. Come down and see if one of them will do. And don't tell me you're wearing the dress from the funeral."

"Yes, I am. It works just fine. It's somber, and has the greatest chance of letting me go unnoticed. To tell the truth, it's the only dress that fits."

Sigrid sighed. "Mamma, you should have said something. Your daughter is a seamstress. It reflects on her when you dress badly! People will think it's my fault! If you'd only told me, I would have made something for you. Something simple but elegant."

"It's no use talking about that now. This will do for tonight. I'll be down in a minute."

Marianne looked at herself in the mirror. She inspected the black dress closely. It didn't look as bad as Sigrid made it out to be. In spite of Sigrid's protests, the black fit her mood. She wouldn't be more comfortable in a splashy, colorful dress. The idea of mourning wasn't that bad, in fact.

Marianne slipped her feet into her high-heeled shoes, draped her black trench coat over her arm, and held her purse in her other hand. She headed downstairs to Sigrid's studio. When Sigrid opened the door, her eyes widened. "Mamma! You look awesome!"

"*Awesome* is not a word one uses to describe one's mother."

"Oh, come on, turn around, and let me take a good look at you."

"I'm not a champion dog at Westminster!"

"Go ahead and turn around! I take back what I said about your funeral dress. It looks really good on you."

Marianne swirled around.

"I have to take a picture and send it to Nina."

"No you won't. No pictures! Where are the scarves?"

Sigrid smiled at her mother and pointed to a countertop boasting a large pile of multicolored scarves with the neatest lace trim. They were fairly large once they were opened.

Sigrid pulled out the top one. "I think this purple with the lime-green lace edging would fit Lola. It complements her darker coloring."

"It'll be perfect, and I promise I won't take credit," Marianne said. "I'll tell Lola you chose it. They're all really beautiful."

Then, Marianne picked up a pretty turquoise one with light-pink trim and a beautiful embroidered flower.

"Emilia is making a collection of these scarves in all kinds of colors and sizes. They're becoming fairly successful, and now she's working on a variation with pearl trim. I think they're unbelievable. Wait a second. I'll find a box for you."

Sigrid returned with a box in the same purple shade as the scarf. It already had a silver ribbon tied onto it. Marianne thanked her and said, "At least Lola won't accuse me of being lazy. She's going to love it."

Marianne looked into her purse for her cell phone and called the number for Taxi Stockholm.

"Mamma!"

Marianne turned to look at Sigrid, and a flash went off on Sigrid's phone.

"Oh, no you don't! Delete that picture at once!"

Sigrid danced out of reach toward the window, eagerly clicking buttons. "Sorry, it's already sent! That's the least you can do after I did this for you! Not to mention the hairdresser! I saved you from Lola's scolding!"

She gestured toward the purple box.

Marianne sighed and extended her arms. "Sorry, I know how much you do for me! I am going to make sure I pay you back somehow! But, please, don't send the photo to Nina!"

"Already done. Why are you so difficult? I get to see how great you look! Shouldn't Nina?"

"Nina is different. She always takes things the wrong way."

"So you think she'll consider you a bad person because you're going out and enjoying yourself even though Pappa is dead?"

Marianne pressed her lips together. "Something like that. Everything that has to do with Pappa is a sensitive issue for Nina. You know that."

"I think you're exaggerating. She's been worried about you lately."

Marianne smiled. She knew that Sigrid was wrong. Still, she drew her close and gave her a long hug and a kiss on her soft cheek.

"Thank you, my dearest, dearest Sigrid. Thank you for everything!"

With a deep sigh, she forced away her worries about her children. They were grown, responsible adults. She should trust them to take care of themselves and ask her for help if they needed it. But that was easier said than done.

Once in the taxi, she rolled down the window. She felt a bit overheated from her conversation.

"I would like to go to Skeppsholmen, please. The old bathhouse right below the Modern Museum."

The taxi driver started down Riddargatan and turned onto Narvavägen. He took a left at the Royal Dramatic Theater and then went past Blasieholmen and Hovslagargatan. As they passed the National Museum, Marianne noticed a young couple standing on the entrance stairs. They were kissing. The young man held the woman around her waist, and she was running her hands through his hair. A small sigh escaped Marianne. How long had it been since she'd kissed someone in public? Well over thirty years. She hardly remembered the feeling. Her time was over. She would have to hope for a bundle of grandchildren to love. She should take on the same hobbies as other women her age: making handicrafts, or tending roses.

The taxi shook as it drove over the wooden planks of Skeppsholm Bridge. Twilight was coming. A cool breeze started to blow through the taxi window. On the hill behind the Modern Museum, outdoor candles had been set out, and Marianne smiled. Lola was an extraordinary hostess.

CHAPTER 69

The girls were laughing at something on television when Paula woke up. She could hardly keep her eyes open, although it wasn't even eight p.m. She realized she hadn't slept more than three hours during the past twenty-four. If that. The girls had been thrilled to have pizza, and dessert in the middle of the week had put them into seventh heaven.

Paula's cell phone rang. She reached for it, still half asleep, and saw it was Jens.

"So, did you take in the car?"

"I didn't have time."

"What do you mean, you didn't have time? I told you to do it! I booked it at the repair shop!"

"I know, but it didn't happen. And I didn't buy groceries, either. I'm sure you find that distressing, too."

There was silence on the other end. A few moments later, Jens's voice returned. "What is the matter with you? What are you up to?"

Paula looked over at the girls. Her heart pounded against her chest, but before she could say anything, Jens continued.

"We won't argue about your shortcomings. It's beneath both of us. But in the future, I need you to do as I say. It's not like you have a busy schedule or anything!"

Paula sighed and walked to the kitchen. "It's not that. We'll talk about it when you get home."

"I'll be home in an hour."

"Good. Bring some milk and bread with you so the girls have something for breakfast."

Jens hung up without replying. Paula took a deep breath and knew that it would all come to a head tonight. She had no choice. Things couldn't go on like this. She teared up as she watched her girls sitting together, sharing a blanket, happily unaware that their world would soon fall apart.

CHAPTER 70

Marianne drew her coat around her as she walked carefully to the entrance of Lola's house. She glanced at her watch to decide if there was time for a Davidoff cigarette, but it was already quite late. Her cell phone rang.

"Hello, Mamma. Nina here."

"Hello, sweetie! How are you?"

Marianne's stomach knotted. She wasn't ready for an argument with her daughter.

"I'm fine. Just wanted to say you're looking fantastic!"

"What?"

"I saw the picture Sigrid sent."

Marianne swallowed with relief. There was no accusing tone in Nina's voice.

"Thanks," she said. "It was about time I did something about my hair."

"It looks really good. Are you going out tonight?"

"I'm invited to Lola's for dinner. But I'm in no hurry. We can chat for a minute."

"I just wanted to tell you that you looked great."

Marianne wrinkled her brow. There was something off—something wasn't as it should be.

"Where are you? I thought you and Robert were going away for the week."

"We're out at Svartsö Manor Bed and Breakfast. But we're coming home soon. Robert said he had a meeting early tomorrow morning."

"Oh, that's too bad. I thought you two were going to rest up all week there. Take time to be a couple."

"Yes, but our plans changed. We just had dinner out in the archipelago instead. I really just wanted to say hi. I love you."

They hung up, but Marianne still had the feeling that something was wrong. Something left unsaid. Nina seemed to have something on the tip of her tongue. She weighed the phone in her hand, wondering whether to call Nina back. But then, if Nina wanted to tell her something, it wasn't good to press her about it. It was better to wait and see. She also had to remember to call Peder tomorrow. She set her cell phone to mute, slipping it back into her purse. She was not on call this evening, and Olle was in the office. But it was difficult for her not being available. Still, she couldn't let her phone ring in the middle of Lola's dinner. How gauche that would be!

Lola lived in a building that had once been a cold-water bathhouse. She'd snapped up the former rental when it went on sale. She converted the ground floor to a gallery, and the second floor was her private residence. The gallery was in a great spot, close to the Modern Museum. The large windows looked out over the water and faced Djurgården.

Marianne hurried up the stairs to the second floor. She rang the doorbell, and it gave off a buzzing sound. She heard clattering footsteps, and the door opened with a creak. Lola smiled widely. She was wearing a bright-red dress, which left one shoulder bare. She looked like a dream. It was hard to tell that Lola was almost sixty. She could hold her own with any thirty-year-old.

"Finally! I was beginning to think you might back out. Hurry up and come in—everyone else is already here. Oh, what have we here?"

Marianne smiled. She handed Lola the purple box and turned to hang up her coat. She buttoned a button on her sweater and pulled in her stomach as best she could.

Lola eagerly pulled off the silver ribbon and opened the box.

"I'll bet Sigrid was behind this! It's beautiful!"

Lola draped the scarf around her shoulders, and Marianne saw that Sigrid had been absolutely correct. The color suited Lola perfectly.

"Yes, Sigrid chose it. I'm such a bad guest."

"You are forgiven. You were clever enough to ask your talented daughter for help. But couldn't she have found a more colorful dress for you?"

"She tried . . . but one step at a time."

"Well, I have to say, you still look pretty good. And your *hair*! *Wonderful*! Going to the hairdresser wasn't a bad idea at *all*! Now come inside and say hello. Stand up straight and hold your stomach in, for the love of God!"

Marianne pinched Lola's arm and laughed. She glanced briefly into the gold-framed mirror and bared her teeth to make sure no lipstick was on them; then she entered the living room.

Lola had recently renovated her apartment. The minute she owned it outright, she'd set to work. It hadn't been changed in over forty years, but Lola had chosen a classic style with a great deal of white, matched to splashes of black and gray. Not surprising for a gallery owner. When it came to clothing, Lola's style was cutting edge, but in interior design, she was much more conservative. The two overstuffed sofas in an English style had white coverings. Six people were spaced out on them, and four more were sitting in armchairs. Marianne looked around in confusion for somewhere to sit before a Gripsholm-style chair was placed behind her. She received a quick kiss on both cheeks.

"Bonjour, Madame! You look stunning tonight!"

"Thank you, Philippe."

Philippe, Lola's partner, winked. "Let me get you a glass of champagne."

Marianne sat down and waved briefly to the other guests. She had already met most of them on other occasions, and it would be rude to make them all stand up and kiss her cheek. Her father had always insisted if there were more than twelve people in a room, it was inconsiderate to go up and greet each one.

Philippe and Lola didn't live together, and Lola loved using the Swedish expression *särbo* to get a rise out of people. Philippe was divorced and lived with his sixteen-year-old daughter, Viki. He only stayed at Lola's place on occasion. He was ten years younger than Lola and ran a successful furniture company, whose designs sold to over twenty countries. He'd started off taking prototypes to furniture manufacturers all over the country, hoping they'd sell his designs.

Philippe loved Lola deeply and had courted her for two years before she agreed to go out with him. They'd been friends at first, but within a year, they were a couple. Lola refused to move in with him, and Philippe said he was fine with that since Viki was still living at home. When Viki moved out, he planned to ask her to marry him and to live in the same home. He joked that it was time Lola made an honest man out of him. Lola always said time would tell. When it came to relationships, she was afraid to commit, and Marianne understood why. The year Lola turned eight, both her parents had died, and she was tossed from one boarding school to another, all over Europe. She met a German count fifteen years her senior and married him when she was thirty. For ten years he beat her, until Lola had the courage to leave him and demand a divorce. She moved to Berlin and worked at an established gallery, specializing in photography. Her former husband stalked her in Berlin, becoming aggressive and violent whenever he tracked her down. Despite reporting him to the police and getting a restraining order, Lola never could hide from him for long, and she lived in daily fear of his reappearance. Then a miracle happened: One October evening after a fancy dinner, he was in a car crash on the autobahn. He passed away two days later at the hospital. He was said to be drunk behind the wheel, but Marianne suspected it might have been a case of suicide. She never talked about it with Lola. He wasn't worth their attention.

Lola finally had peace. She returned to Stockholm at forty-plus after only visiting a few times during her marriage. She opened her own gallery and went right to work. She'd inherited a fortune from her parents and, luckily, her husband had never been able to touch it. She decided she would never be involved with another man again. Philippe had his work cut out for him when he met her, but as far as

Marianne was concerned, Philippe was a gift from Heaven. He treated Lola well and was able to smooth away her rough edges. She stopped battling fiercely just for the sake of getting her way, and she became much warmer and friendlier to other people.

It wasn't strange under the circumstances that Lola had no children. Marianne couldn't imagine any children in her life. Art was her focus, and she took artists under her protective wing. That was enough for her. Lola had also used her fortune to set up a prize for promising young artists. Swedish cultural life had a patron in Lola, and people gladly accepted her assistance.

–□–

Marianne leaned back and tasted the champagne. It was chilled properly, and she could have drunk it all at one go. She'd had only coffee all day, and she realized how thirsty she was. She got up from her chair with difficulty and smiled at the people sitting next to Philippe. He was talking to a red-haired woman who'd been a very popular author but had given up writing for painting. Her work pleased the critics, yet was easily accessible to the average person—a balancing act few could accomplish.

In the kitchen, everything was well under control. The dishes were arranged attractively, and a chef greeted her, asking if he could be of assistance.

"I just need a glass of water, please. I'm going to be too tipsy from champagne if I don't drink some water. I've only had coffee today."

"Of course. Let me get you a glass."

"Everything smells wonderful. What are you serving to-night?"

"For the appetizer: Swedish river crabs with Västerbotten cheese and home-baked crisp bread. For the main dish, I've made saddle of venison with buttered new potatoes. To end the meal, there will be warm cloudberries with fried Camembert."

"It sounds terrific. I haven't had warm cloudberries in over thirty years!"

"I understand that it was a fashionable dessert in the seventies."

"You weren't even born then, were you?"

The young man reddened a bit. "You're right," he said. "I was born in 1981."

Marianne finished her water and smiled. "You're the same age as my youngest daughter. It's a good year. Is there anything I can help with here in the kitchen so I can avoid rejoining the crowd out there?"

The man smiled back and shook his head. "Thanks, but no. Everything is all set, but you're welcome to come back if you need another glass of water."

Marianne snatched her champagne flute from the windowsill and walked back into the living room. She noticed another guest returning to the room and thought there was something familiar about him. Not wanting to give up her chair, she hurried back and sank into the cushions with relief. She had no desire to sit on the sofa with the other guests. Marianne was happy to spot an ashtray on the coffee table. A woman was stubbing out her cigarette in order to light a new one. Marianne dug into her purse for her pack of Davidoffs and discreetly pulled out a cigarette. But then she realized she hadn't brought her lighter.

"Perhaps I can help you," a voice said.

Marianne recognized the voice and looked up. The new guest, who'd looked so familiar, was none other than one of her old college flames—Ralph Nordström.

"Good Lord, it's you! Ralph! What are you doing here?"

Marianne had spent quite some time with Ralph when she was studying at Lund. He had come to Lund from Oxford to get a Swedish law degree along with his British one. Like his father, he was planning to be a career diplomat. Marianne had seen Ralph just once after Lund. It was a brief meeting around Christmas, sometime in the eighties. She'd been outside NK department store with her girls in a twin stroller, looking at the displays for an idea for Hans's Christmas present. Ralph had been well dressed in a dark suit and narrow coat. She was hot, wore no makeup, and her down coat was worn and spotted with oatmeal stains. She'd done her best to keep the girls from fussing too much. Ralph was home for a quick visit with his parents. He asked which prosecution office she was working for, and she had avoided answering, saying she'd find out when the girls were a little older. They'd said their good-byes with smiles and warm looks, and Marianne had treasured that meeting for years afterward.

"Lola and I went to grade school together when we were tadpoles. I had no idea you two knew each other."

"Lola is one of my very best friends."

"But that's strange. Did you know her when you were at Lund?"

"Yes, we'd been sent to the same finishing school in Switzerland one summer. We were supposed to learn typing and French, but we spent most of our time balancing books on our heads and writing comprehensive shopping lists for meals. All the time, they'd yell at us to pull our stomachs in."

Ralph laughed. "It's hard for me to imagine the two of you there."

"We were there all right. We smoked, sneaked out, and got drunk on sweet liqueurs. Girls were supposed to attend finishing schools back in the day, but now I hear they go to language schools instead. But I'm eternally grateful that I was sent there, because I met Lola. We couldn't see each other much when she was living in Germany and, as you know, I was studying at Lund. But . . . what are you doing in Sweden? Are you waiting for a new posting?"

Ralph shook his head as he lit his own cigarette. "No, just the reverse. I'm getting ready to retire."

"You're not that old, surely. And why would you want to retire in Sweden? You've never even lived here except for those years in Lund."

"That's right. Still, I'm tired of traveling from place to place and never settling down. I want a permanent address and a quiet life, where I'm my own boss. My parents have passed away, and for ten years I've longed to return to Sweden. And how are you, the most beautiful student Lund has ever seen?"

"Well, I don't really know yet. Ask away."

"Still married?"

Marianne flinched, almost dropping her cigarette. She tried to keep her voice steady, "No, I'm a recent widow, actually."

"Lola mentioned over lunch that one of her close friends had just lost her husband. So that was you. I am so sorry for your loss, Marianne."

"Thank you," she replied.

They both took a sip of champagne. When their eyes caught each other, Marianne hastened to take another puff.

"Where do you live?" she asked.

"I've bought a house in Gamla Stan. On Drakens Gränd, not too far from the Royal Palace. It needs some renovation, but I think it will be fine once that's done. It was as close to an English townhouse as I could find in Stockholm, and one of the reasons I could leave London. I met my architect today, and he thought it would be finished in a few months. Until then, I'm staying at a hotel on Storgatan near Hedvig Eleonora Church. I have rented the entire top floor. It has a wonderful terrace at my disposal. But that's enough about me. What about you, where do you live?"

"I'm still in my apartment on Banérgatan. It's my child-hood home. I think you must have been there once or twice. I had a big party there, you might recall. Pappa still brings it up. We emptied his entire liquor cabinet that night. He was so angry."

"Yes, I do remember. I especially remember my hang-over the next day. I seem to recall that the apartment was fairly large. Are you living there all by yourself?"

"For now at least. I haven't decided what to do, but I like the apartment."

Ralph roared with laughter. "I should think so! You could go bowling in the dining room!"

"Well, these days my son still comes back every year from Australia. He comes home during vacations. It's comfortable to have enough space so we don't get in each other's way."

"So you have three children? I remember two girls in a stroller when I ran across you outside NK. You looked tired that day!"

"Oh, I was," Marianne said. "I was so exhausted that my whole body ached! Whenever I see pictures from when the children were small, I remember that feeling of never getting enough sleep. All I wanted back then was to sleep through a single night. Now I get all the sleep I need, and then some."

"Did you become a prosecutor?"

Marianne looked down and took another puff. "No, other things got in the way."

"Such as?"

"Three children and a husband."

"You could have worked out a way to share responsibilities with him?"

"Yes, but we didn't. Although the wonderful seventies had just gone by, we were still children of a more conservative era. When the kids came, we found ourselves taking on traditional roles. I had sworn it would never happen to me, but it did. It was hard for him as well, since he hardly saw the children except for weekends and vacations."

Ralph cut in: "Or perhaps he didn't want to spend time at home. I met your late husband. If I may be honest, he wasn't one of my favorite people. But then . . . I was biased. I was so in love with you."

"What? Come on, you weren't in love with me. You were with that Scanian woman! The one from the upper nobility, with the crazy father. Did he really chase you with a rifle?"

"Yes, though I think he just meant to scare me. Perhaps he knew my real thoughts. I was so in love with you. I thought *you* must have known somehow."

Ralph laughed and blew the smoke sideways from his lips. Marianne raised one eyebrow, pretending to ignore his statement. Ralph nodded hello at the other guests.

"Do you know many of these people?"

Marianne shrugged. "I wouldn't say I know them well, but I've met all of them before."

"Let me get a chair, and you can tell me who everyone is. I'm new here, so I don't know a soul."

Ralph found a chair that was upholstered in Svenskt Tenn's popular Tehran pattern. He pulled it close to Marianne's chair, stubbing out his cigarette and taking Marianne's flute. "Let me fill your glass so we don't die of thirst."

She smiled. Ralph didn't look much older than in their student days. Then, as now, he was elegantly dressed and seemed to have taken care of his health. His former light-brown hair was now gray, but he had the same hairstyle. He had a slight tan, which he'd always had no matter what the season. His eyes were more intense than she'd remembered. Perhaps he'd learned how to really use them. Marianne wondered what he thought of her. He certainly couldn't see her as well preserved. She'd always had curves, even in the Twiggy era, but her figure now was more "upholstered." Too many pounds had settled around her stomach—although, for the most part, the weight was distributed throughout her body. A treacherous weight gain. Perhaps she never would get used to it. But what woman would ever be happy weighing so much? Or any man for that matter?

"Now tell me. Who are these people?"

Ralph sat back down beside her. He crossed one leg over the other and lit another cigarette, offering his lighter again. Marianne hurried to pull out another Davidoff, refusing one of Ralph's.

"You have met Philippe, of course?"

Ralph said, "Yes—he's a pleasant chap, but ever since my years in the West Indies I sometimes have difficulties with Frenchmen. He's nice enough, though."

Marianne continued telling him about the other guests, and Ralph listened intently until the young chef discreetly rang a small bell from the kitchen to let them know dinner was served.

CHAPTER 71

The cold air nipped their cheeks as they left the impressive house on Friggavägen. Torsten looked back at the lit kitchen before he hunkered into the passenger seat.

"So what do we say about that encounter?"

Augustin shook his head. "That guy is a real asshole."

Torsten sighed deeply and, as was his habit, rubbed the bridge of his nose with his thumbs.

"How can people be like that? How can they live with themselves? That guy there, he has an extremely beautiful wife, two lovely daughters, and a job that would make most people envious. And what does he do with his time? Heads off to Right Now to *find himself,* leaving his wife and children at home alone, while he develops his inner child, or—not to mince words about it—fuck around with other peoples' spouses. What is it with that place? Do they brainwash people, or give them drugs?"

Augustin said, "This family resembles the Turins, with one exception. Christopher Turin was much more pleasant."

Torsten used the back of his hand to rub away some of the fog from the inside window. "No, Turin can't be faulted for having a bad personality. I wanted to give this guy a punch when he told his wife to be quiet right in front of us."

"Though we must consider that he was under stress. Two police officers had just shown up in the middle of dinner to ask him questions."

"But we weren't there to talk just to him. We also wanted to talk to his wife. She didn't seem a big fan of Right Now," Torsten said.

"Do you think he hits her?"

"No," Torsten said, "but he's not a kind man. I thought she was generally nervous. Did she say anything to you when you went out to the kitchen with her?"

"No. Just that she didn't like the fall weather and the early darkness. She's apparently afraid of the dark. She thinks she hears breaking twigs outside and unusual noises in the house all the time. She says it's gotten worse since Ellen Nyhlén was murdered. She told me her husband thinks she's just trying to get attention."

"Anyone would be afraid of the dark in that mansion," Torsten said. "Especially when there was a murder just a mile away. How do you interpret the husband's reaction to us mentioning the murder?"

Augustin frowned. "He mostly seemed angry that we hadn't found the killer yet. I don't think he fits the profile of a crazy murderer on the loose."

Torsten snorted. "I think he's too taken up with his own sweet self to kill anyone. But, Augustin, can you tell me— what's the deal with all these upper-class women and their sweaters?"

"Their sweaters?"

"Yes, all the weird colors and lace and small roses."

Augustin laughed. "You mean the Odd Molly sweaters?"

"Is that a brand? Why do grown women wear clothes that look like they were designed for children? That woman was dressed just like her little girls. Why's that? I've never seen that style before. I've heard about women who dress like their teenagers, but this is taking it to an extreme."

"It could be a matter of taste, but I see your point."

"It's as if they want to deny their femininity. Diminish their sexuality."

"Aren't you exaggerating just a bit?"

"No, especially considering who these women are. Most of them are completely supported by their egotistical husbands. Let's consider what all these Right Now families had in common."

"We didn't find out all that much. It's a collection of people where at least one spouse wants to find meaning in life because he or she is bored. Though I have to say, that last couple was really in bad shape. I have very little sympathy for that husband."

"He seemed more extreme than most of them. Am I being prejudiced saying that practicing yoga every day is neurotic?"

Augustin laughed. "Maybe, although it's supposed to be an effective way of getting in shape. I've never tried it myself, but I have a lot of friends who have."

"I think exercise should involve sweat and a racing pulse and all that. I can't see standing still with your leg behind your head. How can that be exercise? It's stretching, isn't it—what you do *after* exercising?"

Torsten's phone rang. The conversation didn't last long. He hung up and turned to Augustin. "Change of plans for me. Noah has decided to sleep over at a friend's house. They want to pull an all-nighter before a big exam tomorrow. So, I have a little more time. Why don't we drop in on Ushtanga Erik and Christina Filipsson again? Or do you have other plans?"

Augustin shook his head to indicate he had none. "Why not?"

"Anki and Per have called both Isa Turin and Jonas Carlfors in for questioning tomorrow," Torsten said. "Let's pay a visit to Christina Filipsson. She lives in town. And Erik Bergström has a large house on Lidingö Island—or 'Suffer in Pain Island' as we like to say."

"Ha, ha, funny. What's Christina's address?"

CHAPTER 72

Guests devoured the Swedish river crabs with great relish—and lots of happy slurping sounds. Marianne scraped out every last bit of meat with the attention of a forensic specialist. The crabs were of the best quality and Marianne suspected that Lola had chosen each and every last one herself from Melanders in Östermalm Food Hall. Harry had always insisted that there were top-quality and second-best shellfish. An average customer got second best, but when a top customer was spied, the top-quality stock was hauled out of the back. Lola certainly would be considered an important customer. No one would ever consider trying to pass off second best to her. But Marianne didn't command that level of attention. Whenever she came to the Food Hall to buy game and lingonberry gelée, she was just content when a salesperson remembered her well enough to greet her by name.

The aged cheese had been set on pieces of crisp bread spiced with cumin. Ice-cold schnapps was served, and just one schnapps song was sung in broken Swedish by Philippe. Marianne felt the strong drink burn down her throat. She shivered, both from the harsh taste and a sense of well-being.

"How have you been lately? Has it been unbearable?" The question came from Simon Zetterberg, the famous economics journalist. He had curly golden hair and was looking down at her from his six-foot-three inches. Marianne realized he was bringing up Hans's death. Before she replied, she dried a drop of crab juice from the top of her hand, enjoying the feeling of the napkin's starched linen for a second.

"Yes, it's been extremely difficult," she said. "Feeling loss is an odd state of being. One moment, it feels like you're in a big black hole. The next, you're acting as if the person's still alive."

"I can understand that. What do you miss the most? Or is that an inappropriate question?"

"I'll give you an honest answer. Right now I am extremely angry at him. I want him to come back to life so I can tell him to go to hell."

Simon stared open-mouthed at her for a moment. Then he laughed heartily. "My dear Marianne, what a perfect description! But did you two really have it that bad?"

Marianne looked across the table to where Ralph was laughing with the red-haired artist. Then she answered, "Yes, I guess we did. I've realized that our marriage wasn't worthy of the name. It was hard on both of us."

Simon patted her knee. "Well, I'd already guessed that."

They both nodded, acknowledging this. Marianne remembered several years before when she'd come crying to Lola in the middle of the night. Simon and his wife Kitty, both good friends of Lola, had been there for dinner. They'd heard Marianne's entire tale of woe about one of Hans's affairs. The next day, she'd left Lola's, convinced that it was time for a divorce. But Hans's diagnosis of cancer had intervened. It wouldn't have been fair to abandon him then. She'd been held in the marriage against her will, much like the day she discovered she was pregnant with Peder.

"Marianne, *skål*! May this autumn bring you the happiest time of your life!"

Marianne smiled slightly as she raised her glass. Simon was right: things could only get better now.

Chapter 73

Paula could hardly believe she'd said it out loud. She had told Jens she wanted a divorce.

The living room was dark except for the light from the television. She felt safer with the TV on. She had no idea if Jens was asleep or not. She thought he'd taken some sleeping pills, however. She wasn't going to need sleeping pills tonight. Her entire body ached from anxiety. She felt so physically exhausted that she didn't think she could stay awake another minute.

She had told him while he was showering. At first he was irritated that she'd disturbed his peace and quiet in the bathroom, but she ignored his protests and sat down on the lid of the toilet. When she'd told him what she wanted, he stayed silent a few moments. Then he turned off the water, looking much older as he stepped out and reached for a towel. Old and exhausted, despite his excellent physique.

"Aren't you going to say anything?"

"What do you want me to say? You've already made up your mind."

"But what do *you* want?"

He didn't reply—he just continued his after-shower routine.

"You haven't touched me for two years. Not since you started those courses of yours."

"I have no desire to discuss what you think I've done wrong. If this is how you feel, then we will divorce."

"You can't put all the blame on me. You're also in the wrong!"

"But you are the one who wants a divorce."

"Because I can't imagine living the rest of my life with someone who no longer wants me. You think of me as one of your employees. Don't you miss sex with me at all?"

"Sex is just a surface thing, something you have to control. If you had worked hard to understand the principles behind the power of yoga and meditation, you would know how primitive you seem to me now. Sex is just a tool."

"Stop that nonsense. I don't give a damn how *you* see me. I want sex with my husband—the person I married."

"Let's just divorce as quietly as possible for the sake of the children. I imagine you will be the one moving out."

"And why is that?" she said.

"Because you can't afford to purchase my half of the house. Or do you have some secret income I'm not aware of?"

Paula knew money would be his weapon, but she avoided that bait. "I will look into the best way to divide the property. And what about the children? Especially since you travel so much?"

She felt cowardly, as if she were hitting him below the belt, but she only had so much at her disposal.

"I'll have to think about it."

"Every other week or every other weekend?"

"We'll have to discuss this with experts in the field. You're going to need a lawyer. I have one."

"You already have a *divorce* lawyer?"

"Yes," he said.

Paula felt she should have expected this but thought he might be lying.

The doorbell rang. Paula frowned.

Jens called to the girls to open the door, and they answered that the police were there.

Jens looked at Paula and hissed, "Don't say a single word about your paranoid ideas. If you do, after our divorce, I will make sure you'll never see your daughters again."

Stung, Paula followed Jens downstairs to meet the officers. The girls had politely shown them to the kitchen.

As the two investigators asked Jens about his participation in Right Now, Paula could barely contain her laughter. Still, she kept silent in the face of Jens's threat. She knew very well he was a fierce opponent in law and business, that he was always out to win. She couldn't afford to lose this battle.

When the officers left, the girls could sense that something was wrong. They repeatedly asked what was going on. Jens ignored them and stalked to the bedroom, closing the door behind him.

Paula put the girls to bed and lay down between them while they read for a while.

Then she double-checked the doors. She picked up her cell phone. She wanted to text Passi but was afraid he'd send one back while she slept. Jens could find it in the morning if he woke before she did. He'd never checked her cell phone before, but all bets were off now. Instead of worrying about finding a place to live and what she should do with her life, she thought about last night. Her time with Passi had given her much more than sexual satisfaction. That physical side of things may be fleeting, but she wanted to enjoy it as long as she could. Everything else was much too difficult to think about. She knew she'd feel hit by a ton of bricks in the morning.

Paula fell asleep with the television on, completely unaware that someone watched her every movement, just ten feet away on the other side of the window. Someone who thought he loved her.

CHAPTER 74

Augustin looked up at the grand nineteenth-century building. It was half a block from Strandvägen and not more than a stone's throw away from where Marianne Jidhoff lived.

"How long has Christina Filipsson lived here?" he asked.

Torsten checked his papers. "According to the tax authorities, since January of last year, when she bought her apartment. What can an apartment cost in this neighborhood?"

Augustin shrugged. "About six million crowns. Maybe more. Nothing around here is ever affected by economic downturns."

"Good Lord. That must mean Marianne Jidhoff is really wealthy!"

Augustin raised his eyebrow in amusement. "You think about her a lot, you know."

"I do, do I? Well, why not. She's special."

Torsten looked at his younger colleague and said in all seriousness, "I like her. And I think it's a damned shame that she never became a prosecutor. But none of that changes the fact that we work with her. She is highly capable. We can use her experience. Let me tell you, I know she's part of Olle's plan."

"Olle has a plan?"

"You ought to realize that by now. You're part of it. You don't think you got your job with us through merit alone, did you?"

"But . . . rather . . ."

Torsten lowered his voice. "Olle Lundqvist has decided to bring about some changes, because he won't let all these leaks end his career. Nothing will come between Olle and his journey to the top. That's why he brought us together in the first place. He wanted you because he knows how much you have to give. You don't fit in just anywhere. You were the best candidate to work with me: You're the same type of person as I am, just with less experience. A strange bird that doesn't fit in.

"Now, Marianne Jidhoff may be a wealthy woman from the upper class, but at work, she's also the odd man out. She'll never fit into the department. Also, she was married to Olle's best friend and mentor, Hans Larson. He knows exactly what she's capable of. Quite honestly, everyone knows she was the brains behind Hans Larson's successes in the courtroom. She will never admit it because she's not the type to boast. We three are a unit Olle Lundqvist can trust no matter which way the wind blows, and no matter how hard."

"Has he told you this himself?"

"Are you kidding? Olle is the most careful strategist you can imagine. This is just the first step in his plan."

Augustin laughed and shook his head. "So, according to your little theory, what's the *next* step?"

Torsten lifted an eyebrow and pressed the elevator button. "Go ahead and laugh now, but you'll see. I think he wants to create a separate operating unit with just the three of us."

Augustin turned serious. "You mean, like the Huddinge Group?"

"Yep."

Augustin knew well that Torsten Ehn had been one of the youngest members of the Huddinge Group, an investigative unit that had successfully infiltrated criminal gangs and garnered huge headlines. Finally, the unit became too well known, and so when Hans Holmér was the chief, he put an end to it. People at the Academy still talked about the Group with great respect. Its members were role models for many young recruits.

"You're sure about this?"

Torsten opened the elevator gate and stepped out. "You can't be sure of anything around here, but I know that's what Olle would like to see happen. We'll have to wait and see how long it takes. Well, it's showtime, so let's go."

Torsten pressed the doorbell. Two short rings echoed inside the apartment.

Augustin wondered whether any of what Torsten had just told him was true, or if he'd just dreamed about a return to his glory days in the Huddinge Group. His thoughts were interrupted when Christina Filipsson opened the door.

She looked even more beautiful than when they'd seen her at Right Now. Since it was evening, she was wearing a black silk robe knotted loosely at the waist. Her hair was bound up in a loose bun, with some locks hanging freely over her trim shoulders. Her two round breasts swelled over the low neckline. Augustin noticed the freckles from the sun on her skin. She was barefoot, and her perfume was sweet but not overwhelming. She gave them both a big smile.

"Welcome! I've been expecting you!"

Torsten wrinkled his brow. "How's that?"

Christina continued smiling. "I read in my cards that strangers would be dropping in—strangers who meant well. I sense goodness in you, even though we are strangers right now."

Again she lost much of her beauty when talking. Her clichés were so banal that Augustin wanted to tell her to be quiet. Augustin glanced at Torsten, who also seemed irritated, but Torsten sounded friendly.

"Can we come in? We have some questions we'd like to ask you."

"Of course. Please don't see yourselves as strangers. From now on, you are taken into the circle of souls around me. Come in, please. Just let me change into something more appropriate. Please go ahead and sit down in the kitchen, and I'll be right there."

Christina Filipsson vanished into an apartment that drew from the colors of nature. Torsten whispered to Augustin, "Has she been smoking something? She's even more woo-woo than the last time we saw her."

Augustin sniffed the air. "Perhaps, but this scent could also be incense. It's sometimes hard to tell."

The kitchen was enormous and brand-new. There were high, shiny cabinets, which had never seen a child's handprint. No crumbs or stains were on these counters. Not a single detail had been left to chance.

"How nice that you've made yourselves at home. What can I offer you? I assume you can't have wine on duty? What about tea? I don't have coffee, unfortunately. Or how about a glass of juice?"

"Juice would be fine," Torsten said.

They sat down at the large white Corian dining table.

Christina Filipsson moved lazily. She tried to look seductive as she pulled out a juice press and some oranges. Augustin and Torsten exchanged glances, and Augustin even managed a discreet gesture of puffing an invisible cigarette. Torsten smiled, looking down at the table so he wouldn't laugh. Soon they each had a glass in front of them.

"We're here because we want to know more about your relationship to Christopher Turin."

Christina Filipsson started squirming; she kept her lips pressed together, as if she wanted to control any careless word. After a moment, she said, "He was a careful man. He was stifled by his spiritual blocks."

"Yes, you mentioned that the last time we spoke to you. Now, please forgive me, but I want you to speak to us clearly without all the nonsense. A killer is on the loose—someone who murdered Christopher Turin—and I need direct answers. We don't have time for any fluff."

Augustin looked at Torsten in surprise. He hadn't expected him to be so tough right off the bat. Christina Filipsson seemed caught off guard as well. She was about to say something, when a voice came from the hall.

"Hello?"

Christina was tense as she looked at the officers. She called out: "Hello, sweetie, I'm in the kitchen. A few police officers are here to ask me some questions. Something happened to a guy from work. Do you want anything?"

"No, thanks, I already ate."

A young man stuck his head into the kitchen. He nodded hello to Torsten and Augustin, and they nodded back. He turned away, and it was clear she was his mother.

"Is it all right if I go to my room? We have a big test tomorrow and I should study."

"Sure, but tell me if there's anything you need. How was Adele?"

"She's doing better. It was strep throat, and she got some antibiotics."

"Poor little thing. I'll come in and say good night later."

He smiled and left, and Christina turned back to them. "That's my son, Casper. He's started his first year at the University of Stockholm, and he spends all his time with his girlfriend. It's kind of sweet, actually. She's a lovely girl."

Torsten smiled. "Nice. I have a son the same age. Where does Casper's father live?"

"In Canada. He moved after we separated. Casper visits on his vacations. This past summer, he was there for two months."

"How *is* your relationship with your ex?"

"Pretty good, now that we each live on our own sides of the Atlantic."

Torsten smiled. "Perhaps that's wise. Now I have a few questions about your business. The one you have on the side—in addition to Right Now. What kind is it?"

Christina squirmed again. "The same thing I do there. Coaching."

"According to your website, you're a lifestyle coach. What is that?"

"I help my customers find the right path."

"What does Erik Bergström think about your side business?"

"Not much."

"He's aware of it?"

"Yes, he is."

"So why did you start it up?"

"Because I got tired of so many long ferryboat trips. I wanted to stay home with Casper."

"Was Christopher Turin a customer in this business, too?"

Christina looked down at the table. "Yes," she said quietly. He was one of the first clients outside Right Now that hired me."

Torsten took a deep breath. He looked directly at her. "Did you sleep with him?"

Christina turned to him.

"You don't understand what I do. Sex can be freeing when used the right way. Yes, sometimes I slept with him— when I thought it could be helpful. Sometimes we just talked. It depended on what he needed at the time."

She said this with such conviction that both Torsten and Augustin jerked back.

Torsten's eyes narrowed. "Is sex typically part of your job?"

Christina Filipsson sat up straight and glared at Torsten. "Yes, if it is useful. But it doesn't come up most of the time."

"How many of your customers have you slept with?"

"Only three of them."

411

"So Christopher was one of three."

"Yes."

"Who were the other two?"

"I'm not about to reveal that information. You can lock me up—I don't care. That's extremely private, and it has nothing to do with your investigation. Just because I don't see sex as narrowly as you doesn't mean I should be punished."

Torsten shrugged. "Possibly, but according to the laws of the Kingdom of Sweden, what you are doing is called prostitution. Or, as it was called in the good old days, whoredom. Is *coaching* the modern term?"

Christina didn't take her eyes off Torsten. Augustin drank the last of his juice and put his glass on the table.

"Is there anyone close to Christopher who would have been upset by this? One of your other customers who might have become jealous?"

Christina shook her head. "No. I keep everything I do strictly confidential. The person who would be most upset would be his wife, but I believe she was happy he kept his distance from her."

"Did you know about their custody battle?"

"Yes, everyone did. Christopher spoke about it openly, even to those he didn't know that well. He needed to talk."

"What did you think of their custody battle?"

Christina Filipsson frowned and looked at the table. When she looked up, she turned her gaze to Augustin. "Christopher would never have gotten sole custody. Honestly, he needed the fights with her. He did everything he could to make his wife angry. He just wanted her to react."

"So he liked having a nasty custody battle that affected his children?"

"Yes, I'd say so."

"Did he ever think that his wife might not want to be with him any longer? That she might not love him anymore? Didn't you bring that up during your coaching?"

"Yes, many times. Christopher still needed to internalize his conflicts."

"Did he?"

"Well, unfortunately, he ran out of time."

Torsten changed the subject. "Now about Erik Bergström. How come he doesn't have a share in your extra business?"

"He's one hundred percent engaged in Right Now. He has no time for anything else—he already puts hours into his yoga every morning. He thought it would be good for me to have something else to do. He understood that I was frustrated being away from Casper so much—and that in the long run, it wouldn't work out."

"So how often do you see each other? As a couple, I mean?"

"When we're giving our courses together. Sometimes he comes into the city, but not very often. We do our best to communicate through meditation."

Torsten sighed again and shook his head.

She said, "Why does our spirituality bother you so much? You should look inside yourself and find out."

Torsten smiled. "Yes, perhaps I should. Or perhaps it's all a bunch of crap that makes money off of other people's misery. Add some sexual services, and I find your entire business to be unpleasant and unlawful. But now we won't take up any more of your valuable time."

They both stood up, and Christina Filipsson led them through the hallway toward the door.

"I think you have a much too narrow view of how the world works. People have different needs, and there are different ways to solve one's problems."

Buttoning his jacket, Torsten said, "Certainly, but the one you are practicing is still illegal. Usually, the consequence of that is jail. Have a good evening."

They didn't wait for the elevator but walked down the stairs. Torsten listened to the messages on his cell phone.

"They've found Ellen Nyhlén's bicycle. Someone threw it into a ditch near the crime scene. The tech guys are going over it now, but it probably won't give us much more. We might not even have the offender's fingerprints in the system. If there were no fingerprints on the body, I doubt we'll find any on the bicycle. Do you think Ushtanga Erik is at his house on Lidingö?"

"Actually, I doubt it. He's probably still out in the archipelago. Perhaps we can call him in tomorrow."

Torsten said, "Yes. It's too late to call tonight. And we got all we needed from her."

"Such as?"

"We know what kind of relationship she has with Ushtanga Erik. We know what her coaching is really about. I don't think Bergström is involved in this case, actually. On the other hand, the connection to Christina Filipsson seems clear to me."

"Do you think we should check out her ex-husband in Canada?"

"Maybe, but that's a long shot. You know, the more we find out about the people involved here, the more my head spins. I just don't see the connection yet," Torsten said.

"It's only because you've decided that Christopher Turin's killing is connected to Ellen Nyhlén's. But they're different cases. They have nothing to do with each other."

"They *are* connected. I'm absolutely sure."

"We have nothing to show they are," Augustin pointed out. "Not a single thing. I think you're fixated. You're like a dog staring at nothing."

"How do you know? Dogs see things we can't. At least, they can certainly hear things."

"You're starting to sound just as crazy as Christina Filipsson," Augustin said. "Oh, I get it. That's why you're so upset. You believe in some of that mumbo jumbo yourself, but you're ashamed to admit it."

Torsten replied, "The amateur psychologist has spoken." Then he sighed. "Maybe you're right, and I'm on the wrong track. Let's just go home. We'll write up our reports tomorrow morning and send them to Marianne and Olle."

"I'll drive you home. Unless you want to grab a bite to eat first. I need some dinner."

Torsten beamed. "Are you inviting me?"

"Absolutely. We think the same. What do you want? Expensive pizza? Hamburgers? Gourmet food to go?"

"Pizza sounds fine to me. Where do you get it?"

"Dell'attore. It's on the crossing between Kommendörsgatan and Karlavägen. You can't find more expensive pizza in all of Stockholm."

"Sounds perfect. I promise to invite you for pizza at a place on Verkstadsgatan sometime. They don't make the most expensive pizzas, just the biggest."

Augustin laughed, shaking his head at his colleague. It was almost touching how much Torsten needed company. Augustin had nothing against it since he didn't have a damn thing to do, either.

CHAPTER 75

Have you been enjoying yourself, Marianne?"
Marianne looked up from her perch on the sofa to see Ralph approaching. "Yes, I'm enjoying myself very much. Are you?"

Ralph looked around conspiratorially before sitting down. He lowered his voice and said, "I was next to Cita Theander. She's fascinating, but dear Lord, she is so neurotic I don't know how she can stand being with herself. Even for an artist, she's extreme. Did you know that she decides what to eat each week by the color of the food?"

"She's following the color method?"

Ralph said, "She had a lucky break because red was this week's color. She could eat both the crabs and the fillet of venison with lingonberries. She had to skip dessert because orange is next week."

"Interesting. So I guess you have no intention of trying this diet."

"Of course not! I like a mixed palette. But it was interesting to talk with a person so different from us everyday mortals."

"Everyday? You're hardly common. Aren't you the one who has to sleep with the window open, no matter what the

season? And don't you always purchase the exact same pajamas from Brooks Brothers every time you go to New York?"

"Definitely. I demand the same pattern because the others are of lesser quality. Still, I bear my OCD with a certain
consistency, of which I am proud."

They both laughed. Ralph bent closer to her. "I'm quite
impressed that you remembered that."

"It was so odd that I could never forget it."

"And how do *you* sleep?"

Marianne gave him a seductive look, hearing herself say,
"Naked."

Ralph was startled. Out of the corner of her eye, she saw
him studying her while she searched for her third Davidoff
of the evening.

"Would you think it forward of me," she said, turning to
him, "if I asked you to bring me a gin and tonic?"

"Not at all. Your wish is my command."

Marianne inhaled deeply, waving her hand at the
smoke. She leaned into the sofa and felt the cool night air
sweep through the room through the open balcony doors.
She could smell the sticky sweet scent of the chestnut trees
and hear the sound of the Djurgården ferry picking up tourists. The Gröna Lund Amusement Park was closing for the
night. A few colored lights twinkled from the stilled Ferris
wheel. She could see a lone man walking his dog along the
dock below and the Vasa ship dock and museum, both dark
shadows on the other side of the water. A passing wooden
Delfin boat was illuminated by its party lights.

She held her cigarette between two fingers, letting her
thumb rest on the dampened end. *Naked.* Where had that

come from? She hadn't slept naked in years. Perhaps it was time.

She closed her eyes and listened to the buzz of voices from the party. Someone was in a heated discussion about the corruption within third-world NGOs. She heard Lola explain what her friend who worked at Sida told her. For every donated hundred-crown bill, it'd be lucky if fifty made it to those in need. Marianne hoped Lola was wrong. She fingered the cell phone in her purse and wondered if she should call Olle or Torsten to see how the case was going. But what could she do at this hour of the night? She could hardly go over to the station now: tipsy and dressed for a party. She'd be of more use tomorrow.

"Now, I'd like to know your plans for the rest of your life."

Ralph had returned with her drink, filled to the brim with ice. She smiled at him and then sighed deeply.

"I don't know. I've thought so much about that I feel like I'm going crazy. Ideas just tumble around in my head, and I can't get them to make sense."

"What do you want?"

Marianne shrugged. "If only I knew. Part of me thinks I should just enjoy the time I have left. Retire and leave all thoughts of a career behind."

"And the other part?"

"I should stay at work and take pride in what I'm able to do."

"Aren't you proud of yourself now?"

"I'm proud of how my children turned out."

"But they are not you," Ralph replied.

"No. I'm not proud of myself. I'm not ashamed, but . . ."

"You would prefer not to talk about it."

"Not really, no."

"Then you do know what you want. It's the opposite of me. I've worked hard all my life, and now I want to explore something different. The parts of life you've already experienced."

"You mean you want to start a family?" Marianne looked at him in surprise.

Ralph laughed and shook his head. "No, not with children, no. I mean, I want a relationship with someone. Find someone to love. During most of my life, I pushed that away. I told myself I'd think about it later. Perhaps I was afraid—or, even worse, lazy."

Marianne watched the ice cubes swirl in her glass for a moment. Then she said, "I can understand that. So you think I should keep working?"

"Yes, obviously."

"Even just as a secretary to a prosecutor? Even though I never pursued a big career, the way I'd planned?"

"You are not just a mere secretary to a prosecutor. You do yourself a disservice looking at it like that. Yes, of course you should keep working, my dear Mary. You're not ready to retire."

He looked at her with tenderness.

"But don't you think it's pathetic? To come back to work after years of leave and actually think I'll make a difference? It's not like I need the money."

"It's never been about the money. Most of us from Lund don't need the money. We need to work."

"Perhaps you're right. I shouldn't think like that."

Ralph finished his drink as Marianne took a deep drag on her cigarette. She promised herself it would be the last of the evening.

He took her hand and held it to his lips for a moment. He gently set it back on her knee and said, smiling: "May I offer you another drink? And would it be too forward to ask if you'd like to have it at my place?"

Chapter 76

Torsten waved to Augustin as he drove away. He'd decided to walk the few blocks home to help digest his meal. And yet that wasn't the only reason. The past few days had been filled with too much driving and coffee drinking. He was looking forward to his weekend sailing trip with Noah, hoping they'd be able to get away; but it wouldn't be easy if this case didn't resolve soon. He'd been around long enough to take weekends off, and lately, he'd been able to ensure he had a private life, even though there were times when the workload was heavy. Still, there'd been two murders in a part of town where murder was rare. He wanted to think, to go over everything without anyone interrupting his thoughts.

Augustin was absolutely right that there seemed no connection between the two murders. But Torsten was convinced there was, which meant his subconscious mind already knew—it must be right before his eyes. He was just waiting for the lightbulb to go off.

Leaving Christina Filipsson's apartment, he thought of Marianne Jidhoff. Was she in her apartment all by herself tonight? He was nearby and could drop in for a spontaneous visit, but he didn't think Marianne was the kind who liked that. He also had no idea whether she was seeing anyone. That was none of his business. Still, he looked forward to spending more time with her. He wanted to excel and impress—to walk on the high wire—for her.

He forced his thoughts back to the murders and systematically went through all the information he'd gathered the past few days. He began to toss arguments back and forth in a kind of mental ping-pong. He was so lost in thought that he hardly noticed his surroundings until he found himself at the front door to his apartment building. He glanced at his watch and saw it had taken him an hour to walk from Östermalm all the way to Folkskolegatan. He punched in his entry code and took the stairs.

He knew Noah wasn't home, but he still felt disappointed when he walked into his empty apartment. He didn't like being by himself, and he wondered what his life would be like when Noah moved out for good. He might get used to it, but he didn't know how.

Now slightly gloomy, he brushed his teeth and peered at his reflection in the mirror. He ought to get his hair cut. Probably he should be more regular about shaving. For the past year, he'd shaved only every other day, but now he saw that was a bad idea. He looked too sloppy, and his face itched.

He got his sofa bed ready and opened the balcony door. Shivering, he climbed beneath the blankets and closed his eyes. It was just past ten in the evening, but he was exhausted from all the hectic days. If he got a good night's sleep, he might be able to sort his thoughts on the case.

CHAPTER 77

He checked the alarm a second time before shutting the cover. Their code was a combination of the children's birth years. It had been fairly easy to figure out, and he'd had a good look at it through his binoculars. He couldn't understand why security firms put alarms in such easy-to-see locations. Maybe that would be a good career for him later: to start a security firm that made it impossible for burglars to break in. He'd be the perfect expert.

He quietly took off his shoes and walked through the living room in his socks. The house was absolutely silent. The lamp on the ground floor, which was usually kept on, was off. They had used the fireplace earlier that evening. He placed his hand over it—it was still warm. Her cell phone was on the coffee table.

She breathed deeply on the couch, and he had to resist the impulse to lie down next to her. She looked more fragile than usual, and it was hard for him not to touch her. But he didn't have time—he had other things to do.

He headed up the stairs. The girls were deeply asleep in their bedrooms, and he could hear their regular breathing.

From the master bedroom, he heard nothing. He walked silently to the half-open door, eased it open, and shuddered with a sudden feeling of contentment. He was here, and she could feel safe. He carefully sneaked into the bedroom and stood perfectly still. The man lay on his stomach, his right hand still gripping his cell phone. He smiled crookedly, feeling proud to be standing here watching Jens Steen in the darkness.

She needn't worry any longer. He would take care of her.

CHAPTER 78

To reach Ralph's temporary residence at an exclusive hotel, they had to walk through the lobby to the elevator and exit at the top floor. Ralph escorted her down the carpet-covered hallway to a door at the end.

"Do you eat here at the hotel, too?"

"I have a small kitchen. I do the best I can. I'm not much of a cook, but I can make myself breakfast and a few simple dinners. Most of the time, I eat out. Stockholm has changed quite a bit. Ten years ago, you couldn't find a nice place open for breakfast, but now you can."

They entered the minimal suite. It felt welcoming in spite of its spare interior. Ralph opened the terrace doors, and Marianne stepped outside to enjoy the starry night sky. Excusing himself, Ralph returned with a blanket, which he draped over Marianne's shoulders. Then he went back inside.

Marianne sat down in one of the recliners and continued to stare into the black night. Ralph made coffee in the kitchenette. A heat lamp beside her turned on and she felt warmed right away. She kicked off her shoes and pulled her feet beneath the blanket. A breeze was coming up. She closed her eyes. In the background she heard Chet Baker.

"Am I disturbing you?"

"No, I've just settled in perfectly. Oh! Is all that for me?"

Ralph was carrying a tray with two cups of steaming coffee and round glasses of cognac. There was a bowl with candy—white truffle nougat!

"I can't believe this! White truffle nougat is my favorite!"

Ralph laughed. "I have to admit I knew. Lola told me you love white chocolate and you often shop at Eje's—and once I went there, they knew exactly what to give me. It seems you are a valuable customer."

"I must be responsible for fifty percent of their profits. Mmm. Have you tasted these? They are heavenly."

"I *did* have one in the shop. They are hard to resist, just like you. You go together."

"Stop it! You embarrass me."

"Come on, it's the twenty-first century. You can't embarrass people anymore!"

"Then I will get a swollen head, and I'll be impossible to deal with. You must have been pretending you didn't know I was recently widowed. Shame on you!"

"Guilty as charged!" Ralph held up two hands and smiled.

They both laughed. Marianne sipped her coffee. The hot coffee and the white chocolate blended so wonderfully.

"You're still the same," Ralph said.

"The same?"

"So happy and positive. I don't believe I've ever seen you in a bad mood."

"It's an illusion. All summer I stayed in bed feeling sorry for myself. I enjoyed making myself miserable."

"But you're positive and happy again."

"Happy as I can be. Still, I've gotten back on my feet. I have other things to do these days."

"That's what I mean. You brush yourself off and get back in there. You must have been born with more than your share of positive energy."

"Perhaps," Marianne said. "But it feels strange hearing you say that. It's not the picture I have of myself. I often think I'm troublesome and demanding. But you're right. I don't let grief and worry get the upper hand. Maybe that's because of my mother."

"Your mother?"

"She died when I was born. In childbirth. I almost didn't make it either. Pappa found himself with a small child right after he lost the love of his life, but he didn't wallow in his grief. He was filled with gratitude that I'd survived."

Ralph slowly lifted his glass of cognac. "*Skål* that you survived. And that you are here with me now, although thirty years have gone by and I am no longer that exciting young man you used to know."

Marianne chuckled. "You were never exciting, but you were cute."

Ralph smiled over his glass. "Being cute is good enough. Actually, it's more than good enough."

—□—

Marianne tried to relax. She closed her eyes, but she was still too tense. Ralph noticed she wasn't letting go, but they both pretended she was. When he finally came, she simply felt relieved that it was over. They hadn't gotten into the proper rhythm from the start, although their kisses were full of desire. His mouth had explored her entire body and he seemed to like what he discovered. But she felt awkward and had difficulty remembering how to be with a naked man. His personal odor was different from Hans's. He was soft in the places where Hans was hard. He had hair where she was used to finding soft skin. Marianne bit her lip and tried to think of something to say. She wanted to apologize for not being able to relax. She didn't remember herself like this. Sex used to be exciting, but now it made her uncomfortable.

Ralph lay next to her, stroking her cheek.

"You are wonderful. I can't believe I'm actually lying next to you. It seems unreal. You don't realize how many years I've dreamed about being with you. And here you are, naked beside me."

He began to kiss her on the throat, and they started up all over again. She thought at first that he was kissing her to relieve her from embarrassment, but his kisses became more intense and again he wandered all over her body. Her long-forgotten urges came back to life. All her stiffness disappeared. She wanted this now!

"Please, can you sit on me? I need . . . to look at you."

Ralph's voice was thickening. He groaned as she sat up and straddled his body. She thought being naked in front of him would feel uncomfortable, but when she saw he was aroused, she felt braver. Ralph lay quietly beneath her, his hands on her hips, groaning more intensely. Marianne moved faster and faster, enjoying the fact he was so still. When she suddenly came, she was surprised. Her orgasm didn't last long, but Ralph's image seemed to waver before her eyes and then he shuddered all over. He uttered a long, animal-like moan, and she had to keep herself from laughing. Ralph opened his eyes. For a moment, he stared at Marianne in confusion.

"My God, Marianne, my God. That's all I can say."

They lay in silence for a long time. After a while, Ralph got up and came back with a pack of cigarettes.

"Shall we celebrate with a smoke in bed? This is a non-smoking hotel and it's forbidden. Are you okay with that?"

Marianne smiled and shook her head. "I haven't been moral for quite some time. My humble self has completely forgotten everything having to do with morality."

Ralph laughed and kissed her cheek gently. "How lucky for me!"

They shared the cigarette, gazing at the ceiling. Marianne blew out some smoke. "It's been a long time."

"I didn't notice. You're good in bed."

"I don't believe you for a second," she laughed.

"Well, you are. Just looking at you, like I said, it's obvious you enjoy all the good things in life."

"I guess I should take that as a compliment. But it's probably a good thing that you remember what I looked like when I was young."

"If you think your looks have faded with the years, let me be the first to tell you you're wrong. I was shocked when I saw you at Lola's. I was expecting a morose widow. Instead, a sexy goddess appeared."

Marianne laughed. She couldn't help giving Ralph's arm a pinch.

"That's not nice, putting such thoughts into the head of a woman of my age."

"I'm not flattering you. I'm amazed that you're unaware of your own charisma. Don't you feel sexy?"

Marianne kept looking at the ceiling. She took a last puff from the cigarette, which was dangerously close to its filter.

"No, I seldom do. As I said, it's been a long time."

Ralph shook his head. He took the cigarette butt from her hand, extinguishing it in an ashtray on the nightstand. "Perhaps . . . from what I've heard about your marriage, that's not surprising."

"It's true. Hans's illness made things difficult, and sex had never been a priority. Or perhaps we hid behind his illness. What about you? What about your life?"

Ralph shrugged. He seemed troubled for the first time that evening.

"I don't know how to answer that. My wife and I never talked about sex. She did it like it was her duty to God and her country. It hardly made me feel appreciated as a man. The sex became less frequent until it finally stopped altogether. At that point, we knew it was time to talk seriously about getting a divorce."

"Did you have other women on the side?"

Ralph was silent for a moment, and Marianne wondered if he would tell the truth. Then he replied, "Yes, it happened. I'm not proud of it. It seemed that we were in silent agreement about it. I was discreet."

Her stomach cramped. She could understand Ralph's decision but still felt sad that he'd chosen to go that way. She'd wanted to keep him on a pedestal a little while longer. Ralph turned his face to her.

"Have I disappointed you?"

Marianne blinked. "No, no, I do understand. And did your wife have affairs, too?"

"I have no idea. I doubt it, but perhaps I was just naive."

"What did she look like?"

"She was tall and thin. Light hair, green eyes. She was attractive, but she was somewhat cool. When she was young, she used to be ashamed of her height. She thought she was a giant. It wasn't true. She really was quite pretty."

"Was?"

"Yes, well, she still is, but she died for me. She turned chilly. I never saw that spark in her eye anymore. Perhaps it was all my fault. Now, she probably smiles a lot when she's in the right company."

"I know some people whose smiles have stopped entirely. Many acquaintances my age—the ones in bad marriages. It's sad how we make our lives so complicated. It's hard enough just living."

"Yes, it's sad, isn't it? So let's stop crying and have another cigarette."

"Thanks, but I've had so many."

"Chocolate?"

Marianne laughed. She was unable to answer before Ralph leapt out of bed and returned with the bowl of chocolates and pack of cigarettes.

Chapter 79

Something made him jump.

He realized he must have fallen asleep.

The rest of the house was still quiet.

He sat up slowly.

It was time for him to go home and get to bed. He was needed. Tomorrow. Silently, he stood up from the sofa where he'd fallen asleep listening to her breathing. He walked into the hallway. Tomorrow would be intense. He needed his sleep. He was needed. By her.

CHAPTER 80

Marianne rubbed her finger beneath her eyes to get rid of some smudged makeup. She'd have to take off the rest at home. She realized it was awkward, but she wanted to sneak out without waking Ralph. She had tried to convince herself it was because he was sleeping so deeply, but then she admitted she didn't want to face what had happened that night. At least not here and now. She wanted to take the time to let it all sink in. She was, in all honesty, shocked at what had happened: not really about having sex with him, although it was her first time in thirty years sleeping with someone other than Hans. She just felt unsettled about their conversation afterward. She knew she shouldn't be upset about Ralph's unfaithfulness—but something had been shattered when he'd told her. No matter how good his reasons, some of the glow had been lost. She couldn't ignore her reaction. She didn't know if she wanted to spend more time with someone who was the unfaithful type. That was harsh, but it was a stumbling block. Was there something about her that drew unfaithful men to her? "The gene of unfaithfulness," as Lola called it. She would break that pattern right now. Perhaps she could ignore this emotional response; perhaps she could be with Ralph occasionally, just enjoying the moment.

Still, she wanted to sort it all out, and she didn't want to have to think too hard before her first cup of coffee this morning. She wanted to go home and ponder things.

So she dressed and sneaked out to the suite's living room. Having found a memo pad and a pen, she sat on the sofa and wrote:

Dear Ralph. Thanks for an absolutely wonderful evening. I'm so glad you pulled me out of my shell. Since I'm an early riser, I'm slipping out quietly so I don't wake you. You are sleeping so sweetly. Thanks again for last night. Warmest wishes, Mary.

She folded the sheet of paper and attached it to the bathroom mirror with some tape from the medicine cabinet. Then she walked out the door and shut it as quietly as possible.

The early September morning was chilly, and Marianne saw that frost had settled overnight. She hugged her shawl around her shoulders and strode as quickly as possible in her high heels. A newspaperman had located his cart at the crossroads between Storgatan and Grevgatan. She greeted the young man, who looked just as awake as the hotel doorman. Once she passed Torstenssonsgatan, she realized her phone was vibrating in her purse. She didn't want to pick up but did so anyway. She was certain it was Ralph, but she was surprised to see that it was Nina.

"Hi, Mamma. Did I wake you? Are you home? Did you go out?"

"No, you didn't wake me. I was out. What's wrong?"

Nina didn't answer, but Marianne could hear heartbreaking sobs. She felt her own heart crack.

"Please, Nina, tell me where you are and I'll come get you."

"I'm right outside your apartment! Nobody's opening it!"

Marianne's throat was dry, but she pulled herself together to answer. "I'm right outside the building. I'll be there in a few seconds."

Marianne opened the front door and ran up the stairs to the third floor. She had no patience for the elevator.

Nina was standing in front of her apartment door wearing just an old sweater and torn jeans. On her feet, she wore flip-flops. Marianne realized Nina had thrown on whatever she had at hand. She held a small plastic bag. Her tear-stained face looked as if she hadn't slept all night.

Marianne had braced herself to have to answer where she'd been all night, but instead her daughter rushed into her arms. Nina's entire body shook with sobs. She must have gotten cold. How long had she been waiting outside the door?

"Let's go inside. I'll make you some tea. Or would you like some hot chocolate?"

Nina nodded as they went into the apartment. She put down her plastic bag and then stood there, her arms hanging hopelessly at her sides. Marianne threw her shawl on the hat rack and pulled Nina close to her. She stroked her hair.

"Sweetie, what's going on?"

Nina looked at her, confused. "Where have you been?"

Marianne knew she couldn't tell Nina the truth. Instead, she found herself saying, "I was at Lola's dinner party. You know how late those go." It *was* just before four a.m., so theoretically it was possible.

Nina blinked and then said, in a small voice, "He found someone else."

"Robert?"

Nina nodded.

"What will you do?"

Nina shook her head and wiped her nose with the back of her hand. "*He* doesn't know yet what he wants to do. He says he can't choose between us."

Marianne wanted to scream as loud as she could. But instead she took a deep breath and hugged Nina even closer.

"It'll work out for the best. I promise. It will be for the best."

Marianne knew that Nina didn't need to hear those empty words. She'd been in the same situation all too often. It was incredibly painful to see her daughter enduring the same pain—standing there torn apart with such grief. That feeling of powerlessness. Nina had been betrayed by a man the same way she'd been betrayed by Hans. She took the guilt upon herself. She'd been a terrible role model for her daughter.

"I need to change. Let me tuck you up in my bed so you can warm up. You're freezing."

Nina let herself be led into Marianne's room and crept into her bed. Marianne tucked her in, just as she'd done when she was a little girl. Nina had always had difficulty sleeping in her own room—more so than the other two.

"I'll be right back with something hot to drink."

Marianne hurried to the bathroom but left the door open, just as she'd done when Nina slept in her bed when

Hans was away. Nina had said she didn't like the door closed; she liked to hear Marianne brush her teeth and move around in the bathroom.

Marianne pulled off her clothes and hung her dress on her robe's hanger. She took off her panties and threw them right in the washing machine. The water in the shower took forever to warm up, and she stamped her feet on the cold bottom of the tub. Then she scrubbed her body as fast as humanly possible and even ran some shampoo through her hair, following with some conditioner. She wanted to get rid of the smell of smoke, as well as the last bit of hairspray remaining in her hair. Then she brushed her teeth, which felt fantastic. She brushed her hair and put on her robe. She completed everything in double time, not wanting to leave Nina alone for too long.

Marianne found some flannel pajamas and rag socks, which she placed at the foot of the bed. Then she sat beside Nina and ran her hand over her forehead. Nina was staring at the ceiling and biting her lip.

Marianne spoke gently and softly. "I found a pair of pajamas for you and a pair of warm socks. Come. Let me help you change."

Nina sat up and Marianne pulled off Nina's thin sweater, replacing it with the soft, warm pajama top. Marianne had received the pajamas as a Christmas present from Sigrid a few years back. The flannel was high quality and had light-blue stars. Once Nina pulled on the pajama pants and the socks, they headed for the kitchen.

"So what do you want? Tea or hot chocolate?"

"I'll have what you're having."

Marianne decided to make hot chocolate. Nina didn't need caffeine right now. She needed to sleep. Hot chocolate was the best for that. Marianne found some slices of white bread in the refrigerator and dropped them in the toaster. After a while, she heard Nina say in a fragile voice, "I don't understand why I didn't just tell him to go to hell."

Marianne looked down at the toast she was buttering. She said, "It's not as easy as you think. Never do what other people think you should do. You have to do what's in your own heart."

After a few seconds' pause, Nina asked, "What would you do?"

Marianne placed the plate of toast on the table and filled two mugs with steaming hot chocolate.

"Are you asking me what I would do if I were me, or if I were you?"

"If you were me."

Marianne looked directly at her daughter. "Then I'd tell him to go to hell."

Nina looked right back at her. "And if you were you?"

"Well, if I were young and had no children, I'd do the same. Tell him to go where the sun doesn't shine."

"But if you had children?"

"Then I would wait and see how things develop."

"If you had children, you wouldn't leave him?"

Marianne looked at her mug and swallowed. "No, I wouldn't. You have obligations to consider with children in the picture."

Nina sat still. She was breathing heavily. "Did you want to leave Pappa?"

Marianne felt that question like a fist to the face. She had to hold back her own tears. "Yes. Yes, I did want to leave him. I was a coward."

"But you had us."

"Yes, but if I had faced our problems then, maybe you wouldn't be here now, suffering the way I did. As a parent, one has to be a role model. I certainly wasn't successful there."

Nina sat silently. "Was Pappa unfaithful before we were born?"

"Not that I knew. I don't believe so. I think that came later, though I ought to have seen what kind of a person he was from the beginning. If I had been more attentive, perhaps I would have seen it coming."

Nina chewed her toast, although Marianne could see she wasn't hungry.

"How did you find out?" Marianne asked.

"I didn't. He told me."

"How long has it been going on?"

Nina shrugged. "He didn't want to say. Obviously, for a while or it wouldn't have come to this. A few months, perhaps? Maybe I didn't notice because I was grieving for Pappa."

The words cut Marianne like a knife. She had to blink away her tears. She was also boiling in anger. How could Robert hurt her daughter like this? Just when she needed her husband the most. Instead of support, she got a knife in the back. What an asshole.

Nina shivered. "Do you mind if I go back to bed? I haven't slept much."

"Go right ahead. Just crawl back into my bed. I'll be fine."

Nina slowly headed for the bedroom.

Marianne put the dishes in the dishwasher and thought of having a cigarette. She didn't feel like it. Perhaps she shouldn't have spoken so freely. Nina needed her support now.

She went into the hallway and picked up her cell phone. A text had come from Ralph about ten minutes earlier.

My little runaway. I thought I'd treat you to a good breakfast, but with your heathenish morning hours, I see that was an impossible dream. I am eternally grateful for our evening together. I truly hope we'll get to repeat it another night. Yours for all eternity, etc., etc., Ralph.

Marianne smiled. She took the cell phone into the living room and set it next to the morning paper. She stretched out on the sofa and pulled the blanket over herself, thinking she'd flip through the paper's cultural pages. But her eyes closed as soon as she started, and the paper fell to the floor. She surrendered and let sleep take over.

CHAPTER 81

Paula jerked awake to Jens clearing his throat. He was standing over her with his arms crossed over his chest.

"So, when were you going to tell me you were fucking some damned foreigner?"

She blinked, trying to guess how he'd found out. Did someone call him during the night?

"What are you talking about?"

"Stop playing fucking dumb. Don't think for one second I'm such an idiot. It seems all of Djursholm is aware that you went to Lotta's place to fuck that waiter. How charming!"

Paula took a deep breath. She stared at this man who was her husband. Then she decided to fight.

"Maybe I did. Everyone knows you're sleeping around. All of Djursholm knows our marriage is on the rocks. Now they really have something to gossip about."

"Do you realize what you've done? You won't be able to show your face at the girls' school. Every single person there knows."

Paula quickly calculated that Purran must have started the rumor. Or even Lotta herself. She knew not to trust anyone in this town. She stared right back at Jens. "So what? All the men, with all their little affairs, pick up their children.

They have their au pairs and their whores. What's the difference?"

"You're pathetic. I want you to move out immediately. Today. You'll never share custody of the girls."

Paula felt her eyes burn. She stood up so she could look him in the face.

"Go ahead: call me a whore if it makes you feel better. But let me tell you a thing or two. You will not threaten to take the girls from me, is that clear?"

Jens was shocked by her anger and took an involuntary step backward. Paula continued. "I know exactly what went on in that little Right Now group of yours, and I think the press would be extremely interested, too. All about the sex and the people involved. Just let me make a statement to the press about the whole dirty game and cite you as the source. And send a copy to your friends on that island. They won't be happy about *that* kind of publicity. And when it comes to who has the right to live in this house, I want to remind you of our prenuptial agreement. Remember that? Remember that my father forced us to sign it before we married? As far as I recall, the down payment for this house came from my maternal inheritance."

"Remember, little wife, my salary has allowed us to live here. You don't even have an income."

"I wonder how much you know about family law? I am going to stay here with the children and I'll have main custody. Yes, of course I will, because you're never here, you travel too much. I want *you* to leave *right now* before the girls wake up."

Jens stared, stupefied. Paula had to duck as he threw a punch at her face. She jumped to the side and shook her head.

"If you try to hit me again, I'll call the police."

Jens tried to show he couldn't care less about her threat, but he controlled his outburst. He stomped up the stairs, and she heard hangers banging down as he pulled clothes from the closet. She looked at the clock and realized the girls were already awake. She guessed they were staying in bed, too frightened to get up, and she hoped Jens would just leave as fast as possible. She didn't want to argue any longer; she certainly didn't want to get into a physical fight. She decided to stay out of his way on the ground floor.

Ten minutes later, Jens stormed out of the house. He revved up the Porsche and screeched out of the driveway.

When she was sure he wasn't coming back, Paula ran upstairs to the girls. As she'd suspected, they were hiding in their beds with the covers over their heads. Her youngest was crying. Her oldest wouldn't look at her.

"I know it sounded terrible, girls, but everything's okay."

"Are you and Pappa getting a divorce?"

"Yes, we are," Paula said. "We aren't happy together anymore. You've probably already noticed that. It has nothing to do with the two of you. It's just between Pappa and me. Come downstairs now, and we'll eat breakfast. Then I'll call the school and tell them you have to take a sick day. We can go into the city and do something fun instead. All right?"

Paula had no idea if it was psychologically beneficial taking the girls downtown to do something fun when they faced losing their sense of security. On the other hand, sending them to school seemed worse.

She went down to make breakfast. She picked up her phone and put it on the charger. There was a message on the phone.

"Finally! Just you and me! I'm longing for you!"

First she thought it was from Passi, but then she realized it was from that same anonymous number. Her breath caught in her chest, and she had to hold on to the countertop to keep from fainting. Stars whirled around, and she sat down on the floor. Desperately, she called Passi.

Hi, Passi. You've got to help me. He's starting to send messages again. I don't know what to do! Have you reached that guy you thought could help me?

Chapter 82

Marianne woke for the second time that morning in a place that wasn't her own bed. Her neck was stiff, and her sofa pillows, which had seemed soft and welcoming a few hours before, were hard and lumpy. Shocked, she saw it was already ten in the morning. How could she have slept so long? Nina must still be asleep.

Marianne got up as quietly as she could. She pulled her robe closer around her body and hoped that Harry would soon tell the building manager to turn on the heat. Once she flushed, she listened for Nina's breathing but didn't hear anything. The apartment was suspiciously silent. Without making a sound, she opened the door to her bedroom. Her bed was empty and it had been made. She found a note on the pillow. Marianne thought that the morning was repeating itself in an unusual way. She shook her head and looked for her reading glasses.

Dearest Mams. I'm sneaking back home while you're sleeping. Will be in touch. Love, Nina.

Marianne frowned, feeling a lump in her stomach. She read the note again a few times before letting it fall back on the bed. She wanted to scream at Nina and tell her she had to leave Robert before it was too late. But last night, she'd talked calmly and diplomatically. As usual. To her daughter, she should have been more direct and put her foot down. Probably Nina had slept for a while, dried her tears, and then gone back to Robert thinking they could still work it out. She would tell that disgusting idiot that they could solve everything, that there was no need to rush.

Marianne could hear her own reasoning in those words. She picked up the note and tore it into little pieces, ending up with a paper cut on her forefinger. She tried to call Nina's cell phone, but it was turned off. She went into the kitchen and lit a cigarette, while turning on the coffee machine. She wasn't at all hungry for an egg this morning, but she took out a pan to boil two anyway. The coffee tasted sour, and she boiled the eggs too long. She tried the morning Sudoku with no success. Her brain wasn't working at all. She didn't know whether to blame all the wine she'd had during last night's adventures, or her distress over passing her wishy-washy ways of dealing with men to her daughter, destroying her life in the process. If she'd been stronger and left Hans, maybe Nina wouldn't be going through this now. That was the hard truth. Her telephone rang, and she hoped it was Nina.

"Hi, Marianne. Torsten here."

"Hello!"

Marianne realized her voice sounded harsh. She quickly changed her tone to something more pleasant. "Sorry, you caught me by surprise."

"I did? All right. Well, I've sent over yesterday's reports by messenger. They should be there any minute."

"Thank you, that was kind. Anything specific turn up?"

"No, nothing that hit me right away, but I want to see what you come up with. Are you all right, otherwise?"

"Yes, as I said, I was expecting someone else on the other end, not you."

"So that explains it. I'm heading into the interrogation room now, but give me a call when you've finished reading."

Marianne thought he sounded disappointed about something. She hoped she hadn't put him off.

The reports arrived ten minutes later, and Marianne practically ripped them from the messenger's hands. She had a desperate need to take her mind off things.

−□−

Once her eyes adjusted, she read rapidly. On the fourth document, she frowned. She went back to the first and read them all again, more slowly. Then she leapt to her feet and ran for her phone. She called and asked to be connected to the local station in Danderyd. It took her a few minutes to find the right person and tell him what she needed. Then, taking a deep breath, she called Torsten, who answered after two rings.

"Torsten? Sorry to bother you. I know you're in the middle of questioning someone. I just read your reports and I believe I've found the connection. There's no time to waste. Can you and Augustin get here immediately?"

Chapter 83

Augustin jogged behind Torsten, putting on his jacket as they headed down the stairs.

"What's going on?"

"Jidhoff called. She's figured something out."

"What?"

"She just told us to get right over."

Augustin's telephone rang at the same moment they jumped into his sports car. He looked at the display and hesitated. Torsten looked at him questioningly.

Augustin shook his head, then clicked the call off. He put his phone in his jacket and started the car. "I'll take it later. Which is fastest, Kungsgatan or Hamngatan?"

At that time of the morning, the traffic wasn't bad, and Augustin was parking in front of Marianne Jidhoff's apartment in ten minutes. They hurried up to the third floor, and Augustin's phone rang again. Torsten laughed.

"Must be a girl. Don't worry, you don't have to tell me, even if we're partners."

Augustin shook his head. "I'd tell you if it were a woman. Right now a friend wants something from me. He'll just have to wait a minute."

Marianne opened the door. It was obvious she was thinking about the case. Her hair was a mess, and she was wearing more casual clothing than the day before. She had on sweatpants and a hand-knit sweater with a scarf collar.

"Let's go into the library. I have a map there."

Marianne had put up a number of Post-it notes on a bulletin board. She'd written large letters on them.

"Yes, here, you see, I've found a connection, even though I don't have a solution. Still, now we have somewhere to look, except . . . nothing about the young girl's death. Perhaps that will become clear. Well . . ."

Marianne cleared her throat and pointed to the Post-it on the top left corner.

"Here is Christopher Turin. He is married to Isa Turin. They go to Right Now when their marriage is in trouble. Right?"

Torsten and Augustin agreed.

"Isa Turin decides not to continue and stops. Christopher Turin continues anyway and begins a separate counseling session, if you could call it that, with Christina Filipsson. Christina is single and has a teenage son. She also has a sporadic relationship with the cofounder of Right Now, Ushtanga Erik. He is also single. Christina runs her side project as a form of 'lifestyle coaching,' which also includes sex with certain clients. Clients she's handpicked from Right Now. Am I correct so far?"

Torsten nodded. Augustin's phone rang again. He got up and headed for the hallway, saying, "Please excuse me. I have to take this. He'll just keep calling if I don't. Keep going."

Marianne tapped her pen on the note about Isa Turin. "Yes, here's the interesting thing. Isa Turin said someone had been calling her daughter and leaving anonymous messages a month or so before Christopher was killed. I decided to follow up. The phone was registered in Isa Turin's name, so I began to wonder if the caller was trying to reach Isa, not her daughter."

Torsten looked at her curiously.

"I read through your reports on the Right Now attendees in Djursholm. Nobody mentioned any anonymous calls, but when I called the police in Danderyd, I got a bite. A woman living on Friggavägen reported someone breaking into her house two days ago. She also said someone had been calling her anonymously for some time. The woman hadn't attended Right Now, but her husband—"

Augustin came running back. "Sorry, but my pal just asked me to help him with his new girlfriend . . . well, she's actually not so young . . . but she's being terrorized by somebody calling anonymously, someone who broke into her house two days ago. Guess who she is? The woman we visited last night."

Torsten looked up, saying, "And she lives on Friggavägen."

Augustin looked at him in surprise.

"I'm going to call in a patrol immediately," Torsten said. "Now, who is behind all this? Who are we looking for?"

Marianne said, "Someone close to Christina Filipsson. She's the point around which everything revolves."

Torsten looked at Augustin. "If your pal is having an affair with the woman on Friggavägen, it's pretty damned obvious that her husband is our guy. If he was also one of

Christina's special clients, he'd have a motive for getting rid of Christopher Turin. And he's a very unpleasant person."

"But you said he was too self-involved to be a killer?"

"Yes, but there could be another side to him. I have to call Christina Filipsson. Find her number for me, will you? And I need to send that patrol to Friggavägen right away."

Torsten was reassured after three patrol cars were on their way to Friggavägen. Then he called Christina Filipsson.

"Hello, Christina. Torsten Ehn. From the police. I know you don't want to tell me who your special clients were, but please listen to me. It's a matter of life and death. Just say yes or no. Was Jens Steen one of them? All right, thanks."

Torsten turned to the others, excited. "He was. Put out an alert on Jens Steen. Tell the patrols."

Augustin looked at him. "Can we be sure it's him?"

"Pretty sure. But not one hundred percent. Jens Steen also lives just a few yards away from the café where Ellen Nyhlén worked. Perhaps he had a reason to kill her, too."

Marianne looked at her bulletin board. Something didn't fit. It was too simple, too quick. Though perhaps she wasn't yet used to the fast pace of police work.

Torsten asked to be connected to one of the patrols. He lifted his hand, requesting the others to be silent. When he finished, he turned toward them.

"Jens Steen is dead. He's just been run over right outside his office. The driver backed over him, according to some eyewitnesses. The car used was Jens Steen's own silver Porsche."

The three of them froze. Marianne looked back at her bulletin board and at her Post-it notes, tapping them with her pen. Torsten had sunk into a chair, and Augustin was leaning on the door frame.

"Wait a minute," she said. "Remember our conversation earlier? Torsten, you thought we were dealing with a *young* man. Which young man is connected to Christopher Turin, Jens Steen, and Christina Filipsson?"

Torsten leapt from his chair. "Damn it! Okay, call Josefine, that young woman we interviewed from the café, and ask her to be ready for identification. We have to find Casper Filipsson immediately! Perhaps he's on his way to Friggavägen. But why? Why did he want to kill these men?"

"To protect the women," Marianne said. "And to protect his mother. He wants to save them from these 'evil men.'"

Torsten added, "Some kind of justified killing. We'll probably find out he had a violent father who beat Christina Filipsson during their marriage. Nine out of ten murderers have violent fathers, so that wouldn't surprise me in the least. But how does Ellen Nyhlén fit in?"

Augustin said, "Perhaps she just got in his way."

Torsten sighed. "Could it be so simple? Maybe so . . ."

He sighed again, and Marianne realized he was taking it hard. Torsten turned to Augustin. "Ask Brundin to get ready to inspect a vehicle. I have a feeling that Jens Steen's Porsche was used to mow down Turin, too. If we're lucky, Brundin will find evidence to prove it."

CHAPTER 84

Torsten drove to the station where Casper Filipsson was waiting for his defense lawyer in one of the interrogation rooms. The patrol had spotted him up in one of the trees next to the house on Friggavägen, perched on a branch. When he saw the police, he came quietly. Casper had looked tired, fragile, and very much the adolescent.

Torsten decided not to park on Bergsgatan. Augustin sat beside him, shaking his head, "The guy's not even twenty."

"Yes, but he's been in the children's psychiatric hospital several times. He's been violent toward his mother. A year ago, he attacked a teacher, and that was reported to the police. Later, he stalked the teacher and stood outside his house. The teacher reported him again when he found his daughter's cat dead in the yard. He got a restraining order, and things calmed down. Another thing, just as suspected, his father had been abusive toward Christina."

"Just think, a boy with mental problems knows his mother is engaging in prostitution. She sleeps with clients, for money, in her own home. How did the identification go?"

"Josefine said Casper had been at the café and talked to Ellen Nyhlén a few times. They spoke the same day she was killed. According to Josefine, Ellen took a liking to him—thought he was cute. Perhaps he panicked and thought he'd be recognized."

Torsten locked the car, and they walked to the entrance. Then he changed his mind and started walking toward the café. "Let's have a real cup of coffee? I don't think I can stand one from the machine."

After ordering their coffee, Torsten motioned toward the jail. "I believe the motive is simple. He wanted revenge on the men who took advantage of his mother."

Augustin swallowed. "I can almost understand why."

"Me, too," Torsten said. "What a terrible childhood. I'm glad the local police will be handling the case from now on. I think I'll let them do the questioning and all the follow-up."

Augustin raised an eyebrow. "I thought you wanted this. That's nice of you to let it go. Or was it an order from Olle?"

"No," Torsten replied. "We've solved the case. As far as I'm concerned, I really don't want to deal with someone just a couple of years older than my son. He's still not a hardened criminal."

Augustin raised his other eyebrow. "No, he's just killed three people, including a young girl who got in his way."

"Yes, that's true," Torsten replied. "Well, at least we can look forward to a good weekend. Don't you think we deserve it?"

"Maybe. I'm going to get together with my pal, Passi. He seems to be serious about that widow on Friggavägen. He's going to help me with physical training—get me in better shape."

"Well, that's been a remarkable coincidence, hasn't it? Tell your pal to take his time. Widows need tender care."

Augustin laughed, shaking his head. "Sounds to me you're thinking about a different widow altogether. But I could be wrong?"

Torsten glared at him. "You're too young to know about these things. But you have to admit, she's brilliant, isn't she? Damn, she's a smart woman!"

"I agree, but keep in mind—those widows need special care!"

Torsten couldn't help roughing up Augustin's stylish haircut.

"All right, then! I'm off! Have a good weekend, and stay out of trouble," he said.

CHAPTER 85

Marianne felt gratified that her input had been so important in solving the case. Olle couldn't stop praising her. He was especially happy there had been no leaks—not a single detail of the inquiries had gotten to the press, even though these were the types of cases that the media loved to put on the front page.

She had had no luck with the trap she'd set in her computer, but Lillemor was still her number-one suspect. Perhaps the woman's alcohol abuse was one reason for that. But Olle thought the leaks were coming from more than one person. Maybe some secret inner organization. Lillemor could have been part of that, but that remained to be seen.

Still, Marianne was on pins and needles. She couldn't stop thinking of Nina. Olle had given her the rest of the day off—he'd be on call himself—but she almost decided to go in after all, just to avoid pacing the hall in her own home. Returning to work had been a wise move after all.

When the doorbell rang unexpectedly, she jumped, hoping it was nobody she had to be nice to. She felt like slugging somebody—hard.

"How are you, Mamma?" Nina said as Marianne opened the door. "You look shocked."

Marianne stared at the two suitcases in Nina's hands. She had to force herself to close her mouth.

"Sigrid's downstairs with a truck," Nina said. "Can you help bring up my stuff? I'm assuming that it's all right if I stay with you. It would be hard to fit into Sigrid's two-room apartment. We both know my old room is still empty."

Marianne shook her head. "I was convinced that you—"

Nina laughed. "That I was going to stay with him? No. You can see for yourself, I've left him. I know I might feel bad in a few days, but I'm feeling pretty good right now. You should have seen his face. Come on, let's get moving. I've also asked Grandpa to come help."

"Have you brought all your stuff?"

"Almost everything but the sofa, which I never liked— and the bed. That's not something I want to keep. Let me run down and help Sigrid move things out of the car. Could you please put these suitcases in my room?"

Nina rushed down the stairs and Marianne watched her go. Nina didn't look a day older than she did when she'd come home from high school for a quick lunch.

The suitcases were heavy, and Marianne needed all her strength to lug them into Nina's room at the end of the hall-way. Nina's room had been used for extra storage the past ten years. There was a great deal of junk in there, which, admittedly, should have been taken to the dump years ago.

Marianne left the door open and headed downstairs to Nina. Double-parked on the street was a Statoil rental truck. Both her daughters were working as hard as they could to unload Nina's things: everything including boxes, lamps, and chairs.

"How in the world did you load all that?"

"We started early this morning. Sigrid already had a ton of empty boxes from her move into her studio."

"What did Robert say?"

"Not much. He seemed shocked."

"I can understand that. So who helped you pack the truck?"

"No one. But don't just stand there! We have to get all that junk out of my room this weekend."

"If you want, we can help you sort through Pappa's things as well," Sigrid said. Then we can drive everything to the dump at once. Or is that too much?"

Marianne swallowed. She looked at her rosy-cheeked daughters, sweating from their hard work.

She shook her head and smiled, "I don't think it will be too much for me at all."

CHAPTER 86

Torsten was sorting everything on his desk. He looked up as Per looked in.

"What are you doing this weekend?" Per asked.

"I'm going out on my boat. I think it'll be the last weekend before winter."

"Wonderful plan. This weather has stayed surprisingly good for this time of year. Is Brundin going with you, or are you going on your own?"

"Brundin has to stay home. I'm going with my son. He asked to go out, and you can't say no to that."

"Fantastic," Per said.

Torsten finished up and headed for the garage. He had to admit that he was envious of Augustin's car. Not because he could see himself driving a little sports car, but more because Augustin was able to buy such a vehicle in the first place. Augustin and his car fit the same lifestyle. Perhaps that was their biggest difference.

Augustin had seemed almost downcast when Torsten told him he wouldn't be working on Friday. Torsten told Augustin to take the comp time and stay home, too. He suspected that Augustin didn't have a large circle of friends, but they had also just been through an extremely intense week—it was normal to feel empty and rootless after the adrenaline rush subsided.

Torsten hopped into his Corolla and turned on the radio. He was supposed to meet Noah at their apartment to finish packing food for their trip.

Noah was sitting on the sofa with his laptop on his knees. "Ready to go?" Torsten asked.

Noah pointed to his bag on the hall rug. Together, they put together the last few items, and Torsten found a nylon bag for the food. They drove onto Hornsgatan, and it looked like they were in luck, as most of the traffic was heading in the other direction. Maybe they were beating the rush hour into the city. As they passed Slussen, Torsten rolled down the window and let the fresh air stream over his face. Noah drummed on his legs to the beat of the music.

Skeppsbron Bridge was filled with traffic as usual, but once they reached the Royal Palace, the pace picked up again. As they swung past the Grand Hotel and the Nybro docks, the water glittered. A group of tourists with cameras dangling from their necks were boarding a Delfin boat.

Torsten was able to merge his Corolla into the lot not far from the gates. He'd chosen the Hundudden Boat Club, although he'd had to wait ten years to get a berth. The offer had come through the mail slot right after his divorce, and he'd seen it as a sign. Katrin didn't like the sea or life on a boat, which he could respect. People shouldn't be forced to spend free time doing things they didn't enjoy. Instead, he'd gone to sea when she had to work weekends. They'd done other things when she had free time.

The berth at Hundudden had been a dream come true. It was situated in a good harbor facing the archipelago.

This evening, they wouldn't be able to sail far, since they had to tack across the wind. Still, the winds could change overnight, and at least they'd be able to make it to Grinda. There were a number of small bays there where they could drop anchor.

After they'd loaded everything onboard, Torsten double-checked that they had charcoal for the grill as well as toilet paper.

"So, what do you say? Should we have a sandwich at Kruthuset before we go? Then we won't have to worry about getting hungry too soon?"

There was a buzz of activity inside the restaurant. Many people had come to either haul in their boats for the season or have one more sail, just as he and Noah planned. The owner was pleasant and knew them. He greeted them, announcing that his pâté sandwiches were fresh. He knew they were Torsten's favorite, as he ordered them every weekend.

The name Kruthuset, meaning "House of Ammunition," was from an earlier era. The place had been set a bit away from the storage houses, due to the risk of explosion, and it had been remodeled as a café for the use of the boat club members and for the general public.

A group of dog owners sat at one table outside in the sunshine, the dogs lolling at their owners' feet. Torsten assumed they'd just gotten back from a long walk.

They took their liver pâté sandwiches to a table, and Torsten also had a coffee, while Noah drank a raspberry soda. Like the dog owners, they chose a table in the sun.

Noah grimaced as some bubbles from his soda went up his nose.

"I called Mamma," Noah said.

Torsten looked up from his sandwich. He'd just taken a big bite. "And?"

"I told her exactly what I thought. She went berserk and said I was spoiled. Peo told her I don't behave properly."

Torsten swallowed a lump in his throat. He tried not to show his rage.

Noah continued, "Then she started crying. She said some strange things that I really didn't understand. Finally, she said she was sorry. She said that we could meet in Stockholm if I absolutely didn't want to go back to Oslo."

"Is that how it ended?"

"Yeah, except she asked if I needed any money and said that she could send some over if I did."

"And what did you say?"

"I told her I had my student support and was fine. But she could buy me a winter jacket if she wanted to."

Torsten grumbled. He was too upset to finish his sandwich.

"She said she'll send money for a jacket next week. Then she wondered if we could go to London one weekend in the fall. But I don't understand what she's planning. She's acting like a teenage girl from one of my classes. Crazy."

"Well, I think it was good you tried to talk things out. Your mother was probably upset about how the visit turned out, too. I'm sure you'll have a better relationship now."

"But what does she see in that guy? Not that you two always got along, but he's a piece of work."

Torsten was curious to know what Noah thought about his parents' relationship, but he knew he could never ask. He tried his best to be diplomatic.

"He's probably OK. I think your mother needed someone to look up to, and I wasn't that person."

"But he's nasty."

"Maybe he's just jealous of your relationship with your mother. That's not unusual."

Noah shrugged. "That's stupid to be jealous of a kid."

Torsten couldn't help smiling. And soon he was able to continue eating his sandwich. Noah drank the last of his soda in one gulp and let out a burp.

"Well, what do you say?" Torsten said. "Ready to go? If you take the suitcases, I'll take the food and sleeping bags. I hope you brought enough warm clothes. I heard it's going to frost tonight."

CHAPTER 87

On Monday morning, Marianne walked into her office. She saw immediately that her monitor had been moved again. She had almost begun to look forward to this cat-and-mouse game. Someone was trying to see what she was doing—and sooner or later, that person would be discovered.

Everyone makes mistakes.

Alexandra Baranski stuck her head into the doorway and whistled.

"Wow! You look better each time you come in! Where'd you buy that dress?"

Marianne waved in greeting and stood up straighter. "My daughter is a seamstress. She has a studio where she sells her designs. She gave me this dress as a name-day present. I mean, I don't like to admit it, but Dagmar is my middle name."

They laughed. St. Dagmar's Day had been September twenty-seventh.

"Well, you look radiant. And, congratulations on those cases last week. Torsten Ehn must worship the ground you walk on."

"He's the one who did the legwork that led to the right clue. I would never have seen the connection, but he was absolutely sure of it. It's always good to have a second pair of eyes. Sometimes it's hard to see the forest for the trees in one's own reports."

Alexandra looked at her watch. "Come on, we have to hurry. Olle wants us all in the press room. The new Stockholm police chief is going to be introduced today. It will look good if we all show up."

They hurried toward the elevators. Alexandra lowered her voice.

"The Root is back. Have you seen her yet?"

"I ran into her this morning," Marianne said. "She looked much better."

"I hear she's started a substance-abuse program."

"She has?"

"It was one of the conditions for returning to her job."

"Well, we all have our crosses to bear."

If Alexandra suspected that Marianne knew more than she was willing to reveal, she didn't show it.

The press room was crowded with journalists. Lillemor Rootander stood by the podium next to Olle. She nodded toward Marianne, who took her place by the wall, next to Alexandra. On the other side of Olle was a tall woman with ash-blonde hair in a page cut. She wore a police uniform and was staring intently at a sheet of paper in her hand. Marianne realized she was the person they'd all come to see. The woman was just under fifty. Marianne couldn't decide whether she was attractive. But then, police uniforms didn't make any woman look good. A bit of makeup would have done wonders, she thought.

The press secretary asked for everyone's attention as he came to the microphone.

"Welcome. I will not make a long speech today, but I will give the microphone to our new city police chief. Give a warm welcome to Irene Sundberg."

Marianne almost choked. She looked down at the floor and forced herself to take a few deep breaths. When she raised her head again, she looked to one side and caught Lillemor Rootander's gaze. Lillemor made a discreet nod toward Irene, and she and Marianne smiled at each other in complete understanding.

Yes, Irene Sundberg was *that* Irene.

ACKNOWLEDGMENTS

Writing this book was a prodigious undertaking. I'd like to thank the many people who offered their invaluable help.

Pappa and Maggan, my wonderful parents.

Anne-Marie Bergström. You took the time to help me, and I enjoyed your great expertise.

Carola Faulkner and Alexandra Montgomery. You read the manuscript with great energy and engagement. You're such beautiful friends.

Louise and Jonas Frisén. I asked so many questions of you, and—from your great knowledge—you gave me great answers.

Theresa Westerström, the best.

Ulla and Jan Strömberg, the best parents-in-law a person could wish for. Without you, no books.

Katarina Wennstam, because you're just so darned wonderful!

Mari Jungstedt for your high spirits and your laughter.

Camilla Läckeberg. You're the toughest one of all, and you always yelled at me when I wanted to quit. Thanks for not giving up.

Denise Rudberg

Martina Haag, the Big Star!

Maria Sveland and Mian Lodalen. You both are inspiring.

Johanna Bergenstråhle and Börje Hansson. You believed in this book from its inception, and you were wonderful sounding boards.

Andreas Eriksson. I couldn't have done it without you. You are the most professional of all, as well as being a good friend.

Camilla Hildebrand, because you're the finest friend a person can have. And you have the most attractive legs.

Sara Nyström, because you are the Pride of Piteå.

Björn Häggelin. You are so inspiring and so much fun. As well as the best dressed!

Hannah Widell. You were right. You promised me it would all work out in the end.

Micke Spreitz, such a good friend all these years. You know so much about all kinds of things.

Katti Kjellvertz, one of the most amusing people I know.

Augustin Erba. Because you contributed your name, the best one of all, and because I love talking with you.

Calle Frisell, a very warm person who can answer the most difficult questions in areas I find hard to understand.

Philip Segenäs, a rock and a wonderful cover model for my children's books.

Daniel Mollberg, such a good friend.

Claes de Faire, always so energetic and always in the know.

Harry Faulkner, the most stylish man in all of Östermalm.

Fifi Stehag. Because you are so kind and generous.

Gunnar Holmgren. The best lunch companion, and so much fun.

Cecilia Hagen, so fast answering text messages, with such exciting things to talk about.

Kajsa Herngren, a tough negotiator with social skills who knows how things work.

Liliana Tovar and Anna Höglund, two great breakfast companions.

Lena Patriksson, because you knew what was needed.

Pernilla Alm, because you had the endurance to read.

Pontus Frithiof, the best pub owner in Sweden. You make Stockholm a much better city.

Sven and Cati Hagströmer, such great inspirations, and because Cati knows the deal when it comes to Sudoku.

Lisa Lindberg. My good editor, who handled this text in the best possible way.

Susanna Romanus. My wonderful publisher, who has been both patient and demanding—and who trusted me to deliver. You believed in this book and contributed to it with your energy. You understand.

Calle and Loppsan. Because I was allowed to be your mother.

Johan Strömberg. Because you are my husband and you still love me. You make me laugh every single day.

—▢—

Two people deserve special thanks: Anders Åhlén and Ulf Jonsson at the National Police. You took time to assist me in the best way possible. Your help has been invaluable, and I am eternally grateful!

ABOUT THE AUTHOR

Denise Rudberg is one of Sweden's most successful novelists—crowned by readers as the Chick-Lit Queen of Sweden—and in 2009 she began incorporating her signature sexy, energetic style into mysteries featuring the intrigues of Sweden's upper classes, naming the subgenre Elegant Crime. *A Small Indiscretion* is her eleventh novel, and her first to be translated into English.

About the Translator

Laura A. Wideburg fell in love with the Swedish language as a high school exchange student in Vrigstad, Småland. She returned to Sweden to study linguistics at the University of Stockholm. She received a PhD in medieval literature and historical linguistics from the University of Washington.

Laura began to translate Swedish thrillers and crime novels in 2005 and has translated Inger Frimansson, Lars Kepler, and Helene Tursten. Her translation of Inger Frimansson's *Good Night, My Darling* won *ForeWord Reviews* magazine's Best Translated Novel in 2007. This is her first translation of a Denise Rudberg book.

She is also the Lead Teacher at the Swedish Cultural Center and has written two books in use there: *Swedish—The Basics* and *Swedish—Beyond the Basics.*

Laura lives in Seattle with her husband, two children, and two cats.